To Justice Mike Cavanagh
with best Wishes.

Thomas E. Brennan

THE BENCH

THE BENCH

A
NOVEL

By

Thomas E. Brennan

VANTAGE PRESS
New York

This is a work of fiction. Any similarity between
the characters appearing herein and any real persons,
living or dead, is purely coincidental.

FIRST EDITION

Copyright © 1997, 2000 by Thomas E. Brennan

Published by Vantage Press, Inc.
516 West 34th Street, New York, New York 10001

1997 Publication by Tebco, Inc., East Lansing, Michigan

Manufactured in the United States of America
ISBN: 0-533-13603-2

Library of Congress Catalog Card No.: 00-91562

0 9 8 7 6 5 4 3 2 1

For Pauline Mary

AUTHOR'S NOTES

This story is set in Michigan in the early years of the last decade of the twentieth century. To enhance its credibility and authenticity, I have mentioned some real people, places, and events. These are intended to be apparent and benign. The yarn itself is pure fiction, all the principal characters being figments of my imagination. Any similarity to real persons living or dead is accidental and unintentional, and I apologize for what my subconscious mind may have prompted. So saying, I must confess that I recognize snippets of familiar personalities in some of the things my fictional people say and do. I can only hope that these echoes will help the reader to know and love the fictional characters as I came to know and love the real ones in my forty-five years on both sides of The Bench.

The Author

Telling a tale is the work of an author; writing a novel is the achievement of a team. Mine was largely peopled by family. Polly, my dear wife, to whom this book is dedicated, inspired me to write it, read every page as it came out of the computer, and, as always in our forty-six year marriage, was lavish in loving criticism. Our daughter, Marybeth Hicks, was my editor. She has her mother's flair for correcting my missteps. In spades. Her sister, Peggy Radelet, added more subtle, though not less valuable, suggestions.

Beyond this inner circle, I have benefitted by immeasurable assistance from a host of relatives and friends who have encouraged, critiqued, researched, suggested, approved and disapproved. Donna Morris, Catherine Brennan, Corbin Davis, Ray Brennan, Mary Ann Pierce, Jim and Mary Ryan, Joe Kimble, Fred Headen, Jim Canham, Father Norbert Clemens, the entire staff at Thomas Cooley Law School, and of course, my old nemesis from the Detroit Free Press, Hugh McDiarmid, whose timely public boost breathed life into my manuscript.

To all of you, and to the dozens of others who were kind enough to answer questions, make phone calls, check sources, and cheer me on, I can only say: Thanks so much. I hope that this effort will be as successful as your help and encouragement richly deserve.

The Author

PART ONE

THE JUSTICES

CHAPTER 1

MALLOY

She awoke, naked, lying on her back, her husband's left arm draped across her mid section.

He slept in total satisfaction--slow, steady breathing and soft, intermittent snores echoing the triumphant song of male conquest.

For a moment she flirted with the idea of initiating a surprise reprise of last night's torrid episode, but the thought of morning love-making turned her attention instinctively to the clock on the night stand.

6:05 a.m. Time to return to reality. Time to get the children off to school.

Deftly, she removed his hand, scootched to the edge of the bed, and rolling to the floor on hands and knees, looked around for her clothes.

The trail told an unmistakable story. The bra and panty hose strewn a few feet from the bed. The half slip and the little black cocktail dress tossed hurriedly over the arm of a chair. Her purse dangling from the bathroom doorknob. And her open toed black pumps there on the floor, just inside the door. Interspersed were boxer shorts, a tee shirt, socks, a white dress shirt, a red tie, his navy blue suit coat and trousers, and black wing tips. Only her fur jacket and his top coat had made it to the closet.

She smiled as she gathered up the accouterments of last night's elegant image, and crept into the bathroom. Quickly dressed, she fluffed her hair for a moment, decided to go with a random look, washed her face and patched up her eye shadow and lipstick. No time to shower, she applied a generous dose of perfume to her neck and wrists. It would have to do.

Without a glance toward the bed, she silently slipped loose the security chain on the door and stepped into the hall. Waiting for the elevator, she could see the asphalt street and concrete sidewalks six stories below, wet with chill, autumn rain, reflecting the glow of street lights and traffic signals.

Yesterday--Tuesday, November 6, 1990--would be a day to remember.

The elevator door opened. Two Japanese businessmen stood in the right rear corner, briefcases in hand, overnight bags hung from shoulder straps at their sides. Self-consciously, she stepped inside and smiled lamely at her fellow passengers, who nodded politely in return. Then she turned and stood front left facing the door. She could feel her ears burning. The perfume was overwhelming.

They rode in silence a few floors. Then one of the two men said something softly in Japanese. Both men laughed.

At ground level, she strode quickly across the hotel lobby, addressing the bell captain in a firm voice that could be heard by him, by the half-asleep room clerk, by the maid vacuuming the carpet in the lounge area, by the old man reading the morning paper in the large wing-backed chair, and by the two Japanese businessmen walking behind her.

"I am Mrs. Malloy, Judge Malloy's wife. The Judge is upstairs still sleeping. I have to go home and get the children off to school. Would you please call me a taxicab?"

* * *

Riding through the cold, dark streets of Lansing, Michigan, Margaret Mary Malloy was happy. Despite a nearly sleepless night, she wasn't tired. Indeed, she was still on an emotional high, as she thought of last night's victorious election returns. Her husband was elected Justice of the Michigan Supreme Court. James Patrick Malloy. Her Jim. He made it. Nobody thought he would. Nobody thought he could. But he did. We did, she thought, recalling how she had campaigned beside him day and night since early August.

In many ways, it was a replay of Jim's first election as Clinton County Circuit Judge eight years before. Then, his nomination had been literally by chance. Drinking beer with a group of young lawyers after a local bar association meeting, the conversation turned to the inevitable complaints about the circuit judge who had reigned in Clinton County for more than a generation. A cantankerous old curmudgeon, who was best known for brow beating everyone who came before him, especially the young lawyers, he was up for reelection in 1982. That night, the young lawyers drew straws to see who would oppose the incumbent. Jim Malloy drew the short straw.

No one expected him to win then, either. But he did. Sheer guts and hard work. Door to door campaigning. She had helped him then, too. Licking envelopes. Endless hours on the phone. Endless nights of work and worry.

Now it all seemed worth the effort. A little like childbirth, she thought.

A twinge in her abdomen reminded her of how election day had ended. She and Jim dressing excitedly about 10 p.m. as positive returns began coming in. Arriving at the hotel where the Governor-Elect's victory party was in full swing. The hugs, the kisses, the high fives, the sincere congratulations of so many friends. And strangers. Some people she knew only from news stories. Television personalities. Margaret and Jim had been part of it. Part of something very big and very important.

And Jim, beaming with joy, as early morning final results were broadcast, pulling her aside, with that familiar impish gleam in his eye, showing her the room key, making his prurient proposal. She knew then that she was experiencing what her German grandmother called 'middleschmartz', the monthly message from her prolific ovaries. And she didn't care. It was just one of those magic moments. Whatever will be will be.

The cab pulled up the driveway to the old farmhouse. "Rathcroghan" they called it, summoning visions of a storied

Irish castle, immortalized in *The Tain*. Jim and Margaret had purchased the place soon after he--they-- had set up law offices in DeWitt. She had been a legal secretary at a local law firm, and he a young associate. They had fallen in love. Jim decided to leave the firm. He had asked her to come with him, to be his secretary and incidently, to be his wife. It was a cockeyed way to propose marriage. But he meant it. And she had wanted to be with him. At the office. After hours. All the time.

At first, that's just the way it was. Long days in the store front office, treating every client as though he or she were the only client they had. Which was often the case. Long nights at Rathcroghan, removing calcimine, sanding floors, painting, varnishing, sewing curtains. Jim Malloy, lawyer by day, plumber at night. Margaret Malloy, legal secretary by day, wallpaper hanger by night.

That's the way it was until little Jimmy came along. Margaret had tried going back to the office when Jimmy was about six months old. It didn't work. She had lost the consuming interest in the law practice. And she just couldn't stand leaving the little guy with a sitter every morning. He had quickly realized what was happening, and he made the parting as traumatic as possible. Never mind that the baby sitter said he stopped crying as soon as Margaret was out of sight. His heart wrenching sobs echoed in her ears all the way to the office. It was more than a mother could bear.

***

She paid the driver, fumbled the key from her purse, and entered the house. Just in time. The sitter had overslept. The boys were just getting up. Little Mary Ellen was still sleeping. Margaret dove into the frantic business of school morning mothering. By 7:30 when the bus stopped out in front, Jimmy, 10, and Paul, his 8 year old brother were standing by the mailbox, bundled against the autumn chill, book bags and lunch boxes in hand, eager to tell the bus driver and all the kids who cared to listen that their dad had won the election. Whoopee!

Margaret fussed with Mary Ellen's locks. Unfortunately, she had inherited her mother's rather thin, straight hair. Her daughter's was longer, though, and lighter. Blond, actually.

Mary Ellen loved to dress up. Always went to kindergarten looking like a little princess, which is just what her dad called her. Today was no exception. In fact, Margaret chose the pink, flowered dress and her Sunday-best red coat and hat.

She smiled as she remembered the day Jim bought his daughter the red coat and hat. It was one of those afternoons when Margaret simply had too much to do. Drive Jimmy to his hockey practice. Take Paul to his basketball game. Take the VCR up to the corner repair shop to be fixed. All the usual chores. And Mary Ellen, whose woolen mittens had been mistakenly tossed in the washer and dryer, shrinking them to the size of doll clothes, needed new ones. When was she going to have time to get Mary Ellen her mittens?

"I'll go," Jim had volunteered, and packing his daughter into his Ford Taurus, he drove off toward the mall.

When he came home with coat, hat, boots, AND mittens, Margaret had a field day of good-natured scolding.

"Jim Malloy," she chirped, "Don't you ever, ever, talk to me about spending too much money on the kids' clothes. You went out of here to buy maybe a three dollar pair of mittens, and you come back with at least 150 dollars worth of goodies."

Jim took it in good cheer. He knew that spoiling his only daughter was no sin in his wife's eyes. And she knew that he knew.

***

Returning from the kindergarten run, Margaret finally had time to shower, change clothes, and fix herself some toast and coffee. At age thirty-six, she was pretty satisfied with her life.

Jim was fond of saying whenever he had a couple of drinks, that she was "one damn good looking woman." And she was.

Their home, while not band-box perfect, was getting there. The three bathrooms, four bedrooms, and the kitchen were completely remodeled. The family room addition was half finished, enclosed and insulated, but needing drywall, wood trim and carpeting. The outside remained rural and rustic. An ambitious landscaping plan was relegated to the back burner when the supreme court campaign began.

Their active social life centered mostly around Jim's work. He liked judges as social friends, and she found most of the judges' wives to be good company. Jim and Margaret Malloy were people people.

Both of them had grown up in large Irish-Catholic families in the Detroit area. Jim attended a central catholic high school for boys, where he earned letters in football and basketball, in addition to graduating *magna cum laude* and delivering the commencement speech. The priests and lay brothers, who ran the school, had a way of generating great loyalty in their teen-age charges. Jim was no exception. He counted several of his high school teachers as close personal friends. Still saw them from time to time. One of them had presided at their wedding.

That high school loyalty played other roles in Jim's career. An older alumnus of the school ran for the Michigan Court of Appeals and recruited Jim to work on his campaign. When he won election, he offered Jim the chance to work as a uniformed court officer in the Lansing office of the appeals court. Jim jumped at the chance, even though it meant dropping out of college 30 credits short of graduation. Then, in the fall of 1972, Jim read in the local newspaper that a group of lawyers and judges were starting a new law school in downtown Lansing. Classes would be held in the evenings. By January of 1973, Jim found himself enrolled in the inaugural class of the Thomas M. Cooley Law School, even though he had not completed his undergraduate degree.

The next three years had a profound impact on Jim Malloy. Almost from the first day of class, he realized that the legal profession was his intellectual and emotional home. He read the ancient legal precedents with consummate interest. He loved debating the finer points of law with classmates and instructors.

After graduation, he passed the bar examination and made the adjustment from law student to practicing attorney swiftly and with gusto. Through dint of perseverance, he persuaded a local law firm to take him on as an associate. He proved himself quickly, winning both a major criminal trial and a substantial civil award in his first year at the bar.

While he was a good lawyer and worked long hours, Jim was also a loving husband and a caring father. And if he didn't exactly have a movie star's good looks, he did have a certain fumbling, masculine charm that women found appealing.

Eldest of the four Cronyn girls, Margaret Malloy attended an all-girls' version of Jim's high school. She had also done well academically and had been the editor of the school's newspaper. Like most of her classmates, she followed the fortunes of the boys'-school varsity teams with great interest. But she had never heard of Jim Malloy. Four years her senior, he was ancient history by the time she entered high school.

She had come to mid-Michigan, like so many others, to attend Michigan State University in East Lansing. A desultory four years had evolved into a journalism major, though she really had less interest in working as a newspaper reporter than in being a successful syndicated columnist, a career that permitted more choices in lifestyle. The journalistic job market being nearly non-existent when she graduated, she obtained a low-paying job on a small weekly paper, but had to take a position as a receptionist-clerk in a local law office to support herself. By attending all the seminars offered by the Legal Secretaries Association, she became skilled enough to call herself a legal secretary.

Someday, Margaret often thought, she would get back to

writing. When the kids were grown. And not just to keep busy or make money, though God knows, they could use it. She wanted to write because she had things to write about. Things she wanted to say. Things she had learned and was learning about children, about marriage, about men, about politics. About life.

***

Her second cup of coffee was interrupted by Jim's arrival.
"Hi honey."
"Hi. How do you feel?"
"Me? I'm the greatest!"
He was always the greatest. An inherited attitude. His dad, Joe Malloy, was always the greatest. And everything Joe Malloy had was the best. The best house. The best car. The best wife. The best kids. The best neighborhood. The best church. The best meals, vacations, Christmases, birthday parties, clothes. You name it. Whatever Joe Malloy had, Joe Malloy insisted was the best.

It was the Malloy way of whistling in the dark. The truth was that Jim's parents had very little by most middle-class standards. Eight children. One salary. A two-bedroom bungalow with the attic finished off as a boys' dormitory. And a so-called recreation room in the basement, where most of the growing up took place.

"So what now, Mr. Justice? The answering machine shows you've already had 5 phone calls." As if to confirm her report, the phone began ringing.

"Let the machine answer it, Mag. I need to have coffee with you before I face my adoring public."

They sat at the breakfast bar for over an hour, just talking. Recalling the humorous events of the last months, the crises that engulfed them in the final weeks of the campaign, the people they had seen the night before. They relished the whole experience, and let their thoughts wander recklessly to expansive views of the future. The world was indeed their oyster this day.

Finally the incessant ringing of the phone won out, and they listened to the messages on the answering machine. Ever the lawyer, Jim took out a yellow pad and made notes about the calls. Which needed returning and how urgently. Which would get a thank-you letter. Which calls should be answered by Margaret and which by him. Then he went into the den to go to work.

As Jim called friends, reporters, relatives, and assorted well wishers, he thumbed his way through the small Mexican basket that served as his 'In Box'. A mountain of unopened mail, mostly ominous window envelopes, spilled across his desk. Time to pay the fiddler.

The campaign was a terrible financial drain. It was his own fault. When the Republican nominee for governor, State Senator Mark Edwards, asked him to accept the party's nomination, he said there was no money in the budget for the supreme court race. In fact, that's why Malloy been asked--to fill the ticket with credible candidates. He wouldn't win, he was told, but if he would do this service for the party, he would have first call on a future appointment or nomination.

'Filling the ticket' is a peculiar aspect of Michigan's peculiar system of selecting supreme court justices. Trial court judges and the judges of the court of appeals are all nominated and elected in nonpartisan elections. Supreme court justices, due to a political anomaly, are nominated in party conventions, then elected on the nonpartisan ballot. The parties always feel an obligation to field candidates for the supreme court, even though they often have little enthusiasm for the race.

In 1990, two incumbents were up for reelection, Chief Justice Ed Breitner, a well known and highly regarded jurist from Oakland County, and Douglas Green, a one-time Dearborn Probate Judge, who had achieved fame three decades before as the star of a television program reenacting juvenile delinquency hearings. By 1990, more than half of the voting-age population had never heard of Douglas Green.

As incumbents, Green and Breitner were entitled under Michigan's constitution to re-nominate themselves by filing an affidavit of candidacy. While they did so, just to be on the safe side, both of them sought and obtained the nominations of the Democratic party as well. Neither sought the nomination of the Republican party. In some other states, and in the lower courts of Michigan, good judges are often favored with the support of both political parties. But in the supreme court of Michigan, the tradition of partisan nomination and party identification has a strong grip.

As a circuit judge, and president of the judges association, Jim Malloy knew that Chief Justice Breitner was not well regarded among the trial bench. The chief had never been a trial judge, and his approach to judicial administration was often high-handed, autocratic, and naive. Moreover, Breitner's court was conspicuous for its public wrangling, particularly between Justices Alton Henry and Doris Templeton. Their opinions were often spiked with vitriolic personal references to each other.

Almost every time opinions were released by the court, the newspapers and television would report that the supreme court was 'bickering' or 'bitterly divided'.

Jim Malloy felt that the fallout had been disastrous for the courts and for the legal profession. The impression was that the merits of the cases were not as important to the outcome as the conflicts between members of the court. He felt that Breitner should be replaced as chief justice. And he thought that enough people might agree with him to make a difference in the election.

And so the young circuit judge had challenged the distinguished chief justice to a series of debates. At the law schools. At bar association meetings. On public television. Eventually the major media began to notice. At first, the debates focused on Breitner's leadership of the court. On whether he was responsible for taming the acrimony among the justices. Whether, as chief justice, he should have been able to control the rhetoric in the court's opinions.

But as the debates went on, they began to expand into the important issues of the day--the big issues. The things that matter to the general public and to the media which caters to it. The life issues: abortion, euthanasia, assisted suicide. The economic issues: tort reform, ecology, employment. The social issues: gay rights, affirmative action, domestic abuse.

The more substantive the debates became, the more Jim Malloy became convinced that his election campaign was not just a matter of his own career advancement. He began to see the campaign as a crusade for truth. The good guys against the bad guys. Right against wrong. And the more he saw things that way, the more he believed that he had an obligation to make every effort within his power to win.

He did all the usual things to raise money, appointing a committee, asking his friends and relatives to help. But in the last analysis, he had financed much of his own campaign. First, it was a matter of encroaching into the little nest egg that he and Margaret had started to set aside for the children's education. Then he redirected the proceeds of the home improvement loan, obtained to finish remodeling Rathcroghan. In the final days of the campaign, he began frantically kiting credit cards, opening new ones to pay off old ones and then loading up the old ones again.

In the end, Breitner won easily, leading the ticket by 300,000 votes. But Malloy edged out the second incumbent, Douglas Green, by 12,000 to win the other seat on the court.

***

With a sigh of resignation, on this Wednesday after the election, Malloy began writing checks to pay the accumulated bills. He didn't bother to calculate the bank balance after each check. He knew that he was overdrawn already, and that each additional check he wrote dug a deeper hole. His plan was very simple. Pay everyone. Then go to the bank and borrow enough to cover all the checks. Surely a Justice of the supreme court should have enough credit to pay his bills. The bottom line was well over $20,000. Surely he was good for that.

Margaret interrupted. Chief Justice Breitner was calling. Malloy could feel a sudden quickening of his heartbeat. In all of their previous meetings, Breitner had treated him with cordial disdain, like an unemployed, uninvited, and unwelcome brother-in-law. How would he act now that they were to be colleagues?

Malloy picked up the extension phone and said, "Hello, Mr. Chief Justice."

A female voice responded. "One moment for the chief justice."

Malloy's Irish bubbled up. That old ploy. The power play, he thought. HE calls ME, then I end up waiting on the line for him to pick up the phone. Malloy counted to ten. Then he hung up.

Margaret was stunned. "You just hung up on the chief justice!"

"He'll call back," Malloy said, confidently.

Three minutes later, the phone rang.

"See?" said Jim smiling. He let it ring four more times.

"Jim Malloy here"

"Jim! This is Ed Breitner. We must have been cut off. Sorry about that. This office is a mad house."

"I can understand. Congratulations on your overwhelming victory. You certainly left the rest of us in the dust, Mr. Chief Justice."

"Just a combination of the incumbency designation on the ballot and a well financed campaign. Your victory was more remarkable. I shutter to think of how well you'll do in eight years as an incumbent."

"Thank you, but I have no designs on leading the ticket. A win is a win in my book."

"To be sure. You are now 'Mr. Justice' and not just 'Judge' Malloy. But I have to warn you that we usually leave our formal titles at the courtroom door. I hope you will call me Ed."

"I'll try, but I don't know how easy it will be to call Justice Henry 'Al' or Justice Van Timlin 'Fred.'

The C.J. laughed. "Try 'Alton' and 'Van'. That's real hair down chumminess for those two old codgers."

"Anyway, I'm very much looking forward to getting to know them and the other Justices."

" We have a good court, Jim. I know you'll enjoy working with everyone. You can't help making friends here, because we work so closely on so many really important matters."

"I can see that. By the way, how is Justice Green doing? I've always respected him. He sounded rather low when he called me to concede. Have you talked to him?"

"Yes, we spoke briefly this morning. Transition stuff. He's a survivor. And he bears you no ill will. I suggest you go to see him and have a talk. He'll be flattered. And he may have some good advice for you."

"I'll do that. What else do you suggest?"

"Get a good secretary. Someone with experience in the court, if possible. It's the quickest and most painless way to break in. Also, touch base with the court administrator. She can get you set up with your state car, your laptop computer, cell phone, fax machine, the whole nine yards. There are a lot of toys on this job."

"Sounds like it. Will she also assign me an office.?"

"No, I do that. And Mike Delbert, the clerk of the court, will help you settle in. I'm putting you in Green's office. It has a nice view of the plaza. I think you'll like it. I've talked to Van and to Bob O'Leary. They're the only other associate justices with offices in Lansing, and neither of them want to move."

"Isn't that just across the hall from your suite?"

"Exactly. I'm looking forward to being neighbors."

"So am I, Mr. Chief Justice. I hope my feisty campaign rhetoric will not stand in the way of developing collegiality."

Margaret, who had been sitting across the room listening to her husband's end of the conversation, stood and began pantomiming a tip-toed walk through a barnyard, holding her nose. Malloy threw an eraser at her.

"You haven't seen feisty until you've read some of Alton Henry's memos," Breitner chuckled. "Thick skin is a requirement on this job. By the way, let me fill you in on the agenda for the first Tuesday in January."

"I assume I will be assigned some cases on the January Call."

"True. The clerk will get you the briefs. I think there are 16 oral arguments in January Term. You'll probably end up with two of them. But the first order of business, as required by the constitution, is the election of the chief justice."

"That's for a two-year term, isn't it?" Malloy squirmed. This was going to be a touchy subject.

"Just so. It's a ritual we go through in January of every odd numbered year."

Pause. Uncomfortable pause. Was Jim supposed to say something?

Finally, "So I understand."

"Look, Jim, I know how you feel about me and the way I run the court. You were very candid in your criticisms during the campaign. I never took it as a personal matter. Just a difference in style and philosophy. Frankly, you had a lot of valid points. I wasn't about to admit to any failures publicly during the election campaign, but believe me, I know I'm not perfect. I can do this job a lot better than I have been doing. Frankly, Old Greenie wasn't much help to me. Constantly talking. Constantly voicing opinions about things he didn't know anything about. Frankly, I think you and I will be much more simpatico about court administration than he and I were. Frankly," Breitner coughed.

If he gets any franker, I'm going to feel like a priest hearing confessions, Malloy mused.

"The truth is, Jim, we don't have a whole lot of options. Alton never comes to Lansing unless it's to hear oral arguments or attend a formal meeting of the court. Many years ago, he converted his back porch into an office. That's where he does all his work. The man's a recluse. Nobody on the court would vote for him to be the chief. The chief justice has to deal with the legislature, the governor, the media. Henry's an anachronism.

"How about Van Timlin? Wasn't he chief at one time?"

"Van Timlin is over the hill. He had his time in the chair as chief justice, ages ago. He was totally passive. A ceremonial C.J. Couldn't get a pencil sharpener out of the office of management and budget. Frankly, the whole court was dissatisfied with him as chief justice. That's why they elected me. I really didn't need the hassle, but I felt somebody had to do the job. Anybody but Van.

"What about O'Leary?"

"Bob's just not a candidate. Not interested in the job. Frankly, he's too lazy. He'd rather be on his sailboat cruising around Beaver Island, drinking Tullamara Dew and reading Keats.

"And the women?"

"Doris and Hilda are both first rate lawyers and judges. Both good students of the law. But they are both from Detroit, and they have their offices downtown. As you know, they were both nominated by the Democratic party, as I was, and they have always insisted that I should be the chief justice. Frankly, Jim, Doris can be awfully abrasive at times. Diplomacy is not her strong suit. I think even she realizes that she doesn't have the tact and finesse to represent the court or the business acumen to manage a multimillion dollar court system.

"Is Hilda a candidate?"

"Hilda is a wonderful person. I'm very, very fond of her. There isn't anyone in our profession I respect or admire more than Hilda Germaine. But the plain truth of the matter, Jim, is that the chief justice of the Michigan Supreme Court has to wrestle with Neanderthals in the house and senate, with bigots in the executive office, with citizen groups of all kinds and dispositions, and frankly, very frankly, and I hate to have to say this Jim, but very frankly, I just don't think the leadership in the legislature, even the people from my own party are ready for a female chief justice, especially an African American."

For a moment, just a moment, Jim Malloy was speechless. Breitner had axed every one of his colleagues, in a bold bid to win his support for the chief justiceship.

"Gosh Ed," Malloy sighed in mock consternation, " I guess that narrows it down to you and me."

Breitner burst into laughter. Making his pitch to Malloy was a test of his nerves, and Jim's frivolous reaction relaxed him suddenly and unexpectedly. He coughed and laughed. Laughed and coughed.

Malloy joined in the laughing.

"I'm sure you'll be a great chief justice someday, Jim." Breitner's voice smiled. "You have the one most important qualification. You don't take yourself too seriously."

"I owe it all to my wife, Mr. Chief Justice. Margaret finds a way to deflate me every time my ego swells."

Listening across the room, Margaret flopped her hands at her husband, and shook her head from side to side. Malloy smiled at her and nodded up and down vigorously. She responded by pulling up her skirt teasingly, and Jim wheeled around in his chair so he wouldn't have to look at her. She retaliated by coming up behind him, tousling his hair and kissing him on the back of his neck. He tried to shoo her off.

"I'm anxious to meet ... or rather, see her again," Breitner was saying. "She'll add a very attractive dimension to our social gatherings. By the way, have you thought about your swearing-in ceremony?"

"I'm not looking to do anything big. Maybe just have some family and friends come in on the first day of court."

"We can do that. I'll have my staff set it up. But don't wait for the first day of the term to take the oath of office. You won't be on the payroll until you do."

"Thanks for the advice. That's the kind of collegial solicitude I like to see in a chief justice."

"Anything I can do. Once again, welcome aboard."

Malloy was smiling as he hung up the phone. "Mags, if I didn't know better, I'd think that Ed Breitner was really worried about being reelected chief justice."

"He is?"

"Sounds like it. Doesn't make sense. The Democrats have a majority on the court: Alton Henry, Doris Templeton, Hilda Germaine and Ed Breitner."

"And they elect the chief justice along party lines?"

"They always do, as far as I know. O'Leary, Van Timlin and I won't even be invited to the caucus. It will be a done deal by the first Tuesday in January."

***

Jim and Margaret went back to paying bills. As she sealed the last envelope, the doorbell rang. She went to answer and, in a moment, returned and announced, "We have a visitor." Joe Malloy Jr., Jim's older brother, filled up the doorway as he burst into the room.

"He's not a visitor, he's my brother!" Jim wheeled around in his chair and rose to greet his older sibling.

"Hi lil' bro. How does it feel to be a big shot supreme court justice?"

" It's tiring. They don't let you sleep more than a few hours every night."

"Well, congratulations again. How late did you stay at the hotel.?"

"Got a room and stayed over. Came home after breakfast."

"While Mr. Big Deal Supreme Court Justice here was sleeping

in this morning, I was rushing home to get the kids off to school," added Margaret.

"You mean Jim hasn't hired you a nanny yet?" Joe Malloy asked in mock surprise.

"That's a laugh," said Margaret. "After this campaign, we won't even be able to hire a baby sitter again until 1994."

"As a matter of fact, guys, that's what I wanted to talk to you about."

"Uh oh. Money?" Jim scowled.

"Money, campaign debts, and something else. I've been reading the Code of Judicial Conduct."

Joe Malloy was a lawyer. In the eyes of his kid bother, Joe was the very best lawyer ever to crack Black's Law Dictionary. A top graduate of the University of Michigan Law School, and five years older than Jim, Joe was what they call a transactional lawyer. He never went to court. Well, he seldom went to court. When he did, he didn't lose. Mostly, Joe put deals together. His office was in the Ren Cen, overlooking the Detroit River. His clients were all major corporations. He flew all over the country 'doing deals' that boggled the mind of a small-town trial judge.

"And what have you learned?"

"Mostly, I've learned that a newly elected judge or justice can't hold a fund-raising party to pay off his campaign debts."

"I guess I knew that. I'll just have to suck it up and borrow the money to clean off the slate. I've been sitting here writing checks all morning. I think it's time to call brother Tom, our friendly family banker, and get a loan. You know, consolidate all those annoying little obligations into one massive intolerable burden."

" Tom will do what he can, I'm sure, but the bank may not be so cooperative."

"Oh, come on, Joe. Twenty or twenty-five thousand can't be too much of an unsecured loan, even for a dubious risk like me."

"Twenty or twenty-five thousand?"

"Yeah. I've been robbing Peter to pay Paul for the last three months. Mostly to keep running our TV ads. I've got a stack of melting plastic credit cards." Jim opened the desk drawer, scooped up a handful of cards, and spread them out on the desk top.

"Six kinds of VISA and five different Master Charges. Not to mention Discover and American Express."

Joe whistled.

"And I can assure you, none of that is my doing," Margaret added. "I get all my food budget by taking back the pop bottles."

"Very funny," said Malloy.

"The sad thing," Joe was shaking his head, "is that I could have raised a bundle last night."

"Last night?" asked Jim.

"Why didn't you?" asked Margaret.

"As I read the ethics rule, fund raising has to end as soon as the polls close. Like buying a ticket on a horse race. When the bell rings, the window closes. But there must have been a dozen people who came up to me last night, while the returns were coming in, who wanted to contribute to your campaign. Three guys actually wrote checks. I gave them back."

"You're kidding!" Margaret was shocked.

"I'm dead serious. As a matter of fact, Art Wilhelm, the big lobbyist, wanted to know how much debt the committee had run up. He offered to help pay the bills. Said he'd get us a check for $10,000 first thing in the morning. I said thanks but no thanks."

"Ah the price of scruples." Malloy was philosophical. His wife was not.

"Do you mean to tell me that I'm going to have to wait two or three years to get the family room finished and the landscaping done just because of some silly technical rule about when campaign fund raising is supposed to be done?"

"I am afraid there's no other way. Jim has to make up the

arrears out of his own pocket. You're going to have to borrow the money. And that may not be real easy."

"Why not?"

"Well, as the treasurer of your campaign, I'm the one responsible to file the final reports."

"And?"

"And your 25 G's is not exactly the full extent of the Malloy Campaign's deficit position."

"Not exactly?"

"Not exactly."

"How much not exactly?"

"Well, let's just say it's in a more expensive neighborhood than the 25 grand overload on your credit cards."

"A more expensive neighborhood like maybe Grosse Pointe?"

"Would you believe Bloomfield Hills?"

"Give it to me straight, Joe. How much are we talking about?"

"Well, all the bills aren't in yet, but I've got to think we're looking at pretty close to six figures."

"How much for sure?"

"We're at $97,000 and counting."

Joe left about 2 in the afternoon. Margaret went to the basement to do laundry. That's how she always coped with financial worries. Alone again, Malloy slumped into the leather wing back chair and closed his eyes. No savings left. Two mortgages on the house. And $100,000 plus in unsecured personal debt. Just about a year's salary. And campaign expenses are not even tax deductible. No wonder the brightest and the best of America's young people have no desire to get into public service.

He thought of the politician who, when asked how it felt to be tarred and feathered, replied, "I would not have enjoyed it all, if it had not been for the honor of the thing."

CHAPTER 2

HENRY

BAHBOOM!

Christmas shoppers in the parking lot of the Mall of America in Minneapolis froze in their tracks when they heard it.

So did thousands and thousands more, hurrying to shopping malls in Palatine, Illinois; King of Prussia, Pennsylvania; Bethesda, Maryland; Dublin, Ohio; and half a dozen other bustling American suburbs at exactly 7:14 PM on Monday, December 10, 1990.

Alton and Virginia Henry were in the parking lot on their way to the J. L. Hudson Company in the Twelve Oaks Mall in Novi, Michigan and the justice was in the midst of telling his wife about his many phone conversations with his new colleague. How he and young Malloy were conniving to oust Ed Breitner from the chief justiceship.

Startled by the explosion, they stopped and gaped at the sky. The first boom was followed immediately by another and then another. Each thunderous clap announced a brilliant ball of color, first filling the sky with light, then cascading down in flickering deference to a new burst of a different hue.

The source seemed to a small office complex just a few blocks north of the mall.

It continued for nearly seven minutes, each rocket being launched as the one before it had barely trailed off and faded away. Reds, greens, blues, and dazzling whites. Fireworks aficionados could almost hear the strains of the 1812 Overture.

The surprise spectacular ended as suddenly and as loudly as it began, with one, last, deafening explosion. This time, however, there was no burst of light. Instead, there was a veritable gusher of small, blue and white pieces of paper which scattered in the wind over nearly half a mile. About the size of a standard business card, two by three and a half inches, the missives

21

fluttered lazily to the ground in eerie silence. Several landed on the pavement a few feet from the Henrys as they resumed walking to the mall.

"Who do you suppose is dumb enough to advertise like that?" Alton asked Virginia rhetorically.

"I think it was entertaining, Alton. A lot of people applauded when it ended. Maybe it was sponsored by the mall."

"They must have cut loose a hundred thousand of those leaflets. I expect they will be charged with littering at the very least." Alton bent over and picked up one of the specimens. It turned out to be not exactly a piece of paper. In fact it was a tiny decal. On one side, beneath a clear plastic layer was what appeared to be a miniature flag. Two vertical bars of royal blue separated by a bar of white. In the center of the left blue bar was the letter 'A' in white. In the center of the middle white bar was a blue letter 'O'. The right hand blue bar contained a white 'R'. On the back of the decal there appeared the words, "The Army of Righteousness shall overrun the fortress of Evil."
"Somebody ought to tell those righteous folks it's not so damn righteous to be trashing the countryside," Alton snarled, as he dropped the decal into a trash container just inside the revolving door.

***

December 10th was Michigan Supreme Court Justice Alton P. Henry's birthday. His sixty-sixth birthday. For many years he and Virginia had celebrated it in the same way; with a Christmas shopping trip and dinner at a restaurant. In recent years, the trip was to Twelve Oaks, about an hour's drive from their home just outside of Hillsdale. Except for those birthday outings, the Henrys almost never ate out. They were homebodies.

Their rambling farm house had been Alton's father's home. And his grandfather's. His father, Alton Prentice Henry Jr., better known as Prentice, had given him a deed to the place when Alton and Virginia had their first child. The elder Henry then built himself a new home in town, just a few blocks from his law offices, which quite appropriately, were smack dab in the middle of town.

Prentice Henry was a legend in Hillsdale County. He had grown up on his father's farm just outside of town. He had been a star high school athlete and had played football at the University of Michigan. He graduated from the University's law school, and opened his office in the center of town. A popular, gregarious and handsome fellow, Prentice was an Elder in the Presbyterian Church, President of Rotary, Chairman of the Board of Hillsdale College, and the recipient of just about every honor and award the town and the county had to offer. All this despite the fact that he was a Democrat in an overwhelmingly Republican area.

Prentice had been elected to the state legislature in the Roosevelt landslide in 1932, along with dozens of others who had run for office for the first time, knowing little, if anything, about politics or the government. One of his fellow legislative freshmen, upon learning that he had won the election, promptly purchased a train ticket to Washington D.C. Being a lawyer, Prentice Henry, at least knew that the state legislature sat in Lansing.

Serving his rural district with distinction and dedication, the elder Henry was recruited in 1938 to run for the United States Congress. He won, and appeared on his way to a successful career in politics. Then came 1940, and FDR's decision to seek a third term. Prentice Henry didn't think any president should serve more than two terms. Despite his admiration for Roosevelt, Henry spoke publicly against the third term. Shunned by the party, he was defeated in the primary election, returned to his law practice and never looked back.

In due course, Prentice was elected president of the State Bar of Michigan.

His son Alton was the strong silent type. A good student, an avid outdoors man, a tenacious but not particularly athletic athlete, Alton was known in the small southern Michigan community as a polite, hard working, well behaved boy. To his classmates, he was somewhat of an enigma. He had few friends and no confidantes.

Like his father before him, he played football in high school. Unlike his father, he was not a local hero. For three years, he played guard both on offense and defense. An immovable object on offense, despite his 175 pound size. On defense, he could be downright vicious. But as a lineman, he was always somewhere near the bottom of the pile, usually mud stained so thoroughly that his number 16 could easily have been a 10 or an 18. His name was seldom heard over the public address system or mentioned in the newspaper, even though he was an important factor in Hillsdale High's winning records in 1939, 1940, and 1941, his senior year.

In the Battle Creek game in October of 1941, Henry almost achieved the dream of every mud covered, unsung hero in the defensive line. He actually stripped the ball away from the BC halfback trying to execute a double reverse, and took off down an unobstructed field toward a touchdown and immortality. Unfortunately, the Hillsdale left end was blocked by two players, and being completely disoriented, thought that Henry was running the wrong way. The end was faster than the guard. He caught Henry from behind on the ten yard line. From that day forward, Alton Henry never really trusted anyone.

Alton Henry turned 17 years of age three days after the Japanese attacked Pearl Harbor. He promptly joined the Navy, not because he had any knowledge of ships or interest in the sea, but because the Navy took 17 year olds and the Army didn't.

Henry saw considerable action aboard a battleship in the Pacific. He mustered out in September of 1945, having earned the rank of boatswain's mate.

Alton Henry was a voracious reader. Fiction, science,

philosophy, whatever. He was intellectually curious, and capable of dogged perseverance. During his time in service, Henry read the bible from cover to cover, as well as Webster's New English Dictionary. He easily passed the test which gave him a high school diploma. At war's end, he was entitled to attend college under the GI Bill of Rights. Prentice wanted Alton to go to the University of Michigan, get his degree, then continue on to law school. He longed for the day when the sign over his office door would read, "Henry and Henry, Attorneys at Law."

Alton was accepted to begin classes at the U of M in January of 1946. He attended freshman orientation, and promptly packed up his bags and left Ann Arbor. The whole college experience appeared entirely too juvenile and irrelevant to his career plans. Despite his father's protestations, Alton took up the study of law as a clerk in the law offices across the hall from his father's. He took and passed the bar examination in the summer of 1948. Alton Henry was one of the last lawyers in Michigan to be admitted through the clerkship route, with neither undergraduate college nor law school credits. The clerkship law was repealed later that same year.

If his admission to the bar was quaintly old fashioned, Alton Henry's ascent to the supreme court of Michigan was one of those stranger-than-fiction stories that can only happen to real people in real life.

G. Mennen "Soapy" Williams was elected governor of Michigan in 1948. In the next decade, the Democrats built a powerful dynasty in Lansing, electing majorities in both houses of the legislature, the lieutenant governor, attorney general, and secretary of state, auditor general, and a host of educational and judicial offices.

In 1950, the unions took over the Democratic party. The head of the AFL-CIO in Michigan became a king maker. Every would-be Democratic candidate sought his approval. The endorsement of the union was the *sine qua non* of success in

Michigan politics.

In 1958, Governor Williams sought an unprecedented sixth term. In the days before the Democratic state convention, a handful of Soapy's closest advisors plotted the strategy for a November victory. Unlike many others in his party, Soapy did not rely exclusively on the big, blue collar, Wayne County vote. He wrote off no part of the state, campaigning energetically throughout the geographical mitten and across the Upper Peninsula.

He urged the party leaders to make sure the ticket was well balanced. There were Democrats all over Michigan, he insisted. Hadn't he called square dances in every county?

Talk in the smoke filled hotel room turned to the issue of the sixth term. One of the Detroit papers was already comparing Williams to Roosevelt, and asking editorially, "How long is too long?"

Some of the old timers in the room recalled that a Congressman had criticized FDR, and had paid for it with a primary defeat. A lawyer named Alton Prentice Henry. From Hillsdale, a rural Republican stronghold. Then someone-- later no one would own up to it-- suggested that getting the Roosevelt critic on Soapy's Democratic ticket would be somewhat of a public relations coup. Even this highly principled lawyer who had opposed Roosevelt approved of Soapy's sixth term. It would be worth at least one good story.

And so the plan was hatched to put lawyer Alton Prentice Henry Jr. on the Democratic team by nominating him for the Michigan Supreme Court. A very young second level organizer at state party headquarters was put in charge of feeling out the candidate. The organizer didn't know Alton Prentice Henry Jr. much less his son, Alton Prentice Henry III. He had never been to Hillsdale.

Prentice was out of town. To the young man from party headquarters, the 34 year old Alton looked like a middle aged adult. He simply assumed that Alton Henry III was the lawyer he was supposed to approach about running for the supreme court.

When the senior Henry returned and heard the news that Soapy's people wanted his son Alton to run for the supreme court, he was ecstatic. He immediately wrote a check for $10,000 to the Democratic Party. Thereafter, no one ever mentioned the case of mistaken identity.

Alton Henry became the party's high court candidate and, in November of 1958, was swept into office along with the rest of the followers of G. Mennen Williams.

***

On Tuesday, December 11th, the second day of his 67th year, Justice Henry followed his invariable routine. Up at 5:45 am, he pulled on his old grey corduroys, donned an ancient wool Pendleton shirt and an even more ancient leather jacket, and took a brisk walk down Still Valley Road three quarters of a mile to his favorite diner, where he bought a morning First Press, downed a glass of apple juice, asked after the owner's husband's health, petted her snarling beagle, announced his weather prediction for the day to the several assorted locals who occupied the rickety chairs and leaned on the sticky oilcloth-covered tables drinking coffee and smoking cigarettes, then trudged back up Still Valley in time to shower, shave, dress, eat breakfast, and read the paper before clicking on the television for the 7:00 am network newscast.

This day, the print and broadcast media were in agreement. The headline story was dubbed the 'Christmas Fireworks.' The spectacular display Alton and Virginia had witnessed the night before had, it was reported, been duplicated in 15 different communities throughout the East and the Midwest. All occurred at exactly 7:14 PM Eastern Standard Time. All had been within a short distance of a busy shopping mall. All had ended with the scattering of decals bearing the prediction that 'the army of righteousness will overrun the fortress of evil.'

The 'Christmas Fireworks' had one more thing in common. Each had been launched from the roof of a medical clinic which performed abortions.

The Federal Bureau of Investigation was, of course, taking charge. The president of the United States had already issued a condemnation of the incidents. So had just about every national, state and local public official the media were able to corner between 7:30 PM and 7:30 am.

No one had been hurt. In Pittsburgh, a garage fire was attributed to falling rocket debris, and in Cincinnati, a woman claimed her cat had been burned. None of the pyrotechnics had been doused before climaxing. They were simply too inaccessible and unexpected.

The talking heads on CBS, NBC, ABC, and CNN; commentators, hastily summoned law professors, psychologists and criminologists; all speculated on responsibility for the displays and the identity of the perpetrators. Bible scholars debated the origin, authenticity, and symbolism of the army of righteousness.

And almost every report of the incident included a rehashing of recent bombings, shootings, protest demonstrations and arrests at abortion facilities. Even without saying that there was a connection, the juxtaposition of information sent a strong, chilling message. America's quarter century political division over human reproduction had entered a new and ominous phase. Now there was an organized, interstate, paramilitary organization at work.

* * *

Henry turned off the television and turned his attention to his desk. A solitary file lay in the center of the work surface. Justice Henry never retired until every bit of court business which came to his attention during the day was addressed. One thing at a time.

Thirty years before, Alton Henry had issued the firm and final decision that he would not be needing an office in Lansing. No sir, he didn't need a fancy, expensive office like the other members of the court, the legislature and the executive branch. Waste of the taxpayers' money. He would construct an office wing on his house and work there. The frugality angle played well in the newspapers, and Henry instantly became the darling of all the taxpayers advocate groups, a distinction he cherished, nurtured and played to the hilt every eight years when he was up for reelection.

The voters were less aware that Henry had been among the most insistent lobbyists for state provided automobiles for the justices. In all his thirty-plus years on the court, he had never stayed overnight in Lansing. Long before the coming of the interstate highway system, Justice Henry commuted nearly 80 miles over two lane roads to attend sessions of the court.

He worked at a huge roll top desk which had belonged to his grandfather. It was made more than a century before by some long forgotten Dutch artisan in Grand Rapids. A work of art, really, full of cubby holes, tiny drawers, and built in files, all finished in solid oak, with each piece carefully chosen so that the grain flowed in gracious and continuous patterns.

Beyond the desk, the spacious room was furnished modestly. An old kitchen table surrounded by four wooden chairs served as a library table. It occupied a corner of the room where two sixteen foot, full-wall bookshelves met. When Henry was researching the law, there were usually five or six law books, annotated statutes, cases, and indices scattered on the table.

Opposite the library corner was a door to an ante room which served as his secretary's office. The mail was delivered to the Henrys' road side mailbox at about 10:00 am every business day. At 10:15 am, his secretary would drive up in her blue Oldsmobile Cutlass, clean out the mail box, park her car at the side of the house, and using a key that fit only the side door, enter the office ante room.

Unless the justice had some pressing matter that needed to be typed immediately, she would leave at precisely 4:00 PM. When she did, every piece of mail which had arrived that day and every faxed message would have been answered.

Like all of the secretaries in the supreme court, Henry's was skilled in the use of the personal computer. She used the latest version of Word Perfect, which had become the lawyers' word processing software of choice. Her boss did not, could not, type anything. Neither did he use the Dictaphone which had been supplied to him by the court administrator. He did not know how to operate a fax machine. Never had done it. He did not have a law clerk. He wrote all of his own memoranda and opinions. He wrote them using a number two lead pencil on eight and a half by thirteen inch yellow legal foolscap. Some people go down hard. Alton Henry's stubbornness had not changed since his days at Hillsdale High.

There was a window next to Henry's desk. It overlooked the treated wooden deck that wandered around the corner of the house from the office to the kitchen. The Anderson window cranked open, swinging from left to right. In the summer, there would be a screen on the inside. Now, in December, the screen was stored in the garage.

Next to the window, leaning against the wall, was Alton Henry's 22 caliber rifle. Fully loaded with long cartridges. The justice glanced out at the deck. It was habitual. He probably glanced out at that deck a hundred times a day. He knew the intruder would return. He still bristled whenever he thought of the damage done last summer when the sneaky little vandal actually got into the house. Lamps overturned and broken. Upholstered furniture ripped apart. One day he would kill that little black bastard. Put a 22 slug right between his beady eyes.

* * *

Henry was working on his opinion in the case of *Silus v Grand Haven Consolidated Hospital*, when the phone call came. Silus was an interesting matter. A so-called wrongful birth case, one of a new genre that had followed inexorably in the wake of the U.S. supreme court's decision in the case of *Roe v Wade*. Martha Silus, the plaintiff, had been abandoned by her drinking, gambling, abusive husband. Penniless, pregnant, and single parenting three toddlers, Martha sought the aid of the Women's Health Center in Saugatuck. Since she was already in her sixth month, she was referred to the defendant hospital, where she was scheduled for a late term abortion. As the attending physician began the procedure, complications developed, Martha went into shock, and feeling that she was further along in her pregnancy than they had originally believed, the doctor decided to perform an emergency cesarean section, to save the lives of both the mother and child.

Saddled with another mouth to feed and no breadwinner, Martha brought suit against the hospital and the doctor for malpractice and breach of contract. During the trial, the defendants sought to introduce evidence that Mr. Silus had returned to the home after the litigation was commenced and was, in fact, living there at the time of trial. The trial judge sustained objections to the offer of proof, and the jury returned a verdict of $500,000. The court of appeals affirmed, and the supreme court granted leave to appeal. Mostly to consider the evidentiary issue.

The call was from the chief justice.

"Hello, Alton. How are you?"

"Just dandy, Ed."

"And Virginia. How is she? All through Christmas shopping?"

"I guess so. She never tells me."

"Please give her my regards, and say hello for Elizabeth, too. She's very fond of your wife, you know." Breitner had a very stilted way of trying to be cordial and friendly.

"That's nice. You can tell her the feeling is mutual. Elizabeth is a wonderful lady. I don't know how she got mixed up with the likes of you."

The chief justice ignored Henry's good natured barb. Clever repartee was not Breitner's forte.

"Do you have a minute, Alton? I'd like to talk to you about our January term."

"Go ahead, Ed. It's your nickel."

"As you know, we have 16 oral arguments on the calendar, which is a full docket. But we also have a number of administrative matters that are pressing, and I wonder if we shouldn't plan on sitting all day Thursday and maybe even on Friday morning."

"C'mon, Ed, you know how I feel about Fridays in Lansing. What are all these administrative matters?"

"We have a new colleague on board. Malloy is going to want to be sworn in. Frankly, we're going to have to spend some time orienting him to our methods. And then there is the matter of voting for the chief justice."

"That shouldn't take long."

"Electing the chief?"

"Yeah. That's always a done deal by the time the court meets."

"It should be. We still have a four to three majority."

"Do we have a candidate?"

"This job is no fun, as you know Alton, and frankly, I don't know why I keep letting you people stick me with it, but so far, nobody else has expressed any willingness to take it on, and for better or worse, the girls seem to think I have been doing a good job."

"I'm not sure that's a favorable recommendation. I certainly don't think that Gloria Steinem and the Queen of Sheba would want ME to be the boss. I don't know how you keep those two in line, Ed. You must be more of a stud than you let on."

"It's not my charm, believe me. The fact is that Doris and Hilda both live in Detroit. Frankly, neither of them want to move to Lansing."

"Heck Ed, what's a little commute? I hear you live in Bloomfield Hills. Or is it Northern Ontario?"

Breitner's face reddened, but his voice remained matter of fact. "I keep an apartment in Lansing, as you know. I'm here every week. And managing Michigan's One Court of Justice is a pretty demanding job. Surely, you wouldn't begrudge the chief justice few days at his fishing cabin."

"Go fishin' all you want, Ed, but you have to find someone to mind the store when you're gone."

Breitner grew defensive. "Van and Bob have offices here in Lansing. They're available for emergencies."

"Maybe one of them should be the chief." Henry cut to the quick with the comment.

"Personally, I'm glad the Republicans don't have enough votes to elect O'Leary. He has too many bad habits. And we certainly don't want Van back again, for Heaven's sake. Remember how much trouble you and I had getting Van out of the center chair after I came on the court?"

"Those were the good old days, before you became leader of the girl scouts and took up Canadian citizenship. What about the new guy? Will he be trying to round up votes?"

"No way. I've talked to him. He doesn't even know where the bathroom is yet, but he can count noses. I'm sure he expects us to make the decision."

"I suppose so."

Henry sounded resigned to the reelection of Breitner as chief justice. Seizing on that impression, Breitner felt it was time to push for a commitment. The truth was that he was afraid of losing Henry's support. As long as Green had been on the court, the Democrats enjoyed a five to two majority, and Breitner didn't need Henry. Now Henry was the swing vote. Philosophically, he was more conservative than most Republicans. He had little use for Hilda Germaine, and was downright hostile to Doris Templeton.

And he had been increasingly critical of the incumbent chief justice.

Michigan's Constitution of 1963, it's first since 1908, established what was then thought to be a revolutionary concept in the administration of justice. It provided that Michigan was to have one court of justice, consisting of a supreme court, an intermediate court of appeals, trial courts of general jurisdiction called circuit courts, probate courts in every county to handle estates and juveniles, and local courts of limited jurisdiction called district courts.

The supreme court was to be at the apex of the new system, which was seen as an integrated court. No one knew what that meant exactly. The more progressive view seemed to be that the supreme court would make court rules and issue administrative orders to assure that the court system really worked. It was to take all necessary steps to eliminate backlogs, enforce ethical standards, discipline errant judges, modernize clerical functions, supervise staff employees.

And on and on.

Alton Henry was a court management hawk, most of the time. Being himself an extremely hard worker, with no life to speak of outside of his work on the court, Henry was impatient with any trial judge whose docket got behind. He kept lecturing Breitner on the supreme court's responsibility to make the trial judges work hard. He was no fan of modern methods of litigation. In particular, he hated the process known as discovery.

Discovery by taking sworn depositions of witnesses prior to the trial was introduced in the late 1930's. It was originally intended to speed up court trials and make them more fair and just by eliminating surprise testimony. Over the years, however, discovery grew like the proverbial beanstalk to the point that it often overshadowed the trial itself. Lawsuits of any magnitude spawned mountains of typewritten depositions, the expense of which was astronomical. Financing a legal action became an impossible hurdle for average people and small law firms to clear. Henry thought the supreme court should do something.

But whatever Breitner proposed, Henry opposed. When Breitner sought to install a state wide computer network, Henry said it wasn't necessary, would cost too much and probably wouldn't work. The necessity and cost were debatable. The many obvious failures of the new system were grist for Henry's mill.

And then there were Breitner's frequent fishing expeditions. Every time he went to his Canadian cabin, Henry would make some sarcastic crack about him being a wet back, or needing a green card, or going into semi retirement. They had never been close, but since Kosman was replaced by O'Leary, Henry had become downright difficult.

Breitner wondered how much Henry knew about the O'Leary-Kosman election. He still felt a rush of satisfaction whenever he thought of it. Breitner first became chief justice in 1981, when he, Alton Henry, Douglas Green, and Bernie Kosman as a Democratic majority, had ousted long time Republican chief justice Fred Van Timlin from the chair. Breitner was reelected as Chief in 1983, and things were going very well in his career.

Then in 1985, Kosman challenged him saying that the chief justiceship should rotate among the justices. In truth, Kosman himself wanted to be chief. Breitner persuaded Green to go to Kosman and tell him that he did not have the support of the Democrats. Kosman promptly went to the three GOP justices and, pushing his plan for rotation, got their three votes, which, together with his own, made him the chief justice.

Furious, Breitner vowed to make Kosman pay for his defection. He worked behind the scenes trying to deny the Democratic nomination to Kosman when he stood for reelection in 1986. He failed. The convention nominated Kosman and Doris Templeton. Two weeks later the Republicans nominated Robert Allen O'Leary, a well regarded Upper Peninsula Congressman. The polls showed that Templeton, one of the first women on the supreme court, was going to lead the ticket by a wide margin, but that Kosman and O'Leary were in a horse race for the second seat. Breitner saw his chance. He placed a clandestine call to Bob O'Leary, offered substantial financial help for the campaign if O'Leary would back him for chief justice.

The Congressman was very receptive. "Ed, you're my favorite Democrat justice. I'd be honored to be your new best friend," he had said. Whereupon Ed Breitner whispered to his wife Elizabeth Whitney Rutherford Breitner, who in turn whispered to the Whitneys of Grosse Pointe Shores and the Rutherfords of Birmingham and Rochester, and voila! there was a sudden influx of big bucks into the O'Leary campaign coffers. The rising tide of his television commercials in the final week of the campaign swept the Munising Irishman out of the lower House in Washington, D.C. and into the highest court in Lansing, Michigan.

Despite their secret alliance, Breitner wasn't too sure that O'Leary would back him under all circumstances. A defection by Henry could easily upset Breitner's tenuous majority. So he sought to pin Henry down.

"Frankly, Alton, I think it would move matters along much more quickly and smoothly if you would be good enough to put my name in nomination. I mean, you are the senior member of the Democratic contingent. Your nomination of me would certainly be well received by Justices Templeton and Germaine, and to be perfectly frank about it, I think our Republican colleagues would be impressed by seeing you take a leadership role in this matter."

"You flatter me, Mr. Chief Justice. I'm not so sure that the ladies wouldn't abandon you if I make the nomination. Let me think about it."

"Take your time. By the way, what are you going to do on that wrongful birth case? We didn't have much time to discuss it at conference."

"Some interesting legal issues there. Wrongful birth cases are usually predicated on the doctor's failure to inform parents of birth defects. They claim that if the doctor had given them the straight skinny they would have had an abortion. And since our screwy United States Supreme Court says that abortions are legal, people are collecting money for having deformed kids. Then there are the so-called wrongful life actions. Same thing, only this time it's the deformed child who wants damages for living. There are two other variations on the theme. Wrongful pregnancy and wrongful conception, where birth control pills, vasectomies and the like don't work.

"What we've got here is the delivery of a healthy baby. It might be called a wrongful delivery case. It may in fact be a case of first impression. The plaintiff's not blaming the defendant because she got pregnant or because she didn't have all the information necessary to decide whether to have an abortion. She had already decided on the abortion. That's what she went to the hospital to get. That's what she thought was going to happen. That's what she was paying for. It may be nothing but a simple breach of contract."

"Wasn't there some evidentiary problem?" Breitner was glad to get the discussion away from the chief justiceship. When they were talking about the law, he and Henry were much more comfortable and friendly.

"Yup. Defendants wanted to prove that the plaintiff's husband, who had walked out on her, had come back home before the trial. Apparently they had two ideas in mind. First, she testified that his leaving her when she was pregnant and had three other little kids was a main reason why she decided on the abortion. If he came back home, maybe she really wasn't so unhappy about having another kid. Second, they wanted the jury to know that the breadwinner was back, and if he was the scoundrel she said he was, maybe he would gamble away whatever she got from the lawsuit."

"The trial judge excluded the evidence?"

"And the court of appeals affirmed."

"Sounds like a good start for 1991. Oh say, did you hear about what the right wing kooks did last night?"

"Hear about it? I heard it. Virginia and I went to Twelve Oaks last night. I must say it was a darn good show, but they sure dumped a lot of trash on Oakland County."

"They dumped a lot more than trash. I tell you Alton, these people pose a real threat to our country. I sometimes think we're in for the kind of religious wars they have been having in Ireland for so long."

"And in Israel?"

"That's really a different thing. Has to do with national sovereignty."

"A bomb's a bomb, Ed. They're all nuts."

"Maybe so. Let's stay in touch. And think about that C.J. thing."

"OK"

"And don't forget to give my regards to Virginia."

Justice Henry hung up the phone shaking his head. Ed Breitner was a fool, Henry mused. Did Breitner really think he could dump on people for years and then ooze a little charm on the telephone and get himself reelected? Henry dialed the number for the Clinton County Circuit Court.

"Jim Malloy here."

"How's it going, Jim?"

"Good enough, Mr. Justice." Malloy knew the voice. They had been on the phone with each other every day since the election. "Trying to wrap up all my business here in circuit court. Gotta give the county their money's worth."

"Have you talked to O'Leary and Van Timlin yet?"

"Just briefly. Nothing really substantive. They have both been very friendly and helpful. So have Templeton and Germaine. I've called both of them as well."

"I'd be careful if I were you when you talk to the ladies. Especially Doris. Whatever you say to her is going right back to

Breitner."

"I figured they were pretty close."

"Speaking of the chief, I just got off the phone with him. He is pitching me hard to support him for another term. I can't tell whether or not he has gotten wind of what you and I have been discussing."

"What did you tell him?"

"Not much. I let him assume that I expect him to be reelected. If he thinks it's in the bag, he won't be putting roadblocks in our path."

"Was he looking for a commitment?"

"Definitely. He played the old 'we Democrats have to stick together' song. Then he asked if I would nominate him."

"And?"

"Well, I just told him I thought getting a nomination from me might lose him some votes with the Detroit crowd. I told him I would have to think about it."

'You know Alton, that donkey and elephant business doesn't play very well with me. I've never held, or even been a candidate for, a partisan political office. When Mark Edwards asked me to run for the court, I told him I didn't like the process of party nomination. He agreed. Thinks we ought to have a Missouri Plan, or some other appointive system. I'm not opposed to electing justices, just so long as it is truly a non-partisan election."

"The Missouri Plan stinks. Imagine running for reelection on a Yes or No ballot. All the people I know would vote No on every incumbent."

"Maybe so. My beef with the present method of party convention nominations is precisely what is happening with the chief justiceship. It divides the court. Creates a We - They mentality that interferes with collegial decision making."

"The court is always going to be divided, Jim"

"I suppose that's human nature. But it shouldn't be automatically along party lines. When I accepted the Republican

Party nomination, I told the convention that my only qualification for their partisan nomination was my monumental non-partisanship."

Henry chuckled. "Sounds like you were backing into the campaign bus."

"Actually, it was a take off on Fiorello La Guardia's famous quip, 'My only qualification for public office is my monumental ingratitude'."

"I certainly agree that there is too much politics on the court. Breitner is a political animal. That wife of his thinks he ought to be president of the United States. She's always parading him around for her toady friends at the Hunt Club, or wherever they hang out. And Templeton is a hack. A political groupie. She thinks Breitner shits ice cream."

"What about Hilda? She seems like a very level headed person. And highly regarded, from what I hear. The first black woman on the court. Always comes across measured and thoughtful."

Yeah. Yeah. I know. Everyone loves her, but I think she'd make a lousy chief justice. She's always late for court. Never gets her opinions in on time. Has trouble making up her mind. That's what happens when you try to please everyone."

"O'Leary's got a good head on his shoulders. And he used to be in Congress. Has some experience dealing with the legislative branch of government. We ought to work on him."

"You can work on him if you want to. But he's not my first choice."

"Why don't you take the job?"

Henry's peals of laughter were genuine, even if slightly forced. "No thank you. I would have a revolt on my hands by the end of the first day."

"I think you would do a fine job." Malloy knew he was pressing, and hoped he sounded more sincere than he really was.

"You flatter me. But I know my limitations. Being chief

justice is not my ambition. But you, Jim-- I keep telling you--
you are just what this court needs. You're young. You're new.
You've been a trial judge. The trial bench knows you and they
like you. Your home base is right there in Lansing. You're on
good terms with our new governor. It just makes good sense."

"I'm starting to think you're serious about this, Mr. Justice."

"Damn right I'm serious."

"And you really think a rookie justice can handle the job?"

"Listen. In the United States Supreme Court, the president
appoints the chief justice. Rarely is a sitting member of the court
appointed. The chief justice of the United States is almost
always a rookie."

"I still have my doubts, Alton. But if you want me to, I'll talk
to the other Justices and see what they think. I'm going to feel
awfully presumptive, though."

"Forget how it makes you feel. If you haven't got the
testicular fortitude to grab the brass ring when it comes around,
you shouldn't be chief justice anyway."

"Will you help me?"

"The only one I can talk to is O'Leary. Van Timlin hates my
guts. He is still smarting over the fact that we took him out of
the center chair a decade ago. He was a disaster then and he'd
be a worse disaster now. Don't even think of urging him to run.
Even Breitner would be better than Van."

The two agreed to keep in touch. It was getting late in the
day. Henry's secretary poked her head in and announced that
she was leaving and did he have anything that needed to be
done before she left. No, he didn't. And she should drive
carefully on the way home. In forty-five minutes Alton's wife,
Virginia would ring him on his office phone line and inform him
that dinner was ready. He never ate lunch, but always had
dinner at exactly five o'clock.

At dinner, they usually talked about their two sons and their
families. About once a week the boys would call their mother.
She kept up on all the grandchildren, the boys' careers,

vacations, health, general gossip. None of the family ever called the justice just to talk. Alton was no good at small talk. He wrote letters full of sage advice to his children and grandchildren and they wrote back to thank him.

Before the meal was over, the talk would turn to the supreme court. Alton shared everything with Virginia. All the gossip. All of his opinions, ideas, and feelings. He talked and she listened.

Virginia called. Dinner is on the table.

Alton took one last glance at the deck. There he was. Standing starkly still in the fading daylight. Staring boldly, challengingly at him not more than thirty feet outside his office window. His face expressionless. His eyes unblinking.

Alton moved with infinite patience in tiny increments until he was at the window. With consummate care, he turned the crank until the window was three inches open. Keeping his eyes fixed on his target, he reached over with his right hand and grasped the rifle. Still moving slowly so as not to startle the intruder, he lifted the gun, rested it on the casement, slid the barrel through the opened window, took careful aim, inhaled deeply, let out about half of his breath and squeezed the trigger.

As if guided by some surrealistic instinct, the thirty pound woodchuck scurried off of the deck a fraction of an instant before the rifle fired.

"Damn you." Muttered the Honorable Alton Henry.

CHAPTER 3

GERMAINE

On this cold December morning, like so many others, Ben Tuttle and his son Josh had breakfast together at 6:00 AM. Toast and orange juice. Coffee for the doctor. Milk for the 13 year old eighth grader. They didn't talk much. Just a few softly spoken comments about the Pistons or the Bulls or about school or the family. It was a special time for them that Josh had suggested because his father was so busy at the hospital, gone so much, and well, a guy needed to talk to his dad once in awhile.

Ben left for the hospital at 6:30. They parted, as always, with a big bear hug and a jovial, fatherly punch to the shoulder.

It was dark and cold outside. Inside, the five bedroom brick two story home was churchly quiet. Josh's sister Melissa, asleep in her room, would need vigorous waking at 7:15. Grandma would be up by 7:45, doting over her granddaughter, lecturing Josh, and scolding her daughter, the Honorable Hilda Tuttle Germaine, Associate Justice of the Supreme Court of Michigan.

Josh was big for his age. Five feet eleven. 160 pounds. A good looking boy with an infectious, toothy smile. He was, by anyone's standards, a very promising young man. Almost an 'A' student. A competent, if not excellent athlete. Active in the Boy Scouts. Steady. Responsible.

What he was to do this morning was typical of his thoughtful and affectionate nature. With an armload of firewood from the back porch, he tip-toed into his parents' massive master bedroom, and silently built a fire in the fireplace. Across the room, covers pulled halfway over her head, Hilda opened one eye and watched her teenager at work. Then she pretended to be asleep as he turned away from the cozy flames and left the room.

A few minutes later, Josh returned with a tray. Orange juice, coffee, toast with butter and strawberry jam. And the morning First Press.

"Brought ya breakfast, mom. Dad says you gotta get up by 7:30."

Hilda sat up and smiled. She thanked him for the breakfast, for starting the fire, for being such a wonderful son. He sat on the edge of the bed and they talked, as they often did, about his future. What high school. Which college. What career he would follow. It was a running family joke that he was being torn between law and medicine. He would always insist that he wanted to be an engineer, so as not to take sides between his mom and dad. That morning Hilda thought the engineering thing was starting to get serious.

They were soon distracted by Grandma's noisy fussing over Melissa. Her hair wasn't right. Her dress needed attention. "Here child, let me just press it up a bit. You can't go off to school with such a wrinkled old dress darling. No way."

Josh and Hilda knew what was coming. They looked at each other knowingly.

"Melissa honey, your momma is a Justice of the supreme court. You can't be going off to school looking like some old welfare child."

Josh giggled. Hilda shook her head. Cindy Hawkins Germaine, 74 years old and proud of every day of it, would never fully adjust to the most exciting, rewarding, self affirming day of her life when she, a one time New Orleans jazz club dancer, sat in the chambers of the supreme court and watched her only offspring sworn in as a member of the highest tribunal of the sovereign state of Michigan.

Within the hour, Josh and Melissa had trudged off to school. Hilda had showered, dressed, and come downstairs to join her mother in the kitchen. It was Tuesday, December 18, 1990. A week before Christmas. It was difficult for Hilda to leave Cindy in the morning. Her mother always wanted to fix a big breakfast. Pancakes. Eggs. Bacon. Just like down home. Hilda rarely wanted anything but a piece of toast and some juice. The ritual never varied. Hilda would get her coat out of the closet, pick up her brief case, and go out in the kitchen to say goodby. Her mother would scold her for not eating enough, pour her a cup of coffee, insist that she take off her coat and sit at the table like a civilized person with good manners.

Then Cindy would serve up a lumberman's breakfast. Hilda would adamantly refuse to eat anything. Her mother, after scolding her about wasting good food, would take off her apron, pull up a chair and dive into the pancakes with unabashed gusto.

Hilda thought she understood the psychology of the process. Her mother had grown up in poverty in New Orleans. Fourth in age of nine siblings borne by her mother's mother of three different fathers. Cindy would never quite outlive the gnawing sense of guilt that accompanied looking into a full refrigerator. She could not bring herself to cook pancakes, bacon, and eggs for herself. Only the fiction that she was feeding her daughter alleviated enough of the guilt to permit her to prepare the meal; only the pretense that her daughter was wasting valuable nutrition would justify her own appetite.

Cindy was dark skinned. In her younger days, she had fought to be recognized as a Negro. With a capital 'N'. As opposed to the many common descriptions which seemed to carry negative overtones. Colored. Darkie. Nigrah. Black. And, of course, the almost universal slang word, nigger. She was a proud woman who, despite minimal, indifferent education, and a childhood in dirt poor slums, never felt the least bit inferior or deprived. She was, in her day, a strikingly beautiful woman, with flashing, flirtatious eyes, an almost wicked smile, and a figure to die for. At the age of 18, she was an accomplished jazz club entertainer. She had the moves. And she could sing the blues. When the horns wailed, the pianos rattled and the thumping bass vibrated on the wooden platform, Cindy could let out a mournful howl or a soul shattering trill that would stop the traffic on Bourbon

Street.

One of the boys who stopped was a French sailor. Pierre Germaine was an able bodied seaman assigned to the destroyer 'Provence' at anchor off the coast of Portugal when the news came that France had surrendered to Nazi Germany in 1942. The captain had convened his senior officers, informed them that he had no intention of sailing under the flag of the Vichy government, and offered to put anyone ashore who did not want to join DeGalle's free French movement. No body left, and the 'Provence' sailed for the gulf of Mexico, in due course, putting in to the port of New Orleans.

There she idled for two years while the American navy department tried to figure out what to do with the ship, how to supply it, who would pay the men, and under whose command she would sail. Finally, in the spring of 1944, the 'Provence' was assigned to the United States Coast Guard, and she spent the rest of the war patrolling in the Caribbean and the Gulf, based in New Orleans.

Pierre was born in a small town on the northern coast of France. Until he joined the navy and got a week end pass in Marseilles, he had never seen a black person. Whatever baggage of bigotry may have been carried by other sailors, this one was unfettered and free to see in the lovely ebony singer the helpmate of his heart's desire. They were married in November of 1944.

After the war, Pierre was naturalized as an American citizen. He worked as a bartender in the French quarter. Cindy sang and danced. In 1947 they bought a small restaurant, and opened a club of their own. In 1948, Hilda was born. In 1949 Pierre died. Ulcers. Pneumonia. Undernourishment. Overworking. Who knows. A good man. The good die young. Pierre was 29.

Cindy struggled to keep the club open herself. It was a constant battle. She cooked, waited tables, sang, and danced. And grew old, fat, and tired counting coins, paying taxes and putting her daughter through Southern University and Tulane

Law School.

Hilda loved her mother. Without reservation. It warmed her heart to have mamma living with her and Ben. Ben loved the old lady too. They shared good natured banter whenever they were together. The fact was that Cindy was lonely. By nature, a gregarious person, she loved to talk. "Have a lil' chat" as she would say. Hilda always found it hard to break away.

This December morning, the 'lil' chat' lasted until almost 9:30 AM. Hilda leaned on the gas pedal of her state owned Oldsmobile, as she entered the John C. Lodge freeway, and headed downtown.

Traffic was still heavy on the Lodge, though it was past prime drive time. Hilda called her secretary and informed her that she would be a little late. Again. Passing Henry Ford Hospital brought the face of her husband into sharp focus in her mind. He was a struggling med student at Columbia when they met. It was September of 1975. She was a new associate at a Manhattan mega law firm, having just completed a two year stint as a law clerk in the United States Circuit Court of Appeals for the sixth circuit. She was glad to be out of Cincinnati and back to the big apple, where she had spent an exciting 18 months earning her LLM at NYU.

They met down in the village on a Saturday morning in June. She was just out for a stroll, a stunning mulatto lawyer in tight blue jeans and a halter top. He was playing basketball behind a twelve foot link chain fence, shirtless, his ebony chest dripping sweat, as he muscled his way through a mass of grunting, cursing, elbowing weekend jocks to contest for a rebound. Raw manhood. Enough to make a lady swoon. She didn't really swoon. But she did start hanging around. First pretending to be waiting for a bus. When the bus came and went, she bought a newspaper, and pretended to be pouring through the want ads. Eventually the newspaper ruse grew wearisome, and she feigned interest in the basketball game. Soon enough every player on both teams could tell she was watching Ben Tuttle, and Ben himself flashed her an appreciative smile.

As she was about to give up her vigil, the ball skidded out of bounds just inside the fence where she was standing. Ben jogged over to in bound the ball. He was close enough to savor her perfume. He made eye contact with her. Big time. With a wink, he flashed her a disarming smile.

"Wanna see me dunk?" He asked boastfully.

She did.

He flipped the ball to a team mate and charged toward the basket. His team mate lofted a perfect ally-oop pass which Ben snatched from the air two inches above the rim and slammed into the net, as his body thumped against two monster defenders planted beneath the basket. The three of them sprawled on the asphalt and the feisty referee raced to the heap, blowing his whistle, pointing at Ben with his left hand while slapping the back of his head with his right hand. You. You. You. Charging. No basket.

That's how they met. The black and tan. Detroit and New Orleans. Man and woman. Lovers. Friends. Partners in living. Husband and wife. Mom and dad.

She had chosen to keep her maiden name, adopting Tuttle as her middle name. Not hyphenated. Just Hilda Tuttle Germaine. Her mother always told her she was half French. Made it sound special, like being royalty or something. Hilda wanted to keep that identity.

When Ben finished his internship at Sloan Kettering, they moved to Detroit. It was Ben's home town. He had always wanted to practice here. For some reason, he loved the Motor City. Motown. It had a siren call to African Americans.

Detroit was originally a French town. Founded in 1701 by Antoine de la Mothe Cadillac. He can be seen in all the old oil paintings with Alphonse de Tonty, standing along side their canoe on the south bank of the river they called de Troit, meaning 'the straights'. Talking to the Indians. Planting the flag of France. Starting a city. Behind them, at the top of the hill, more Indians. Their arms heavy with furs, waiting for the trading post to open for business.

They called it Fort Ponchartrain. It was a French town for almost 60 years. The street names still echo that Gallic tradition. Beaubien. Rivard. LaFayette. The French settlers established their farms along the Detroit River. Long narrow strips of land running south from the river bank. Later the fences separating those farms became the boundaries of the city's political wards from which were elected councilmen, congressmen and bailiffs of the common pleas court.

An Ottawa chief named Pontiac was one of the first suburbanites. Like many who came two hundred years later, he parked outside of Detroit and tried to take over the city. After 135 days, he gave up. That was in 1763. In 1805 the city burned to the ground and got rebuilt with a whole new design. A judge named Woodward drew up the plan. It was to be a series of hubs with streets running out from each like spokes on a wheel. It never quite happened. The frustration of urban planners is not a purely modern phenomenon.

In 1812, General Anthony Wayne surrendered Detroit to the British. After the war of 1812, it became part of the Northwest Territory of the United States of America.

Detroit was the capital of Michigan for awhile. The first home of the University of Michigan. The terminus of the underground railroad that carried black men and women from slavery in the south to freedom in the north.

In the 20th century, a man named Henry Ford came along and built an automobile, and he figured out a way to build a lot of automobiles and sell them cheap. He decided to pay all his workers $5.00 a day, and then lots of people wanted to come and live in Detroit. They came from Ireland and Germany and Poland. From Italy and Hungary.

The town got bigger and busier. And bigger and noisier. And bigger and dirtier. And bigger and richer. And bigger and bigger. The village of Woodmere was annexed in 1905. The village of Saint Clair Heights was annexed in 1918. The village of Oakwood was annexed in 1923. The village of Redford was annexed in 1927. Then, like a boiler with no safety valve, the city stopped spreading out and the people simply crowded together. Density equals pressure.

The African American population of Detroit mushroomed during the second world war. They came to work in the former auto factories which had been converted to military purposes. War production it was called. Blacks came from the south in droves along with Appalachian whites from Kentucky, West Virginia, and Tennessee. It was an explosive mix. In 1943, in a part of the city known as Paradise Valley, the mix erupted in a bloody race riot.

The following year, on December 30, 1944, a man named Orsel McGhee bought a house on Seeboldt Street, a few blocks from Northwestern High School. One of his neighbors, a man named Sipes, sued Mr. McGhee. Said he couldn't live on Seeboldt Street because he was not of the Caucasian race. The case went to the Supreme Court of Michigan. A man named Thurgood Marshall filed a brief there on behalf of Mr. McGhee arguing that the Negro population of Detroit had increased from 40,000 in 1920 to 210,000 in 1944, and Mr. McGhee and his family and others like them had no place to live.

McGhee lost his case in the Supreme Court of Michigan. All eight justices said the law was against him. But on the third day of May, 1948, the Supreme Court of the United States ruled otherwise. McGhee stayed on Seeboldt, and nobody talked about Paradise Valley any more.

In the 1950's black families drove up and down the streets of the twenty-first and twenty-second wards, the sprawling northeast and northwest residential areas, every weekend, looking at houses. No need to look for 'For Sale' signs. Almost every house was for sale. Just go up, ring the doorbell, ask to take a look, and if you like it, make an offer. Street by street, block by block, the racial composition of Detroit changed.

One of the last bastions of white middle class exclusivity lay between Six and Eight Mile Roads on the south and north respectively, and Woodward Avenue and Livernois on the East and West. The Detroit Golf Club and the University of Detroit anchored the south end of the area. The State Fairgrounds guarded the Eastern edge.

Most of the homes in the posh Palmer Woods subdivision, and the upscale Sherwood Forest area west of it were built in the 1920's and 1930's. They were spacious and gracious. Quality workmanship. Marble. Oak. Lots of oak. Their original owners were for the most part WASPs. The street names harkened to their English roots. Canterbury. Cambridge. Berkeley. Fairfield. The architecture did the same. Brick and stone. Classic Victorian lines. Leaded glass windows.

When the inner city black bubble burst, the ethnic populations moved like the shifting sand dunes along the shores of Lake Michigan. Usually, they didn't leap frog. They stayed in formation. First the Germans and the Belgians, then the Italians, then the Poles seeped out of the east side of Detroit and filtered into the nearest Grosse Pointe communities one by one. Keeping the same order, they drifted across Eight Mile Road into Macomb county. East Detroit. Saint Clair Shores. Roseville.

On the West side, the Jewish neighborhoods around Twelfth Street, LaSalle, Elmhurst, and Dexter Boulevard began moving north. The WASPs went to Birmingham, Farmington, Bloomfield Hills.

In the 1940's and 1950's people used to drive through Sherwood Forest and Palmer Woods during Christmas season to see the beautiful lights which decorated the mansion houses. By the end of the 1960's, there were only a handful of Christians in the neighborhood.

In the late 60's and 70's the next wave came. Catholic baby boomer families. They bought from the Jewish home owners, who headed for Southfield and Farmington Hills. They converted the maids' quarters into fifth or sixth bedrooms for their big families. They stayed for twenty years and might have stayed longer, but the riots of 1967 spelled the end of the city fathers' dreams of a long term bi racial city. By 1990, the City of Detroit, once the nation's fourth largest at 1.8 million residents, had shrunk to roughly 900,000. The public schools were well over 90% black. The white minority consisted largely of retirees. Never boasting much of a high rise apartment population, the Motor City was, and is, a home owners town. By the last decade of the millennium, those homes were owned by the descendants of Africans brought to the new world in chains.

Hilda and Ben had purchased the five bedroom Tudor on Chelsea Lane the year after she went on the court. They were the paradigm of the emerging African American middle or upper middle class. She had won an appointment to the faculty of the Wayne State University Law School when they moved to Detroit. It was the start of a meteoric rise in the profession. In three years she made full Professor. Two years later, with strong support from her colleagues on the faculty, Hilda Germaine became the first black female law school dean in Michigan. And one of only a handful throughout the United States.

The Deanship had given her the visibility that resulted in her being tapped by the Democratic Governor for elevation to the state supreme court when Justice Gustavson was nominated for a Federal Judgeship by the then Republican President.

She could see the law school from the freeway as she headed for her office overlooking the Detroit River and the City of Windsor on the 22nd floor of the Woodward Tower.

***

A mile west of Wayne State University, houses built by Irish and German immigrants nearly a century before stood like forlorn sentries against the winter chill. Many were boarded up. Most of those still occupied housed the trapped victims of the ghetto. Surrounded by crack houses, frightened by day and terrified by night, they lived a tenuous existence. Sustained by food stamps, fueled by welfare checks, hypnotized by television sets, the local residents shivered in drafty kitchens, and slept in unheated bedrooms that were often only a few degrees warmer than the snow covered automotive relics parked or abandoned at curbside.

One of those boarded up houses this December 18, had become the headquarters of the Crocks. It had a still functional fireplace into which had been thrown a motley mixture of trash, broken furniture and baseboards ripped from the walls. The fire blazed a circle of warmth in the living room, empty but for four ancient mildewed mattresses and some torn blankets. They had been there since Saturday, sharing a treasured supply of crack cocaine. They were statistically, the harbingers of the New Detroit. Ezra Johnson, age 14. Big Dog, they called him. Michael Hollow, age 12. He was known as Puncher. Delano Roosevelt, 'The Prez', was the same age. And their unchallenged leader, Rat Tail, whose real name, unknown even to these, his closest comrades, was Jeremiah Wheatley. He would be eleven years old in one month.

Rat Tail had been born tough, and had spent the last 500 weeks getting tougher. His mother, Arliss Wheatley, was a drug addicted prostitute. His vocabulary was vividly violent, abusive, obscene, and reckless. In another culture, he would have tested out to be a budding genius, with an IQ pushing 160. In the ghetto, his wit made him the leader. The boss man. It was Rat Tail who had christened their quartet "The Crocks," and had carefully stenciled the head of a crocodile on the back of each of their stolen black leather jackets.

This 18th of December, Rat Tail had a trophy he was triumphantly brandishing about to impress and entertain his little band. A nine millimeter hand gun known as a Tec-9. The street gang's weapon of choice. He had plenty of ammo. They took turns blasting away. First at beer cans. Then out the window at birds sitting on telephone lines. Then at the smiling faces of smokers grinning down from the billboards that lined McGee street a half block away.

This was a rush. They needed more fun. More targets. They went in search of transportation.

***

Hardly settled into her leather chair, Hilda answered a call from Chief Justice Breitner.

"Merry Christmas, Hilda. Are you and the family ready for the holidays?"

"Happy Holidays to you, Chief. I think we're about ready. If I can keep my mother from baking too many pies."

" Your mother's a wonderful woman, Hilda. Elizabeth and I are very fond of her. Please say hello for us." Breitner's opening was always stilted, stuffy.

"Thank you, Ed. What's happening in Lansing today?"

"Just getting things lined up for our January Term, and trying to clean up all the cases currently in process. Whatever we can decide while Green is still on the court between now and the end of the year, should be disposed of. Some of the others may have to be reargued, especially if we are not unanimous. You were assigned that fraternity case weren't you?"

"*Braxton v Central Michigan*? Yes, that's mine."

"I really feel badly about that, Hilda. Frankly, I should have caught that thing before the clerk divvied up the docket. In view of the sensitive nature of that matter, it really should have been given to one of the other justices. Maybe Van or Bob."

Hilda stirred in her chair. "No need to give me any special treatment, Ed. I think the cases should be assigned by blind draw. That's our rule. I am happy to take whatever comes my way."

"Oh, I'm not suggesting anything irregular. Frankly, I prefer the blind draw. As a matter of fact I insist on it in almost every case. With very few exceptions. I mean the only time I would take a case out of order is for some very special reason."

"Well, there's nothing very special about Braxton. It involves racial issues, but there is no reason for me to be uncomfortable with that. Any more than any other justice."

"I understand that Hilda. Believe me. And that's why I respect you so much. You've got guts."

"Let's just say I may be too naive to see any problem with it."

"Frankly, Hilda, you make my job a lot easier. I wish I had five more Associate Justices as cooperative as you."

"Just doing my job, Chief. That's why they pay me the big bucks."

"Well, I want you to know I appreciate it. I really do. That's one of the reasons I called. As you know, the first order of business at our January meeting will be the vote on the chief justice. With Greenie gone we're going to have to stick together. We only have a one vote majority."

"We?"

"I mean those of us who appreciate and respect the liberal tradition of the court, Hilda. I don't mean to suggest that we ought to be voting along political party lines. Frankly, I think we ought to have a non partisan Missouri Plan. I've said that many times. But it is important that the leadership of the court system not be handed over to people who want to turn back the clock."

"I wouldn't be in favor of that."

"I didn't think you would. I just hope we can keep Henry from doing something foolish."

"Like what?"

"I don't know. He could line up with the Republicans...er, the old guard. I wouldn't want to see Van back in the chair."

"I don't think that will happen, Chief. Henry isn't too fond of him."

"Well, I hope not. Anyway, it's comforting to have you in my corner, Hilda."

"I've supported you in the past, Ed, and I can't think of any reason why I would change my mind."

"Thank you Hilda. Thank you very much. Please remember me to your mother and to Ben."

"Sure. Say Hi to Elizabeth, Ed."

***

At the gas station on Grand River, a patron was refueling his 1988 Camero at the self serve pump. The gas cap was laid on the trunk of the car. The keys were in the ignition. Donning the innocent face of a ten year old cherub, Rat Tail approached the man.

"Gimme a dollah, Bro."

"Go ask yo momma."

Rat Tail snatched the gas cap from its perch on the trunk.

"Gimme a dollah, mufuka."

The man, visibly annoyed, looked at the meter on the gas pump. Twenty dollars worth. Enough. He hung up the hose, and held out his hand toward the grinning urchin who had his gas cap.

"That's enough, boy. Gimme the gas cap."

"A dollah." Rat Tail backed up.

"Gimme the gas cap."

"Two dollahs." Rat Tail backed up again.

The man stepped forward threateningly. "I said, gimme the gas cap."

"Three dollahs, mufuk." Rat Tail was starting to run. The man began to run after him, then froze in his tracks as he heard the engine of the Camero rev up. He whirled around to see Big Dog drive off in his car. By the time he looked back, Rat Tail had disappeared. The gas cap lay on the pavement.

***

While Hilda had been talking to the Chief, Bernice had taken a message from Justice-elect James Malloy. He was at home. Hilda returned the call.

"How are things in Lansing?"

"I'm looking out my den window at a perfect winter scene. A foot of snow everywhere. Sunshine. Makes me want to put on the cross country skis."

"You do that?"

"Sometimes. It's fun."

"Are you getting ready for January Term?"

"I'm a little nervous about it. What are these Morning Reports that I've been getting? How important are they?"

"Morning reports are just summaries of the cases prepared by our Commissioners. They don't take the place of the Briefs filed by the lawyers. But they help to remind you of the salient points involved in the case. Sort of a point of reference on the day of oral argument."

"That's about what I thought. Do you have a moment to talk to me about the chief justiceship?"

"Certainly." Hilda was surprised at Malloy's directness.

"Alton Henry wants me to go after it. I'm sure you know that during the election campaign I criticized the chief justice's leadership of the court. Henry seems to agree with me. He thinks we need a change. Obviously, I do too, but I don't think I should be the candidate to oppose Breitner. After all, I am a total neophyte."

"So who do you think should take it?"

"I was hoping you would be interested. I think you would make an excellent chief justice."

"That's very flattering, Judge. If you mean it."

"I do. I think you have the balance and the political skills to project a very positive image for the court."

"Would Henry support me?"

"That would be a question. But if he is serious about making a change, he should go along."

"He's pretty unpredictable. You flatter me, Jim, and I am really touched by your expression of confidence in me, but I don't think I would ever want to be the chief justice of a divided court."

"Is there such a thing as an undivided court?"

Hilda laughed. "I suppose not. But I wouldn't take the job unless I were drafted by a solid majority of the court. Substantial unanimity. That's what I would want."

"Substantial unanimity? That's a phrase the governor likes to use. I always thought it was an inconsistent understatement. Like a rather round circle. Or a slightly pregnant woman."

She laughed again. "Whatever. I'll know it when I see it. Meantime, I'm afraid I have already made a commitment to Ed. He hasn't been all that bad in my book. He wants the job very much. Would be deeply disappointed if he lost it. And, in my view, it doesn't really matter who the Chief is, if we all get behind him and try to make things work."

"Maybe so, Hilda. That is certainly the right attitude."

They said goodby after a few more pleasantries. Hilda hung up the phone and watched ice chunks float down the Detroit River. This fellow Malloy might just be a good addition to the bench.

***

The brown Camero screeched around the corner of Six Mile Road and Winchester Drive. The Crocks were in their element. Big Dog at the wheel. Prez and Puncher in the back seat. Rat Tail up front next to the driver. Prez took aim out of the left rear window with the Tec-9. WHAM! The porch light of a large red brick home splintered into a thousand pieces. The Crocks screamed with delight.

"My turn." Yelled Puncher. He took the gun and rolled down the right rear window. Two blocks later, a young woman was walking her three year old sheep dog. POW! The animal leaped straight up, flipped over on its side and fell squirming into a bank of snow. More peels of laughter from the Camero. More fun.

"Gimme that thing," demanded Rat Tail. "I'll show ya shootin'"

***

Josh Tuttle was smitten with Keesha Morris. She sat near the front of the room in English class, and he couldn't take his eyes off of the back of her head. But he was thirteen and shy, and so he did what shy thirteen year old boys have always done. He followed her home from school. At a distance of nearly half a block. When she disappeared around the corner of Santa Paulo and Winchester, he hastened his steps so as not to lose sight of her. When he rounded the corner, she was right there, just a few yards in front of him. Waiting.

"Josh Tuttle, are you following me?"

"Jeez no, Keesha. I was just... I was hoping I could walk you home from school some day."

"You could have walked me home from school today, Josh Tuttle, if just you would learn to walk a little faster." She flashed him a taunting smile, and darted into the side door of her house.

Josh swallowed down the rush of excitement that only comes from a first meaningful encounter with the opposite sex. His pace quickened as he crossed the street and began walking north toward his home. Whistling.

The bullet entered the left side of his face 3 centimeters below his left eye. It obliterated his pituitary gland, severed his optic nerves and exited his cranium just a little below his right ear. Josh's knees buckled, and he slumped in a heap to the sidewalk. His head rested on a pillow of blood soaked snow.

The mood in the Camero changed instantly. They had seen thousands of people shot and killed on television. Blood spilled everywhere. But there was always the unstated reality that what they were seeing was unreal. That everyone who died would get back up and live to die again tomorrow or next week or whenever. They filled the air with curses and obscenities. They screamed with terror.

Big Dog was the first to panic. He slammed the accelerator to the floor and raced to the next intersection, skidded around the corner, headed west, the car swerving wildly as he continued to accelerate. Ignoring the stop sign at Livernois, he whipped the car north on that wider and busier thoroughfare, and sped toward Eight Mile Road.

A Detroit Police car was parked at the curb half a block away, and as the Camero roared by, the two officers immediately took up the chase. It was not a long chase.

Three quarters of a mile away, the Camero entered the Eight Mile intersection against the red traffic signal, abruptly turned left, as it took a broadside hit from a west bound pick up truck, flopped over on its left side, and skidded 113 feet along the highway, spewing gasoline from its capless fuel tank and generating sparks as metal scraped on concrete. The trail of gasoline burst into flames. Like a gigantic fuse, it chased the car until it stopped and exploded in a ball of orange fire and black smoke.

Big Dog, Prez and Puncher were trapped inside and immolated. Rat Tail somehow extricated himself from the top of the overturned vehicle, and ran from the scene, flames leaping from his hair and clothes. A newsboy and a gas station attendant tackled him and rolled him in a bank of snow that had been piled between the sidewalk and the apron of the service station. He was still clutching the Tec-9. In the scuffle, the weapon was discharged and the bullet shattered Rat Tail's left ankle.

***

Ben Tuttle was making his afternoon rounds at 4:10 PM when he heard himself being paged at Bethlehem Mercy Hospital. He was wanted in emergency. Strange. It was not his time to be available for emergency duty. He hurried to the first floor, east wing. The nurse on duty appeared agitated.

"Doctor Tuttle, a boy has been shot. They brought him in just about twenty minutes ago. I think it is your son, Josh."

Ben raced to the emergency operating room. He was already wearing a green surgical gown. He didn't bother to scrub. As he burst through the door, he was instantly aware of what had happened. That eerie, somber, defeated silence was something that every surgeon experiences. What was a roomful of frantic motion and desperate action just seconds ago was now a tomb of slow moving, other-world creatures. Mopping. Cleaning. Reorganizing.

He approached the lifeless figure still on the gurney. Two colleagues, their surgical caps soaked in sweat and their gowns splattered with blood, mumbled condolences and stroked his back. Ben stood in stunned silence for nearly five minutes looking with disbelief at the mangled skull of his only son. Then he tenderly punched the lifeless shoulder and slumped sobbing to his knees.

Bernice took the call from Doctor Tuttle. No, he didn't want to speak to the Justice. Just tell her that I'm on my way downtown, and to wait at the office.

At 4:51 PM, Ben Tuttle entered the lobby of the Woodward Tower. He walked painfully, deliberately to the elevator, stepped in and pushed the button for the twenty second floor. His mind was a dizzy blur. Rehearsals were impossible. He had to tell her. But how could he? How could he do this? Help me Jesus. Help me now.

Hilda suspected something was wrong as soon as Bernice gave her the message. Ben just never came to her office. Maybe it was a man thing. When he came downtown, which he did occasionally, they always met at a restaurant. As soon as she saw his tortured face she knew something was very, very wrong. She rushed into his arms.

"What is it Ben? Has something happened to Grandma? Is she dead? Oh God, Ben, tell me."

" It's Josh, Hilda." He groaned in agony. "It's our son. Our baby. Oh God, Hilda, he's been shot. He's dead. Why do I have to say those words? Why? Why Josh?." Ben slumped to the couch and pulled his wife down with him as she screamed. "Not Josh, Ben. Please God. Not Josh. No. No. No. No." She clutched at Ben's chest so hard that her fingernails dug through his shirt and into his skin.

In time, the wailing turned to sobbing and the sobbing turned to empty numbness. Eventually, they talked in low, hushed, monotones. They talked of what had happened and what must now be done. But neither one of them could bring themselves to say the word 'Tomorrow.'

CHAPTER 4

VAN TIMLIN

On Wednesday, December 19, the press and the television were consumed with stories about the Josh Tuttle murder. Not just Detroit. Not only Michigan. National television, network news, all the major commentators featured the story. The son of a supreme court justice killed by a ten year old gang leader. It burned up the wires of the wire services. Children and guns. Children and drugs. Children and gangs. No one is safe.

The Detroit papers mentioned that Josh had been on his way to his home at the corner of Winchester Drive and Chelsea Lane. Within hours of the delivery of the morning edition, cars began cruising past the Tuttle home. Slowing to a crawl. Gawking at silent, mourning bricks and mortar. At ten thirty, a Cadillac stopped, and a teen age girl got out and planted a bouquet of red roses in the snow covered front lawn. By noon, the lawn was alive with a dozen floral displays. By the time Ben and Hilda returned from the funeral home, the barren, snow covered front lawn was a riot of color, with more than 120 bouquets, baskets, and flower displays trumpeting the community's heartfelt sympathy for the Tuttle family.

Cindy sat on the window bench in the front room, hugging Melissa, rocking gently back and forth, staring at the flowers, and softly singing, "Where you there when they crucified my Lord?..."

***

Justice J. Frederick VanTimlin was home from the office, had removed his shoes, assumed a comfortable position in his favorite chair, feet on the coffee table, browsed remotely through a dozen TV channels, and just dozed off when Gertie juggled through the front door laden with Christmas packages.

63

Van stirred and looked up. "Good evening, Gertie my love. You look like Mrs. Santa Claus!"

"Get your feet off the coffee table."

One of her packages fell to the floor, as she struggled to set the rest down on the table in the front hall.

"Would you mind getting the rest of the things from the car. I'm simply exhausted."

"Why certainly." Van complied.

"And don't track a lot of snow in here. I just cleaned the floor this morning, and I want it to look nice for Christmas."

"How come you came in the front door?"

"Because you have your car parked on my side of the garage."

"Well, why not park on the other side? You wouldn't have to walk through the snow."

"Freddie will be home in a minute. I had to leave space for him."

Van harrumphed as he put on his coat. She was always thinking of Freddie. Freddie will be hungry. Freddie will be tired. Freddie needs this. Freddie wants that.

Jasper Frederick Van Timlin, Junior, born April 7, 1949 was an only child. In many ways, at age 41 he was still a child. He lived at home with his mother and father. He had never been married. His mother did his laundry, made his bed, woke him up in the morning, once in a while even tucked him in at night.

The man was clinically obese. He claimed he weighed 295. In truth, he was well over 350 pounds. He ate all the wrong things, and in gross quantities. He sat around. He sat around a lot. In fact, all the time. Sat and ate. Sat and talked. Sat at work. Sat at home.

Gertrude indulged Freddie's every whim. She weighed 107 pounds. She never sat. She worked incessantly. Cooked. Sewed. Washed. Ironed. Cleaned.

In most things they were exact opposites, but Freddie and his mother had two things in common; they were both obsessed with Freddie's comfort and convenience, and neither one of them had any sense of economic reality or financial responsibility. Freddie paid his parents no board and room. His entire paycheck went for his personal needs and wants. His car. His computer and it's peripherals. Restaurants. Movies. Psychic readings. Lottery tickets. Football pools. Magazines and junk food. While he had virtually nothing to show for it, Freddie's credit card had reached its limit more than once. Van, of course, was expected to bail him out every time. Which, on orders from Gertie, he always did.

Years before, when Freddie was a two hundred pound graduate of Western Michigan University, Van had hoped his son would follow in his footsteps and study law. Gertie never had much use for lawyers. Thought they were all, with the possible exception of her husband, charlatans and crooks. Gertie had urged Freddie to seek a respectable position. Over the next five years, Freddie had half a dozen respectable positions. Each time he was laid off or let go, he ballooned a little more. Finally, when his son's unemployment compensation ran out, Van interceded with the head of the state highway department, an old friend, and got Freddie a civil service job. That cocoon proved invincible, and Freddie remained on the state payroll.

In college, the younger Van Timlin had dated a little. It rarely got past the first visit to his home. Sensible girls had no desire to compete with Gertie. The one or two who tried were quickly out maneuvered by Freddie's mother.

The file on Associate Justice J. Frederick Van Timlin, printed annually in the Michigan Manual, was simple and straightforward:

"Associate Justice J.(Jasper) Frederick Van Timlin was born on October 9, 1921 in Zeeland, Michigan, the third son of Otto Van Timlin, a journeyman cabinetmaker, and his wife, Bertha, nee Zehnder. Justice Van Timlin, after attending public school in Holland, Michigan, was admitted to Hope College, where he earned a BA degree in 1948. Subsequently, he studied law at the University of Michigan, which conferred its Juris Doctor degree upon him in 1951.

"Justice Van Timlin served his country during the Second World War, 1941-1945, as a sergeant in the Field Artillery in the European Theater of Operations. He was awarded the Bronze Star for meritorious conduct.

"On returning to civilian life and completing his education, the Justice was employed as a law clerk for Justice Leland Carr, 1951-1953. He then entered the practice of law as an associate in the Grand Rapids firm of Rollins, Forester, and Brace. In 1956 he became a partner in Rollins, Brace, and Van Timlin. Justice Van Timlin was elected Attorney General of Michigan, in which office he served until his elevation by the electorate to the supreme court in 1960.

"Justice Van Timlin was chosen by his colleagues as the chief justice in 1971, and served in that capacity until the end of 1982. The Justice and his wife Gertrude have one son, J. Frederick Jr. Justice Van Timlin is a member of the Lansing City Club, and the First Christian Reformed Church, where he has served as an elder. He was nominated to the supreme court by the Republican Party."

The bare bones biography published in the manual did not, of course, tell the whole, human story. Van and Gertie met at Hope College when they were both active in the Christian Students' League. It was a typical post World War II campus romance. He, a returning veteran with a year of college under his belt before enlistment; she, a member of the high school class of '47, seven years his junior, embodying everything he had dreamed about and prayed for while he was being jostled aboard an LST crossing the English channel toward Normandy and a rendezvous with destiny.

But somehow, their marriage didn't follow the baby boomer script that governed the rest of America in 1950. Gertie had developed a tumor on her ovary after Freddie was born. In those days they did radical hysterectomies on relatively inconclusive evidence. Her tumor was benign, but her child bearing years were over.

That event had been the defining episode of their marriage. Van was in law school, on his way to becoming a stuffy, cerebral, somewhat pompous professional. He was not good at expressing his own feelings or divining the feelings of others. He was a hard worker, an honest man, a good provider. He paid his taxes and his bills. Went to church. Loved his wife. All duties. All performed without complaint and without noticeable enthusiasm.

Now, after 42 years of amiable if not ecstatic togetherness, Van and Gertie played their roles by rote. Freddie crowded them apart like a massive internal growth. But Freddie was benign. Radical excision was not indicated. They could live with each other and they could live with him.

The phone rang. It was the chief justice.

"Van, I'm sorry to bother you at home. Are you eating dinner?"

"No, Gertie's just starting to fix supper now."

"Please give her my regards. Elizabeth and I are very fond of Gertie. We really must get together sometime during the holidays. The four of us."

"Well, that would be very nice, Edward. Very nice indeed."

"Van, the reason I'm calling is to discuss Hilda's son's funeral."

"Oh yes. The Tuttle boy. Tragic thing. Really terribly tragic."

"Devastating. I talked to Hilda this morning. I think she still hasn't felt the full impact. She seems to be going through the motions, making arrangements, responding to the press, giving instructions to her staff like she was in a trance. Just methodical, calm, self contained. I don't know how long she can keep it up."

"Well, I should think her husband will take care of her. Isn't he a doctor?"

"He's a doctor, but he has also lost his son. It's got to be tough on both of them. Anyway, I called to tell you that Hilda wants her friends in the judiciary to be honorary pall bearers. We are going to wear our robes and sit behind the family in the church. supreme court in front, judges of other courts behind."

"Wear our judicial robes to a funeral? I never heard of such a thing."

"Hilda wants it. She thinks it will give the ceremony a solemn, special kind of dignity. Kind of a recognition that the whole state is mourning. I think everyone is going."

"Even Alton Henry?"

"I think so. I talked to him this afternoon."

"Well, Ed, I'll have to think about it. Gertie and I have already sent some flowers to the funeral home, along with a sympathy card. I'm not so keen on driving all the way to Detroit in this weather and with all the Christmas shopping crowds and the office party drinkers on the road."

"The roads are clear," Breitner spoke sharply "And Friday is suppose to be sunny and warmer."

"I'll think about it, Mr. Chief Justice. But don't count on me."

At dinner that night, Freddie downed sixteen ounces of beef, two large baked potatoes drenched in butter and crowned with sour cream, a large salad swimming in creamy dressing, and two pieces of apple pie buried under sheets of cheddar cheese. He pushed the string beans to the side of his plate and ignored them. He whined about his travails at the office, his callous coworkers, his inconsiderate supervisor, the uncooperative paving contractors he had to deal with.

Justice Van Timlin wondered why Hilda Germaine was orchestrating such a big funeral for her son.

$$***$$

On Thursday, the morning edition of the Capital City Tribune carried an editorial calling for the adoption of tough new laws to put an end to street gang terrorism. To political terrorism. To religious terrorism. Let it be the Josh Tuttle Law. That he may not have died in vain. That this decent, innocent young boy scout may be for all of us a symbol of hope for a future of peace in our neighborhoods. Peace in our cities. Peace in the world.

Justice Van Timlin's secretary for twenty-eight years handed him the paper as he passed her desk. This would be a short day she was sure. The Tuttle killing had brought the work of the court to a standstill. Van would not be handing her anything to do today, and he did not have a law clerk to annoy her with memoranda as most of the other Justices did. He always did his own research and wrote his own opinions. Today she expected him to read the paper, read his mail, talk on the phone to some of his colleagues, and take a nap. Maybe she could get away early for some Christmas shopping.

The first call was from Justice Green. Was Van going to Detroit for the funeral? Maybe they could get together for a drink afterwards. He would miss their frequent lunches. It had been a pleasure to serve along side of him for so many years.

Van said he hadn't decided whether to go down or not. There would be a lot of Christmas shoppers on the road, and drunks coming home from office Christmas parties. And God knows what kind of teen gang gauntlet you'd have to run getting to a church down there in no man's land.

Van Timlin called Alton Henry.

"Are you going to Detroit for the funeral?"

"Sure. Aren't you?"

"Do you think it's safe?"

"Of course not. But that won't keep me out of there. I'm up for reelection next year. I expect I'll be in Detroit for lots of things."

"Well, that's no motive for me. Remember I'll be over seventy when my term is up. Ineligible to run again. The main consolation is that I don't have to cow tow to the voters."

"By the way, have you talked to Judge Malloy about the chief justiceship?"

"No, does he want to talk to me?"

"I'm sure he does. He and I have been cooking up a little surprise for Ed Breitner. I liked what Malloy said during the campaign about the chief. Maybe it's time for a change."

"And he wants to talk to me?"

"Aren't you and he both Republicans? Who else is he going to talk to?"

"Well, that's very interesting. Very interesting, indeed. I'll be happy to talk to the young man if he calls."

Hanging up the phone, Van Timlin leaned back in his high backed leather chair and mused about his conversation with Henry. If Alton Henry, nominally a Democrat, was ready to dump Breitner, the chief justiceship could be back in the hands of the Republicans for the first time in many years. He had been the last Republican chief justice. He was the senior GOP nominated Justice. He had given no thought of being a candidate, as long as the Democrats had a majority. But this was a new ball game.

Van had relished being the chief. Sitting in the center chair in the courtroom was a place of honor and importance. First among equals. Like the Bishop of Rome. Like the Prime Minister. A psychologist might have seen a deeper reason why Van enjoyed being chief justice. It was a personal affirmation of worth that dwarfed the demeaning commands Gertie gave him when he came home. Allowed him to chuckle patronizingly when she ordered him around, and to obey her instructions without giving up his belief that he was indeed, still her lord and master.

Yes, Van thought to himself, it would be nice to be the chief justice again.

Malloy called just before lunch.

"I understand that Justice Germaine has asked her colleagues on the court and a number of her friends on the trial bench to serve as an honor guard at her son's funeral tomorrow," said Malloy.

"That's true. The chief justice called me at home last night,"

Van Timlin replied. "Are you going?"

" Not being on the court as yet, I don't think I belong up with the Justices. But I am planning to go to the funeral and sit with the trial judges. "

"Well, perhaps that would be appropriate."

"I was thinking that you may want to ride down with me," Malloy offered. "You and I haven't had much of a chance to get acquainted. I would be pleased and honored to be your chauffeur."

"Well, that's very nice of you. Very nice indeed. I hadn't decided whether or not to go, but your kind offer has tipped the scales in favor of making the trip."

Trip? Malloy smiled. The 90 mile run to Detroit was hardly what he would call a trip. He had driven it so many times he could predict, within minutes, his time of arrival from any place along the route going in either direction.

"Good. I've had a few interesting conversations with Justice Henry, and I think you and I have a lot to discuss."

"Well, I do too. I'm looking forward to the ride."

They made arrangements to meet at the Okemos entrance to I-96 the following morning at 8:00 AM. When they did, Van Timlin suggested that Malloy drive the state owned vehicle issued to him rather than Malloy's own car. No need to wear out your own tires, Van said. We'll be doing the people's business all the way there and back.

***

Interstate 96 between Detroit and Lansing is one of the nation's busiest and fastest moving freeways. And free it truly is. There are no toll roads in Michigan. None. The welcome mat is out for millions of vacationers from other states and from Canada, who pour into the beautiful mitten shaped peninsula year after year. Summers, to swim, boat, fish, golf, and wiggle their toes in miles of soft warm sand along the shores of the

Great Lakes. In winter, to ski, hunt, snow mobile, shanty fish and record on film glistening snow laden evergreens and rugged wind carved sculptures where waves of freezing fresh water have cascaded over random shapes of broken ice along the deserted beaches.

On Friday, December 21, 1990, Jim Malloy was behind the wheel of a state owned Oldsmobile for the first time. The license number, MSG 006, signaled two important facts. That the vehicle was part of the fleet assigned to the top brass in Michigan state government. And that this particular car was issued to the sixth person in the MSG pecking order. After the governor, the attorney general, the secretary of state and the chief justice, came the members of the Michigan Supreme Court by seniority. With thirty years on the bench, Van Timlin was second in seniority after Alton Henry.

Malloy took advantage of the chance to visit with the veteran jurist. Van Timlin after all, had been on the court when Malloy was in law school. Some of his opinions were in the case books that Malloy and his classmates had studied. As students, they had criticized, praised, evaluated, distinguished, and debunked his opinions. Now, here he was, in person, sitting in the passenger's seat, looking more like someone's retired uncle than a legal icon.

Malloy told Van about a meeting he had with Douglas Green, the justice he had defeated in November.

"Really a very nice man, you know. And very helpful to me. He suggested I retain his secretary at least for a while. Recommended her highly for her professionalism and loyalty."

"You would serve yourself very well by keeping her, Judge. She is an excellent employee, with a very pleasant, cheerful disposition. That, believe me, is important."

"Green was awfully forthcoming with me. Didn't seem to be bitter at all. He told me something that struck me as rather profound."

"Well, yes, Green does like to pontificate at times."

"He said that a court, that is a multi judge court like the supreme court, is like a chemical formula. If you change just one of the ingredients, you change the entire molecular structure of the substance. Different people affect others in different ways. People change their attitudes, their opinions, their biases even, depending on who they work with, according to Justice Green. Have you found that to be true?"

"Well, I think that may be true of some folks. I never thought I changed very much through the years. I've worked with a lot of justices. Some of them were darn good lawyers. Some of them wouldn't know a rule of law from a rule of thumb. But you will have a chance to learn a lot on this job."

Malloy wondered how he could steer the conversation around to the election of the chief justice. He decided to take the long way. Ease into it.

"I'm looking forward to the job. And I'm certainly glad to have the campaign behind me. I hope being on the supreme court will prove to be worth all the work and money it took to get here."

"Well, yes. I understand campaigns are getting more expensive than they used to be. I never spent more than ten thousand dollars on a judicial campaign. Of course, the Republicans sent out letters on my behalf. I don't know what that cost."

"Ten thousand? Is that all? My campaign cost more like three hundred fifty thousand."

Van Timlin whistled. "Three hundred fifty thousand dollars?"

"Oh yes. And the worst part is that the party gave me very little help. Less than a hundred grand. The rest I had to raise or pony up myself."

"Well, you must have really depleted your savings, I should think."

Malloy laughed. "Depleted isn't the word. It wiped me out. And then some."

"You went into debt?"

"Would you believe a hundred and twenty five thousand

dollars of debt?"

Van whistled again. "That's a mountain. And ethically, you can't do any more fund raising can you.?"

"Nope. Just got to suck it up and pay the fiddler."

"How in the world do you propose to do that? Don't you have a couple of kids?"

"Oh yes, Margaret and I have all the accouterments of the American Dream. A house in the burbs, two cars, two mortgages, overloaded credit cards, three point two children...."

"Three point two?"

"Oh yes, I just found out last night that Margaret is pregnant. She got that way the night of the election. It was kind of a surprise present for winning."

"Well, well. Congratulations. I think."

"We'll get by. I pray a lot. Especially the part about 'give us this day our daily bread'."

"Seriously, and you don't have to answer this, it's none of my business, but what are you going to do about that campaign deficit?"

"I've already done it. My brother Tom works at the Automotive National Bank in Detroit. He used his good offices, and a couple of cosigners, and I borrowed the money on an unsecured loan. Starting in January, I'll be teaching an elective course at the law school, and I'll make enough to cover the payments. Just."

"Sounds like you are going to be a busy young man."

"I've always worked hard." Time to get to the meat, Malloy told himself. Here goes. "Speaking of the campaign, you may have heard that I criticized Chief Justice Breitner rather severely during the election. I said then that I thought he should be replaced as chief. It seems that there may be some support on the court for that proposition. What do you think.?"

"Well now, I've always liked Ed. Just like Douglas Green. I always liked him too. Good lawyer. Good fellow to have a drink with. But I never voted for either of them. Not for chief justice.

Not for justice of the court. I never voted for any Democrat. Not ever, in my whole life. Never did. Never will."

Malloy couldn't keep from laughing. "Is that the way they do it in Holland?"

"That's the way they do it in the western part of the state. Ottawa County. Kent and Berrien, too. You don't see any Republicans getting elected in Detroit or Wayne County do you?"

"Not lately."

"Well, I should say not. Politics is politics. That's life."

"But there have been some switch overs in the court every so often, haven't there? I mean, didn't you and the other Republicans elect Kosman once?"

"Well, by gum, that's so. I had forgotten. Of course, we didn't have any choice about that. The Democrats had the majority. All we could do was decide which Democrat we wanted to be the boss."

"It looks like there will be another aberration in January. Alton Henry says he won't vote for Breitner. "

"I thought that is what he was getting at. Now I suppose he wants me back in the chair. That's ironic, after he and Breitner dumped me a dozen years ago."

"I don't think so."

Van Timlin swallowed hard. He was truly confused. Truly at a loss for words.

"You. You. You don't....think so?"

"No, I'm afraid Henry still has you on his shit list, if you'll pardon the expression. But he is anxious to dump Breitner. He wants me to oppose him."

"You? You aren't even sworn in yet. He's got to be kidding."

"That's what I told him. He insists that in the federal system, the president appoints the chief justice, and it almost always is a rookie. I couldn't argue with that. But I told him I still think it should be someone else."

"If not me, who?"

"I suggested Germaine or O'Leary. I think Henry would go for O'Leary. I'm not sure he'd support Germaine."

"I wouldn't. She's a Democrat."

"So was Kosman. Isn't it a matter of who will be best for the court?"

"Well, the best thing for the court is to have a Republican chief justice. That's what I think."

"That kind of boils it down to O'Leary, doesn't it?"

"I suppose so. Do you think O'Leary wants it?"

"I don't know. We've talked a few times, but I haven't really tried to pin him down."

Van Timlin grew silent. He had decided to come to Detroit only because he thought Malloy wanted to approach him to be chief justice. His disappointment was palpable. As the car turned off the freeway onto Seven Mile Road, Van Timlin stirred uneasily. Stores that were not vacant were heavily barred. There was an eerie, war zone kind of quietude along this once thriving commercial street. Van Timlin relocked his door.

As the two men neared Livernois Avenue, it was apparent that they had come to the right place. Flashing blue lights announced the presence of several police squad cars stationed in the center of the road, diverting passing traffic to a single lane in the middle of the roadway, and directing mourners to park in the two southbound lanes. For fully three city blocks, the street had become a parking lot for the New Philadelphia A.M.E. Church.

Originally built as Saint Mark's Episcopal Church, the imposing Gothic structure was sold in 1978 when most of its parishioners had migrated to the northern suburbs. The building was purchased by a new congregation, organized and presided over by the Reverend Billy Cutler. The same Billy Cutler who had labored for 11 years in the National Football League as a defensive tackle, first for the Pittsburgh Steelers, later for the Bengals. He threw in the towel after his third knee operation, earned a Master's Degree in Theology and was ordained in the discipline of the African Methodist Episcopal Church.

It was Billy who suggested the name New Philadelphia. For two reasons. First, and most obviously, because Philadelphia means brotherly love, and the founding trustees wanted their church to be a beacon of love and hope in the community. There was a second reason, though. The African Methodist Episcopal Church itself was founded in 1816 in the city of Philadelphia by the Reverend Richard Allen. Born in slavery and sold to a Delaware farmer, Allen purchased his freedom and was ordained a Methodist minister. When white church members pushed them back into the gallery, Allen and his followers built their own house of worship. The New Philadelphia Church under Billy Cutler exuded the same pride, self sufficiency, and independence as had Bishop Allen two centuries before.

Malloy parked the car as directed, then he and Van Timlin walked to the parsonage adjoining the church. There, the front parlor had become a temporary judicial robing room. Two dozen judges, most of them black, milled quietly about, greeting each other in hushed respect for the place and the occasion. The service was to begin at 11 AM. About 10:35, Hilda Germaine entered the room. She was completely composed. She moved deftly through the assembled jurists, greeting them each by name, and thanking them for serving as honorary pall bearers. Her smile, tinged with sadness, gave her face a particularly beguiling beauty. Her eyes widened just a little as she recognized Jim Malloy.

"Judge Malloy. How nice of you to come. I hope you will sit up front with the supreme court."

"That would be somewhat presumptuous, I'm afraid." Malloy paused. "I know I was not invited, Hilda, I just wanted you to know how much I feel for you and your family."

"You're very kind, and not at all presumptuous. Please sit with the court. You're one of us now."

In a moment, she was gone. An aide to the funeral director appeared, officiously lined up the judges, and led them down a hallway which connected to the vestibule of the church. There, the robed men and women formed an honor guard on either side of the main entrance and waited for the casket to be brought in. Soon it was. Behind it, shuffling in stifled anguish, were the actual pall bearers. Eight Boy Scouts, in crisply starched uniforms. Wearing the light grey gloves that would be left on top of the casket at the grave site.

There followed the mourners. Hilda, Ben, Melissa, and Cindy, and a winding line of weeping men and women, boys and girls. Mostly black. All somber.

Of course, the media was there. Remote broadcasting equipment. Trucks. Aerials. Heavy cables draped across the road. Flash bulbs popping. On-the-scene TV reporters mouthing their intros into whirring cameras. But there was none of it in the church. Hilda and Ben had made it clear. Billy agreed and issued strict orders to the blue blazered ushers. No pictures in church. No cameras. No flash bulbs. New Philadelphia was a House of Worship. And never more so than on this day of agony.

When the church was full, the ushers led the judges to their reserved rows of seats, behind the family. Across the aisle, several rows had been reserved for dignitaries. His Honor, the mayor of Detroit. Members of the city council and county supervisors. Mayors of several suburban towns. Highland Park. River Rouge. Oak Park. Leaders of the boy scouts. Of the bar. Of the medical profession.

Behind the reserved seating, the church was packed wall to wall with people. School children. Neighbors. Uncles, aunts and cousins. People who new the Justice. People who knew the doctor. People who knew and loved Josh Tuttle.

Billy Cutler was nervous. He had played football before tens of thousands of fans. He had performed on Monday nights before audiences in the millions. But this was different. Josh Tuttle and Billy's son had been pals. Classmates for four years. Always at each other's homes and in each other's refrigerators.

And in the hearts of each other's parents. This would be hard.

"My dear friends," Billy began when the last strains of the Old Wooden Cross faded away, his voice low, and expressionless, as he tried to assume a formal air in the presence of so many distinguished visitors. "We are gathered here this morning with heavy hearts. Our hearts are heavy because the heart of this one boy, this boy scout, this son and grandson and brother and neighbor, and schoolmate, and friend, has stopped beating. We are gathered here today because Josh Tuttle is dead. And because we are not dead. We have come to honor Josh Tuttle, and to think about, and to talk about, and to commemorate, not his death. But his life. Josh is gone, but we are still here. We are the living. We must go on living. Almighty God has given us this mysterious gift of life. It's ours. Ours to treasure. Ours to use. How are going to use it? How are we supposed to use it? How does God expect us to use it?" Billy Cutler paused, nodding his head up and down. When he resumed speaking, his voice quivered, just a little.

"Josh Tuttle knew what he was supposed to do with his life. And he was doing it. Josh Tuttle lived in the Lord Jesus. Every day of his life. He lived in the Lord Jesus."

Someone near the back of the church, speaking loud enough for everyone to hear, said *"Amen."* The 'Amens' always inspired Billy to new heights of oratory. His voice rose, his tempo quickened, as he resumed. "His whole life was a song of praise to his friend and savior, Jesus Christ. He let that song of praise be on his lips and in his heart."

Amen. Amen." Voices in the congregation responded.

Billy's heart began to thump in his chest. "You could hear that song. You could feel the pounding of the music of salvation. When Josh was around, Brothers and Sisters, Jesus was around. You knew it. You could tell."

"Yeah, yeah, sing it Reverend." A heavy set woman was on her feet.

"In Mark 10:14, the Gospel tells us that Jesus said, 'Suffer the little children to come unto me.' Josh has gone to sit at the feet of the Lord. And we have suffered. Oh Lord, we have suffered. We have suffered this boy to come unto you, Lord. This innocent boy."

"*Lord, Oh Lord,*" A woman sitting across the aisle from the Justices wailed. Alton Henry and Bob O'Leary glanced at each other. Spontaneous response from the congregation was not the norm in the Presbyterian and Catholic churches they attended.

" He didn't do anything to anybody," Reverend Billy went on, beads of sweat forming on his brow. "He didn't hurt anybody. Josh Tuttle couldn't hurt anybody. He just wasn't that kind of a boy. He wasn't one of them that hangs out in the alley behind the drug store and smokes cigarettes, and uses dope, and takes things that don't belong to them. Takes things away from old people walking down the street. Takes things away from the supermarket without paying for them. He wasn't that kind of a boy."

"*No. No. Amen.*" "*No, not Josh*" "*Not that kind.*" Responses came from some of Josh's friends, and their parents.

"Josh was a good boy. He loved his momma. He loved his dad. And his sister Melissa. And he loved his Grandma. He surely did love his Grandma." Cindy Germaine's shoulders began to shake, as her silent tears gave way to audible sobbing.

"Thirteen years old. Maybe he was in the February of his lifetime. You and me Ben, we're in September. Hilda, I guess you're back there someplace in July or August." Justice Germaine's tear streaked cheeks rose in a sad smile, as she acknowledged Billy's intended compliment. "But Josh was way way back in February. Maybe one sixth of his normal life expectancy was used up. He still had a long road ahead of him. He still had a lot of living to do. He still had a lot of life coming to him. Time. The gift of time. That's what was snatched away from Josh Tuttle last Tuesday. And we can't understand it.

Billy Cutler's forehead furrowed in an expression of bewilderment. "*Amen. Can't understand,*" said a voice from the assembly.

"You and I, we can't understand why God lets these things happen. Why would a merciful, loving Creator just come down and grab this one boy, this good boy, and take him away.? Why deprive Josh Tuttle of his May and his June and September? Never to lie beside his woman. Never to hold his baby boy or his little girl. Never to see his parents grow old or to send them off to be with Jesus when their time has come."

Now the *Amens* and the *Lord, Lords* were coming fast and furious. Reverend Bill was rolling. His words flowed with passion. With conviction. He was speaking from his heart. From his very soul. He was saying what the people wanted to hear. "It makes us angry. ANGRY," he roared, the veins in his neck protruding. "We feel like Josh has been cheated. It's not right. It isn't fair. It isn't just. Justice. That's what we want. Justice. Exodus 21:24 'You shall give life for life, eye for an eye, tooth for tooth." Someone has to be punished for doing this to Josh. For doing this to us. To Josh's family. To his friends. To the whole community. To the whole city. That's how we feel, isn't it?"

A deep masculine voice from the back was heard. "*Uh hu,*" it said.

"We can feel it deep down in our bones," cried Billy. "Somebody should have to pay for all this hurting. For our pain. Somebody is responsible for our grief. And we need to have them suffer as we have suffered."

Billy was lashing out at evil. Giving voice to the frustration, the pain, the shear maddening wrath shared by every person in the room. Almost simultaneously, they burst into applause. In the middle of the church an elderly man stood and shouted. "*That's right Reverend Billy. You tell 'em.*"

Suddenly, Billy was silent. He stood wringing his hands, and shaking his head back and forth, back and forth. The church responded by hushing into a tomb-like quiet. When he spoke again, Reverend Billy's voice was low, almost a whisper. But it reached to the furthest corner of the great, soundless nave.

"And all that hungering for justice turns into hate and an appetite for revenge. That's what causes people to go crazy. Go into a killing frenzy. That's why wars get started and neighbors get to shooting one another. And nations drop bombs on other people's houses and schools and hospitals." His voice rose again, to a new crescendo. " Romans 12:19 tells us, 'Do not avenge yourselves, beloved, but give place to the wrath, for it is written, 'Vengeance is mine; I will repay, says the Lord.'' We aren't the score keepers. We aren't the referees in this game of life. It's not our job to even up the score. That's God's job. He knows what needs to be done and he knows how and when to do it."

Softly, again, he continued, looking around at his audience, as though seeking the answer to a paradox. "Anyway, who are we to blame for Josh's death? Who ought to pay the price for killing him? A ten year old boy? Are we going to lock up a ten year old boy for the rest of his life and say, there, we fixed that. Say we punished Josh Tuttle's killer, now we can rest easy. No, my Brothers and Sisters, that's not the way it should be. That's not what Josh would have wanted us to do. That's not what the example of his good and kind and God fearing life should have taught us to do."

The congregation fell silent. Reverend Billy had gone from preaching to teaching. Now he was not speaking to their hearts, but to their heads. Now he appealed to reason, asking them to reach beyond the hurting and the sorrow.

"The killing of Josh Tuttle is a lesson, Brothers and Sisters. A lesson to you and to me. It's a lesson about life. About how precious life is. And how fragile it is. It's a lesson about how life doesn't belong to you or to me or to anybody. Life belongs to God. Life comes from God. And life goes back to God. That's the way it is in this world. We can't do anything about it, no matter how hard we try. Folks talking about freezing their bodies so they can get wakened up fifty or a hundred years down the road and warmed up again and given all the new pills and drugs to make them live again. That's shameful. That's the devil talking. The devil himself. Folks claiming that they own their bodies, and saying they have the right to kill themselves. And to help each other kill themselves. Or putting sick people and old people out of their misery by killing them. That's the devil talking. The very devil himself." Billy was back on his bully pulpit. Rolling again.

"Amen, Reverend Billy, Amen. Amen." Encouragement came from all around the room.

"These bodies of ours are just loaned to us. Loaned to us by an almighty, loving Creator. They don't belong to us. These bodies, these hands, these feet, this head and hair and eyes and nose." Reverend Billy was grandiloquently gesturing to the parts of his body. "This blabbering mouth of mine. It doesn't belong to me. It's God's. It's all God's. He can come along with a bolt of lightning, or a heart attack, or a great big lump of cancer, or an eighteen wheel truck crossing over the yellow line, and he can just wipe us out like snapping his fingers. Or he can let a little ten year old boy have a 9 millimeter gun and shoot us right through the head, just like he did to Josh. And we'd be dead, too. Just like Josh."

"Like Josh, Reverend Billy. Oh yeah."

"Human life doesn't belong to human beings. We didn't invent ourselves. We didn't just say one day 'I'm going to start to be' And then come into existence. No. We came into this world, every single one of us according to the plan that God made up. We came about, each and every one of us because our daddies and our mommies loved each other. We were conceived in an act of love. Each and every one of us here in this church today came into being because two people loved each other. And in the miracle of God's creation, that loving caused another person, another somebody who can love and be loved, to come into existence.

"Amen," said Ben Tuttle.

"*Amen*," sobbed Hilda Tuttle Germaine.

"*Amen*, " whispered Jim Malloy.

"So here we are folks. Here we are still on the face of this green earth, still living." Reverend Billy Cutler was looking at the mayor, and the supreme court justices, and the other public officials before him. "What are we going to do to protect and preserve this wonderful gift of life the Creator gave us? What are we going to do so that other mothers and dads don't have to bury their sons and daughters when they are still in the January or the February of their lifetime? I don't know, Brothers and Sisters. I just don't know what we're going to do. I don't know what we can do, except to make just laws and try to get good people into our public offices, who will have the wisdom and the courage to do what has to be done."

His Honor, the mayor said "*Amen*." The city councilmen said "*Amen*." The judges said "*Amen*." Everybody in the church could hear them say it.

"One thing all of us can do for Josh and for our city," Billy concluded. "We can all pray. We can pray hard. Ask the good lord Jesus to be with us. To open our hearts. To enlighten our minds. To show us the way. For he has said to us, in John 14:6, 'I am the way and the truth and the light' And again in John 11:25, 'I am the resurrection and the life; he who believes in me, even if he die, shall live.' So, let us pray."

The Reverend Billy Cutler led them in prayer and there were no dry eyes in the church.

When they finished and the choir sang another hymn, Ben Tuttle rose from his place in the front row, and walked haltingly to the pulpit.

"I just want... Hilda and I just want... all of you to know how much we appreciate you being with us here today. Your kindness has been a source of strength for all of our family. And I want to thank Reverend Billy for his beautiful talk here today. Josh would have liked it."

For a long time, Ben stood in silence. Finally, he looked up again.

"One more thing. Hilda and I have been putting some money aside for Josh's college education. Our Josh, he won't be needing it anymore, and we thought that maybe it could be used to help some young kids to stay off the streets, and play on teams or stay in school. We decided to donate Josh's college money to the Police Athletic Association, and we wanted all of you to know that, so if you want to do something in Josh's memory, that would be a good place to put it."

Ben walked back to his seat with deliberate solemnity. As he did, the choir burst into their final hymn. Out of the corner of his eye, Malloy could see Van Timlin reach into his suit coat pocket, remove his checkbook and pen, and begin writing a check. It was for five hundred dollars, payable to the Police Athletic Association.

CHAPTER 5

TEMPLETON

Cheryl Templeton braced herself against the wind whipped snowflakes that clung to her eyelashes and crusted her wool Burberry scarf. The walk from her grandfather's apartment on the second floor of the stately old brownstone building on Addison to the lively warmth of Nick's Near North Nook was only a few blocks, but it was hard going this December evening.

She had hoped that Roger would ask her to go to Boston with him over Christmas break to meet his parents. He didn't. She hinted and teased, cajoled and even pouted. No deal. He had all kinds of excuses. Money. Time. Commitments. Bottom line was that he just wasn't ready. She knew that but she didn't want to believe it.

Now she was hoping at least he would stay in Chicago a few more days and meet her family. Her grandfather with his significant other had descended on the apartment two days before. With his usual flourish, Grandpa had announced that he was hosting a family dinner on Saturday night. A kind of ersatz Hanukkah celebration with secular neon lights and no mention of the Maccabees victory over Antiochus of Syria. Sara and Sam were flying in from New York. Her mother would drive over from Detroit. Everyone was welcome to bring a guest. It was to be great fun.

Cheryl was sure her grandfather would like Roger. Heck, maybe her mother would like Roger, too. Of course he wasn't Harvard, Yale, Penn, or NYU. But he had done his undergrad work at Northwestern. And he was at or near the top of their class at Chicago-Kent. That should count for something.

Cheryl turned into Nick's, shook the snow from her hair, scarf and coat, stamped it from her boots, and looked around for Roger. The room, illuminated only by tiny tree lights ringing the soffit above the bar and outlining the frosted front windows,

86

was dim. Even so, she could see his smile from the door.

Although she was from the middle Atlantic and he was a New Englander, Cheryl and Roger had much in common. Both claimed political families. Both were liberal, culturally Jewish non believers. They liked the same music, movies, and Merlot. He exercised regularly. She attended aerobics classes sporadically, and was always promising herself to do more.

As she reached the booth, they kissed so matter-of-factly that they could have been married. Or brother and sister. As always, it was done on her initiation. Pushing her coat, scarf, and purse along the bench, she slid into the booth, relaxed her shoulders and grinned.

"So."

"Merlot?"

"Merlot for sure."

Roger motioned the waitress over and ordered two. His needed refilling.

"So. Have you been here, waiting breathlessly for me to make my grand entrance?"

"I was for a while, but then this woman with huge pointy jugs came in and I forgot you entirely."

"That's not funny."

"True. It wasn't funny. It was tragic. I fell instantly in love, joined her at the bar, plied her with liquor and whisked her away to my apartment for an incredible tryst. Then she told me she was married and had to stop seeing me. I came back here heartbroken to drink myself into a stupor."

"In your dreams, funny man."

"Thank you, ma'am."

"Anyway, when are you supposed to leave for Boston?" She knew he had a flight in the morning at 8:15.

"Bright and early in the AM. Back to Beantown, traditional turkey, apple pie, Chevrolet, and baseball. And a houseful of screaming nieces and nephews. Then we do drugs. Tums and Excedrin. You wouldn't like it."

"Try me."

"I'm saving you for Spring break." Roger broke into a corny Groucho Marx imitation. Eyebrows bouncing up and down, flicking an imaginary cigar. "How would you like to go to Fort Lauderdale, little girl? I hear the beaches are paved with condoms."

"You are impossible." She shook her head in exasperated amusement. "Well, if Boston is so awful, why don't you stay here a few more days. My grandfather is hosting a dinner party at the Pelican down on Wells. Mother will be there. So will my sister and her husband, the genius stockbroker. Could be fun."

"The Pelican is out of my league. My credit card has a pulmonary embolism every time I walk by the place."

"Hey, this is a freebee, Mr. Stafford-Loan-Laden-Law-Student. Grampa megabucks is picking up the tab."

"Now you are getting my attention. I'm nothing if not a mendicant." Her smile melted in a sudden mood change. He sensed that the conversation was about to take a turn. Probably for the worse. He would have pierced the silence with another of his inane comedy routines, but something about the way she held her mouth made him feel uneasy.

They both sipped wine. She ran her index finger around the rim of her glass. Finally the words came.

"I'm pregnant, Roger."

For a few seconds, Roger said nothing. Did nothing. His mind and his expression went blank. Then his head began to turn back and forth.

"Are you sure?"

"Yes. I've been sure for a couple of weeks. I didn't want to tell you during exams. It's all my fault. I know I told you I was on the pill. Actually, I had been when I was in college, but not in law school. Not until we started, like, seeing each other, like, you know, regularly."

"Gosh, babe, this really is a bad break for you. I never suspected ... I mean, if I had thought ... I never would have..."

The usually glib Roger Foresberg was speechless.

"I know. I know, Roger, and I don't blame you. I just wish this hadn't happened so soon. I mean I thought that you and I had a good thing going."

"We did, Cher. We did, and we still do. You know how I feel about you. You're the best. Tops in my book. I've never known anyone who makes me feel the way you do. You know how much I care for you."

"I know. I know." She thought she knew. "I mean if this were, like, two or three years from now, and we were both practicing law, maybe it wouldn't be so bad to have a cute, little law clerk of our own."

"Try nine or ten years, Cher. I'm still a confused adolescent."

"C'mon, Roger. You're thirty-one and I'm twenty-seven. We don't even need our parents' consent."

He ignored the comment. "So what are you going to do? Do you need some money?"

She understood the offer. Wounded pride and fierce independence mingled in her eyes.

"Don't be crass. I told you it's my problem."

They sat a long moment in strained silence. The she forced a smile.

"So, are you going to let my grandfather buy you a scrumptious New York sirloin tomorrow night?"

"Gosh, Cher, I'd love to, but I've already got my ticket, and I promised my mother I'd be home this weekend. And you know how mothers are."

"Oh yes." She sighed. "I know how mothers are."

***

Justice Doris Cummings Templeton let her law clerk, Warren Adams, drive the Oldsmobile. As they sped along I-94 this sunny Saturday morning, she could not help but notice that he had a fine, firm jaw line. He was indeed a good-looking, young man. And a truly nice person, in addition to being terribly bright, well educated, and well connected.

Most of all, her clerk was absolutely loyal and trustworthy. And discreet. She never had to worry about his overhearing telephone conversations or seeing confidential memos. It wasn't that he lacked interest or didn't pay attention. Quite the contrary, Warren was an intellectual sponge who soaked up every bit of information around. But he knew when to talk and when to keep his mouth shut.

Yes, indeed, the young man was a great catch. The kind of bachelor who gets written up in the women's fashion magazines. Cheryl will swoon. Absolutely swoon, she mused, giving in to a surreptitious smile. It was all she could do to keep from humming or whistling a tune from 'Fiddler on the Roof.'

The role of Yenta was not a familiar one for Justice Templeton. She was, in fact, no great fan of the institution of marriage. Her own venture upon the seas of matrimony had lasted a scant two years. Just long enough to deliver two baby girls.

Doris had met her husband when he was a young assistant professor of political science at Brown University. She was in his class, 'Contemporary American Democracy', an elective seminar. Ahead of his time, advocating a revolution in civil rights and a war against poverty, he was an icon to Doris and her classmates. He was the quintessential Kennedy clone, in the year of JFK's ascendency. Caught up in the romance of Camelot, Doris overwhelmed the young professor with her enthusiasm for his lectures and her zeal for his pet causes. The barrier between teacher and pupil melted with the snow in the Spring of 1961. By the time she donned her cap and gown in June, she was carrying his child.

Doris Templeton and her poly sci teacher were married just two weeks after commencement. It was a nuptial contract in form, but not in substance. Their clandestine courtship yielded no time or occasion for settling on the axioms of marriage. Or of life, for that matter. They were smitten with each other. She got pregnant. They got married. That's the way it was in those days.

There followed a year which, if not idyllic, was at least an adventure. Sara was born before Doris learned that her husband hated asparagus. Doris was already pregnant with Cheryl before her spouse discovered that she thought women were biologically, intellectually, morally, politically, and psychologically superior to men.

Doris' fierce independence and uncompromising certitude soon pushed the man out of her life. When she went into labor with Cheryl, in November of 1963, she didn't even bother to call and leave a message for him at the University. She just hung a sticky note near the phone saying, "I'm in labor. Don't forget to pick up Sara at mother's" Then she got in the car and drove herself to the hospital.

Doris delivered Cheryl almost without feeling. Yes, the usual pain of childbirth was there. Yes, she worked hard, bearing down, pushing down, focusing all of her strength and concentration on the difficult business of expelling her intimate stow-away. But there was none of the emotional high. None of the rush that had come with Sara. There was no partner to share the moment. Just an efficient physician, barking orders and two nurses who crabbed at her and cooed at the baby.

The sleep of her post partum exhaustion was rudely interrupted by the suddenly blaring television on the opposite wall of the room. A shocked and weeping anchorman was heralding the day of dreadful mourning.

"John Fitzgerald Kennedy, 35th President of the United States died at 1 PM today."

For Doris Templeton, the agony of the nation dwarfed the accomplishment of her delivery. So puny a new life. So large and significant the life she watched expire on the television.

In the dirge-filled days that followed, Doris was glued to the tube. She felt somehow like a soldier being rushed into battle to replace a fallen comrade. Someone had to pick up the Kennedy standard. The torch had passed, as he had said, not to one man, but to a whole new generation of Americans. Doris felt compelled. Her sense of civic duty hardened into an irrepressible need to 'get involved'. To 'do something.'

And so Doris did something. She joined the Peace Corps. Left Sara and the infant Cheryl with her 57 year old mother, divorced her husband, resumed using her maiden name, and packed off to a remote village in Ecuador to teach English. Over the next three years, she learned more than she taught. She learned about intractable poverty, indomitable optimism, stoic resignation, and inexplicable perseverance in the face of insurmountable obstacles. And she learned that the only sure reward for total dedication was total frustration.

Near the end of her three year commitment to the Peace Corps, her father wrote to say that her ex husband had remarried and was going to seek custody of the girls. The next day a registered letter arrived. It carried notice of a custody hearing. Doris had already known it was time to go. And so she went home.

The custody battle was a bruising, protracted tug of war. Her husband's lawyer charged that Doris had abandoned the children. Doris argued that her parents had acted as her surrogates. She compared her time in the Peace Corps with the military obligation of draft age males. When your country calls, you go. You make the best possible family arrangements, and you answer the call.

The outcome of the litigation had almost as much to do with who Doris's father was as it did with the arguments made by respective counsel.

Arthur Cummings Templeton III, Andrew Hamilton Distinguished Professor of Law at the University of Pennsylvania, was, in 1967, at the peak of his illustrious career in the legal profession. A fabled teacher, prolific writer, and outspoken advocate of popular reforms in American jurisprudence, Templeton could be counted among those few academics whose views were sought with equal frequency by congressional committees, the Brookings Institute, the American Enterprise Institute, the White House, the American Law Institute, the Commission on Uniform State Laws, and every American Bar Association blue ribbon committee worthy of favorable mention in a newspaper editorial.

It would have taken monumental courage for any American trial court judge to hold that Arthur Cummings Templeton, or his wife, or their daughter, were unfit parents.

And of course, it didn't hurt their cause that the children's father was remarried to a woman who had two children of her own, and was manifestly lukewarm to the idea of taking on two more.

So, in 1968, Professor Templeton, his wife, daughter, and two granddaughters moved to the nation's capital, where Arthur served a visiting fellowship at the Brookings Institute. Doris secured a job as a congressional staffer, working on a House committee chaired by an influential congressman from Michigan. That year two more tragedies tore at Doris Templeton's heart. Her mother, a victim of Alzheimer disease, passed away and Hubert Horatio Humphrey lost the Presidential election.

Through the Watergate years, Doris remained on the staff of the House of Representatives, but decided to pursue a law degree. Her father, whom she admired without reservation, signed on as a distinguished adjunct professor at The National Law Center at George Washington University when Doris was accepted there. His teaching fees paid her tuition. His interest in her studies made the law school years a time of intense bonding. The model single parent and the paradigm of fatherly and grand fatherly nurturing. Happy years for both of them. Sara and Cheryl would later remember the brownstone house in Georgetown as a safe harbor.

In the years after she became a lawyer, Doris's duties on the

Hill multiplied. She worked hard on the Carter campaign in 1976, and was rewarded with an appointment as under secretary of Health Education and Welfare. A good record there, her congressional contacts, and her father's clout combined to win her a nomination to the federal bench in July of 1980. The Republicans in the Senate, however, stalled her confirmation hearings until November, and when Ronald Reagan was elected, the Templeton nomination died on the vine.

Her mistreatment at the hands of the GOP senators gained her a measure of notoriety and sympathy among the Democratic faithful, and led to a position as associate General Counsel of the United Automobile Workers Union in its national headquarters. Then, in 1982, her former boss in the Congress tapped her on the shoulder. He was running for Governor of Michigan. The UAW assigned her to its Detroit office, and she spent the next six months working on the gubernatorial campaign. Arthur didn't go with his daughter to Michigan. Instead, he kissed Doris, Sara, and Cheryl goodby, and moved to West Palm Beach, saying it was time he learned how to play golf.

Her candidate won and his first opportunity to fill a vacancy on the Michigan Supreme Court came in 1983. He named Doris Cummings Templeton to be a member of that August body.

In 1988, her father came out of hibernation to accept a visiting Professorship at Northwestern University Law School. He leased an apartment in Lincoln Park, took up with a librarian 26 years his junior, and within two years, had retired again to West Palm Beach, this time with a trophy significant other.

Arthur's leaving Chicago came at a fortuitous time. While Sara made her way well in the world, working as a staff psychologist for a New York marketing firm, marrying a hustling Wall Street stockbroker, and generally living the 1980's D.I.N.K. life style, Cheryl's road to maturity traversed a number of major chuckholes. The younger sister had celebrated her seventeenth birthday by getting pregnant. Doris took charge, arranged an abortion, black listed the boy, put her daughter on the pill, and in the Fall, shipped her, bag and baggage, to the University of Wisconsin. In Madison, Cheryl took advantage of the raucous Badger social life, and graduated with a 'B' average and no career track in mind whatsoever.

Always decisive, Doris sent her to Chicago to live with her grandfather and look for work. Always rebellious, Cheryl chose instead to apply to the Chicago-Kent School of Law. That was about the time Arthur and his lady friend left for Florida. Always indulgent, Grandpa continued to pay the rent on his Chicago apartment.

Arthur was unpredictable, but invariably fun. He had called two days ago to announce that he was in Chicago, and wanted to host a holiday party. She never said 'No' to her father. Nobody did. And so Justice Templeton was on her way to an impromptu family reunion.

***

The Oldsmobile passed the curiously named town of Climax, Michigan, when Justice Templeton set aside the briefs she was reading and picked up the car phone. She had not talked to the chief justice in several days. She found him at home in Bloomfield Hills.

"Breitner residence, who's calling please?" It was the housekeeper.

"This is Justice Temp ..."

"I've got it, " Elizabeth broke in.

."..leton calling."

"Oh, hello Doris. How are you?" The 'o' in hello and the word 'are' were elongated and emphasized. When Elizabeth Breitner greeted someone, it was with affected gusto. When she asked after someone's health, it always sounded as though she really wanted to know.

"I'm fine, Elizabeth. On my way to Chicago for a family get

together. How were your Holidays?"

"Smashing. Simply smashing, my dear. Exhilarating but tiring. I think I have run poor Edward into the ground."

"Ah yes, the weaker sex. The fellows just can't keep up can they?"

Elizabeth giggled. "You are so right. I suspect he'll soon be sneaking off to that fishing cabin of his to loaf around and recuperate. But I won't let him go until after the black tie New Year's Eve party at the DAC. That's always such a lovely affair, and I have a perfectly scrumptious new dress."

"Sounds *tre' elegante*, Elizabeth. Should make for a Happy New Year. Is the Chief around?"

"He's in the study. I'll rouse him. Happy New Year to you, Doris and to your family."

It took a few minutes. Just when Doris thought she might have been disconnected, Breitner came on the line.

"Doris, how are you? Where are you?"

"I'm fine. Over near Kalamazoo."

"I heard you were going to Chicago."

"Yes, my father is in town with his trophy. Should be a hoot."

"Tell him I said hello and that his piece in the Colorado Law Review about the right to privacy was masterful."

"He doesn't need ego boosting, Ed. He'll only want to know if his article will be cited in one of your opinions."

Breitner laughed. "I would be honored to cite him, but I'd have to stretch the law in one of our banal Worker's Comp cases to do it. What's on your mind?"

"Just wanted to touch base on the C.J. thing. Any new developments?"

"Henry's making noises like he might nominate O'Leary. We need to make sure O'Leary is not a candidate."

"O'Leary would be a disaster. He'd need to down three martinis just to get up the gumption to convene the court. Can you imagine the publicity we'll get if he gets stopped for drunk driving again? You can bet the State Police won't drive him home next time."

"I shudder to think of it."

"Why don't you call Henry and tell him we'll go to the newspapers if he pushes O'Leary?"

"Alton's not easily dissuaded. He would probably play chicken with us."

"What about laying it on O'Leary himself?"

"No way, Doris. That won't fly. Bob's in denial. He'd think we were threatening to make up stories about him. It just might cause us to lose him altogether."

"You think there's a chance he'll vote for you?"

"I think so. Bob and I are good friends. We have a little history together."

"Fishing buddies, eh? Do I hear the wires humming on the good old boy network?"

"Something like that, Doris. You could call it a guy thing."

"I hope that's not all you have going. If Henry nominates him, Bob may just get an attack of machismo."

"Maybe so, but I don't think I can scare Henry off with a phone call. Perhaps we could accidentally let him intercept a memo from you to me."

"Or better yet, plant a story with a friendly reporter to the effect that court insiders are worrying about Justice O'Leary's health."

"That's too hard ball, Doris. That kind of publicity could hurt all of us."

The conversation ended without resolution. She rode in silence for a dozen miles, then uncradled the phone again.

"Justice Henry? Doris Templeton here."

"Who?"

"Templeton, you old fart. Don't pretend you don't know me."

"For goodness sake, it is you. I'd recognize the flattular reference anywhere. To what do I owe this singular honor?"

"Politics, brother Henry. Sheer politics."

"Now you've got my attention. Are we going to burn our

bras?"

" Burn anything you don't need, Alton dear. I suggest that you start with your jock."

Henry stifled a laugh. She was quick and he had no ready retort. "What kind of politics, pray tell?"

"Judicial. I want to talk to you about the chief justiceship."

"Is your boy Breitner stepping down?"

"No way. But I hear you're trying to stir up a mutiny."

"Me?" Henry assumed a tone of mock innocence. "I'm harmless. Impotent. You've said so yourself. More than once."

"I've also said that you are untrustworthy and not a team player. Are you trying to dump Ed?"

"Could be."

"And just who do you think is qualified to take his place? Van Timlin?"

"Get serious, Doris. I led the charge against Van ten years ago."

"Who then? O'Leary?"

"He would be better than Breitner."

"You can't be serious."

"I am serious. Bob chaired some important committees in congress. He has leadership experience. And you have to admit, he is an amiable fellow."

"He was always a minority member. Never chaired a committee. A sub committee, maybe. Hardly anything comparable to the C.J.'s job."

"I still think he is qualified."

"What about his drinking? We certainly can't afford to have a chief justice who lives on booze."

"I don't know anything about that. I never saw him drunk. He always shows up for work sober, as far as I can tell. And he gets his cases written, which is more than I can say for some of the mouthy liberals on our court."

Justice Templeton grimaced. "You never miss a chance to needle me about the Hertzberg case, do you?"

"Never, dear lady. It's my sacred duty."

"Well, some of us think we have a sacred duty to maintain the prestige and dignity of the Michigan Supreme Court. That means keeping your amiable Irish sot out of the center chair. If you nominate O'Leary, the news media will expose his excessive drinking, I promise you."

" I can't help what the media chooses to say about him or anyone else. Anyway, what makes you think that the media would be more tolerant of an alcoholic associate justice than an alcoholic chief justice? And they've never hit him on that score that I know of."

"He hasn't been hit because the chief justice has covered for him. You know that Ed has good rapport with the papers and TV. Whenever they come to him with rumors about Bob, he puts out the fire. Who will do that if Bob is Chief?"

"Anyone who doesn't honestly think he has a drinking problem, I suppose."

"That will be an awfully short list, Alton. An awfully short list. Think about it. And have a Happy New Year."

Doris tilted her seat back, closed her eyes, and smiled. She sure enjoyed playing good, old-fashioned, country, hard ball with the boys.

***

Professor Templeton's dinner party was less than a social triumph. Cheryl and Warren showed no interest in each other. Sara's husband, who had the least of substance to talk about, dominated the conversation. The host actually fell asleep waiting for dessert to be served, while Doris eyed his flashy significant other with a mixture of disbelief and disdain. Justice Templeton's law clerk left the restaurant to join his Chicago friends as soon as he could do so without offending. Arthur and his squeeze took a cab back to the apartment. Doris was left to drive Sara and her husband back to their hotel. Cheryl invited herself along for the ride.

When she was finally alone with her mother, Cheryl talked about Roger.

"You remember the fellow I said I was seeing? The one from Boston?"

"Yes. Roger somebody. That the one?"

"Roger Foresberg. We really like each other. I think this could get serious, Mom."

"Why don't you bring him around. I'd like to meet him."

"He had to go to Boston over break. But he really wants to meet you."

There followed an awkward silence. Doris had a million questions. The kind women ask each other when they talk about a man. But Doris, being Doris, waited for Cheryl to volunteer.

"I'm pregnant." She said it almost conversationally. No cause for alarm.

"Jesus Christ!" Her mother was alarmed. "Don't you take precautions?"

" I got back on the pill as soon as we started dating steady. But I guess it was too late."

"I thought you learned your lesson in high school. Really, Cheryl, you can't keep on doing this."

"I know, Mom. I know. But ..." Cheryl was not accustomed to sharing her inmost feelings with her jurist mother. ."..I really do love him. I really do."

Cheryl started to sob. "I think about him all the time. And when I think about him, I hurt all over. I just love him so much, Mother."

Doris reached over, took her daughter's hand and squeezed it firmly, reassuringly.

"I understand, sweetheart. Believe me, I really do understand." She squeezed Cheryl's hand one last time, patted her on the knee, and regripped the steering wheel.

"Get it taken care of right away, honey. You don't want to miss any classes."

***

The old year was about gone. Auld Lang Syne was in the air. Stepping off of the ' El,' Cheryl felt a poignant sense of things coming to an end. As each step brought her closer to the Women's Health Center, she felt her bond to Roger slip away another notch. Walking introspectively, she did not notice the uniformed man and woman until she was almost between them.

They wore shiny black helmets, fastened with chin straps, blue Eisenhower jackets, which exposed the blue shirt collars and black four-in-hand ties worn beneath. Crisply creased grey slacks touched the top of militarily spit-and-polished black oxfords. Black Sam Browne belts stretched diagonally from their right shoulders to their left hips, where each carried a holstered cell phone. Their hands, gloved in white, were clasped behind them, as they stood in motionless parade rest on either side of the walkway leading into the clinic.

Security guards. Cheryl felt an added chill to her already cold arms and shoulders.

"Excuse me, ma'am." The male guard addressed her politely. "Do you mind if we check you for metal. Just a precaution."

"No ...uh ... go ahead."

He reached around to his back and brandished a familiar metal detector, with which he quickly scanned her legs, arms, front and back. Her purse caused a beep. She opened it.

"Just coins."

"Thank you ma'am. Sorry for the inconvenience."

As she resumed walking, the woman guard handed her a card of some kind. It looked like a greeting card. Cheryl took it, and advanced several more steps before examining it. The front of the card bore the endearing picture of an infant, perhaps two months old, with wide, blue eyes, set above a downward tilted mouth. Tears streamed down both of the round, pink cheeks.

Cheryl assumed it was a brochure about family planning,

perhaps detailing the services available at the clinic. She opened the card. Inside was the sickening, full color photograph of a mangled fetus and the message, "Please, Mommy, don't kill me."

Suddenly nauseated, Cheryl turned on her heel and ran back toward the 'El.' She brushed past the guards too abruptly to notice the emblem on the back of their jackets.

It read, "Army of Righteousness."

CHAPTER 6

O'LEARY

Some secretaries don't have to be told to do it. Like Nike athletes, they just do it. Evelyn Mentash was one of those.

An attractive forty-something brunette who had never married, Evelyn was desperately, longingly, in love with her boss. Had been from the day she came to work for him ten years before. Her boss was widowed, eligible, handsome, witty, outgoing, and available. And he was the kind of a man who needed a woman. Someone to attend to all the details of living, like food, clothing, lodgings, medical care and so forth. Thus would the Honorable Robert Allen O'Leary be liberated to ponder the greater things: philosophy, jurisprudence, political science, history, theology, art, and of course, the Law.

But Evelyn had never been able successfully to compete with her rival. It was quite impossible, really, for Bob O'Leary had a crush on the Muse of Melancholy. And nobody does melancholy like the Irish. Not that he did not have good reason. He had seen enough sorrow to down any ordinary man. Still, there was hope for Evelyn. O'Leary was no ordinary man.

Eldest sibling in an Upper Peninsula Catholic family, O'Leary was an avid hockey player in his youth. In spite of several other offers, he accepted an athletic scholarship from Northern Michigan University, located in his home town of Marquette. A high scoring wing, he led his team to two consecutive NCAA titles. Team captain and star, he basked in the admiration that Yoopers, as residents of the upper peninsula of Michigan often call themselves, reserve for those of their own who make it big in the overpopulated world down below the Mackinac Bridge. Carrying a low number in the Viet Nam draft, and being somewhat familiar with the service branch because of nearby Sawyer Air Force base, O'Leary applied for and was accepted to flight school. Now he was a dashing fighter pilot, and an

103

officer to boot. His personal stock in Marquette skyrocketed.

Then in 1965 he was shot down. The army sent a helicopter behind enemy lines to rescue Lieutenant Colonel O'Leary. They got him out, but not before his right leg was chopped off two inches below the knee by automatic weapons fire. In the hospital in Saigon, he met Sohgn Nyegyn, a hauntingly beautiful Vietnamese nurse. Their storybook romance could have been scripted by Earnest Hemingway. After the sweet sorrow of their parting, O'Leary returned to the States, was fitted with a prosthesis, and enrolled in law school at the University of Notre Dame.

Despite the artificial leg and foot, he played hockey for a very good law school team that actually beat the varsity in an off season charity game.

O'Leary wrote Sohgn often at first, but mail delivery was suspended as the war reached its weary climax. He lost touch with her, and while she still lingered in his fantasies, he became more and more resigned to the finality of their separation. He finished law school, passed the Illinois Bar examination, and won a position with a respected Chicago law firm.

Then one day, he returned from court to find Sohgn waiting in his office. She had survived a horrendous escape, including weeks of inhumane wandering aboard an unwelcome, overcrowded boat. Their reunion was steamy and brought them quickly to the altar. Shortly thereafter, the young lawyer and his new bride left the big city for the shores of Gitchee Goomi at Munising, there to raise a family in the shadows of pictured rocks, and get involved in politics.

By Christmas of 1979, Bob had served two years as county prosecutor, and was ending his first year as a Republican member of the United States House of Representatives. That year, there were five stockings hanging from the mantle. In addition to the big ones for mom and dad, smaller stockings proclaimed that they belonged to Bobby, 5, Kathleen, 3, and Nancy Ann, 1.

But Camelot was not to be a lasting home for them. On Christmas morning, Kathleen woke with a temperature of 102. Sohgn called the doctor, who phoned a prescription to the town pharmacist. He, in turn, offered to go down to the store and make it up, even though he had not planned to open at all on the holiday. Sohgn was dressed, while Bob was still in pajamas. She insisted on driving up to the pharmacy to pick up the prescription. As she backed the Bronco out of the garage, Bobby ran out the front door, hoping to go with her. She did not see him. The car slammed him to the ground, and the back tire had rolled over his throat by the time Sohgn could stop the vehicle.

Bobby's tragic demise completely devastated Sohgn. She had been so proud of the three children she had presented to Bob. Especially the boy. Especially Bobby. She never regained emotional stability. On January 25, 1980, just one month to the day after Bobby's death, Sohgn was found in the Bronco, motor running, in the garage, her soul gone to apologize to her first born son.

On the surface, O'Leary seemed to recover from the double blow to his heart. He continued in the Congress, winning re-election in 1980, 1982, and 1984. In 1986, the GOP recruited him to run for the supreme court, and with secret help from Breitner, he was elected. The girls were of school age, so O'Leary rented a house in Lansing, where the family stayed during the school year. Summers always meant Munising and Lake Superior.

O'Leary's secretary, Evelyn Mentash, had been extremely helpful with his two teen age daughters. They would often go to his office, especially when he was out of town, and pass the time with the glamorous assistant. She listened to them, gave boy friend advice, cheered them up, shared their triumphs, and tried to interpret their father to them when he seemed an unfeeling Neanderthal ogre.

When he was in Congress, a young boy in Ishpiming lost a leg when he was struck by a train. His father, a friend of O'Leary's, asked the Congressman to visit the boy in the hospital, to show him that he could have a productive life with an artificial leg.

After that, O'Leary made it a practice to visit new amputees whenever he could. He would demonstrate his agility with his artificial leg and foot. The big finish was always a ninety second demonstration of Irish step dancing. It was great politics, but that's not why he did it. He made no effort to get publicity. His reward was in the gratitude of his fellow amputees. After he went on the court, O'Leary expanded his visitations to the entire state. Evelyn routinely watched the papers for news stories about amputations. In addition, a number of hospitals, having learned of the justice's willingness, used him to bolster the spirits of people who were abnormally depressed after amputation surgery.

On this late December day in 1990, Evelyn performed her customary chore with an unaccustomed uneasiness. She clipped the story from the Detroit paper and left it on his desk. She wondered what he would do.

TUTTLE KILLER LOSES FOOT

The juvenile allegedly responsible for the December 18 drive-by shooting and death of Josh Tuttle, son of Supreme Court Justice Hilda Germaine, underwent surgery yesterday for the removal of his left foot, a spokesman for Ponchartrain Receiving Hospital confirmed today.

The boy, approximately ten years of age, was taken in custody when he fled from a burning stolen car in which three other juveniles were trapped and killed. When apprehended, he was carrying a nine millimeter pistol. Scuffling with his captors, who were trying to extinguish his flaming clothes and hair, the boy shot himself in the foot. He has been hospitalized since the incident for third degree burns over much of his body. Doctors expect he will make a complete recovery. Under Michigan Law, a ten year old cannot be tried as an adult for committing any crime, including murder.

***

O'Leary stopped at a sleazy bar near Greek Town on his way to the Hospital. These amputee visits were never fun. At best, there was a sense of having done some good for someone who was really hurting, emotionally as well as physically. At worst, it was a real downer, reminding him of his own post-operative depression and all the heart wrenching experiences that followed in his life.

He downed the first martini before the bartender could finish a tirade against the management of the Red Wings. A second critique took a longer. The subject was Bill Ford, owner of the Detroit Lions. By the time O'Leary looked at his watch and decided he could delay his mission no longer, the Tigers were being excoriated.

There was a fair amount of security to be passed before the justice could get to the boy known as 'Rat Tail.' Although Jeremiah Wheatley was not considered a criminal, he was in the custody and control of the Wayne County Probate Court, Juvenile Division. A uniformed officer was posted near the door to Rat Tail's room. The guard did not recognize O'Leary. Supreme court justices are not celebrities. But he announced himself, and the officer was too intimidated to challenge him, so the justice was allowed to pass into the windowless private room.

The boy was restrained. Despite his burns, and the surgery he had undergone, Rat Tail was feisty, rebellious, and uncooperative. He put on quite a show of temper tantrums when he first arrived. The nurses and orderlies soon learned that his hands had to be tied down whenever there were less than two people in the room to subdue him. Lying on his back, his face still partially bandaged, Jeremiah appeared a pitiful sight. Small. Helpless. Hurting. Scared. As soon as he opened his mouth, however, all of those appearances faded out as the brassy, nasty, spit-in-your-face Rat Tail was revealed.

"Hello there young fellow. How are you doing today?" A standard friendly greeting from the friendly public official.

"Wudzitlooklikefuk.?"

"Looks like you're not quite ready to play basketball. But you will be pretty soon. Who's your favorite basketball star, Jeremiah?"

Rat Tail looked at the tall stranger quizzically. Was he for real? Didn't look like a doctor. Who was he and what did he want?

"Ainnevagwineplaynobaskaball. Gotnomufkinfoot."

"Hey, you still have one real foot. And I bet it still feels like you can wiggle the toes on the other one. Go ahead. Try it. Wiggle your toes on both feet."

Rat Tail didn't answer. For a moment, his face was expressionless, as he sent the neurological messages down both legs commanding his toes to wiggle. The sheet above his right foot stirred as his toes began to move. There was no similar sheet response on the other side, but in Rat Tail's head, and all the way through his nervous system, it felt like his left toes were wiggling, too. The boy's lips parted in a shy smile, then in spite of himself, gave way to a wide, toothy grin.

"Sheeemanahkinfeelit."

"So can I." O'Leary sat on the chair a few feet from the bed.

He raised his right pant leg to display his artificial foot and leg. He unstraped the prosthesis, exposing the sock covered stump that protruded below his knee. The he bared the knob of smooth scarred skin that had held the plastic limb. Rat Tail's eyes widened. The Justice rolled the leg around so the lad could see it from every angle. He quietly explained its parts, how he put it on, washed it, changed shoes and socks, and walked on it.

Then he put it back on, stood up and did his famous Irish step dance.

Jeremiah Wheatley laughed out loud.

***

As O'Leary left the hospital room, the white police officer stationed at Rat Tail's door was engaged in a heated exchange with a heavy set, elderly, black woman.

"Sorry, ma'am, my orders are 'no visitors', without a court order."

"Well, why don't you be a good brother and go get us a court order? I told you I'm here to see that boy and I'm going to see him. Didn't come all this way on a smelly old bus just so you can shoo me away. Now get out of the way an let me go in there."

It took a moment before Justice O'Leary recognized the lady. He had never seen her angry, but on the few occasions when they had met, he had been impressed by her outspokenness. He had last seen her less than two weeks ago at Josh Tuttle's funeral.

"Hello, Mrs. Germaine," O'Leary began, "It's nice to see you again."

She eyed him questioningly. "Do I know you?"

"Bob O'Leary, ma'am. Justice O'Leary of the supreme court. I work with Hilda."

"Well, for Heavens sake, so you are! I'm very, very glad to see you, sir, at this very moment. Seems like this here

gentleman, this police officer here, doesn't understand that I am
going in to see that little boy in there."

O'Leary turned to the policeman. "I'm sure that Probate
Judge Morrison won't mind if Mrs. Germaine goes in for a little
visit. I'll be happy to wait here while she does." Then,
addressing Cindy, O'Leary added, "I'll be happy to drive you
home when you're ready, Mrs. Germaine. My car is not quite as
smelly as the DOT bus."

The officer quickly backed down. "Just doing my job, Judge.
You understand, don't you?"

***

Cindy walked steadily to the edge of the bed and let her eyes
take in the full sight of this person who had snuffed out the life
of her precious grandson. She was struck immediately by the
fact that he was young. Too young to be a murderer. Too
young to go to hell. She looked him in the eye. He looked back
defiantly, not knowing who she was or why she was there,
except that she was another adult to be defied.

"I'm Cindy Germaine. Josh Tuttle was my grandson. You
killed that boy, and I'm his grandmother. I came to see you to
tell you that you are gonna have to make it right with Almighty
God for what you did to Josh."

Rat Tail said nothing. Didn't move a muscle.

"You hear me what I'm saying, boy? You took the life away
from my daughter's only son. He was a good boy. Didn't hurt
anybody. Didn't hate anybody. Didn't do anything bad. Didn't
do anything to you or to your momma or your daddy or any of
your people. What you did was a sin, boy, and God Almighty
He punishes sinners in the fires of hell. And you gonna burn in
the fires of hell for all eternity, twisting and calling out for Elijah
and cursing your own momma for birthing you in the first place.
You going to be so full of pain and hurting your skin is going to
peel off like an old ripe banana and your soul is going to dance

on them hot coals for longer than it takes a tree to grow or an ocean to dry up."

Rat Tail's eyes were getting wider.

"The only thing that's going to keep you out of that place of hellfire and damnation boy is you turning over yourself, body and soul to the Lord Jesus. You're going to have to spend the rest of your born days praising the name of the good Lord Jesus every single minute. You took and sent an innocent man back to his God and Creator when it wasn't even his time to go. You did that. Now he's dead and you're still living and now you got to take his place and do all the good in this old world that Josh Tuttle would have done if you hadn't shot and killed that boy. You understand what I'm saying?"

Rat Tail thought he had heard enough.

"Gitthufukoutahere."

Cindy was a church going, God fearing, Jesus praising, good Christian woman. But she had lived in New Orleans long enough, and listened to enough roughhouse sailors so that the language of the street was no stranger to her. She heard what he said, and she knew how to deal with it. She walked deliberately to the bathroom, just inside the door, returning in a moment with something in her left hand. Without hesitating, she sat on the edge of the bed and, making a fist with her right hand, squeezed Jeremiah's nostrils between the knuckles of her third and fourth fingers, twisting his nose so far clockwise that his eyes watered. When he opened his mouth to yell for help, she used her left hand to jam the bar of soap between his teeth, forcing it so deep into his mouth that it pressed against his tonsils. He couldn't breathe. He couldn't cry out. His hands fought helplessly against the restraining devices that held them securely to the sides of the bed. All he could do was taste the acrid soap. And see the stern black face of the old woman whose eyes pierced to his very soul. And listen, however unwillingly, to her diatribe.

"Now you listen to me little nigger boy, and you listen good.

You already have done all the bad in your life that the good Lord God in Heaven has got for you to do. Starting right this very minute you're going to start doing good, because you haven't got time enough before you are going to pass over the River Stix your ownself that you can waste one single minute away from doing a whole powerful lot of good things. You're going to start right now having a clean mind and a clean body and a clean mouth. Right from this minute you're going to praise your sweet Lord Jesus every time you open your mouth. Every time. You hear? You're going to praise the Lord Jesus and ask him to forgive what you did to poor Josh, and ask Jesus to make you a man like Josh was and to do just some of the good things for God's people that Josh would have done if you hadn't killed him. You listening to me boy? You hear what I'm saying to you? You made all the mothers and daddies cry on the green earth that you're going to make cry in your whole life. You're going to learn to love people. You hear? And you're going to learn to love the Lord Jesus, and you're going to praise Jesus every day an every hour and every single time you open that smart little nigger mouth of yours. You hear me what I'm saying to you, boy? You hear what I'm saying? Now let me hear you say "Amen" little brother, and let me hear you praising Jesus."

She released his nose and mouth. He coughed and spit the bar of soap into her left hand.

"Amen" He whispered.

"I said, let me HEAR it, boy."

"AMENPRAISJESUSAMENDAMIT"

Cindy leaned down and kissed Jeremiah on the cheek. Then she laid a copy of the New Illustrated Children's Bible on the table, and left the room.

***

Art Wilhelm was waiting for O'Leary in the grill room at the Detroit Athletic Club. Although they had been on opposite sides of the aisle in the Congress, the two men were close friends and managed to get together frequently for dinner, drinks, discourse, and dessert.

Wilhelm had taken up the lobbying profession since leaving Congress. He had a way of being the first to know about nearly everything. He maintained offices in Detroit and Chicago and divided his time between his automotive and insurance industry clients.

Wilhelm didn't look up from the Wall Street Journal as O'Leary eased into the chair across from him.

"You're late"

"What's new in the world?" asked O'Leary, ignoring his friend's gibe.

"Guy in West Virginia's buyin' winning lottery tickets, it says here. Justice Department's in a tizzy."

"How so?"

"Guy buys tickets at a discount from winners before they get cashed in, then sells 'em at a premium. Apparently makes millions." Wilhelm pushed the paper across the table, pointing to the story.

O'Leary motioned to the waiter to bring two of what Wilhelm was drinking. He pushed the paper aside. "Why would anyone want to sell a lottery ticket?"

"Winners want to sell to him because he doesn't withhold any income tax. He'll pay you off in cash, or put the money in a Swiss bank account. Whatever you want."

"O.K. I see why some people might want to sell to him. But why would people want to buy those tickets for more than they're worth?" O'Leary was shaking his head.

"Basically because it's clean money. The lottery commission withholds income taxes. Everything is on the up and up. You don't have any trouble explaining to the IRS or anyone else where you got the money. It's not as much money as you had before, but it is after taxes and strictly legitimate."

"So if I'm a crook, and I've got $105,000 in cash from a bank hoist or whatever, I can go to this West Virginia guy and buy a $100,000 winning lottery ticket, cash it in and walk away with maybe 60 or 70 grand in after tax, clean money."

"You got it."

"Is it legal?"

"Well, there's nothing to prevent somebody from selling a lottery ticket. If we were talking about buying a lottery ticket with clean money, I can't see where there is any legal problem. The problem comes when the scheme is used to launder illegally acquired funds, or achieve some other illegal purpose."

"So what you're saying is that this is a way for people to buy legitimate, taxable income. Right?"

"You got it."

They ordered more drinks and had a good old time developing comical scenarios about senators, presidents, and congressmen who might win large lottery pay offs. Richard Nixon, in his familiar pose, both hands in the air full of winning lottery tickets, proclaiming, "I am not a crook." Lyndon Johnson, shoving lottery tickets into the pockets of senators in the cloak room, saying, "Come let us reason together." Silly stuff that comes easily to the minds of long time political junkies, especially when the bartender is mixing the fourth round of cocktails.

***

Dinner with Wilhelm was always great fun, O'Leary thought as he steered onto I-75 north out of downtown. The man could make you laugh. And for a lobbyist, Art was remarkably discreet. If any of his clients had a case in the supreme court, Art would never mention it. Oh, he might steer the conversation a little to get in his two cents worth about overweening bureaucrats, or intractable zoning boards, or whatever was annoying his banks and insurance companies, but it was always so subtle that the connection to his clients' economic interests was unrecognizable.

They had lingered over dinner until about 10:30 PM. When they parted, they agreed to meet in Lansing on Friday night, for one of their frequent gin rummy sessions. Harry Flynn, O'Leary's cousin, and a long time member of the Attorney General's staff, was usually the third player, and the fourth would be someone Art or Bob would suggest. The games were usually held at Flynn's house, he being divorced and living alone. Ever since his older daughter was married and the younger one packed off to college, O'Leary had no need for the rented house in Lansing. Basically, he lived in Munising, but stayed with his cousin whenever court was in session and he was in the capital.

O'Leary asked the new justice, Jim Malloy, to sit in with them for gin rummy this week. O'Leary was looking forward to spending time with the latest Gaelic addition to the bench. They were already being called, in some irreverent circles, the 'Michigan Murphia.'

O'Leary accelerated to 75 miles per hour soon after he entered the Chrysler Freeway. Near the Warren Avenue exit ramp, the right wheels ran up onto the shoulder. O'Leary quickly righted the car, and made a mental note to drive more carefully. Crossing the southern Oakland County suburbs on I-696, he had difficulty keeping the vehicle in the center lane, at one point encroaching so far into the outside lane as to warrant an angry horn blast from another motorist. By the time he reached Brighton, he was cruising between 88 and 92 miles per hour, with the window open to fight sleep. At the Grand River exit ramp, he veered off of the interstate to make a pit stop, and fell asleep sitting on the toilet.

The twenty minute nap put his legs to sleep, but woke up his brain. From Brighton to Lansing, O'Leary drove no faster than

55 miles per hour. He kept the Oldsmobile in the exact center of the right hand lane. He bit his lip, slapped his cheeks, yanked his earlobes, and twisted his nose to prevent himself from dosing off. Parking the car in Harry's driveway, O'Leary promised himself, again, to control his drinking. No more four martini dinners. No more.

***

"Shut up and deal."

Art Wilhelm was addressing Harry Flynn, who was in the penultimate phase of another long story about Upper Peninsula lawyers.

"Ever since you guys in Marquette went Hollywood, we've listened to your cornball stories about lawyers who would rather go fishing than go to court. Get some new punch lines, would ya?"

The remark drew groans and guffaws from Justices O'Leary and Malloy. There was a spark of truth in it. In the 1950's John Voelker, an associate supreme court justice from Ishpeming authored a novel called, "Anatomy of a Murder." Written under the *nom d'plume* of Robert Traver, the book sold well, and, in due course, the movie rights were acquired by a Hollywood producer. The film, shot on location in the Marquette County courthouse, starred Jimmy Stewart, Ben Gazara, George C. Scott, Lee Remick, and Eve Arden. Among others in the supporting cast was a novice actor named Joseph Welch. Welch achieved notoriety as counsel for the United States Army in the epic televised congressional hearings in which muckraking Wisconsin Senator Joseph McCarthy accused the army of giving aid and comfort to the nation's enemies. The movie was a singular success, winning several Oscar nominations.

Marquette's legal community was never quite the same after that. 'Anatomy' lore occupied much of the conversation at bar meetings. Details of the filming were rehashed and embellished in the retelling. How they had painted the courtroom grey, only weeks after the board of supervisors had spent thousands sprucing up the building, including two coats of green paint. And how they had to shore up the second floor of the courthouse to hold the weight of all those cameras. And how the story line of the film followed the facts of an actual case that Voelker had tried as a young lawyer.

Yoopers are great story tellers. Maybe it comes with being cooped up for winter seasons that last from September to May, or maybe it has something to do with carrying pasties -- yesterday's meat, potatoes and vegetables -- under your shirt to keep them warm enough to eat for lunch in a mine hundreds of feet under ground. Maybe it's the ethnic make up. The Swedes, Norwegians, and Irish dominate. And they love to laugh at themselves and each other.

Flynn and O'Leary brought that spirit with them. Malloy and Wilhelm became jesters out of self defense. They had been paired against the cousins by cutting cards. The game began at 8 PM. It consisted of a series of hands played alternately with each opponent across the corner of the table. By 11 PM, a case of beer was emptied and O'Leary and Flynn were each $62.00 to the good against Malloy and Wilhelm.

To Art Wilhelm, $62.00 was a pittance. Chump change. And it was deductible. He was, after all, building relationships with public officials. His clients liked that. Sixty-two dollars was quite another matter for Jim Malloy. His carefully planned family budget allowed him only $250 a month in cash for personal expenses. That included lunches, haircuts, the cleaners, and every other cost that was normally paid out of pocket as opposed to writing a check. His losses for the evening represented a week's allowance.

Malloy coughed it up with some good natured moaning and groaning.

"I hope Margaret doesn't look in my wallet tonight and see how you bandits have cleaned me out. She's liable to come after you fellows with a writ of arousal."

"Doesn't your wife know that you're a big shot supreme court justice now, and rolling in moola?" Wilhelm asked it with a wink to O'Leary.

"That will be the day." Malloy shook his head. "Show me any other hundred thousand dollar a year job that costs three hundred thousand to get."

Wilhelm was amused. "Hey, a seat in Congress only pays about that, and candidates spend millions to win. I'll bet you still have a couple hundred grand in your campaign fund. You'll probably donate it to some worthy cause like the Ancient Order of Hibernians or the IRA."

"Don't I wish. I was hoping to make enough from this gin game to pay off the bankers who bailed me out after the election. You know judges can't raise campaign funds after the polls close."

"That's crazy. After the election is when everybody wants to give." Wilhelm was serious. On Capital Hill, that's the way it works.

"That's the very reason why the court rule forbids it." O'Leary chimed in. "People who give money to winners usually want something in return."

The conversation continued as the men downed one more for the road. As they were breaking up, the losers pulling on goulashes, coats, scarves, and hats against the howling darkness outside, O'Leary tried to set up a future rematch.

Wilhelm demurred. "I'll be basking in Florida sunshine on the shores of Marco Island while you turkeys are wallowing around in three feet of snow and slush."

More moans and groans from the fellows.

"How long will you be in Florida?" Flynn had a reason for asking.

"Two months," answered the lobbyist. "We'll be there until the first week in March."

"Good," said Flynn. "You can help me parlay tonight's

winnings into a major fortune." He handed Wilhelm forty dollars. "Buy me some Florida Lottery tickets."

"You don't have to do that, you have a lottery right here in Michigan." Advice from Malloy.

"Nothing like Florida, Jim," Flynn replied. "The Florida Lottery is the biggest in the United States. They started it just three years ago. In the first six months of last year, they did 1.1 billion dollars of business. I said billion. With a 'B' as in boy. That's a lot of lotto money. Some lady just won 105 million dollars in Florida. You don't hear about those kinds of pay offs anywhere else. And all of their games are parimutuels. The Fantasy Five, where you hit five out of five numbers sometimes pays more than a million, if there are only one or two winners."

"O.K. Harry, I'll waste your money for you. Any of you other suckers want to buy in?" Wilhelm turned to O'Leary as he spoke.

"Damn right I do, Art. Do you know how hard it would be to live with Harry if he is the only millionaire in the family?" O'Leary handed Wilhelm a twenty.

"How about you, Jim? Want to pay off all those campaign debts?"

Malloy may have been a little mellow. His usual limit was two bottles of beer. He had nursed them all night, and taken only a few gulps of the obligatory nightcap. He joined the game at O'Leary's request, mostly because he wanted to work on O'Leary to accept the nomination as chief justice. Unfortunately, an occasion to discuss it had not presented itself. In that sense, it had been a waste of time. Certainly it had been a waste of money. But what the heck, Malloy thought, I've lost a bundle tonight anyway, what's a few dollars more. I don't want these fellows to think I'm cheap. Or worse, that I'm afraid to take a chance. And who knows? What if lightning should strike? Somebody has to win the lottery. Why not me?

He had succumbed to the siren call of hope. Hope, it is said, springs eternal within the human breast. Hope and the ability to dwell in fantasy. Two indicia of the higher nature of humankind. The gurus of the Internet talk of virtual reality, a condition achieved by duplicating sights, sounds, and sensations through the use of computer technology. But virtual reality has existed since the dawn of creation in the play of children, in the plans of grown ups, in the memories of the old.

And in the dreams of people who buy lottery tickets. Indeed, that's what you get for your dollar. A chance to spend 48 or 72 hours daydreaming about what you would do if you were rich.

"Count me in." Justice Malloy removed the last bill, a twenty, from his wallet.

***

The next day was Saturday. The matter of the chief justiceship was getting down to the wire. Henry and Malloy spent most of the morning on the phone. Finally the older jurist convinced his junior colleague that if O'Leary would not accept nomination, Henry would nominate Malloy.

Neither of them knew for sure what Van Timlin would do if Malloy were nominated. Neither of them knew what O'Leary would do in a Malloy v Breitner contest. Both agreed that if O'Leary would accept the job, it would be a lock. Malloy told Henry he would make one last effort to persuade O'Leary to accept the center chair. He called O'Leary, and they agreed to meet for lunch at a Mexican bistro on the west side of town.

"Look Bob," Malloy spoke intently as soon as the pleasantries were over. "Ed Breitner has been Chief for how many years now, six? What has he done, really? Are we any closer to computerized dockets? Are we any closer to getting the filing mess in Wayne County cleaned up? Are we making any headway with statewide funding? More importantly, how is the supreme court perceived by the trial bench? How do we get along with the court of appeals? I think you know it's time for a change and I think you know what we have to do to make things better. You are the logical person to lead the court, and we have the votes to put you in the center chair. Last time you and I talked we got nowhere. You said you had to think about it. You promised me you would give the matter careful consideration. Bob, we need a horse. We need a credible candidate, someone with experience and savvy. Alton and I agree. We think you're it."

O'Leary stirred his martini. "Very flattering. Very flattering indeed. And believe me, Jim, I'm tempted to say yes. I really am. Being chief justice is as high as you can go on our totem pole. It assures you a place in the history books, I suppose. But I don't know. I just can't seem to see myself in the role. I can't picture it."

"What can't you see? What is there to see? If you are chief justice, you sit in the center chair in the courtroom. You sit at the head of the table in conference. You preside when the court is in session. You speak for the court at legislative committee hearings. You speak for the court when the media calls and wants to know what we are doing. You crack the whip on your colleagues and on the trial bench to make sure that everyone is working hard. Can't you see yourself doing those things? I can see you in that role."

"I can't envision it so easily, Jim. I didn't seek this job to be an administrator. I love the law. Love to debate the finer points. Love to weave logical arguments, and expose errors. I like the substantive part of this job, but I don't give two hoots about bossing people around or being some kind of media personality big shot. I say leave that stuff to the super egos on the court like Breitner. He eats it up. Let him issue the memos and make the public statements. My opinions speak for me. I don't need anything more than that."

"Look, Bob, this isn't just me or my idea of what the court should do. Alton Henry has been on the court for longer than anyone, and Van is a veteran as well. Both of them want you to take this. That is what persuades me. They ought to know what is good for the bench."

"I have a high regard for both of those fellows. But they are only two out of seven."

"And you and I make four. A majority. What are you going to do if Henry nominates you on Monday?"

"I hope he doesn't."

"And if he does?"

"I don't honestly know what I'll do, Jim. I just don't know."

***

Bob O'Leary was back home only a few minutes from his three martini lunch with Jim Malloy when the phone rang. It was Chief Justice Breitner.

"Bob, I am going to need your vote on Monday. Alton Henry is trying to oust me as chief justice. He is a bitter old man who simply can't tolerate being put in his place. I think he has mesmerized young Malloy with his conspiratorial whispering. And Van is nothing but a mindless party hack, who will do anything to defeat a Democrat. I have always considered you my friend, Bob, and a man who can, and does rise above partisan considerations in the business of the court. You know me. You know that I put partisanship aside just as you do in these things."

"Ed, I always said you are my favorite Democrat."

"I remember that line. And I hope you remember what it cost me to get you to say it."

CHAPTER 7

BREITNER

On Saturday, May 19, 1990, Chief Justice Breitner was in Lansing. He stayed at the apartment Friday night because he had a pile of paper work to clear away. Saturday, without phones ringing or court personnel around to interrupt, he would be able to accomplish quite a lot.

He was due home in Bloomfield Hills at five. Another of Elizabeth's mandatory social events. He worked until after 12:30 PM, then dashed over to the Country Club of Lansing to meet Bill Tenner, an architect who was working on a conceptual design for a new court house for the supreme court. Talking about a supreme court building perennially occupied the energies of Michigan's chief justices. Despite a half dozen different plans, the court continued to sit in the Law Building, to which it had been relegated in 1969 when the legislature decided to take over the lovely old supreme court chambers on the third floor of the State Capitol.

A well known Eaton Rapids attorney, passing through the grill on his way to the men's locker, stopped at the chief justice's table to pay his respects. Breitner introduced him to the architect, then inquired why the lawyer was wearing his business suit on such a golf-able Saturday afternoon.

"I'm on the Board of Directors of Cooley Law School, Judge. We have a graduation this afternoon. As a matter of fact, our guest speaker is your counter part from the state of New York."

"Please give Judge Wachtler my regards." Breitner felt disappointed that he had not known of Wachtler's visit. The two men had a nodding acquaintanceship as fellow members of the Conference of chief justices. Wachtler would not have recognized Breitner if he saw him on the street. Breitner, on the other hand, would know Sol Wachtler anywhere. The New Yorker was, in many ways, Ed Breitner's idol and role model.

A profound jurist, eloquent speaker, and prolific writer, Wachtler embodied everything Breitner admired and wanted to be. Wachtler had been appointed to judicial office by governors of both parties, Nelson Rockefeller a Republican, and Mario Cuomo, a Democrat. He enjoyed the universal respect of the bench. His name was beginning to be mentioned in the same breath with the great ones of their profession. Learned Hand. Benjamin Cardozo.

Walking to his car in the parking lot after saying goodby to the architect, the Chief glanced at his watch. Almost three o'clock. Maybe he could squeeze in a quick visit to the law school to say hello to Judge Wachtler before the commencement exercises began. He drove to the parking ramp on Capitol Avenue. It was almost full. He ended up parking on the top level. By the time Breitner crossed the street and caught an elevator to the sixth floor auditorium, the ceremonies had begun.

Too late to greet Sol personally, Breitner slipped into the cavernous room, unnoticed among the one thousand or so relatives and friends of the law school graduates. The college's president introduced Judge Wachtler, and the handsome visitor from the Empire State took the microphone with assurance and poise.

After a few introductory comments, Wachtler began warming to his subject.

"I recall that when I graduated from law school, I went to Albany as a young lawyer, and I saw the seven judges of the New York Court of Appeals, which as the President told you, is the high court of our state. I saw these seven judges having dinner together and I said, "Look at these giants. I wonder what they are talking about.

"Well, I've been on the court now for seventeen years, and I have dinner with my colleagues every night, and I still find myself wondering, "What in the world are they talking about?

The room filled with laughter.

"But just to give you an illustration of the kind of things we talk about, I had just read a book by Leo Rosten called, "The Joys of Yiddish." In this book he defined various Yiddish terms and the first one he defines is the term 'Ah-Hah.' He defines it by telling the story of a fellow who goes into a restaurant and orders a bowl of soup and the waiter brings the soup and the customer says to the waiter, "Taste the soup." The waiter says, "What's the matter, is it too hot?" The customer says, "Taste the soup!" The waiter says, "What's the matter, is it too cold?" The customer says, "Will you please taste the soup?" The waiter says, "Alright, where's the spoon?' The customer says, "Ah-Hah.""

The audience roared even louder. The kind of laughing approval that is confirmed by a rousing round of applause. Some were still chuckling as the judge continued.

"So I told this story to my colleagues and the very next day in the courtroom during oral argument there was this young lawyer arguing his first case before our court. And he is somewhat intimidated, because it is an awesome courtroom. All hand carved out of solid oak. Much of the work done by prisoners a hundred years ago."

Wachtler digressed with a short anecdote about a prisoner's appeal, then went on.

"At any rate, this young lawyer is arguing his first case before our court. Looking at the seven judges, he says, 'And the evidence went in, and the evidence was tainted. But the prosecutor sat back and said to himself, 'Ah-Hah' Well, the whole court started to laugh. This poor lawyer. The first thing he does was to look down to see if his clothing was properly attached.

Peals of laughter from the responsive crowd.

"And the chief judge said to him, 'Oh, you must forgive us.' The young lawyer answered, 'I understand, Your Honor.' And the chief judge says, 'How could you, you weren't at dinner with us last night.'"

More raucous laughter shook the room. More applause.

Breitner was spellbound. Sol Wachtler could capture in a humorous story the essence of collegiality. The pure pleasure of living and working and eating with a small group of elite lawyers. Sharing experiences. Sharing laughs. Sometimes even tears.

Breitner glanced at his watch. He might be a little late, but he wanted to hear more.

"And the courts are now handling matters that were never dreamed of by past generations. When I went to law school, whoever thought of consumer protection or environmentalists using the courtroom for a battleground; student unrest moving from behind the barricade into the courtroom.

"We've decided cases in all of our state courts, and in the federal courts which boggle the imagination. We decided in our court last month who won the America's Cup. Who would think that we would decide such a case? Deciding that a terminally ill elderly patient has the right to die. That a young, infirm infant had the right to live. That a husband could be found guilty of raping his wife. Again, these are cases that are born in the imagination of the most imaginative lawyers in the world."

Driving east on I-96, Ed Breitner mulled over Sol Wachtler's remarks again and again. The man had a gift. To be like him, to have his ready grasp of the big picture. That would be something.

***

His pulse quickened as he saw the towers of the Mackinac Bridge rising up on the horizon before him. It always did. The bridge signaled two important things; he was halfway there, and he was about to enter his own special world.

The cabin up north beckoned Ed Breitner. A simple, rustic structure, with a bathroom, a bedroom, and a larger room to live in, it offered shelter from the elements, from the pressures and anxieties of his professional life, and from the ennui of his marriage.

New Year's Day, 1991. In three weeks, he would be sixty years of age. Driving alone on a clear, bright winter day over roads deserted by a population still sleeping off last night's celebrations or glued to football saturated television sets, Breitner reminisced. About his father, Max, who had immigrated from Russia in the last decade of the nineteenth century, married Emma Goldstick in New York City and opened a neighborhood grocery store. About how his parents had worked, and saved and worked some more to build their business. About how his father had squirreled away enough cash in the 1920's so that during the Great Depression he was able to buy when everyone else was selling. About how Max had parlayed savings gleaned from a crowded city block into a real estate empire scattered over three states.

He thought, too, of his sisters. Florence, the quiet, steady, graceful one, had married a dentist. They lived in Philadelphia; had two grown daughters, three grandchildren, and a full, comfortable country club and synagog-centered life. Ada, the wild one, had gone through four husbands, a half dozen live-in lovers, two abortions and a botched career as a concert pianist. Currently she lived in San Francisco with her only child, a twenty-two year old homosexual bartender.

Ed loved both his older siblings, and knew them well. Because inside his own skin, he could feel the urgings that made them each such distinct and special individuals. There were times when he was Florence, feet planted firmly in the community, basking in the respect and admiration of good and decent folks, warmed by the affection of family, and secure in the knowledge that tomorrow would be another today.

But there were also times when he was Ada. Then he longed for the rush of risk, the headiness of adventure, the excitement of uncertainty. Then he hated the mundane, the banal, the hum drum daily drudgery of commitment to people and places and organizations. Then he wanted to be alone. To be free. To be where no one could find him.

Ruminating about entering his seventh decade, Breitner could review an active and successful career. A BA in Political Science from Northwestern University. A law degree from the University of Michigan, where he had been editor of the law review, and enrolled in the Order of Coif. His two years clerking for a Judge in the United States Sixth Circuit Court of Appeals in Cincinnati. Making partner at Beauford, Lemon, Winsock and Quinn after only five years. The hectic, rewarding term of office as Oakland County prosecuting attorney, which led to election as judge of the Michigan Court of Appeals in 1968. Elevation by the voters to the supreme court in 1975. And the crowning achievement of becoming chief justice in 1983.

Except for the unfortunate blip when Kosman ousted him from the center chair for two years, Breitner's career had been an unbroken, sometimes meteoric rise to the top.

Of course, Breitner could never dwell on his career success without thinking of Elizabeth. He met her in Ann Arbor when they were both at the University. He a supposedly mature law student; she a teen aged undergraduate freshman. An eastern Jew and a Grosse Pointe WASP. The things they had in common were money, ambition, brains, drive, and charisma. Their religious differences, doubting families, and his job in Cincinnati kept them apart until 1958 when he returned to Michigan to join Beauford, Lemon. Then their commonality won out. Never a devout or Orthodox Jew, Breitner simply identified himself with that vast multitude of Americans whose cultural roots are planted in all of the world's great faiths, but who answer to the description 'unchurched.'

Edward and Elizabeth had two children; John, now a marine biologist living and working in Maine, and Clara, a graduate student studying Fine Arts in Paris, through an overseas program sponsored by Yale University. The Breitners were socially prominent, financially secure, politically correct.

There were times when the propriety and perfection of his life with Elizabeth made Breitner want to barf. That's when his sister Ada's personality took control. And that's when he went to the cabin.

***

An hour after leaving the original Big Mac, the Mackinac Bridge, Breitner crossed over the locks at Sault Saint Marie into the larger Canadian city of the same name. The streets were clear, but snow was piled high enough at curbside to justify displaying the ubiquitous orange flags which hovered over the locals' automobiles.

Breitner turned north on Queen's Highway 17 and headed toward Wawa. In summer, he would sometimes opt for the more adventurous route along 556, but that road is closed in the winter. He recalled his first trip to this fabulous country. The raw beauty of it. Forested mountains sloping majestically down to the ominous grey waves of Lake Superior, one of the world's largest and deepest fresh water seas.

Introduced to Northern Ontario by his bother-in-law, an avid fisherman and poker player, Ed found himself totally charmed and intrigued by the area, its climate, its peacefulness and its people. Soon he was arranging fishing expeditions of his own, often spending long weekends at campsites on lakes accessible only by air. Sometimes with a few other men. Sometimes alone.

On one of these trips, he purchased the cabin. His Shangri La on Whitefish Lake near Hawk Junction. He had spotted the place while fishing. A sudden thunderstorm had caught him far from camp. Dragging his small boat ashore, Breitner looked around to see if anyone was home. Seeing no sign of life, he tried the door. It was unlocked. He spent a dry afternoon inside, poking around, getting acquainted. As the rain continued, he decided to stay the night, got the fireplace working, cooked his day's catch of bass, and found a home in the north woods.

On his return to camp, Breitner studied the map to see how one would get to the cabin by car. There must be a way, he reasoned, as the place was wired for electricity. Ultimately, after a number of dry runs through dense forests on winding gravel roads, he found it. By inquiring at a local real estate office, he learned that almost all of the recreational lands in that part of Ontario were owned by the Algoma Central Railroad. At their office in Sault Saint Marie, Breitner discovered that the cabin he had found was available, the prior lessee having defaulted on the rent. He wrote a check on the spot, and became another of the thousands of U. S. citizens who own or lease summer homes in Canada.

Later that same summer he returned for a month long vacation. It was 1985, the year he was ousted from the center chair by Kosman. Elizabeth had taken the girls to Europe. He had demurred, pleading that he had several important opinions to write, and could not spare the time. Which was partly true. He did have opinions to write. But his underlying need was to return to Wawa.

Breitner worked up a sweat and an appetite that summer, clearing underbrush, fixing up the cabin, gathering, cutting, and stacking firewood. Doing the chores. Dishes, flatware and cooking utensils had to be found. And bedding. When, somehow, all the chores got done, Breitner was tired, but exhilarated by the strenuous activity.

During his third week at the cabin that first year, the justice went exploring along the shores of Old Woman Bay on Lake Superior. He parked the truck, and walked down to the water's edge. Then he wandered south, sometimes walking easily, sometimes picking his way among slippery, wave washed rocks. It was one of those incredible summer days. Three dimensional. A day that beckoned him away from reality and responsibility.

Stopping to rest, he took off his shoes and wiggled his toes in the sand, feeling somehow giddy and juvenile. Abruptly, he jerked his foot upward when his large toe struck an object just beneath the surface of the sand. Brushing sand away, he realized that he had just found a man's shoe. Curious, he continued to poke around. Another shoe turned up. Then, between the rock he was sitting on and another just inches away, he discovered cloth. A tee shirt. Then denim. A pair of blue jeans, a leather belt still drawn through the loops. In the jean pockets he found Canadian coins, car keys, and a wallet.

Sixty seven dollars in small Canadian bills, water soaked and stuck together, a Visa card, the registration for a 1982 Dodge Van, an insurance certificate for the same vehicle, and an Ontario driver's license told a chilling story. The license, which would expire in June of 1986, a little over a year away, identified one Earl Boatman, born July 16, 1937, a resident of Sudbury, Ontario.

Breitner instinctively looked around. There were no footprints but his. No sign of any human life in sight, nor had there been during his entire hike along the shore. The condition of the clothing and the wallet, and their burial under several inches of sand made clear that their owner had been gone a very long time.

Breitner returned to his pick up truck with the wallet in hand. He left the shoes and clothes. At a restaurant just south of town, he found a pay phone, dialed Sudbury information and obtained the home telephone number of a Clyde Boatman, that being the only listing of that surname in the 705 area code.

"Hello."

"Hello. Is this the Boatman residence?"

"Sure is." A man's voice.

"Could I speak to Earl Boatman, please?"

"Not unless you're a spiritualist or a psychic, eh?"

"I'm sorry. Say again?"

"Earl Boatman's dead. Drowned in Lake Superior more'n a year ago. Body washed ashore buck naked near Old Woman

Bay. He was my uncle, sad to admit. Never done much but gamble, drink and whore around. Owed most everyone in town when he died. I suppose yer lookin' to collect from him too, eh?"

"Not really. I owed him sixty seven dollars and change from a poker game, and I wanted to even up with him."

"Keep it. I just got through closing up his affairs. Sold his van and that run down shack he called a house. Didn't get enough for the whole lot to pay ten cents on the dollar to his creditors. If I get another sixty bucks, I'll have to reopen the estate, eh? Just isn't worth the trouble. So I say, keep it."

Ed Breitner had no desire to get further involved. He hung up the phone, got back in the truck, drove to the forlorn, white clapboard sided Presbyterian church around the corner from the pizza parlor in Wawa, and deposited Earl Boatman's sixty-seven dollars and thirty nine cents in the poor box. Then he drove to the cabin, day dreaming about a new life as Earl Boatman, woodsman of the north.

Earl was six years his junior. From the photo on the license, Ed could see that their faces were roughly the same shape, though his eyes were set a bit wider. Earl wore a beard, which made it difficult to compare mouths or jaw lines. Breitner had not shaved since arriving at the cabin, but his beard grew slowly, and was still in the stubble stage.

Thus began, however innocently and haphazardly, a strange and thrilling chapter in the otherwise staid life of Justice Ed Breitner. He began to think of himself as Earl Boatman. The initials were his. That must have been a sign that it was meant to be. He called himself Earl in the café, at the gas station, in the grocery store. People accepted it. He began to build an identity. He was a seaman. A pilot on the Great Lakes. The Whitneys and the Rutherfords, his in laws, were in the shipping business. He had picked up enough of their gossip to talk rather knowingly about the long narrow freighters which plied the inland seas from Duluth to Cleveland. Each time he did it successfully, he ventured further into the fantasy. When he finally headed south, it was with sadness, satisfaction, and a firm determination to return again as soon as possible.

The following summer the resurrected Earl Boatman renewed his driver's license, a harrowing experience, which required Breitner to pose for a new photograph and make a plausible explanation for the change in his appearance. On balance, it had been a surprisingly easy thing to do once he had identified the busiest time of day to approach the office of the Ministry of Transport. With the driver's license for identification, he easily opened a bank account and purchased a jeep. Meanwhile, as Ed Breitner, he purchased and erected a ten by twenty foot aluminum storage shed next to his hideaway cabin. The cabin, of course, was leased in the name of Breitner. When he was at the cabin, he was Ed. Only when he was out and about could he don the personhood of Earl. The only time he had to play both parts at once was when he towed the Oldsmobile back to the cabin after buying the jeep.

That autumn he drove to the cabin in his state owned car. Its cellular phone, though equipped for roaming, was useless north of the Soo. He bought a phone at the cabin to stay in touch with court personnel and with the affairs of state in Michigan. Unfortunately, it had no answering machine. It was a radio phone, a party line, and answering machines won't work with radio phones. Once at the cabin, he stowed the Oldsmobile in the storage shed and revved up the jeep. That became his regular *modus operendi*.

Now, on the first of January, 1991, Breitner was making one of his few mid winter sojourns to the cabin. Fortunately for him, a fishing lodge several miles beyond his cabin conducted snow mobile expeditions in the off season, taking advantage of more than four hundred miles of trails which meandered north and east out of Wawa. They paid to keep the gravel road plowed, and Breitner was the beneficiary. Arriving at his retreat, Breitner did not enter the cabin. Instead, he opened the storage shed, drove the jeep out, put his Oldsmobile in, closed and locked the shed door, and sped back out to highway 101. Even though he had left Detroit before day break, it was growing dark as he wheeled the jeep south and east toward the small lumber mill town of Chapleau, some eighty miles away. At 7:05 PM, the jeep pulled up in front of a two story, shingle sided house in mid block of one of the four dozen residential streets in the village. Breitner got out of the jeep, pulling his duffle bag behind him, and walked toward the front door. As he ascended the eight steps leading to the dilapidated front porch, the face of a three year old boy appeared at the window for just a fleeting second, then disappeared from view.

Seconds later, Billy Boatman burst into the kitchen excitedly calling to his mother.

"Daddy's home, daddy's home."

* * *

Valarie Talmei had come into his life and he into hers in the summer of 1985. They met at the White River Flea Market on Highway 17. He was there to purchase a bed, mattress, chair, table and all the minor trinkets that daily living requires. She had gone to buy a rose colored overstuffed chair that wouldn't fit in her decaying Ford Escort.

The roadside market was crowded, at least by local standards. Perhaps a hundred people milled around among the several dozen make shift booths. Most of the shoppers were vacationing city folk from the States or the more populated eastern reaches of Ontario. Most of the merchants weren't really merchants. They were local mill workers' wives, Indians, and assorted itinerant peddlers hawking cheap or homemade jewelry, used clothing, housewares and furniture, and selling coffee, soda, doughnuts, and hot dogs. To Breitner, it seemed hardly more than an overgrown garage sale, but you could find an occasional deal on something valuable, if you knew what you were looking for.

He noticed her early on. Her shapely oak brown legs, connecting a pair of dirty sneakers to tightly stretched cut off blue jeans, caught his eye. A vacation relaxed eye. A lonely fisherman's eye. A far-from-home-where-nobody-knows-me eye. And, of course, he noticed her firm, round ass.

Browsing among the used, abused, confused array of merchandise, Breitner's attention kept returning to the girl. Jet black hair, worn shoulder length. Bright, dark eyes beneath long, lovely lashes. A pouty mouth begging to be bitten. And the mystery of a baggy, too large sweatshirt which hid what he could only imagine. And did.

The furtive looking, the sometimes outright gawking, came with being fifty-something. Late fifty-something. After the ego shock of passing the half century mark, the better part of a decade roars by at break neck pace. Incessant demands of career drown out the call of testosterone. Copulation failures become common. A wistful, gnawing, fantasy life creeps in. Grey haired men do a lot of looking, wishing, even hoping. But they don't score very often.

On this partly cloudy, late summer day, in the rapturously romantic expanse of Northern Ontario, the capricious gremlin of opportunity knocked on Ed Breitner's door. He had filled the bed of his truck with his new, old stuff, and was about to drive off, when, looking in his rear view mirror, he saw the black haired girl struggling to jam the chair into the back seat of her car. He watched for a moment, then prompted by chivalry, if not by lust, he climbed out of the truck and walked back to her.

"Excuse me, young lady, you seem to be having some trouble there. Can I help?"

She looked up, still pushing against the chair. "I'm afraid it just doesn't fit. Guess I'll have to try to put it in the trunk. Do you have some rope?"

"Better than that, I have a pick up truck and time on my hands. I'll be happy to haul it for you."

"Thanks, but I'm afraid I can't pay to have it delivered. I live more than a hundred miles from here. Took my last dollar just to buy it."

Breitner laughed. "I'm not in the common carrier business, and I'm not looking for work. Just thought I would offer to help a lady in distress. A very lovely lady, I might add."

She stood, grinning, looked him in the eye, gave him a brazen wink and accepted his kind offer.

Following her rusty car down Highway 17, through Wawa and east on Route 101, he mused that she must not live far from his cabin. He could feel his face flush as he gave in to more and more explicit fantasies. Periodically, he calmed himself down by reflecting that she was probably married, and no doubt had four snot nosed kids and a seven foot lumberjack husband, not to mention a screaming hag of a mother, and a possessive, tobacco chewing, shotgun toting, father. Then the persistent vision of nubile breasts above a heaving belly would come back.

She led him to Chapleau at the intersection of Routes 101 and 129. Three thousand people, most employed by one of the town's three mills or the Algoma Central Railroad. Through the four corners they went, eventually turning down one of the last residential streets before civilization gave way to boundless forests. She stopped in front of a ramshakled two story house. It appeared to be an unimaginative variation on the standard north country residence. A twenty four foot square basement rising two or three feet out of the ground supporting a frame structure, capped by an A shaped, asphalt shingled roof. The front elevation consisted of two windows upstairs, marking two equally small bedrooms, and two contiguous windows downstairs in the living room next to a front door set atop a six by six foot front stoop eight steps above grade level. There were no shutters outside nor curtains inside. The whole impression was one of stark, unadorned shelter from the elements.

He helped her lift the chair into the house and place it in the otherwise unfurnished living room. She made coffee and they chatted about nothing and everything. She learned nothing about him. Not even his name. He learned a lot about her. He asked all the questions. Skillfully, as only a good lawyer can, without arousing any suspicion that his interest was more than idle curiosity.

Thirty-one years old, she had moved to Chapleau only weeks before to take a job as a waitress in one of the town's five restaurants. Actually, Myrtle's Cafe was more aptly classified as a diner. Run by a widow whose only employee and only daughter up and quit one day to move to Timmins and make something of herself, have some fun, meet some real people and have a life of her own, Myrtle's boasted five four tops, a counter with six stools and one eight top in a tiny windowless alcove. For private parties.

Her name, he discovered, was Valarie. She grew up in Thunder Bay, fifth child of an abusive half Indian father and an equally mixed blooded alcoholic mother. Like her four older siblings and three younger ones, she left home as soon as she was able. At sixteen, without a high school diploma, she worked at several minimum wage jobs, lived in crowded boarding houses with other rootless young adults, and generally made her way as best she could. During one particularly long stretch of unemployment, she hitch hiked east to Wawa and lucked into a clerical job at the trucking company whose eighteen wheeler had stopped to give her a ride. Two years of harassment by the married truck driver and his married boss convinced her to move on. The waitress job at Myrtle's, posted in the lobby of the Wawa supermarket led her to Chapleau.

Breitner didn't press on their first meeting. In truth, he didn't dare. Considering who he was, the thought of a romantic affair was ludicrous. CHIEF JUSTICE BREITNER SHACKS UP WITH ONTARIO WAITRESS. It wouldn't play in the Detroit Evening Paper. Reluctantly, he put the girl out of his mind. Or tried to, until he found the Boatman wallet. Then everything changed. Then every possibility became possible.

As Earl Boatman, the question was not whether to approach her, but how. Courtship was a thing in his distant past. The age difference between them was both good and bad. On the one hand, she was comfortable talking to him, just being friendly. On the other hand, she might never see him as a potential lover. Then there was the education gap. He had to use his jury vocabulary on her.

One of his first acts as Earl Boatman was to have dinner at Myrtle's. Valarie waited on him, of course. He was pleased that she remembered him, and while she flirted good naturedly with every man who came in, he persuaded himself that she gave him at least as much attention as anyone else. He managed to inform her that his name was Earl. The tip he left her exceeded any other she received that night. Or that month. She would remember him.

The next summer, Breitner had a plan. He worked feverishly to breathe life into the Earl Boatman identity, and to establish his cabin as a safe haven for the missing chief justice to be periodically reincarnated as a rough hewn Great Lakes sailor and north woods sportsman. He began to haunt Myrtle's. Soon he was waiting for her to finish work. Driving to Sultan or the Shoals for a beer.

The relationship truly exhilarated him. She made him feel like a man. Smarter, stronger, richer, younger. He bought her things. Things she couldn't afford. An iron. A vacuum cleaner. A new television with a VCR. Before August was over, he had moved in. With Valarie, he was truly a different person. Rough. Masculine. Unshaven. Breitner avoided belching, perspiration and flatulation. Boatman could burp, sweat, and fart. Their love making was primitive, uncomplicated, brassy. No need to be sweet and tender. In her bed he was primal, hungry, relentless. He had forgotten what it was like to be throttled between a woman's legs. It was every bit as erotic as he had imagined.

Their parting was mutely emotional. He explained that he was assigned to captain a lake freighter, the Kingston II, from Marquette to Chicago, then back to Cleveland and Buffalo. He didn't know how long he would be gone. He promised to call often and to write. He gave her a Detroit P.O. box where she could write to him. Then he went back to the real world.

It wasn't until July of 1987 that Breitner, installed once more as chief justice, was able to get away again to his northern retreat. In the meantime, he had called Valarie with decreasing frequency. After writing a rather torrid love letter in September, he decided not to put too much in writing. He tried unsuccessfully to create a distinct handwriting style for Earl. Her letters were few and stilted. She had never written anyone before, and had no confidence in the medium. Driving over the Soo locks, he reflected that they had not communicated for more than two months. He wondered if she would be waiting.

It was dark when he got to the cabin, but he managed to store the state car and liberate the jeep rather easily. The drive to Chapleau, windows open to the chill night air, brought back visions of last summer's ecstasy. He drove like a madman to Myrtle's Cafe.

Through the store front window he could see the blonde waitress. No Valarie she. Beefy and bellowing, she appeared more to be distributing feed to barnyard animals than serving restaurant patrons. Breitner didn't go in to ask about Valarie. Instead, he jumped back in the jeep and spun away to her house.

The lights were on. He still had a key and used it. Across the dimly illuminated living room, she sat in the old farmhouse rocker he had purchased for her last year. An infant sucked at her right breast.

Her voice was steady and soft. "He's beautiful, Earl. I call him Billy."

Earl Boatman was nothing if not a man of honor. The following week, they were married in Thunder Bay.

PART TWO

YEAR ONE

CHAPTER 8

JANUARY 1991

When the telephone rings at three o'clock in the morning, your heart rate becomes immediately elevated, and your mind races through horrible thoughts of impending tragedy or doom. Some one was in an accident. Somebody died. Something awful is coming my way.

These impulses seized Jim and Margaret Malloy in the early morning of January 8, 1991. They didn't need much to be awakened. This was already marked as a red letter day in their lives. Jim's first meeting with his new colleagues on the supreme court. The first formal session of the court in which he would participate. The public administration of the oath of office and donning of the judicial robe that had come to be known as a "Swearing In" ceremony.

In spite of Jim's wishes that the ceremony be kept low key, it was quite impossible to prevent his large family and Margaret's from making a big thing of it. There would be speeches, a reception, and afterwards a luncheon 'just for family.' That meant between sixty and a hundred people at least.

Margaret had been on the phone to Detroit until nearly midnight. Jim worked on his speech, and didn't get to bed until after 1 AM.

"It's for you," said Margaret, handing the phone across the bed to Jim. "O'Leary."

"Hello, Bob. Are you alright?"

"I'm OK. Sorry to disturb you. I know it's late. Or early maybe. I haven't been able to sleep. This chief justice thing has got me totally addled."

"Have you decided what you are going to do?"

"Yes. And I'm sorry, Jim. I know you're not going to like this. But I've made up my mind, and it's final."

"You're not going to take it?"

141

"No, I'm not going to take it. More than that, I do not want to be nominated."

"I know that. You told me that before. But you can't stop Henry from putting your name up."

"That's true, Jim. I can't stop him. But I don't have to vote for myself. If Alton nominates me, I'm not going to vote for myself."

"So where does that leave us?. I see a deadlock. Three votes for you and three votes for Breitner. What will happen then?"

"I'll have to make the decision. If Henry nominates Van, I'll stay home and vote for Van. If he doesn't, I'll cast my vote for Ed."

"That's final?"

"Set in stone."

"Thanks for the call. Get some sleep. I'll see you at nine o'clock."

Malloy reached over his sleeping wife to cradle the phone, then rolled onto his back and stared at the motionless ceiling fan. Wide awake, he wondered if supreme court j ustices ever get any rest.

***

Malloy called Alton Henry's car phone precisely at 7:30 AM. He figured Henry would be somewhere south and east of Jackson.

"It looks like the rebellion is doomed, Mr. Justice," Malloy got right to the point. "O'Leary is not only refusing to be a candidate, or to accept the position if elected, he called me at three o'clock this morning to say that he is going to vote for Breitner, if Van isn't nominated."

"Damn. I can't believe that Bob would do this to us."

"He doesn't leave us much room. How about this scenario. What if we put Van back in the chair for one term. Tell him that is all he's going to get. Maybe in 1993 O'Leary will accept it.

Or somebody else."

"Are you the somebody else?"

"I wouldn't take myself out of it. Maybe in two years, Van will think I've had enough seasoning and be ready to pass the gavel to a new generation of Americans, as Kennedy called us."

"Don't be too sure of that. If we put Van back in, he'll think he is there by the Divine Right of Kings. You'll have to take him out feet first."

"Give me two years, I can charm anybody."

"Or make a bunch of enemies in the effort," Henry laughed as he said it.

"Anyway, think about it. I don't know what else we can do. I'll see you in court."

"I'll be there early."

"Maybe we can talk some more."

***

The Michigan Supreme Court is located on the second floor of a glass and limestone monstrosity known as the Law Building. It was constructed in the 1960's as state government burgeoned out of available office space in the State Capitol. The Law Building was not originally intended to house a court. Its design reflected the intended use for general office purposes. Ceilings and floors were divided in six foot square grids, making it possible to move interior walls quite readily. Twelve by twelve offices, twelve by eighteen offices, work areas that measured twelve by twenty-four or eighteen by twenty-four or thirty were easily configured. Anything else was impossible. The smallest possible room was six by six. Too tiny for an office. Way too big for a closet.

The courtroom itself occupies a windowless space directly north of the elevators, and separated from the elevator lobby by a twenty-four by thirty foot foyer. The courtroom itself is 36 by 42 feet. The ceiling, only 14 feet high is finished with plain drywall. The paneled walls are topped with a modest cornice. While the room is not exactly stark, it fails to project the image of reverence for the law that many county courtrooms around the state do so effectively.

The supreme court's move to the Law Building in 1969 flowed from negotiations with the legislature. One important bargaining chip: the Justices were to have free, covered parking below their offices, rather than the traditional outdoor parking spots reserved for them behind the Capitol Building. That gain proved to be illusory and costly. The Office of Management and Budget imposed a parking fee of fifty cents per day for all state employees. The justices refused to pay, insisting that they had the same right to free parking as they had enjoyed outside the Capitol. The imbroglio which followed generated massive media attention and occasioned some of the worst publicity in the court's history.

Nonetheless, the court issued an order restraining the collection of parking fees, and never backed away from it. An example, many said, of the nine hundred pound gorilla rule. Or as Justice Alton Henry was fond of observing, "If we do this thing, who is to gainsay us?"

The court's conference room, unlike the courtroom, has windows on two sides, facing west and north. It is a large room, containing lockers for judicial robes, a lavatory, a sink and small refrigerator, and of course, a massive conference table around which are posted seven, high backed, black, leather, swivel chairs. The table is light oak, as are the baseboards, doors and other wood trim in the room.

Traditionally, the chief justice sits at the head of the table, on the south end. The associate justices are stationed, again by tradition, on either side of the table, the senior associate to the right of the chief justice, the next senior on the opposite side of the table at the chief justice's left, and continuing back and forth along the table in the same fashion as to the other members of the court. One exception, also traditional, though no one seems to recall how or when it began; the most senior justice who wishes to do so, may move his chair to the opposite end of the table from the chief. The result is an imbalance, with three members of the court along one side of the table, and only two on the other.

On Malloy's first day on the job, he found his chair on the west side of the table, the third seat down from the chief justice. Lowest on the totem pole. To Malloy's left, occupying the foot of the table was Alton Henry. First to arrive, Henry was busily pouring through documents, when Malloy entered the room.

The two men shook hands. In the United States Supreme Court, the Justices always shake hands with every other member of the court when they meet in conference. That salutary practice has not taken hold in Michigan. But today was Malloy's first day. And it was the first time Henry had seen him since the election. They were still making small talk, when Doris Templeton swept in and took her place to the right of the chief justice. Since Henry had opted to move to the foot of the table, she was able to slide closer to the head. This gave her the appearance, indeed the badge of being the second in command. Malloy got up, walked around the table and shook her hand. She greeted him politely and cordially, but did not stand. Van Timlin arrived next, with O'Leary on his heels. Malloy wondered if they had been talking in the corridor. Or caucusing someplace. If so, what were they discussing? Would they tell him? More greetings. More handshaking.

At precisely nine o'clock, the chief justice entered the room. He placed his black, embossed, leather ring binder on the table, and proceeded to greet each member of the court individually and warmly. As the chief edged closer to Malloy, the junior justice could not help but think that Breitner appeared to be working the room, in the manner perfected by office seekers. After shaking hands with Malloy, Breitner returned to the south end of the table.

"We'll wait a few more minutes for Hilda. When I left my

office, she had not yet called in on her car phone. That suggests that she may be only a few minutes late."

"Today." Henry chuckled sardonically.

"I'm surprised Hilda didn't ask to be excused altogether after what she has been through." Templeton leapt to the defense of her sister justice.

Breitner changed the subject. "Jim, how many people do you expect for the swearing in today?"

"I'm afraid they'll fill up the courtroom, Mr. Chief Justice. We Irish, you may know, have a way of proliferating like rabbits. Between the Malloys, the Fitzsimmons, and the Cronyns, there may be nearly a hundred."

Van Timlin whistled. "A hundred relatives?"

"I don't even know all their names. But most of them voted for me, so they want to be here."

"We will be taking a break right after the ceremony," said Breitner, in businesslike tones. "That will allow the courtroom to be cleared. Then, I would like to get started with oral arguments. We have a long call this month."

"After the ceremony, we have a reception and luncheon planned at the Radisson Hotel." Malloy was concerned that hearing cases would keep him away from the reception. "All of you are welcome to join us. I sent a memo around inviting everyone."

"What time is the reception?" O'Leary could see a time conflict developing.

"Well, we figured it would take maybe forty five minutes for every one to get over to the hotel. I thought the reception might start at eleven fifteen or eleven thirty, with lunch served at twelve."

"If we take the bench at ten, and the ceremony consumes an hour, I don't see how we can hear oral arguments on a case and still get to the hotel much before noon. Do you Ed?" O'Leary was looking for the chief to cut some slack.

"Perhaps we could hear the appellant before lunch and the

appellee after lunch, but I don't like to do that," replied Breitner.

Templeton leaned forward. "Neither do I."

At that moment Hilda Germaine swooshed through the door and hurried to her place at the table.

"So sorry everyone, the traffic coming up here was abominable. A little snow, and some drivers slow to a crawl."

She looked at Malloy. "Welcome, Jim. It's nice to have you on board. Will we meet your family today?"

"Only about a hundred of them."

Germaine's eyes widened. "A hundred relatives? No wonder you won the election."

"I doubt that they all voted for me, Hilda." Malloy replied, with a grin. "The Irish are rarely unanimous. Besides, most of them are Democrats."

"Could you give me the mailing list, Jim?" asked Henry, laughing. "I have to run this year."

The moment of frivolity passed, and an uneasy silence set in as the justices' awareness of Germaine's recent tragic loss made them all uncomfortably speechless.

Hilda cleared her throat. "Mr. Chief Justice, before we get into things here, I would like to take just a moment to tell all of you how very much I appreciated your kindness and thoughtfulness to me and my family over the past few weeks." Her voice, while low, was well modulated, and didn't crack. "It really is a comforting thing to have colleagues who care enough to share the burden of grief with Ben and me. All of you have been like family to us. The flowers, the memorial gifts," She looked squarely at Van Timlin. "your generosity and concern have bolstered us a great deal." Just a hint of a quiver. Tough lady, Malloy thought.

"Justice Germaine, uh, Hilda," Breitner was taking control. "On behalf of the court, frankly, I know I speak for all of us when I say that you have our utmost sympathy and most sincere condolences. We can only speculate on how much you must have suffered."

An uncomfortable silence set in.

Van spoke first. "What are they doing about the gang that killed your son? Are they going to be tried as adults?"

It was inappropriate. Germaine did not reply. Templeton jumped in. " There was no gang. Just four children all under fourteen. Three of them died after being chased by the police. The only one who survived is ten years old. Too young to be waived over to circuit court."

Breitner took charge again. "Since we are all here now, I think we ought to get on with the first order of business. As you know, the constitution requires that on the first meeting of the court in odd numbered years we are obligated to designate one member to serve as the chief justice to preside at hearings, and sweep the floor, and carry out the trash, and generally do all the nasty little jobs that nobody likes to do. Does anyone have a motion?"

Doris Templeton took the floor. "I have a motion, Ed. You are too damned humble and self-effacing. I my opinion you are the best chief justice the court has had in this century. I consider it an honor and a privilege to nominate you for another two year term and I think we ought to close the nominations and cast a unanimous ballot for Ed Breitner as chief justice. And I so move."

"Support," said Germaine. No one else spoke.

"Well, I'm truly flattered Doris, and justices for your vote of confidence and support for my administration. I really have tried to do a good job over these past years. And I think we are making very excellent progress. The courts of Michigan were busier last year than at any time in their history. A record number of new filings have created a tremendous burden on our resources. We have taken our needs vigorously to the legislature, and I think we are seeing real progress on that front." Breitner paused, sensing that the justices were not interested in hearing a rehash of his last state of the judiciary speech.

"There being no other nominations," the chief continued, "The question is upon Justice Templeton's motion to close nominations and cast a unanimous ballot. Those in favor?"

Justices Templeton and Germaine raised their right hands. Breitner looked around and reflexively raised his own hand. His gaze settled on O'Leary. O'Leary stared straight down at the table in front of him.

Silence.

"Well, what do you fellows want to do?" Breitner asked impatiently.

More silence.

Malloy, Van Timlin, and Henry all looked at O'Leary. O'Leary continued to look down. Breitner and Templeton looked at Henry. Germaine looked at Malloy.

Finally, Alton Henry slammed the palm of his hand flatly on the table with a smack. "All right. All right. Dammit Bob, if you won't take the chair, we are just going to have to do something none of you really want. I nominate Justice James Malloy to be chief justice."

Van Timlin sat bolt upright. "Malloy? I thought we were going to elect O'Leary. Nobody told me..."

"There's nothing to tell, Van." Henry was crisp and blunt. "If you want to know what's going on, all you have to do is pick up the phone. Now what are you going to do, give us two more years of Laughing Whitefish or take a chance on the governor's boy here?"

Van didn't need to be reminded. He knew the way the game was played. He had helped to invent it. "I'll second the nomination of Judge Malloy." Using the trial judge title on purpose, Henry thought. Just one last dig.

Breitner lowered his eyes and sighed. "All those in favor of electing James P. Malloy, please raise your right hands. Henry's hand shot up. Van lifted three fingers of his right hand. Malloy turned the palm of his right hand toward the chief justice.

Everyone's gaze fixed on Bob O'Leary. Still not making eye contact with anyone, O'Leary leaned back in his chair.

"Ed, I voted for you in '87 and in '89. I think I have been as good as my word. I like and respect you personally and as a colleague on the court. I count you as my friend, and I hope we will continue to be such. But I just think at this time in the history of the court, with a new Republican governor coming into office, if we want to make progress on state wide financing of the court system, or computerization or any of the other things we want, like a supreme court building, we ought to use a little political acumen in our selection. I've known Jim for a long time. Watched him come up in the circuit judges organization. I think he enjoys the confidence of the trial bench and I think if we all get behind him, he can and will do a good job for us and for the state of Michigan." With that, he raised his right hand high, lifting the right elbow with his left hand.

Breitner slammed his ring binder shut. He gathered up the briefs that were piled next to the binder, stood pushing his chair away with the back of his legs, and looked around the table in bewilderment. Templeton moved her chair to the north, making room between herself and the south end of the table for Breitner to occupy. He put his books back down on the table, slid them over to the right, wheeled his leather chair around the corner of the table and sat down next to Doris and across from Van. The place of the chief justice was empty.

Malloy tried to gather his books and papers quickly and deftly. He failed in this, his first function as leader of Michigan's judiciary. Briefs tumbled to the floor. Memoranda careened off the edge of the table and fluttered under the feet of the justices. With a skewed bundle of books under one arm, he tried to maneuver his swivel chair to the head of the table. No one moved to help him. No one said anything. No one laughed.

It seemed to Jim Malloy that it took twenty minutes to set himself aright at the head of the conference table. When he was ultimately able to compose himself, he felt that some opening comment was appropriate.

"I am truly humbled and honored that the court should put me in this chair on my first day here. I know that I will make many mistakes. I already have, as you saw from the graceful way I moved myself around the table. But I ask your patience, and your help. Together, I believe there is very little that we cannot accomplish."

"We ought to start by getting out in the courtroom and going to work like the taxpayers are paying us good money to do," said Henry gruffly.

"Good thought, Alton," Malloy answered while turning toward Breitner. " Ed, would you be kind enough to keep the gavel and preside over my swearing in ceremony ? I would be very pleased if you would do that for me."

Breitner nodded affirmatively, but said nothing.

***

The Michigan Supreme Court hears oral arguments on cases during the first full week of every month except July and August. It convenes on the first Tuesday after the first Monday. Usually there are between 12 and 16 cases scheduled for hearing during the term. The court hears three to five of them each day. The appellant and the appellee are each entitled to one half hour to present their cases. Typically, court sessions begin at 10:00 AM. Two or three cases are heard, and the court recesses for lunch. More cases are argued in the afternoon, beginning at 2:00 PM. On the weeks when there are no cases being argued, the court meets only on Thursday. These are called conference days, when opinions are shared, discussed, voted upon, and signed.

The conference room is behind the courtroom and across a narrow hallway. Inside the courtroom, but behind the marble wall which rises in back of the tall leather chairs of the justices, there is another hallway, actually a three foot wide, ramped passageway, which connects the back hallway with the bench in the courtroom. When court is to be convened, the seven justices line up in that passageway in order of their seniority after the chief justice. Upon the signal of the court crier, the door is opened, and the justices file into the courtroom while the crier announces them in the familiar chant, "Hear ye, Hear ye, Hear ye. All persons having business before this honorable court draw near and you will be heard. The supreme court of the State of Michigan is now in session."

On this Tuesday, Justice Malloy, dressed in a navy blue suit, white shirt, green and navy tie, black wing tips and a nervous smile, slipped into the courtroom through the clerk's door just moments before the crier began. He sat at the counsel table.

As the justices filed in by seniority, they seemed somewhat disoriented, as though unfamiliar with the seating arrangement. A new colleague was to join them. Time to play musical chairs As in the United States Supreme Court, Michigan and most other state appellate tribunals observe strict seniority in the arrangement of their seating in the courtroom. The chief justice, of course, sits in the middle chair. The senior associate justice sits to the chief's right. The next senior member to his left. The next senior justice sits to the right of the most senior, and the next sits to the left of the second in seniority. The process continues with the junior associate sitting to the farthest left of the chief justice.

Justice Breitner entered first and took the center chair. Justice Henry sat to his right, and Van Timlin to his left. To the right of Henry, was an empty chair. To the left of Van Timlin, Justice Templeton took her place. Justice Germaine sat at the far right of the chief, and Justice O'Leary was at the far left. Breitner spoke.

"The court is very pleased this morning to welcome the family and friends of our newest colleague, Justice James Patrick Malloy. It is my pleasure to call upon Mr. Joseph Malloy, a member of our bar, and the justice's brother, to say a few words. Mr. Malloy."

Joe Malloy stood nervously and addressed the court. He began by introducing the Malloy family. His father, Joe Malloy, senior. Mother Malloy, born Anna Marie Fitzsimmons. Of course, the new justice's wife, Margaret Mary, and their three children, scrubbed and shining for the occasion, James Patrick Junior, Paul Francis and Mary Ellen. Joe continued with Jim's siblings, their wives, husbands, children, children's spouses. Siblings' in-laws. Then he started in on the Fitzsimmons clan. More spouses, more children. More children's spouses and children's children. Then it was time for the Cronyns. Same pattern. Cousins by the dozens.

Finally, Joe Malloy turned to the court and addressed them. "Mr. Chief Justice, Honorable Justices, I'm mighty happy to be here as are all the members of our families. We are proud of Justice Malloy. That's why we have come here to help him celebrate. We thank you for the opportunity.

"For myself, I just want to tell you this. My brother Jim is about as good a man as you are going to find anywhere on the face of this green earth. I'll tell you one story to show you something of his character, then I'm going to sit down.

"When I was twelve years old and Jim was only seven, our mother sent him out to tell me to come home for supper. I was already late. He found me playing with some boys down at the end of our block. One of them was the neighborhood bully. A little older and bigger than the rest of us. He was the kind who was always breaking things that other youngsters built. If we made a soap box cart, this boy---his name was Clyde something as I recall---Clyde would jump in it and run it down a hill until it hit a tree and smashed to pieces. Clyde was a one man wrecking crew. Anyway, on this particular day, Clyde had taken me prisoner and had tied me to a tree. He was amusing the other boys by throwing handfuls of mud at me. Suddenly, little brother Jimmy appeared, and saw my predicament. He simply put his head down, and began running toward Clyde as fast as he could. Now Jimmy, as I said, was only seven years old. At the time, Clyde was probably thirteen, and much taller than Jim. As a matter of fact, bent over as he was, Jimmy's head didn't even come up to Clyde's belt, if you get the picture. Now it just so happened that Clyde was too busy laughing at me to see Jimmy coming at him full speed. Suffice it to say that Jimmy's head made contact with a very vulnerable part of his victim. Clyde was still writhing on the ground when Jimmy untied me and we took off running home. That night, I told the story at the dinner table, and my dad nicknamed him Jimmy the 'Nutcracker'. We still call him that sometimes." The courtroom exploded with hearty guffaws and irrepressible giggles.

"May it please the court, my good wife, Theresa, counseled me against telling that story here today. She said it wasn't dignified enough. And if I'm out of order, I certainly apologize to the court. But I think that story tells so very much about your new colleague that you and the people of Michigan ought to know. Jim Malloy is a fighter. He's a fighter for the underdog. He's a fighter for those who are being picked on and bullied, for people who are deprived of their freedom or victims of injustice. He is afraid of no one. He will back down for no one. He will do what he feels he has to do, no matter the danger, no matter the risk, no matter the odds. You can count on Jim Malloy, may it please the court. You can count on him to do the right thing, no matter who has to get cracked in the process.

"In these times of sleazy politics, public officials who make every decision with a wet finger in the wind, and their eyes glued to the popularity polls and the newspaper editorials, it's refreshing to have someone like my kid brother come along and exhibit some good old fashioned courage and integrity." His voice cracked as he turned to his brother sitting at the counsel table. "Sock it to 'em Jimmy. I love you."

"Thank you Mr. Malloy." Justice Breitner responded. "The court-- at least some of us on the court-- have already seen a demonstration of his unique prowess. Now I would like to ask

Mrs. Malloy, the Justice's wife to step forward and assist our honoree with his robe. Margaret stood, carrying a new black robe. Jim walked to the podium and slipped his arms into the robe, zipped it up, then took Margaret in his arms and kissed her lavishly. The audience thundered its approving applause. Breitner asked Malloy to raise his right hand.

"Do you, James Malloy swear to uphold the Constitution of the United States and the Constitution of the State of Michigan, and that you will faithfully discharge the duties of the office of ... "Breitner hesitated, unsure of the next word. " ...the office of chief justice of the supreme court according to the best of your ability, so help you God."

"I do."

The usual and expected applause was mingled with overtones of voices asking each other if they had heard what Breitner had said. Was it a slip of the lip?

"Congratulations, Mr. Chief Justice."

"Thank you, Justice Breitner."

Now the applause was renewed with incredible intensity. Breitner had called him Mr. Chief Justice. Malloy had called Breitner 'Justice.' It was true. Jim Malloy was the chief justice! The message raced through the room to all those who had not perceived the significance of the words. The clapping continued unabated. Minute after minute. Like the end of a symphony.

Jim Malloy had written a speech, which seemed appropriate in the wee hours of the morning, when he was not thinking like the chief justice. Now, in light of the need to get on with the docket, he folded the speech and holding it in his left hand, walked slowly and deliberately around to the end of the bench, climbed the three steps, and strode behind the chairs of the Justices toward the center seat. Breitner was standing. They shook hands. Breitner moved to the second chair on the right, and Jim Malloy sat in the chair reserved for the chief justice.

"Ladies and Gentlemen, we thank all of you for coming. We will have the opportunity to thank you more personally at a reception at the Radisson Hotel in about an hour. In the meantime, however, I will ask that everyone clear the courtroom as quickly and quietly as possible, as the court has a full docket this week and we would like to get started. Would the clerk please call the first case?

***

Near the end of the day, Hilda Germaine stopped by Jim Malloy's office. He had not yet moved into the chief justice's quarters.

"Congratulations, Jim. You are going to have a busy two years. There is much to do."

"Thanks, Hilda. I'm going to need lots of help."

"I know that, and I'm going to do everything I can to make this a banner time in the history of the court. I know Ed is disappointed, but deep down, he's a very solid person, and a judge who really loves this court. Ed can help you tremendously, and you will be making a big mistake if you don't involve him as much as you can. You know, committee assignments, that sort of thing. And it wouldn't hurt just to keep the lines of communication to him open, so you can seek his counsel from time to time."

"That's very sound advice, Hilda. But I wonder how I should approach him."

"Directly and soon. As a matter of fact, he is in his office right now. Why don't we go and see him. The two of us."

"You'll go with me?"

"Sure, right now."

"Great." Malloy was already out of his chair and walking toward the door.

Moments later, Justices Germaine and Malloy stood in the office of the former C.J. Ed Breitner sat behind the wide authoritarian desk. He was sitting straight up, both hands on the desk top, holding a sheaf of papers. He did not invite his colleagues to be seated. Malloy shuffled his feet uneasily. Germaine spoke.

"Ed, we would like to talk to you. For better or worse, Jim here has been elected chief justice. I didn't vote for him, as you know. I voted for you, because I thought you deserved to be reelected. But the majority of the court has decided otherwise. It's the decision of the court, fair and square. Now I have told Jim that I am going to do everything I can to make his administration as successful as possible. I know you share our concern about this institution, this court of ours, and the administration of justice in Michigan. So we've come to ask you to join with us, and pledge your support to our new chief justice."

Breitner was scowling and looking at the papers in his hand all the time Germaine was speaking. He never looked up. His words, spoken slowly through nearly clenched teeth, brought the interview to an abrupt ending.

"He'll get no help from me."

CHAPTER 9

FEBRUARY 1991

Oral arguments in the Michigan Supreme Court seldom attract many spectators. Mostly, the Justices do their important work in relative obscurity. The courtroom seats about 150 people, tops. During most oral arguments, there are no more than six people in the courtroom in addition to the seven justices and the court crier, who operates the electronic recording device.

The two lawyers arguing the case for the appellant and the appellee, respectively, occupy the two counsel tables which flank the lectern in front of the bench. If there are co-counsel, as is sometimes the case, they sit at the tables as well. In the spectator section of the room, lawyers whose matters are further down on the call, the occasional law student, perhaps a litigant or two, one or more of the justices' law clerks, and a curious citizen or group of school children constitute the usual crowd.

Unless, of course, the matter at hand is a newsworthy case, which is maybe one out of fifty. But when spectators come, they come in droves. They hang from the rafters. Reporters, TV interviewers, interested citizens and advocacy groups, gaggles of law students, all the law clerks for all of the justices, and just plain curious people. The kind who slow down to gawk at an accident on the highway.

Such a case was *People v Durnacky*.

Morris Durnacky billed himself as 'Mr. Death.' He claimed that during the Viet Nam war, he had personally killed more than five hundred people. He claimed that he had dispatched more people than any practicing physician or surgeon in Michigan. He claimed to be an expert on death and dying. And putting that expertise to work, he had gone into the assisted suicide business.

Of course, the name Jack Kevorkian was a household word

not only in Michigan but throughout the United States if not the world. Doctor Death's troubles with the law, and his unbroken record of success in warding off the legal system are the stuff of American folklore. Whether or not you like him, whether or not you agree with him and his flamboyant lawyer, there is no ignoring either of them. Assisted suicide is a topic of universal social concern. No one knows for sure where it is all going. The judgment of history will surely not be pronounced until well into the twenty first century.

But Morris Durnacky, above all an astute businessman, saw no need to wait for the wheels of justice to grind out a final answer to the moral and legal dilemma, because he clearly perceived financial opportunities in the arena of assisted suicide that Kevorkian eschewed. His foray into the virgin meadow of economic daisies began with a two column, six inch newspaper advertisement.

ASSISTED SUICIDE
NOW YOU CAN DO IT YOUR WAY!
NO WAITING. NO RED TAPE. NO PUBLICITY.
If you are looking to exercise your God-given constitutional right to control your own life cycle, you need to call 1-800-GOODBYE and talk to the only person in the world who can help you the way you want to be helped, no questions asked.

CALL MR. DEATH TODAY
AT
1-800-GOODBYE

Our rates are reasonable. Our service is fast, friendly, and discreet. Member in good standing, United States Hemlock Society.

Unlike Kevorkian, Durnacky did not wait around after he did his business. He did not deliver bodies to hospitals and morgues, and he did not call 911. Consequently, it was not very easy to prove that he had in fact assisted in any suicide, or that he had played any role in the death of one of his customers. But in due course, the Wayne County Prosecutor's office sought a criminal warrant for Durnacky's arrest, based upon circumstantial evidence gathered by the Detroit Police Department, under the watchful, goading eye of the Detroit Evening Paper.

The recorder's court judge refused to bind the defendant over, even on the charge of manslaughter, and the prosecutor appealed to the court of appeals. The defendant's attorney sought what is known as a By-Pass Appeal. That is, he asked the supreme court of Michigan to take the case even before the court of appeals has heard and ruled on it. By-pass applications are often media sensitive. Everyone on the court agreed that this case would be appealed to the supreme court eventually anyway, that it was a matter of grave public interest, and that the administration of criminal justice would be best served by truncating the procedure.

And so the matter was the first celebrated case over which young Chief Justice Malloy presided. The courtroom was packed. Television stations asked to be allowed to set up cameras in the courtroom, and Malloy, allowing this, appointed one station to be the feed, in order to keep the disruption at a minimum. The arguments were heated, passionate, and controversial. The audience was partial and involved. Malloy was challenged to keep order. As a result, he had, in the days that followed, little recollection of the substance of counsels' debate.

So he did what members of the court occasionally do when preparing opinions. He ordered a transcript of the oral arguments. Now, on this frigid February morning, he sat in the quiet expanse of the chief justice's office, protected from telephone and other callers by his secretary, reading the typewritten pages, making occasional notes.

***

CHIEF JUSTICE: Are counsel ready to proceed in the matter of *People v Durnacky?*

MR. GORDANIAN: The People are ready, if the court please.

MR. WOLMAR: The defendant is ready.

CHIEF JUSTICE: You may proceed, Mr. Gordanian.

MR. GORDANIAN: Good afternoon, Your Honors. My name is Vincent Gordanian. I am the chief assistant prosecutor of Wayne County, and I am here representing the People of the State of Michigan in the matter of *People v Durnacky*, case number 48437.

If the court please, this is an appeal from an order of the Recorder's Court of the City of Detroit rendered by Judge Horace Chandler, dismissing the criminal complaint against one Morris Durnacky. The People have charged that the defendant, did on the 19th day of October, 1990, in the City of Detroit, kill and murder one Bernard Epsiloff, a human being, with malice aforethought, contrary to the statute in such case made and provided. This open charge of murder in the first degree carried with it, as the court is well aware, the included offenses of second degree murder and manslaughter.

The evidence here, if the court please, is really undisputed. Mr. Epsiloff checked into the Gateway Motel on Cass Avenue early in the evening of October 18. The defendant was seen entering room 104, Mr. Epsiloff's room, the following morning at approximately 6:45 AM. At 7:32 AM, the proprietor of the motel, a Mister Aldrich, heard a loud noise, which he believed to be either an automobile backfiring or a gun shot. He observed the defendant leaving the deceased's room several minutes later.

At about 10:15 that morning, the housekeeper knocked on the door of Room 104. There was no answer. She knocked again and a third time. Then, assuming the room was empty, she used her master key and entered the room. There she discovered the body of Mr. Epsilof, lying on the bed in a pool of blood. The police were summoned immediately.

From the description of him and his car, the defendant was identified and a warrant for his arrest was issued. He was taken into custody, fingerprinted and questioned concerning the death of Mr. Epsilof. He was fully advised of all of his constitutional rights. His attorney was present at all times during his questioning. A video tape of the interview was generated and has been retained by our office.

A search warrant of Mr. Durnacky's home was issued and executed. There, a number of weapons were seized, including a 347 magnum pistol. A bullet found imbedded in the floor beneath the bed was compared with one fired from this gun and the ballistic tests by the police forensic department confirmed that the defendant's pistol killed Mr. Epsilof.

During questioning by police, the defendant admitted that his gun was used to kill Mr. Epsilof. He insisted, however, that Mr. Epsilof committed suicide, by placing the weapon at his right temple and pulling the trigger. In support of his claim, the defendant presented a written document entitled "Assisted Suicide Contract." That paper was filed with our brief, if the court please, and I am sure the justices have all had an opportunity to read it.

CHIEF JUSTICE: Yes we have, counsel.

MR. GARDANIAN: This case presents a very knotty question, if it please the court, on which the prosecutors of this state need sure guidance from this August body. It is our opinion, and has been from the very beginning, that the defendant is at least guilty of manslaughter under the laws of Michigan.

Manslaughter has been defined as the taking of the life of another by actions which are grossly negligent, careless, or exhibit reckless disregard of human life. It is not necessary that the perpetrator of the crime of manslaughter be the direct and immediate agency causing or bringing about the death. The cases hold, for example, that keeping a vicious wild animal in a careless and negligent manner so that the animal gets loose and kills someone will support a conviction for manslaughter. Likewise...

JUSTICE TEMPLETON: Excuse me, Counsel, but this is hardly the same thing. Here it was the deceased himself who was the immediate and proximate cause of his own death. Don't you think there is a difference?

MR. GARDANIAN: Your honor, the People contend that the defendant supplied a lethal weapon to a man who was in a state of severe depression. We take the position that Mr. Epsilof was not in full possession of his faculties, and that giving him a gun under those circumstances was an action in gross and reckless disregard of his safety. We look at it this way: if the defendant had given a four year old child a loaded pistol to play with and the child killed himself with it, wouldn't we be justified in charging the defendant with manslaughter? This is the same thing.

JUSTICE TEMPLETON: How do you know the deceased was in a severe state of depression? Certainly the coroner can't psychoanalyze the deceased.

MR. GARDANIAN: Madam Justice, the People are prepared to prove at the trial of this case that suicidal impulses are a classic symptom of mental illness and depression. We....

CHIEF JUSTICE: Order. Order in the court. The court will not tolerate any further outbursts or reactions by spectators of whatever persuasion. This is not a political rally. This is a court of law. If there are any more disruptions of these proceedings, I will have the courtroom cleared immediately. You may proceed, Mr. Gardanian.

MR. GARDANIAN: Thank you, Your Honor. The people are prepared to present competent, credible expert testimony from distinguished and recognized physicians and psychiatrists to support the conclusion that a person like Mr. Epsilof would have been suffering severe depression, that he would not have been in a position to make a rational judgment about his actions, and that giving a man in that state of mind a 347 Magnum is tantamount to putting a gun to his head and pulling the trigger.

MR. WOLMAR: That's a bunch of nonsense Gardanian, and...

CHIEF JUSTICE: Mr. Wolmar...

MR. WOLMAR: ...you...

CHIEF JUSTICE: ...Mr. Wolmar...

MR. WOLMAR: ...know..

CHIEF JUSTICE: ...the court...

MR. WOLMAR: ...it.

CHIEF JUSTICE: ...is addressing you sir. Be good...

MR. WOLMAR: (inaudible)

CHIEF JUSTICE: ...enough to hold your tongue when I am talking to you, sir.

MR. WOLMAR: I'm sorry, Judge, but I can't just sit here and let this man say things that are absolutely untrue without speaking up to protect my client's constitutional rights. I have an obligation...

CHIEF JUSTICE: You have an obligation to behave yourself as an officer of this court. Stand up Mr. Wolmar. Stand up when the court, when any member of this court addresses you or whenever you address this court. That's better. Now you will remain standing in absolute silence while I am speaking to you. Do I make myself clear? Do you understand me? Answer me.

MR. WOLMAR: I thought you said I was to remain absolutely silent.

CHIEF JUSTICE: I did and you will, except when I tell you to speak. Mr. Wolmar, your reputation precedes you here. Among the seven justices sitting up here, there are some who will agree with your legal position and some who will not. But I assure you sir, there will be seven votes from this bench to have you jailed for contempt of court if you persist in this unprofessional conduct. You will have an opportunity to make your oral argument in this case when the People have finished.

Now before you sit down, we would like to hear an apology from you to the court, to Mr. Gardanian, and to all of the people in the courtroom who have come here expecting to see the dignity of the judicial system being upheld by the members of the bar.

MR. WOLMAR: I apologize, Your Honor. I am sorry. I got carried away. I'm afraid I get too passionate for my clients' causes. I apologize to the court, to Mr. Gardanian. To everyone.

CHIEF JUSTICE: Thank you, Counsel. The court will measure the sincerity of your apology by the manner in which you conduct yourself from this point on. Now please be seated and let's have no more departures from the proper conduct of these oral arguments. You may continue, Mr. Gardanian.

MR. GARDANIAN: Thank you, Your Honor. We believe this defendant should be held criminally responsible for the death of Mr. Epsilof. As a matter of fact, we are not conceding that the charges should even be reduced to manslaughter. After all, if you take this so-called Assisted Suicide Contract out of the picture, and disregard the testimony of the defendant, which is after all, completely self serving, what do we have?

We have a nearly open and shut case of murder one. We can put the defendant in the motel room at the time of the shooting. No one else was present. His gun was used. A bullet from his gun pierced the deceased's head and was the obvious cause of death. What else do we need to make our case?

JUSTICE BREITNER: Motive, Counsel. What's the motive here?

MR. GARDANIAN: As the court well knows, the people do not have to prove any motive. It is enough if we prove the deliberate taking of human life. But there is plenty of evidence here that will support a determination that the defendant's motive was money, pure and simple. Greed. No different than robbery, fraud or any other crime in which a defendant tries to obtain money by illegal means.

We can show, and we will show if we are allowed to go to trial on this case, that the deceased cleaned out his bank account on the day before he died, October 18, 1990. He took more than ten thousand three hundred dollars in cash. When his body was found, he had a little less than three hundred dollars in his wallet. He had paid for the motel room in cash. It would be reasonable to conclude that he was short exactly ten thousand dollars.

In his statement at the time of his arrest, the defendant admitted that he was paid ten thousand dollars for his so-called services to Mr. Epsilof. Even if we didn't have that admission, even if we had never talked to the defendant, or he had never talked to us, a jury could easily find that the missing money was the motive for the killing.

If the court please, there is only one person in the world who really knows whose finger was on that trigger on October 19. But this we do know; without the defendant's active involvement and participation, this gruesome homicide would not have occurred. Without the actions of the defendant, there never would have been a shot ring out that morning, no pool of blood on the bed, no dead body in the motel room to be discovered by the housekeeper.

If the court please, this man must be brought to justice. Civilized society just cannot have hired killers advertising in our newspapers and preying on pathetic, emotionally disturbed citizens who really ought to be given help and love and support by the community. We maintain crisis phone numbers and all kinds of mental health services to assist people who are thinking of taking their own lives. That's what society ought to be doing, not killing innocent people who need help.

If the court please, I would like to reserve a few moments of my time for rebuttal.

CHIEF JUSTICE: Mr. Wolmar, you may proceed with your argument.

MR. WOLMAR: May it please the court, my name is Perry

Wolmar, and I am here representing the defendant, Mr. Durnacky, but in a more important sense, I am here representing all the people of this great nation of ours.

Your Honors, this isn't a case about murder or manslaughter. This is a case about freedom. This is all about the most basic fundamental freedom that you or I or any other person can possibly have. The freedom to do what we want to do with our own bodies. Because there isn't any government and there isn't any church or religion, there isn't any pope or president that can take away from any one of us the right to do what we want to do with our bodies.

That's what freedom is all about. Being able to think what you want to think. Go where you want to go. Be what you want to be. Do you see this hand? This is my hand. I am the only person in the world who can tell this hand what to do. Whether to feed my mouth, whether to scratch my head, whether to tie my shoe or button my shirt. These vocal chords. My voice. My tongue. My words. Owning yourself and all you are and all you do, that's the very essence of freedom.

Nobody owns my body but me. Nobody owns your body but you. Nobody can tell you that you must breathe or eat or bathe or sleep without interfering with your freedom. Nobody can lock you up, or keep you from going where you want to go without interfering with your freedom. Where is it written that I can't pluck out my eye if I want to. It's my eye. Who says I can't cut off my hand if I choose to do that? It's my hand. And what law says I can't take my own life? What legislature has ever been so despotic as to forbid a man or a woman from exercising their God-given constitutional right to terminate their own life in any way at any time and for any reason they may choose? Not the Michigan legislature. Not the United States Congress.

No, if the court please, it is not a crime to commit suicide. It never has been, under any government in the English speaking world or in the rest of the world for that matter. No one, no government, no congress, no court, no religious congregation can own a human being. That horrible practice, Your Honors, was ended in America over 100 years ago when the thirteenth amendment was adopted. It's called slavery. We are not slaves. We are a free people. And we are free to deal with our own lives as we see fit.

And if suicide is not a crime, how can it be a crime to assist someone to do what he or she has a perfect legal right to do? How can it? How can this court or any court presume to deny a person who has lived a full and productive life, who finds himself or herself living like a vegetable, writhing in pain every hour of the day and night, with no relief, no end to the torture in sight--how can we deny to such a person the simple civil right to have the assistance of a licensed doctor of medicine to achieve a quiet, dignified, painless release from all that agony?

JUSTICE O'LEARY. Mr. Wolmar, we are not talking in this case about physician assisted suicide are we?

Mr. WOLMAR: Your Honor, I don't see why someone who has only a few weeks to live, who is suffering untold agony and pain should not be able to ask their doctor to give them something that will put them out of their misery. We show that much sympathy to domestic animals. Dogs. Cats. Horses. We put them out of their misery. But we make poor old grandma suffer. It's inhumane.

JUSTICE VAN TIMLIN: Are you telling us that assisting in suicide is a function of the practice of medicine?

MR. WOLMAR: Mr. Justice, only the most naive person doesn't know that doctors put people to sleep all the time. It's being done every day in hospitals all over America. It's being done because people want to do it, and they have a right to do it. Pull the plug. Cut off the IV. Double the dose of morphine. Doctors make decisions about who lives and who dies every day. Who gets a heart transplant and who does not. Who gets a kidney. These are all life and death decisions and they are all part of the day to day practice of medicine.

JUSTICE O'LEARY: But this case of Durnacky has nothing to do with physician assisted suicide does it? Your man wasn't-- isn't-- a doctor. Doesn't claim to be a doctor, does he?

MR. WOLMAR: That's right, Judge. He's not a doctor. But what does that have to do with Mr. Epsilof's constitutional right to control his own body? If he was up in the north woods and there was no doctor within miles, would that change anything? It's his body, and his constitutional right.

If the court please, this is a very simple case. Mr. Epsilof and Mr. Durnacky made a contract. A very simple, straightforward contract. Mr. Epsilof wanted to kill himself, which he had a perfect right to do. He rented a motel room for that purpose. The owner of the motel made a contract with him. That assisted him with the suicide. But the motel owner isn't charged with anything. If Mr. Epsilof went to Sears and Roebuck and bought a shot gun to kill himself with, would that make Sears guilty of manslaughter? That's nonsense. The man had a right to buy or rent a gun from the defendant and the defendant had a right to loan it to him for whatever price they were willing to agree upon. That's freedom, Your Honors. Good old fashioned Republican freedom of contract. And that is what this case is all about. The God-given right that each and every one of us has to be the masters of our own lives. To be in control of our own bodies.

CHIEF JUSTICE: And when Mr. Epsilof's cadaver was lying on the bed in a pool of blood, who owned his body then?

MR. WOLMAR: He did, Your Honor. Mr. Epsilof owned it.

CHIEF JUSTICE: Mr. Epsilof still owned his body after he was dead?

MR. WOLMAR: He still had the right to do what he wanted with it. Be cremated. Buried at sea. Whatever he wanted.

CHIEF JUSTICE: Leaned against a lamp post in the center of town and left there to rot?

MR. WOLMAR: He didn't ask to do that. Nobody would want to do that.

CHIEF JUSTICE: But are you telling the court that organized society, the state, has no authority to make laws about what people can do with their bodies? Even after they are dead?

MR. WOLMAR: Well, perhaps I wouldn't go so far as to say after they are dead. After all there are considerations of public health that make it necessary to have some kind of sanitary disposal.

CHIEF JUSTICE: And there are considerations of public health and safety that warrant the exercise of governmental power over people's bodies when they are still living too, aren't there?

MR. WOLMAR: I say no, Your Honor. No government is justified in interfering with our freedom and privacy to do what we want with our own bodies.

CHIEF JUSTICE: So I take it that you oppose seat belt laws, and laws requiring motorcyclists to wear helmets, and laws which require children to be vaccinated, is that correct?

MR. WOLMAR: Most of those things are things that people voluntarily comply with. And I don't see any reason why government can't run advertising campaigns to encourage people to do those things. But I don't think the coercive power of the state, the criminal justice system, can be used to enforce those kinds of things.

In conclusion, May It Please the court, let me just say this. You can reverse the trial judge, and you can make Mr. Durnacky go to trial on charges of murder or manslaughter or whatever you want, but there is no way, no chance whatsoever, that he will ever serve one single day in prison. Under our system of criminal justice, every defendant is entitled to a trial by a jury of his peers. And no jury you can empanel in Wayne County or in any county in Michigan is going to convict Mr. Durnacky. The people of Michigan want to be able to end their lives whenever and however they choose to do it. And they want to be able to ask anyone they want to help them do it. You are not going to stop them. The newspapers are not going to stop them. All the churches and bishops and cardinals in Christendom are not going to stop them from exercising that right and protecting their fellow citizens who choose to exercise that right. You can try my client, but you cannot convict him. Only a jury can do that. And no jury ever will. Never. Never. Never.

CHIEF JUSTICE: Mr. Gardanian, do you have anything in rebuttal?

MR. GARDANIAN: Just a couple of points, if it please the court. The first is this: what my worthy opponent trumpets as a basic human right is not a right at all. The deliberate taking of a human life, homicide, under the common law is, and has always been a capital felony. When a person kills himself, he commits that crime. Every element of the crime is present. The crime is complete. There is only one catch. By definition, the perpetrator of the crime is deceased. There can be no prosecution for suicide, not because no crime has been committed, but because there is no one to prosecute. And typically, no one is ever prosecuted for attempting suicide, though technically, that may well constitute attempted murder. The reason again is simple and practical. The victim does not choose to prosecute. Moreover, suicide being so often a symptom of mental imbalance, the necessary *mens rea* is unlikely.

Finally, if the court please, I want to address my worthy opponent's last comment about the unwillingness of juries to convict in these cases. Two points need to be kept in mind. First, it is not a matter for us to speculate about. We are here to determine the law, not influence jury decisions. Juries are often swayed by passion or ignorance or community outrage or sympathy. We know that. But it is not for the courts to throw up their hands and give credence to jury rule. Many times trial judges give stern lectures to juries who disregard the instructions they are given. We must argue, and you must decide what the law is, not what the jury will do. If we were to do otherwise, the criminal justice system would soon degenerate into mob rule. The function of the law is to instruct, to guide the determination of the fact finders. We have an obligation to continue to do that, whatever the jury panels do in any particular case.

***

Cindy Germaine stepped off of the cross town bus and trudged along the slushy sidewalk to Henry Ford Hospital. At the reception desk, she inquired as to the location of a new patient, Jeremiah Wheatley, who had just been transferred that morning from Ponchartrain Receiving Hospital downtown. Cindy knew about the transfer because she had been largely responsible for making it happen. She had been visiting Jeremiah every week since the first of the year. Reading him bible stories. Talking to him about Jesus. Praying with him that God would forgive him his sins and that he would get a plastic foot that would make him good as new.

The probate court was going to put Jeremiah in the Michigan Training Unit, a place for the keeping of juvenile offenders who are too young to be convicted as adult criminals and sent to prison. Cindy didn't want Jeremiah to go to the unit. She was hoping the judge would find a good foster home for Jeremiah. Someplace where he could be loved and could learn to love. He never knew any love in his life. Cindy could see that. She could see how he responded to the simplest signs of affection.

So she took it upon herself to go and see the judge, and see if something could be done. The judge was impressed with Cindy's interest in the boy. After all, Jeremiah killed her grandson. Befriending him was an act of heroic proportions. With no little effort, the judge finally was able to get Jeremiah transferred to Henry Ford Hospital for the purpose of being fitted with a prosthesis, and learning to use it. It took several calls to top hospital administrators, and the involvement of a community trust fund, but the deal was made.

Now Cindy wanted to see if Jeremiah was being properly cared for in his new environment. She found his room, which he shared with another boy, a leukemia patient undergoing long term chemotherapy. The roommate was completely bald.

"So how are you doing in these new digs, Jeremiah?"

"AhmdoinOK. Gotsumbody to tawk wit hea."

"So you have. And what's your name young fella?"

"Byran Hatcher. Ever body calls me Skinhead tho"

"Been here long?"

"A week now. Be here for two more I guess."

"Well, you sure have a nice round head. That where you got the name?"

"I guess so."

Jeremiah chimed in. "They call me 'Rat Tail'"

"That's a funny name," Cindy was curious. "How did you get it?"

"A ratjump inmahbed wenAhz twoyearzold. Ahbitoff histail mahmamma said."

"Your mother said you bit off a rat's tail when you were two?"

Jeremiah grinned proudly. "Yessm. Shodid. Bitoff histail. Rightoff."

"Well I don't think you'll have to do that here. And I think it's about time you two boys stopped using those nick names. Bryan and Jeremiah are good, solid names for good solid young men. From now on that's what I'm going to call you."

"Hey Bryan." Jeremiah yelled.

"Hey Jeremiah." Bryan yelled back.

They both laughed, and so did Cindy. Then she picked up the Illustrated Children's Bible, now getting somewhat dog eared, and began, for the third time, reading the story of Jonah and the whale.

***

Friday night in the Chicago loop, everyone rushed to the train early. The little bar on Wacker where the law students hung out was nearly empty at 5:30 PM. Roger Foresberg hoped he wasn't too late to catch Cheryl. They had not dated since Christmas break. He felt guilty about getting her pregnant. She seemed very distant and cold. Probably angry, he thought. But now it was February, and there seemed to be a thawing of the chill. She had seemed to be coming on to him a couple of times during the week, and he felt the coast was clear for another sortie. So he had slipped her a note in Civil Procedure, and suggested they rendezvous here. Tonight. For coffee, or whatever.

She was at a far booth, buried in case books. Writing furiously in her spiral notebook. He slid in across from her. No kisses like the old days. At least not yet.

"So how are you feeling?"

"Overwhelmed with Property mostly. I don't get this future interests stuff."

"Doesn't matter. I hear it's never on the bar exam."

"You don't get to take the bar exam until you graduate, is what I hear."

"Oh yeah. That's right. Guess you better keep on reading about lives in being and twenty one years."

"Ugh."

"Anyway, it's Friday. How about a glass of Merlot?"

"Make it diet coke for me. Caffeine free."

"Wow. Are you in training for a marathon or something?"

"No, just trying to be good to your son or daughter."

Roger gulped. "Didn't you have that taken care of?"

"Nope. Started to one day, but I changed my mind. The more I thought about it the more I thought it was not what I want to do."

"You're going to have the baby?"

"I'm going to have your baby, Roger. Yours and mine. The baby we made together."

"Then what? Put it up for adoption?"

"No way. I'm going to keep him or her."

"And raise it yourself?"

"If I have to, yes. There are lots of single parents in the world. I don't want to be one of those frantic females who hear their biological clocks ticking and go doing something foolish. Grab the first stud that comes along and makes an indecent offer. No sir. I found a real good sire for my child. Smart. Healthy. Good teeth. Good sense of humor. A little short in the maturity and responsibility department, but you have to make trade offs to get one with good teeth."

Roger felt a little uneasy. A little trapped. And more than a little studly. He wondered if it was a boy.

***

When supreme court justices retire to the conference room after hearing oral arguments, the process is not quite like a jury entering upon its deliberations. Juries have only one case to decide. They stay together and keep talking about it until a decision is reached or until the judge sends them home or a hopeless deadlock develops.

Not so with the court. The justices will have heard four or five cases during the day. They will take a few moments to discuss each matter, followed by a non-binding straw vote. Then the clerk of the court, who sits in on their meetings, assigns the job of writing the court's opinion to one of the justices. These assignments are done by rotation among the justices whose straw votes put them in the majority on the case. If the justice next in line to be assigned is not aligned with the majority, he or she is passed over, and the case is assigned to the next person on the clerk's list.

On Wednesday, February 4, 1991, about four in the afternoon, the justices filed into the conference room, doffed their robes, poured coffee, settled into their conference chairs, and heard the chief justice announce: "*People v Durnacky*. Justice O'Leary, would you like to lead off the discussion?"

"That was quite a show out there. But I don't think this case is very complicated. In my opinion, it's just another murder case. All of this stuff about assisted suicide, who pulled the trigger and why, that's all for the jury to decide. I would be for reversing and remanding for trial."

"On the murder one information as originally charged?" Breitner asked.

"I think so. After all, the jury doesn't have to believe Durnacky."

The chief justice intervened. "Justice Germaine. What's your view.?"

"I tend to agree with Bob. I might go even further and make it clear in our opinion that we think the defendant should be convicted at least of manslaughter on his own admissions, I know a jury might always ignore the court's instructions. But I think we ought to require that the instruction be given."

"I think that would be a terrible mistake," Doris Templeton barged in without waiting to be called upon. "This is our opportunity to establish a very important principle of law, and stand up for the fundamental human rights of the people. We should come down hard on the side of Mr. Epsilof's right to decide how and when his life should end. He could have gotten that pistol anywhere. Supplying the weapon doesn't make Durnacky a party to the act of using it. Even if it did, what crime did Epsilof commit? None. We ought to declare in no uncertain terms that life termination is a basic civil right of every citizen. And nobody should be convicted for helping or enabling somebody to exercise their basic civil rights."

"Justice Breitner,' said the Chief.

"This is a very, very sensitive and provocative issue. We have a heavy burden here to protect the basic constitutional rights of the people, while at the same time insuring that criminals are convicted and punished, when and if a crime has been committed. Frankly, I think we ought to err on the side of people's freedom. Of course, I'll want to see all of the legal research on this. I have asked my law clerk to give me an extensive memorandum. But if I had to vote today, I would probably tend to favor the defendant's position here."

Typical, Malloy thought. "Justice Van Timlin, what is your view?"

"Well, I don't see any big problem here. I sort of like what Bob had to say about this."

"Three to two. Justice Henry, where are you on this?"

"I've read this whole record very carefully. The first thing we have to think about is this: we are not sitting as a police court on this. We are an appellate court. Our job is to review the record made in the lower court and decide if the judge down there did or did not do the right thing. It's not a matter of what we think the right thing is. It's a question of looking at what he did on the basis of what he had before him at the time. When the trial judge refused to bind the defendant over for trial he had nothing in the record about severe mental depression. There were no psychiatrists called to the witness stand down there. I think the recorders court judge had to assume, and we have to assume, that Epsilof was in complete control of his faculties when he borrowed the gun and shot himself. We're reviewing here the trial judge's discretion. I don't think it was an abuse of his discretion to do what he did, considering the record he had before him."

Malloy took a deep breath and closed his eyes. "Three to three. Why did I know it was going to turn out his way? There are some risks in voting last. Of course, I will reserve final judgment until I see the opinions pro and con. But I must say, I am leaning toward remand. You have a good point, Alton. But I think a court should be able to take judicial notice of the mental state associated with suicide. We don't need to have expert testimony to prove that a person who coughs and sneezes and blows his nose has a cold. Juries can conclude things like that from their own ordinary experiences in daily life. And I think courts can take judicial notice of such things. Anyone whose life has been touched by suicide would, I think bear me out on this."

Bob O'Leary moved uncomfortably in his chair. "You're absolutely right, Jim. I don't see how the point can be honestly disputed."

CHAPTER 10

MARCH 1991

Jim and Margaret found a pathetically decorated Chinese restaurant on the main four corners of Laingsburg, a tiny village 16 miles east of Rathcroghan. It was the only eatery in that town, and one could easily drive past it without seeing it at all. Had it not been for the time they scoured the area for antiques and came up empty handed but hungry, the Malloys, like the rest of the civilized world, would never have known of the place or of its owner, chef, waiter, and cashier, Sun Ying.

Since finding the place, however, Jim and Margaret grew attached to the garish black and red wallpaper, the great gold mandarins in the corners, and the wonderfully authentic Cantonese meals which Sun Ying presented. There was no menu. No prices. You didn't need a reservation, but if you called ahead, it helped a lot.

"You eat what I bring. You don't like it, you don't pay. You like it, you pay me what I say, no more."

Fair enough. And then some.

On this billowing day in early March, with winter still clutching Michigan in its icy grip, Margaret Malloy announced that she was suffering from cabin fever, the universal code phrase that suggests to any husband with functioning antennae that it is time to dust off his credit card and invite his spouse out for dinner. So they called Sun Ying and set out for Laingsburg.

The feast met their expectations. Egg drop soup. Pressed Duck. Mu Shoo Pork. Stir fried Vegetables. Steamed rice. Soy sauce. Plum sauce. Chop sticks. And of course, the traditional fortune cookies. Jim's read, "Children are a poor man's riches."

That night, over their second cup of tea, Margaret told Jim that she had been to see Doctor Carnahan, and the ultra sound showed that she was carrying twins. A boy and a girl.

***

Opinion day in the Michigan Supreme Court is usually on a Thursday. It is the day when the die is cast, the cheese becomes binding, everyone must fish or cut bait, shit or get off the pot. So to speak. After a case has been argued, discussed in chambers, assigned to a justice for opinion writing, and a draft opinion circulated to the bench by the assigned writer, the other members of the court have two weeks within which they are expected to respond by written memorandum to the submitted draft. Will you sign it or not? Do you have reservations which might be cleared away by further research, or by amending the language of the opinion? Do you intend to dissent or concur in a separate opinion of your own?

Once the responding memos have come in, the matter is placed on the court's docket for action, and the clock starts ticking. If dissenting opinions are not completed and circulated within a set period of time, the court will go ahead and issue its final decision and the justices simply have to sign one of the opinions which have been timely submitted, or be shown in the official reports of the court as not participating in the case.

On this opinion day in March, the matter of *Silus v Grand Haven Consolidated Hospital,* the so-called wrongful birth case in which a half million dollar verdict was awarded for delivering rather than aborting a healthy baby boy, was ripe for decision. Since the case was heard and submitted in November, before Malloy took his place on the court, the chief justice was not participating in the case.

At the time the straw vote was taken, it appeared that Justices Green, Templeton, Germaine, and then Chief Justice Breitner were in agreement that the five hundred thousand dollar verdict awarded to the plaintiff in the trial court should be left to stand, and the judgment of the trial court affirmed. O'Leary, Van Timlin, and Henry disagreed. Henry was chosen to write the dissenting opinion. Breitner's name was drawn by the clerk to write the opinion on behalf of the majority of the court.

"I don't know what you want to do on this thing, Jim. " Breitner was saying. "My opinion is ready to go and so is Alton's. With Green gone, and you not participating, we appear to be divided three against three. That means affirmance by a divided court. If there is not a majority deciding to reverse the decision in the trial court, that decision cannot be overturned. I say lets go ahead and sign the opinions we have on the table, put this thing behind us, and go on to other things."

Malloy looked at O'Leary. "Which opinion do you plan to sign, Bob?"

O'Leary leaned forward, his elbows on the table and his chin resting on both fists. "There really is more to it than Ed's opinion and Alton's. Alton wants to send the case back for a new trial to let the defendant show that the husband came home. That might reduce the size of the verdict. But Van and I are taking a more substantive position. We don't think, as a matter of public policy, there ought to be any damages awarded at all where a healthy baby was delivered. I'm prepared to write just such an opinion."

Templeton interjected. "What good will that do? We'll have two votes to reverse and throw the case out of court---you and Van. One vote to go back for a new trial---Alton. And three votes to affirm---Hilda, Ed and I. You can't get a reversal with two votes, so why bother to write anything?"

"Well, it seems to me,"O'Leary, still leaning on his knuckles, continued, "that we ought to simply start all over again here. After all, we have a new justice seated with us. This is a new court. We ought to order the lawyers to come back and re-argue the case, resubmit it, and then let us see where the decision will go."

"Surprise, surprise," Templeton was chortling. "The conservative block wants a recount now that they have another voter on the rolls."

"You are certainly entitled to do that, if you think it would make a difference." Breitner rejoined, in a somewhat exasperated tone of voice. " Frankly, though, I don't think it will do any good. If Jim joins in my opinion, the trial court is affirmed, just as it would be if we go ahead today with only six Justices participating. If he signs Alton's opinion, it will be three to affirm, two to reverse, and two to remand. The trial court will be affirmed, because no majority agrees on any other course. If Jim joins with Bob and Van, the same result will follow. No four votes for anything. And that means affirmance any way you slice it."

Van Timlin crossed his arms and leaned back. "Maybe so, but I still think we should go through the process," he insisted. "I move that we order the Silus case resubmitted."

"Any discussion?" The chief justice was looking at Hilda. She shook her head from side to side.

"Those in favor of resubmitting?" Van and Bob raised their hands. Henry spoke. "I don't see any point in rehashing this thing. I don't like the size of the verdict, but I don't see how we can say that the lady doesn't have a breach of contract case under our decisions."

"That settles it, " Breitner began taking his original opinion out of his file to pass it around the table.

"If Alton won't vote to resubmit, I will." Hilda Germaine announced to everyone's surprise.

"What, Hilda? I thought you were with us on this." Breitner was clearly agitated.

"I was. Maybe I still am, but I see no harm in taking another look. We haven't heard where Jim is on this or what his reasons might be. He ought to be given a chance to participate in our deliberations and we ought to hear his thoughts."

Malloy spoke up. "The chair will vote yea. That makes four votes for resubmission. The clerk will direct counsel to resubmit or waive their right to re-argue the case."

Chief Justice Malloy scanned his docket for the next matter to be acted on. This job certainly is full of surprises, he thought.

***

The Loyal and Ancient Order of Gin Rummy Buffs gathered at Flynn's apartment on Friday night. As it so often did, the between-hands conversation turned to the doings of the supreme court. Justices of the supreme court are under no obligation to keep their deliberations secret. As a matter of history, tradition and sound discretion, however, they rarely discuss court business when their conversations might be overheard by persons who might publicize the court's impending actions, or otherwise make improper use of such knowledge.

Malloy and O'Leary saw nothing wrong with discussing matters which were either public knowledge or about to be public records in front of Flynn and Wilhelm. Flynn, was totally trustworthy, and totally uninterested in what the justices did. Wilhelm had his lobbying clients, and needed some guarding, but he could be counted on to be scrupulously discreet.

"I was really surprised about Hilda's vote to resubmit Silus, weren't you?" Malloy asked O'Leary.

"Yes, I was. Of course she had trouble with the thing the first time around. I think it was a hard decision for her."

"So you think she may rethink this case?"

"Sounds like she is willing to listen."

"What about Henry?"

"Loose cannon on the deck, to quote our beloved immediate past chief justice. It's hard to tell where he will go. But once he writes a dissenting or concurring opinion of his own, you can pretty much cross him off. He'll sign his own, and that's all."

"Silus? Did I hear somebody say Silus?" Wilhelm butted in.

"Yeah, do you know the case?" asked Malloy.

"I've heard of it, and I'll have to warn you gentlemen that you don't want to talk about it in front of me. I'm liable to run out and sell all my stock options in Missaukee Mutual. And get incredibly rich."

"You already are incredibly rich," O'Leary looked up from his cards. "Look at that gaudy sun tan you got in Fort Lauderdale. What has Silus to do with Missaukee Mutual?"

"Don't they carry the liability insurance on Grand Haven Consolidated Hospital?" asked Wilhelm. " I thought I read that somewhere."

"We wouldn't know about that." Malloy commented without looking away from his hand. "The name of the insurer is never mentioned in the court file. Where did you see it?"

"I dunno. Someplace. I've done some work for Missaukee from time to time."

"Ah ha" Malloy grinned. "Now I can see why the vote is going the way it is. You old rascal, Art, you've been salting the mine again, haven't you?"

"I'm a veritable cornucopia of graft, corruption and payola, Mr. Chief Justice." He laid down his hand. " Gin."

"Nuts," said Malloy, as he counted out twenty seven points in his hand.

Silus was not mentioned again that evening. As the game broke up, Wilhelm got his top coat from the bedroom and returned with a fistful of envelopes. "And here in my hand, gentlemen, I hold the answer to all of your dreams and schemes. Florida lottery tickets as promised. I invested all of your ill gotten gains in the educational trust fund of the Sunshine State, and I herewith present you with the evidence of my faithful servitude."

"Tickets? Who wants tickets? What did we win?" Flynn demanded in mock anger.

"Hey, what do you expect from me? Do I have to do all the dirty work for you guys? I told you I would buy your lottery tickets for you. I didn't say I would buy newspapers and look to see if you won. That's for you to do. Heck, that's all you get for your lottery dollar. A chance to look and see if you won. I wouldn't want to deprive you losers of the delicious pain of discovering that you blew the rent money on another piece of pie in the sky." Wilhelm was laughing derisively as he distributed the envelopes, marked with the names of his three companions.

Malloy grinned. "This is no waste of money for me. Margaret and I are going to Florida next month. She always makes me buy her a Florida lottery ticket every day we're there. I'll just dole these babies out one at a time. They should last me for the whole trip."

Wilhelm left first. Malloy hung back, taking time with his coat. "Did you see the First Press editorial about Duracky?" he asked O'Leary. "They used so much of Breitner's opinion, they should have given him a byline."

O'Leary slapped Malloy on the back. "Give it time, kid. It gets worse."

***

Sergeant Firbacher of the State Police Capitol Security detachment took the call.

"Firbacher. Capitol Security. Can I help you?"

"Yes. This is Sandy in Chief Justice Malloy's office. I don't know if I have the right department. We don't get into this stuff much in the supreme court, but we've got the chief justice of the supreme court of Guatemala coming in here tonight or tomorrow morning, and we would like to have the Guatemalan flag hoisted. Is that something you folks do?"

"You're in the right place. Did you say your name is Sandy?"

"Yes in Chief Justice James Malloy's office. I'm in charge of public relations here. Where do you normally fly foreign flags when the governor's office requests them?"

"All depends. Sometimes they only want one or two poles. Sometimes more. What did you have in mind?"

"We only need one Guatemalan flag. It should be displayed, or hung or whatever you do, on the pole in the plaza between the Law Building and Treasury."

"Can do. When do you want it?"

"It should go up late this afternoon, so it will be hanging early in the morning. That site is lighted isn't it?"

"Yes Ma'am. All night. We'll have Guatemala flying just below Old Glory by five o'clock. Is that O.K.?"

"Perfect. Then you can take it down any time after noon tomorrow."

"Good to go. By the way, Sandy, may I have your extension number? Just in case I have any other questions."

"Uh. Er. I'm not at my desk right now, and they just gave me a new phone. I think it's 437, something like that."

"437? Doesn't sound right. It should be four digits."

"Oh yeah. I think it's 4371. Pretty sure. I'll call back when I get to my desk if I got it wrong."

"Thank you."

"No problem. And thank you so much. The court will be pleased."

* * *

At 3:15 AM on Tuesday March 26, 1991, a Chevrolet van pulled to the curb on Allegan Street just west of Walnut. Two workmen, dressed in denim bib overalls got out, removed a box about the size of a large steamer trunk, placed it on a dolly, maneuvered it up the twelve concrete steps leading to the Law Building Plaza in the block immediately west of the State Capitol Building, and wheeled it to the center of the plaza, directly beneath the thirty foot aluminum flag pole, at the top of which two flags fluttered. The familiar stars and stripes, and right below them, the three vertical stripes, two blue and one white, of the flag of Guatemala. After placing the box on the concrete walkway, one of the men set a timer on the side of it, and both men walked back to the van and drove off. No one saw them.

At five minutes past five, as the darkness of the night was just beginning to give way to the faint promise of dawn, the top of the box swung open, revealing the heads of two dozen powerful rockets, the first of which launched immediately, rising nearly eight hundred feet in the still, cool, murky, morning air, before exploding with a frightening, thunderous clap. There followed a pyrotechnic display worthy of the Fourth of July. Chrysanthemums. Willows. Red. Green. Blue. White.

Residents of Lansing Towers, in the block to the north, stumbled groggily from their beds and gawked out of windows as much as ten stories above the street. Bursts of color greeted them with every new rocket blast.

Capitol Security went on red alert. The three men on duty dashed to the stores room, donned helmets, bullet proof vests, and inter-com head sets. They signed the log, and issued themselves automatic weapons, tear gas, and bull horns. Then they rushed out to the plaza. The drill was accomplished in the record time of six minutes, forty-seven seconds. They arrived in the plaza just in time to see the last rocket launch. The one which dumped two thousand familiar blue and white decals of the Army of Righteousness all over downtown Lansing.

Channel 5 was already on the scene. Their remote truck had been driving north on Townsend Street after covering a shooting incident a few blocks south of Interstate 496.

All day Tuesday, Michigan television stations carried full color pictures of the Guatemalan flag waving proudly beneath the flag of the United States of America outside the quarters of the Michigan Supreme Court. They never mentioned Guatemala. They called it the flag of the Army of Righteousness.

Newspapers reported that state police were investigating to see who was responsible for placing explosives on state property. The log at the capitol security office showed that a call had come from the office of Chief Justice James P. Malloy, asking that the Guatemalan flag, which exactly matched the decals of the Army of Righteousness, be raised. A woman identifying herself as Sandy had issued the directive. Her extension was 4371. There was no such extension in the State phone system. There was no one named Sandy employed in the chief justice's office or anywhere in the supreme court.

Chief Justice Malloy told reporters he knew nothing about the incident and had no idea who might have been responsible.

The Detroit First Press ran a headline on its second front page.

CHIEF JUSTICE DENIES ROLE IN CAPITAL BOMBING.

***

Van Timlin and his wife, Gertie, took off their shoes and socks and wiggled their toes in the warm sand. For longer than they could remember, the last two weeks of March were spent in the restful setting of the Florida panhandle. They had been coming here long before San Dustin became a golfer's Mecca. Long before the clean, white, sand beaches were discovered by the hordes of Midwesterners who swarmed over the more southerly shores of Florida.

Once, they had talked of retiring here. Buy a little condo. Nothing pretentious. Just two bedrooms, one for themselves and one for guests. As the years rolled by, it became apparent to Van that the second bedroom would not be for guests. It would be for Freddie. The more Van thought of it, the less he thought of retiring.

This sunlit March morning, walking hand in hand with Gertie, in comfortable silence, just the two of them, Van felt the old urge to escape. Finally. To get away. To steal Gertie from the toils of mothering and homemaking, to leave behind the stress of judging, and just get away. As they splashed along the beach, feeling the warm Gulf waves wash over their feet, Van looked down at Gertie and squeezed her hand. She looked up and smiled. Right there and then, he decided to buy a condo.

That afternoon, while Gertie was reading a novel on the lanai of their rented unit, Van drove down the beach to a new development, a high rise condominium whose foundations had not yet climbed above ground level, but whose interior design was lavishly displayed in a temporary structure surrounded by fluttering, colorful flags and urgent, blaring billboards.

Once inside, despite the irritating, over zealous salesmanship of the developer's agent, Van Timlin made a deposit on a condominium in a building to be constructed in Phase Two, sometime in 1992. His unit would be on the fifteenth floor, overlooking the Gulf of Mexico. It would contain eleven hundred square feet, a large screened-in balcony, vaulted ceilings, a fully electric kitchen, a gas fireplace, a formal din·ng room, and a Jacuzzi tub in the bathroom.

It was, in the words of the salesman, "The most deluxe one bedroom condo on the beach."

CHAPTER 11

APRIL 1991

Joe Malloy, Senior, was sixty-six years old. He and his wife Anna were both in pretty good health, considering that they had raised eight children and worked their fingers to the bone doing it. It was worth it. Now their children were all educated, and gainfully employed or married to solid breadwinners, and Anna and Joe enjoyed and bragged about their two dozen noisy, endearing, precocious grandchildren.

Joe had even been able to put away a modest nest egg for his retirement years. Part of it was represented by their Florida home. One of thousands of such places in the Sunshine State, it consisted of a three bedroom mobile home augmented by a screened extension -- the obligatory Florida lanai-- and another extension used as a carport. Joe and Anna had acquired the place in run down condition a decade before, when they could manage only a few weeks of vacation during the harsh Michigan winters.

Typically they went to Florida to work on the house. Fix up, clean up, paint up. Plant flowers, mow the lawn, trim the hedges. By the time Joe was ready to retire from the auto dealership, where he had sold cars for 32 years, the Florida place was a doll house. Last year, the senior Malloys made the big decision. They spent the entire winter in Largo. Joe augmented his social security by selling a few cars for a dealer on US 19. Anna spent most of her time fussing over those of her eight children who, with their spouses, were able to come for a visit.

The Malloys were a close family. Everybody knew everyone else's business, and how they felt. Joe and Anna were concerned about Jim. The publicity linking him to illegal activities the Army of Righteousness was clearly hurtful. They

190

were happy that Jim and Margaret would be getting away for a week later this month to visit them. Joe planned to get his famous chief justice son out on the golf course, to see if the Nutcracker still knew how to compete with his old man.

***

Silus v Grand Haven Consolidated Hospital was resubmitted by stipulation of counsel, without being rebriefed or reargued. If effect, the lawyers for both sides simply agreed that Justice Malloy could participate in the decision of the case, even though he was not on the court when the matter was first appealed. It was obviously easy for the new jurist to read all of the briefs and acquaint himself with the record in the case. If he wished, he could also obtain a transcript of the oral arguments. There was no point in the parties incurring the additional expense of starting over again.

Having studied the file, Malloy contacted O'Leary as a first order of business.

"I am going to be with you and Van on this Silus thing. But I don't like to see a three, three, one split. Can't we get Henry to come on board?"

"He's a hard sell, " O'Leary observed. "Once Alton has written something, he doesn't like to scrap it."

"You haven't written anything yet have you?"

"No. Been awfully busy with other things. But I mean to get to it soon."

"Why don't you hold off a bit longer. Let me see if I can get Alton to reconsider. Maybe we can persuade him to write an opinion we can all sign."

"He seems pretty well convinced that the plaintiff should have some kind of a lawsuit."

"O.K. Suppose she does. Isn't the real question one of damages? I mean if she were given only a nominal award, something that says, 'Alright, technically, you have a case, but you have suffered no real damages' couldn't you and Van sign that kind of an opinion?"

"I can't speak for Van, but I might be able to go along, if the damages were truly nominal."

"Good. I am going to ring up brother Henry. I'll let you know how it goes."

Alton Henry was at his roll-top desk when his secretary announced that the chief justice was calling.

"Hi there, Jim. Have you planted any bombs in the legislature lately? I hear they need a little excitement over there."

"Very funny, Mr. Justice. The truth is they are now considering adopting an anti-terrorism law. I hear it was introduced yesterday simultaneously in both houses with substantial bi partisan support."

"Who was it that said that no man's life, liberty, or property are safe as long as the legislature is in session?"

"So true. We'll have to wait and see what they do. Whatever it is, no doubt it will end up in our laps."

"Ah yes, the abominable advisory opinion clause in the 1963 Constitution rears its ugly head again."

"So be it. I called on another matter." Malloy wanted to get down to business. "You know I am now going to participate in the Silus case."

"So I hear. Really a foolish exercise. I don't see how you can affect the result."

"That's what I called you about. I've read your draft opinion in the case. It's really good, Alton. I think with a few changes, you might be able to get enough names on it to be a majority holding."

"That would surprise me."

"It shouldn't. As I see it, you, Bob and Van are all in agreement that the verdict is simply too large. Way out of line."

"As I understand it, they don't think there should be any right to sue at all."

"I understand that, and if this were solely a case of alleged malpractice, you probably couldn't get their signatures. Malpractice is a tort. Without damages, there is no tort liability. But you have written that you think the plaintiff had a contract with the hospital, and that they breeched their end of the bargain by not performing an abortion."

"That's the way I see it, Jim."

"O.K. So you want to send it back for a new trial so that the defense can call the husband as a witness, or otherwise prove that he has come back home, right?"

"Yes."

"And you think that testimony will cause the next jury that hears the case to be less sympathetic to the plaintiff, and give her a much smaller verdict, right?"

"I think that's what would happen. That's what should happen, anyway."

"What if you could conclude, as a matter of law, that the damages she suffered are limited to the difference in value, if any, between an abortion and a cesarian section?"

"I don't follow you."

"Well, if we are talking contract, then the damages for breech of contract ought to be limited to the lost benefit of the bargain she made with the hospital. If you order a 21 inch television set, and the store delivers you a 30 inch set for the same price, what have you lost? If you contract for a small hotel room, and they put you in the Presidential Suite for the same price, what have you lost?"

"So you are suggesting she got more than what she paid for?"

"Sure. Take a look at the 1960 case of *Wycko v Gnodtke* in volume 361. I never much liked that case, but it very clearly holds that the loss of a child entitles the parents to money damages. So if you lose money when a child is taken away, don't you gain something of value when you get a child? Aren't there all kinds of people who pay out all kinds of money to adopt babies? They travel all over the world, Romania, Korea, South America, just to find babies they can adopt."

"You're not suggesting that we approve the buying and selling of babies, are you?"

"Of course not. I don't like the Wycko holding precisely because it takes such a monetary view of human life. But the case is in the books. And it is a precedent in Michigan. We ought to be consistent. If losing a baby costs money, then gaining one should be a plus."

"Do you think that if I changed by opinion to simply reduce the award to one dollar, I could get four votes?"

"You'll get Bob and me. And I suspect Van will sign it too, though I haven't talked to him."

"Well, let me take a look at Wycko. I'll see if it has any relevance."

Within a week Justice Henry had submitted a new draft opinion, and Justices O'Leary and Van Timlin and the chief justice had all indicated by memos to their colleagues that they were ready to sign the revised Henry opinion. Thus, there were four votes, a majority of the court, to remand the Silus case to Circuit court for the entry of a remittitur of $499,999.

The plaintiff, Mrs. Silus, got one dollar in damages from the hospital.

***

Jim and Margaret flew to Tampa International Airport on Thursday, April 18th. They caught the five o'clock flight, right after the supreme court's regular opinion conference at which the Silus case was signed and released.

Joe and Anna, wearing shorts, tennis shoes, golf shirts, sun tans and wide, welcoming smiles, were waiting at the curb outside the airport baggage return area. They joined the sidewalk tableau of shirt and tie snowbirds hugging and kissing grey haired locals, while luggage was stacked in car trunks, news of families rehashed, and tales of traveling mishaps laughingly shared.

April is prime time in Florida. Easter vacation. Sometimes Spring break for the college kids. And the weather is predictably sunny, hot, and dry. The thousands of Midwesterners who sojourn to the land of palmettos and pines come because they are wintered out. The graceful drifts of sparkling white snow that make December and January a Winter wonderland in the north lose their allure by April Fool's Day. Freezing rain and slushy snow in April are emotionally draining. Too much of a good thing. Way too much.

Jim and Margaret settled in at mom and dad Malloy's, kicked off their shoes, and prepared to get into a vacation mood. They had almost achieved it, when the eleven o'clock national news came on with a wire service story about a decision of the Michigan Supreme Court depriving a single mother of four children of the half million dollars she had been awarded by a jury of her peers. Complete with sarcasm and raised eyebrows from the anchor man.

On Saturday, Margaret asked Jim to buy her a lottery ticket. After all, the drawings are on Saturday night. We should have something to look forward to, she had insisted. While the clerk was cranking out five one dollar tickets, Jim asked her an innocuous question.

"How do you find out whether a ticket purchased some weeks or months ago was a winner?"

"Easy. Just bring the ticket in and we'll run it through the computer. Or call the 900 number on the back of the ticket."

Sure enough, on the back of the lottery ticket was the message that winning numbers and pay outs could be learned by simply calling 1-900-737-7777, and paying seventy-seven cents a minute for the call.

Malloy returned to his parents mobile home, rummaged through his briefcase, found the envelope given him by Art Wilhelm, spread the twenty tickets out in chronological order, and placed a call to the Florida Lottery hotline. He reached a recording, signaled that he was using a touch tone telephone, and began entering the dates of the twenty tickets purchased for him by Art Wilhelm.

The first eight tickets were losers. The ninth ticket was not a loser. The recording informed him that the Fantasy Five ticket purchased on February 12, 1991, bearing numbers 2, 7, 13, 14, and 20 was a winner. The pay-off was $183,200. Malloy reacted numbly. He simply continued to punch in the dates of the other twelve tickets from Wilhelm's envelope. The rest were losers.

That night, Malloy took his father, mother, and wife out to dinner. They went to a famous, pricey steak house in Tampa. Over dessert he gave his family the good news. Joe Malloy was not really too surprised. He always knew his son Jimmy would do well.

***

Doris Templeton assumed that her daughter Cheryl had an abortion in January. They never talked about it, true. But Doris felt that it was better to let the matter be simply forgotten than to dwell on it. Once the thing was done, Cheryl should have returned to her law school studies, and put the whole episode out of her mind. Especially, she should forget about the young man who had so thoughtlessly caused her the discomfort and expense associated with terminating an unwanted pregnancy.

So when Cheryl called in late April to tell her mother that she was seeing Roger again and by the way, she was still pregnant with his child, Doris nearly went ballistic. She quickly packed a bag, got into her car, and drove to Chicago. By the time she approached the Skyway, she had calmed down. Nothing was to be gained by an emotional encounter. She was sure that Cheryl would see the wiser course, if only they could talk the whole thing out.

The evening began with dinner at a Lincoln Park bistro. Chit chat about law school and about the supreme court would not hold their interest long. They both knew what had to be said, and all the while other matters were discussed, they were both rehearsing speeches in the back of their heads. Making conversation, Doris mentioned that Chief Justice Malloy, vacationing in Florida, had just won more than a hundred thousand dollars in the Florida lottery.

"Some people have all the luck," she concluded.

"Don't they, though," Cheryl agreed. "Just the other day there was a big story in the Chicago papers about some of our local politicians, aldermen or whatever, who had a lottery pool that won over a million dollars. According to the paper, it was not the first time those same guys had winning tickets. There have been calls for an investigation into the Illinois Lottery."

"Well, I suppose if anyone would tamper with a state lottery, it would be here in the Windy City."

Cheryl nodded. An uncomfortable silence set in. Both women stared at their drinks, like chess masters studying the board before their first moves. Finally, Doris opened with pawn to king three.

"I thought the last time we talked about it, that you were going to have the thing taken care of before the January semester at school. What happened?"

"You're right, Mom. I was going to do it. I went to the clinic with every intention of going ahead and getting it over with."

"So what happened to change your mind?"

"There were these two guards out in front of the place. As I approached, one of them asked if he could check me for metal. It was a little scary. I thought, gosh, if they have to check everyone for metal, maybe it's not safe to go in."

"I can see that. I suppose I shouldn't be surprised, but I never heard of guards being posted by abortion clinics. Maybe they had some threats. But after all, we get checked for metal every time we fly on an airplane, and that doesn't keep us from flying."

"That's right, and the metal checking business isn't what

stopped me. I was going past the guard when the other one, a woman, handed me a small brochure, with the picture of a sad baby on the outside. I thought it was something from the clinic, maybe telling about family planning services, something like that."

"Wasn't it?"

"No. I opened it up, and inside was this terrible photograph of a mangled fetus, with the message, 'Please don't kill me, mommy'."

"Oh my God, that's awful. It must have made you sick."

"It really did, Mom. I almost threw up. I honestly thought I was going to. All I knew was that I couldn't go in there and have that abortion. Not then. Not that day."

"So what did you do?"

"I went home and I cried. For the longest time. Maybe two days. I just couldn't get out of bed. I wanted to call you, wanted to talk to you, but I just couldn't. I knew you would be mad. I didn't know where to turn."

"You should have called me. I would have understood. And I sure would like to find out who the hell those so-called guards were, and who they were working for."

"I knew you would. That's one of the reasons I didn't call you. I didn't want to get involved with police, with an investigation, with newspapers and television publicity. My pregnancy was my problem; a very personal and private thing."

"Yes, I can see that. But we can't let these people get away with this kind of thing. Don't you see? We have an obligation to fight, to defend ourselves, to stick up for our rights."

"You always were a crusader, Mom. I'm not. I just want to be left alone. Anyway, after three days, I called Grandpa."

"Grandpa? What did he say?"

"He was very understanding. He asked me a lot of questions about Roger. What was he like, where was he from. Why did I start dating him. Did I still like him. We talked a very long time. He made me feel much better. Grandpa made me feel that he really cares about me and about how I feel."

"And I don't? Is that it?"

"Don't start on me, Mom. You know how busy you are and how much I love and admire you. You are, and always have been, my idol. My role model. I want to be just like you. I wish I could be just like you. But you had babies. You were a single mom. You made it work. Why can't I?"

"That was different. I had no choice. Abortion wasn't legal when you and your sister were born."

"And if it had been?"

"Don't be smart with me. Those were just different times, that's all."

The two women finished their meal in silence and took a cab back to the apartment. There ensued a long, stressful, sleepless weekend during which Doris insisted that Cheryl was making a huge mistake; that it was not too late to terminate the pregnancy; that single parenting was not a sensible option, and that if she persisted in this course, she should not expect her mother to support her and her illegitimate child, while Cheryl accused her mother of abandoning her at birth, putting her career and her causes ahead of her children and family and trying to control everybody else's love life when she hadn't been all that successful in her own relationships.

Doris shouted and Cheryl cried. Then Cheryl shouted and Doris cried. By Monday morning the matter was still unresolved. Doris left because she had work to do in her office in Detroit. Cheryl went to school because finals were only a few weeks away. The child in her womb kicked mightily, as if angry about being excluded from all the shouting and crying.

***

Probate Judge Neil Morrison looked up from the file in his hand, peered over his reading glasses, and asked who was present in the courtroom on the matter of Jeremiah Wheatley.

The County social worker stood, identified herself, and introduced Cindy Germaine, Benny Oldsmer and Nora Oldsmer, his wife.

"If the court please, I am recommending that the juvenile be placed in the foster care of Mr. and Mrs. Oldsmer. I know this is an unusual course in a case of this kind, Your Honor, but I believe the best interests both of the minor and of society will be served by this placement."

The judge looked at Cindy. "Mrs. Germaine, you are Justice Germaine's mother, are you not?"

"I am."

"And are you in agreement with this placement?"

"I surely am, Judge. This lil boy needs the firm hand of a loving father and mother, and I think these folks are just the kind of good, clean living, Christian folk that can bring Jeremiah to make something of himself."

The case worker broke in. "Your Honor, I think it would be very helpful for the court to hear from Mr. Oldsmer. He has developed a very special relationship with Jeremiah over the last months, and I think you should hear about it from him."

"Mr. Oldsmer, would you care to address the court on this matter?"

"Yes I would, Your Honor. I work at the Henry Ford Hospital in physical therapy. Been there for eleven years. Jeremiah was assigned to me when they gave him the new foot. You know, a prosthesis to replace the leg and foot that were amputated. I never saw a boy learn so quick how to get along on an artificial limb. He was walking and running within a few weeks. He even started to dance. You know break dancing, like the kids do. He was good at it, too. Judge, you can't believe how this boy has learned how use his new foot. He has a lot of courage. We have gotten very close to each other over these months. The hospital even let me take him home with me a couple of times for the weekend. Nora wants him to come and stay with us, too. We never were able to have kids of our own. We want to make a home for Jeremiah with us."

Judge Morrison sat forward in his chair. "I've given this matter a lot of thought since the petition was filed. I think the department has done a very fine job of evaluating the Oldsmer home and the arrangements that would be made for Jeremiah's schooling and discipline. I am particularly impressed that Mr. and Mrs. Oldsmer are committed to sending the boy to Holy Trinity School. The court is personally familiar with the good work they are doing in the inner city, and the success they have had with children at risk. I have also had the benefit of the report of the staff psychologist on this matter. I know that the newspapers are very interested in this case, and I hope they will respect the fact that Mrs. Germaine and the rest of the justice's family concur in the placement that is being recommended here today. Everyone has agreed that this will be in the best interest of the juvenile. That's what I really care about. So I am ready to take the heat of adverse publicity if it is to come. I will sign the order placing Jeremiah with the Oldsmers for an initial period of four months, and I will want a full report to review at that time to decide whether to continue this foster home placement. Mr. Oldsmer, good luck to you and your wife."

Jeremiah was not in the courtroom. He was waiting in the case worker's office two floors above. When she came to tell him the news and take him downstairs to his waiting foster parents, Jeremiah asked if Cindy was going with them.

"I don't think so, Jeremiah," the social worker answered. "But she is waiting downstairs to say goodby to you."

"Sheez notgonna say gooby noway. MissCindy promise shegonna bemy gramma."

CHAPTER 12

MAY 1991

The Malloy Florida vacation ended on a sour note. Walking on the Pinellas Trail near Dunedin on the morning of their last vacation day, Margaret was being passed by an elderly gentleman on roller blades, when the skater suddenly lost his balance, instinctively grabbed her arm, and pulled her with him to the ground, causing an ugly contusion on her hip. And of course, worry about the babies.

That afternoon, on the ride home, when the Northwest Airlines 757 was over northern Ohio, and about to begin its long descent in preparation for landing at Detroit-Wayne County Metropolitan Airport, she felt a sharp surge in her abdomen, reminiscent of labor pains. The feeling continued intermittently for the rest of the flight, subsided somewhat while they waited for their connecting flight to Lansing, then began again over Howell.

At Capital City Airport, a law clerk was waiting for them with the C.J.'s car. Malloy had him drive directly to the hospital, while calling Doctor Carnahan on the car phone. The doctor wasn't in. Jim left a message. By the time they arrived at the emergency entrance, Carnahan was waiting for them. A cursory preliminary examination, then the decision to admit her immediately.

Some hours later, after more thorough examination and the intravenous injection of a labor impeding drug, Carnahan informed Jim and Margaret that she was going to have to spend the rest of this pregnancy in the hospital, under medication. He felt that if they could hold off delivery for four or five more weeks, the babies would develop enough to give them a fighting chance. Better than that. A good probability of survival, given the sophistication of the neo natal unit in Saint Robert's

202

Hospital's pediatric department.

Malloy went home, relieved Alice, hugged the kids, took them to MacDonald's, and then brought them to the hospital to see mom. Jimmy, Paul, and Mary Ellen did not remember ever being in a hospital before. They walked almost on tip toes, eyes wide with curiosity and concern. Jimmy lectured Paul on proper decorum, while Mary Ellen tugged at her father's pant leg every seven seconds with another unanswerable question.

Shortly, they entered the private room where Margaret, her dinner tray still cantilevered above her, was idling through a magazine filled with pictures of good things to eat, beautiful ladies obsessing over perfume and lingerie, and rooms replete with perfectly matched or complementary curtains, pillows, bedspreads and throw rugs.

The reunion with their mother was not as boisterous or vigorous as that with their dad a few hours earlier. The children approached her deferentially, tenuously, as though afraid to hurt her. She was, after all, in a hospital bed. She must be either sick or hurt. Margaret sensed their concern and sought to put them at ease by letting them feel the babies kicking. Unfortunately, the twins weren't in much of a kicking mood. Paul particularly, seemed very worried.

Jim and Margaret had long since made a conscious decision to educate their three little ones about the impending births. It was an occasion to tell the story of life's beginning in a way that avoided all the erotic overtones. Simple biology simply told and simply understood. More questions would come later, they were sure. But at least when questions came, there would be a solid foundation to reference.

Jim disappeared into the hall, and shortly thereafter a nurse came in and supplied a dapler with which Jimmy, Paul, and Mary Ellen, each in turn, were able to listen to the babies' heartbeats. The exercise reassured them. And it was fun. Even more fun when they tested the dapler on themselves.

***

Art Wilhelm's appearance in the Law Building was unexpected. He had no known business there, and lobbyists do not hang around courts. Still, he was a friend of the C.J., and announcing his purpose to be entirely social, he was ushered into the chief's private chambers.

"Nice digs, Mr. Chief Justice. Very nice."

"Just a modest gesture of respect for the office from the grateful taxpayers. To what do I owe the honor of this truly unexpected and unwelcome intrusion into the sanctum sanctorum?"

"Oh, I was just in the neighborhood and thought you would like to have someone to play gin rummy with while the general public thinks you are holed up in here reading Blackstone's Commentaries."

"A truly enlightening tome, brother Wilhelm. You should read it yourself sometime."

"I have the kiddie version with cartoon pictures at home. I never miss a night...."

"Come off it, you clown," laughed the C.J. "What's really on your mind?"

"Hey, if I'm intruding, I'll go. Just wanted to drop off this card." Wilhelm handed Malloy a get well card for Margaret. "How is she doing?"

"Well enough. She'll have to stay in bed till the babies come, though. It's rough duty."

"I'll bet. I just wanted to send along my good wishes. And, by the way, to congratulate you on winning the lottery, or Fantasy Five or whatever it was in Florida. I thought maybe you'd like to share your winnings with me, since it was I who bought the ticket for you."

"With my money, don't forget."

"Too true. I was just looking for gratitude, not justice. Believe me, if I had known one of those tickets I gave you was a winner, I would have kept it and given you some of the losers I bought for myself."

"I am truly grateful to you, sir. Indeed, I have here in my drawer a fistful of lottery tickets for you, if you would like them." Malloy opened the drawer with a flourish.

"Forget it. I don't need wallpaper, you lucky Irish clown."

"O.K., so I owe you. Believe me, I do appreciate your suggesting the lottery and whatever hocus pocus you may use to buy winners. It sure has made a difference in my life."

"No doubt, and I'm glad, Jim. You deserve it."

"You're too kind. What's the other matter on your mind?"

"Silus. I saw the opinion that came out on that case. Bob tells me that you did a real job on Henry, got him turned around, and then managed to bring Van along for a majority decision."

"A simple matter of looking for common ground. But I'm a little confused. I seem to remember that you had some connection with the Silus case, but I can't remember what it was."

"No big thing. Our firm occasionally consults for Missaukee Mutual. They had the liability insurance on that case."

"Oh yeah. I remember you said something about that at Flynn's."

"Anyway, I just wanted to let you know that the folks at Missaukee Mutual were also very happy to hear that you won the lottery."

"Why would that be?" Malloy felt his pulse quicken. Was there some connection between Missaukee and the lottery?

"Let's face it, you saved them a lot of money. You're a big hero over at Missaukee."

"Are you telling me there is some connection between my winning the lottery and what we did in the Silus case?"

Wilhelm stood, waving his arms like an umpire ruling a base runner safe at second. "No way. Not at all. That wouldn't even be logical. Why in the world would anyone pay two hundred thousand to fix a five hundred thousand dollar case?"

"I don't know. I have no experience with such things."

"Neither do I. I assure you. All I meant was that there are lots of good people in Michigan who think you are doing an excellent job as chief justice and they are very happy to see you have some good luck. That's all I meant. Don't get all uptight about it for heaven's sake."

"I just don't think I like the juxtaposition."

"I'm sorry." By now, Wilhelm was at the door. "See you Friday night at Flynn's?"

"Can't go. I'll be visiting Margaret in the hospital."

Wilhelm left, and the chief justice sat for a long time, wondering.

***

As he entered Margaret's room, Malloy realized that his wife was not alone. Bob O'Leary's stentorian voice rumbled from around the corner. He was telling some inane, romanticized tale of life in the Upper Peninsula.

"Ah Ha! Caught you two finally. What have you to say for yourselves?"

"Temporary insanity, if the court please. I simply had an irresistible urge to cheer up this lovely lady."

"A likely story, " Malloy feigned drawing a pistol.

"Enough," said Margaret, in her best Maid Marian voice. "I will not have you two dueling over poor little me."

"Puts me in mind of a story." Everything put O'Leary in mind of a story.

"Seems that a gentleman farmer in Sicily gave his son Pasqualli a hunting rifle as a birthday present. A few days later, the boy rushed up to his father and showed him a very expensive jeweled watch. 'Where dida you gida da watch?' asks the father. 'I trada my rifle with Guido to gida da watch.' says the boy. 'Stupido!' cries the father, 'some day you gonna coma home and find you wife ina bed with another man. Whadda you gonna do, looka you watch an say 'you times up?' "

Malloy, laughing, pointed to his wristwatch. "You times up, O'Leary. My turn to entertain the lady."

"I was just leaving anyway. Margaret, take care of yourself. Don't let this big lug overwork you."

He squeezed her hand and started for the door.

"Just a minute," Malloy had a sudden thought. He told Margaret that he would be right back, and walked O'Leary to the elevator.

"I had a conversation with Art Wilhelm this afternoon that got my antennae up. He seemed to be making a connection between the *Silus* case and my winning the lottery. You don't think there might be something fishy about the lottery ticket do you?"

"Fishy?"

"Yeah. He acted like, you know, like maybe I owed him something for getting me the ticket. You don't suppose he knew that was a winning ticket when he gave it to me do you?"

"What do you think?"

"I can't believe that he would buy a ticket, discover that it was a winner, and then give it to me. Makes no sense."

"Didn't he tell you about 1-800-I WON BIG?"

"No. What's that?"

The elevator arrived. O'Leary stepped in. As the door was closing, he shrugged his shoulders. "I don't know anything about it. That's between you and Wilhelm."

***

Curiosity was eating him alive. Malloy punched the buttons on his touch tone phone. 1, 8, 0, 0, 4, 9, 6, 6, 2, 4, 4. 1-800-I WON BIG. He got a recording.

"You have reached the American Lottery Exchange. If you have a winning ticket to sell, please touch one now. If you are interested in purchasing a winning ticket, please touch two now. If you wish more information about the American Lottery

Exchange, stay on the line, and an operator will assist you momentarily. Thank you for calling the American Lottery Exchange."

Before being disconnected, Malloy punched the number 1 on his telephone key pad.

"Congratulations on winning a lottery. Please enter the two letter postal abbreviation of the state in which you purchased your winning ticket, and then press the pound sign."

Malloy hit 35 for Florida.

"Please enter the date on which the drawing was held and press the pound sign."

Malloy entered the date of his winning ticket, 2-12-91.

"If your ticket was on the lottery, press one. If your ticket was on the Fantasy Five, press two. If your ticket was on the Cash Three, press three."

Malloy pressed the number 2 on his phone.

"Please enter the winning numbers on your ticket, and press the pound sign."

Malloy pressed 2, 7, 13, 14, and 20. And pound.

After a short interlude of music, the recorded message returned. "Your ticket is a winner. It can be sold through the American Lottery Exchange for 183,200 dollars. If you wish to speak to an agent, stay on the line."

More music. Soft music. Dentist's office music.

"Good afternoon. This is Rob Winslow, exchange agent. May I help you?"

"Yes. I am interested in selling my ticket."

"We will be happy to buy it, and we will make payment in any manner, currency, or medium you prefer. We assume you have discussed this matter with your tax counsel. Excuse me... it appears from our records that your ticket has already been redeemed by the State of Florida. Are you sure you have the correct numbers and date?"

"Yes. I'm quite sure."

"May I have your name and address please?"

Malloy hung up the phone.

He dialed the 800 number again. This time, he selected 2, the route for buying a winning ticket.

"We have a number of excellent lottery pay-offs available," said the recording. "Please indicate the state in which you would like a ticket by pressing the two letter postal abbreviation. If the location does not matter, enter zero."

Malloy entered Florida.

"Please enter the approximate date of the drawing you would like."

Malloy entered 2-12-91.

There followed a recorded listing of dates and tickets available for purchase, their official pay offs, and the amount of the brokerage fee or premium to be paid in connection with each. His winning Fantasy Five ticket was not among them.

Malloy hung up, sat musing for several minutes, then asked his secretary to get the local office of the Federal Bureau of Investigation on the phone.

***

The two agents were out of the Detroit office of the FBI. They looked and acted precisely as FBI agents are supposed to look and act. Gronski, the senior man, had not wanted to discuss the matter on the phone. He introduced himself, and his partner, agent Smith.

Malloy told them everything he knew. How he had come into possession of the lottery ticket. He named Art Wilhelm. He told about his calls to the 800 number. He told them about the *Silus* case, and his concern about a possible connection.

"Gentlemen, I want you to understand that I am making no accusation of impropriety here. I haven't any real reason to believe that Mr. Wilhelm bought that ticket from someone. If he gave it to me for the purpose of influencing any action of mine, he certainly didn't let on in any way. And I can assure you, I have done nothing for Mr. Wilhelm, nor have I allowed my association with him to influence any official act on my part. If he bought that ticket with my money, and simply brought me the ticket as he claims, then I am quite comfortable in keeping the money. If, on the other hand, it appears that he purchased that ticket from someplace like the exchange, I will want to know who paid for it and why, and I doubt that I would keep the money under those circumstances."

Gronski and Smith said they fully understood, and promised to keep the matter entirely confidential. They added that they would report to the chief justice whatever they might discover about the Wilhelm ticket.

Three days later, 'That's Three O', television's most watched tabloid, carried a bombshell expose' about the American Lottery Exchange, accusing it of being a money laundering operation, designed to give drug overlords, crooked politicians, and wealthy income tax evaders a means of explaining otherwise unexplainable income. Many of Chicago's municipal hierarchy were named and pictured refusing to comment, punching cameramen, and otherwise treating the program's field reporters with contempt.

Chief Justice Malloy was not mentioned.

***

On Monday May 6, 1991, the supreme court heard oral arguments in five cases. The last of these, *Braxton v Central Michigan University,* was being argued a second time. The case had been originally submitted in November 1990, at which time Justice Germaine was selected to write the majority opinion. She had not submitted a draft opinion by January 1, 1991, when the composition of the court changed because of the election of Malloy to succeed Douglas Green. After several inconclusive discussions, the court, decided that the best course was to resubmit the case, in effect, starting all over again.

The litigation was what is known as an injunction suit. Leonard Braxton, a student at the University, brought an action on behalf of himself and others similarly situated, to restrain the University from expelling him from school for violation of one of its housing regulations.

The rule at issue was University Housing Policy number 4(a) which provided:

> All freshmen and sophomores shall live in University dormitories during the regular school year, except those students who reside at the home of their parents or legal guardians, and those students who reside in recognized fraternity and sorority houses. For the purpose of this rule, 'recognized' means certified by the University Inter-Fraternity Council.

Braxton and his co-plaintiffs were members of Kappa Nu, a national fraternity with chapters on the campuses of 47 colleges and universities throughout the United States. Thirty-one of those chapters were located south of the Mason Dixon line. University Housing Policy number 4(a) was adopted in 1987. In 1989, the University Interfraternity Council decertified Kappa Nu, on the ground that the fraternity's unwritten policy was to exclude persons of African descent from its membership. In proof of this claim, evidence was presented, and not disputed, that in the 102 year history of the national fraternity, no black person had ever been admitted to membership. The Central Michigan Chapter had a similar record in its twenty two years of existence.

The circuit court and the court of appeals declined to issue the injunction requested. The supreme court granted leave to appeal, the question being one of first impression in the state.

At the hearing in the trial court, it was established that the fraternity had no formal policy or by law prohibiting the pledging or admission to membership of a person of African descent. It was also conceded that there were no black members of the fraternity. The parties agreed to several other facts which may have a bearing on the court's decision.

First, the university allowed fraternities and sororities to be sex specific. That is, fraternities could be limited to male membership and sororities to female membership. It was also conceded that Mu Lambda Chi was a certified fraternity which had a membership consisting entirely of persons of African American descent. In addition, the Newman Club maintained a residence for Catholic students, and had been certified by the Interfraternity Council as an approved residence for freshmen and sophomores.

The court crier announced the case of *Braxton v Central Michigan University*. Plaintiff-Appellant's counsel stood and walked to the podium.

"May it please the court, my name is Wendell Porath. I am the attorney for the Plaintiffs in this matter. My clients are students in good academic standing at the defendant university. They have paid all of their tuition and fees, after being duly accepted and admitted to the university.

"Each of the plaintiffs has received official notification from the university that they are to be administratively dismissed from the university for failure to comply with Housing Policy 4(a).

"That policy provides..."

Justice Templeton interrupted. "We know what the policy provides, counsel, and we know what the university is doing to your clients. What we don't know, and what I would like to hear from you is why you think the taxpayers of the State of Michigan should provide a university education for people who deny to their fellow citizens the civil rights they are entitled to under the fourteenth amendment to the federal constitution. Could you please address that point?"

"Justice Templeton, I will be happy to address it. It is our position that there is no right under the federal constitution to belong to any particular fraternity. By definition, a fraternity is a social organization. Membership is by invitation. When new members are pledged, the existing members are exercising their constitutional right of association. They can accept or reject persons for any reason whatsoever, or for no reason at all. Like most Greek societies, Kappa Nu uses a form of black balling to allow any member to veto the acceptance of any new member."

"There is more than a little poetic injustice in the name of that procedure, isn't there counsel?" Templeton was on the attack.

"If the court please, there is no evidence in this case, nor is there even an allegation by the university that any pledge to this fraternity has ever been vetoed because of the color of his skin. And the record shows that there have been black students who have pledged to Kappa Nu."

O'Leary inquired. "Does the record show how many?"

"No, your honor."

"So we don't know if there were just one or two over a number of years, or if there have been many black pledges who have all been uniformly excluded, is that right?" O'Leary continued questioning.

"That is correct, your honor. And we must remember that this is a social organization, and a residential one at that. These young men live together in very close association. It is important that they all get along. Like brothers. They are fraternity brothers. So the process of selection involves a lot of very subjective evaluation. Does he smoke? Does he drink? How much? How does he behave when he has a few beers? What kind of language does he use? What sports does he play? There are hundreds of considerations. One thing is rather obvious. Fraternity brothers tend to select new members who are very much like themselves. That is entirely natural. And I submit, if the court please, it is entirely within their constitutional rights to do so.

"This is not a case where a constitutional right is being denied to anyone. Certainly sex discrimination is just as offensive to the constitution as race discrimination. But the university officially allows sororities and fraternities to discriminate against candidates on the basis of their gender. And look at Mu Lambda Chi. It is 100 percent African American. Nobody is talking about decertifying them. This is clearly a case of reverse discrimination by the university, if the court please."

Porath paused, looking over his notes.

"Your Honors, I have no wish to make a long speech here today. I am not a particularly good orator anyway. I am here mostly to answer any questions which members of the court may have after reading our written briefs in the case. I would only like to close with this thought. There are a lot of good people, well intentioned people, well motivated people in America, who want to see the terrible specters of racism, race hatred, and racial bigotry completely obliterated from the consciousness of the people of this country. A culture of political correctness now permeates our society which goes far beyond the protection of civil and constitutional rights. It is an effort, through various forms of community coercion, to control the thought processes of our citizens. You have an opportunity today to strike a blow for true freedom in our country. You have a chance to say in this case that no instrumentality of the government of this state has a right to dictate how people must feel about each other, what they must think about each other, or how they must act toward each other in social, as opposed to civic or political matters. I earnestly hope this court will have the courage to rise up and answer this challenge. If the court please, I will reserve a few minutes for rebuttal. Thank you."

Porath gathered up his notes and returned to the counsel table, as counsel for the university rose. Stephanie Fredericks was a matronly, kindly looking woman, early fiftyish, well groomed, conservatively dressed, and thoroughly prepared. Her presentation was scholarly and professional, replete with citations of authorities. Indeed, so laden with citations and lengthy quotations that the chief justice interrupted after 34 minutes.

"Excuse me, Mrs. Fredericks, I don't want to break your train of thought, but you have exceeded the allotted time for your argument. Are there any other matters, not covered by your brief, that you feel the court needs to hear?"

"No, your Honor, I believe we have covered everything. Thank you." She sat down, Porath waived rebuttal, and the crier adjourned court for the day.

The justices were still removing their robes in the conference room when the debate over *Braxton v. The University* began. "So, Doris, how many black members do we tell the boys at Kappa Nu to take in before they can pass the litmus test of political correctness?" Alton Henry was on the attack.

"More than none, you can count on that. We don't need any lily white fraternities in Michigan. Let them go to the University of Alabama."

"How many, Doris?" Henry would not give up. "One? Two? Surely you don't approve of tokenism. Should they have ten percent? Maybe match the percent of African Americans at the University? And how about Jews? Do they have any Jews? Or Catholics? Maybe the University should outlaw all fraternities as being undemocratic, antisocial and un-American. Is that where you want to go with this?"

"Now that's the first intelligent thing I've ever heard you suggest, Alton." Templeton's eyes were flashing. "Is it possible that you are beginning to come out of your nineteenth century cocoon?"

"I have no desire to become the kind of flittering philosophical butterfly that kisses every blossom in the ACLU's garden like you do, Doris."

The chief justice was seated at the head of the table. He cleared his throat rather deliberately.

"That's enough crossfire. Lets get down to some serious discussion. As I recall from our conversations before lunch, we are pretty much agreed upon the two matters that were argued this morning, is that right? If there is no objection, I will ask the clerk to assign those cases, and we can get on with discussion of *Braxton v CMU*."

The clerk drew two names, while the justices opened their notebooks and arranged files to consider the next matter.

"Hilda, you were assigned this case when it was argued here last fall." The C.J. was looking at Germaine. "I assume you have written a draft, or at least completed substantial research in the matter. Would you care to start the discussion?"

"The most difficult part about this case for me has been to identify what action by the university the plaintiffs claim is denying them their constitutional rights. We certainly don't want to be in the business of operating universities from this conference room. On the other hand, the university is an agency of the state government. As such, it is bound by the fourteenth amendment to accord to citizens of the United States the equal protection of the law. If we were talking here about a university policy, for example, that said, 'White students may not belong to fraternities, but black students may,' that would clearly deny to the white students the equal protection of the law. Just as it would be if the University's policy denied specified rights to black students. But here, there is no university policy on the subject of race. As a matter of fact, the record shows that there are at least two other fraternities, and I believe one sorority, which are, or were at the time the case was tried, one hundred percent white. And those other fraternities and the sorority were certified by the Interfraternity Council as proper student residences for freshmen and sophomores."

Breitner looked up from the papers in front of him. "What exactly is the Interfraternity Council, Hilda? Is it an arm of the university, or a separate organization created by the Greek societies on campus?"

"It's my impression that the council was originally nothing more than a private assembly of representatives of the various campus organizations." Germaine responded. "Apparently in recent years, the university has been asked to send a delegate to the council, who seems to be more than a faculty moderator. In any case, the university policy specifies that the council has the power to certify and decertify Greek houses for the purpose of freshman and sophomore residence."

Van Timlin stirred. "Well, it seems to me that if the university relies on this council, whatever it is, to make decisions that are binding on students, then the council is part of the university. Don't you agree?" He was looking at Germaine.

"I'm not so sure, Van. When a given fraternity decides to accept a student, that student will be officially excused from living in the dorms." Germaine leaned forward as she spoke. "Are we prepared to say that the fraternity itself is a part of the university because its decision is binding on the student? If so, then the fraternity is bound by the fourteenth amendment the same as the university."

"And what if it is? Does that mean they have to have so many members of each race?" Van Timlin was following the line of reasoning to the end.

"Not really," Germaine rejoined. "But it does mean that they cannot systematically exclude members of any protected classification from their membership. And if the council decides that is what they have been doing, then the council is justified in finding that the fraternity is denying students the equal protection of the law, in my opinion."

Van Timlin leaned back."That's an interesting analysis, Madam Justice, but I remain unconvinced. It seems to me that fraternities ought to have wide liberty to select their own members. I'll read your draft opinion very carefully to see if the authorities require me to concur with you."

Malloy tried to move the discussion along. "Anyone else want to be heard on this?" Silence. Some heads shaking.

"How many would affirm?" Templeton, Germaine, and Breitner raised their hands.

"And to reverse?" Van Timlin, Henry and O'Leary signaled yea.

"I was afraid of that," said Malloy, smiling. "Does anyone

218   **BRENNAN**

have a coin I can flip?"

"Very funny, Jim," It was Breitner talking. "You're the expert on generating collegiality. Let's see what magic you can work on this one." The tone was bitter. Sardonic.

"I'll want to see what Hilda writes, of course. And any dissent which someone else might be moved to circulate. But my basic reaction to this case relates to one of the first things Hilda said. I think courts get too much involved in minutia. Matters that properly are administrative or political. Judges can't solve all the problems of the world. When we try, we destroy the credibility of the system and reduce our ability to do the things we really ought to be doing. I'm not happy about courts telling schools how long the children's hair should be, or telling prison officials what they have to serve for breakfast. A University is an academic and intellectual community, quite apart from the community at large. It occupies a relationship of *locus parentis* to the students. When people send their eighteen and nineteen year old children to the university, they expect that someone is going to make rules for their conduct and teach them to act like responsible adults. In their capacity as students, these young people are not just like other citizens. They are obliged to comply with university rules and regulations, and to conform to the customs and traditions of the school. Some universities have liberal or libertarian cultures. Anything goes. The parents and students presumably know what they are getting into when they go there. Some are party schools. Some are conservative hotbeds or think tanks. Diversity in our educational enterprise is a good thing. The courts ought not, in the name of enforcing the fourteenth amendment, deprive universities of the right to be themselves, to define their own distinct missions and follow their own road maps. In this, I would not exclude public universities, just because they are supported by tax dollars. Non public colleges get some tax help, too. The bottom line is, I think if the university, acting through the Interfraternity Council, has determined that Kappa Nu is not the kind of a house they want their freshmen and sophomores living in, then that's their business. I would be content to leave it at that."

As the conference ended, Malloy sidled over to VanTimlin.

"Van, I think Hilda will write an opinion which has a very conservative reason for denying relief here. I sure would like to see you sign with the majority on this."

"Well, maybe I can," said Van Timlin. "Maybe I can."

CHAPTER 13

JUNE 1991

"If the court please, my name is Wallace Wilson Wright. I am here this morning representing myself in the case of *People v Wright.* I really don't feel that it is necessary to introduce myself. I was, after all, a member of the state house of representatives for six years and a state senator for ten more years.

"I worked on the political campaigns of a number of members of this court through the years, and I am proud to say that many judges, both Republicans and Democrats regard me as their friend."

"No need to belabor the point, Mr. Wright." The chief justice addressed him sternly. "We all know you, but that has nothing to do with why you are here. I will say this, however, in deference to you, Senator, the court would be much more comfortable if you were represented by counsel."

"I thank you for the advice, your Honor, but I prefer to handle my own appeal."

"Go ahead, sir. But remember, you will be required to abide by the rules, whether you know them or not."

"I understand." Wright didn't understand, really. "Your Honors, this is a very simple case. Ridiculous in fact. All I was doing was standing out in front of this abortion clinic in Kalamazoo, trying to protect them from the screwballs and terrorists who have been making so much trouble all around the country. At the same time, I was trying to do what I could to educate the young women going in there that there are reasonable alternatives to having an abortion. I think that it is my right as a citizen of the United States of America, to go out there on the public sidewalk, not interfering with anyone, not making any noise or trouble, and exercise my right to freedom of speech in that manner."

Justice Templeton charged into the fray. "Isn't it true, Mr. Wright, that you were wearing a police uniform? That you were dressed to look like a police officer? And isn't it true that you were stopping people, making them undergo a security check with a metal detector before you permitted them to go past you and enter the building? Do you call that just exercising your right of free speech?"

The Senator bristled. "That's a lie, Judge. I never wore a police uniform. I know what a Kalamazoo police officer looks like. I could have looked like that if I had wanted to. But I didn't. I was wearing a white jacket. They don't wear white jackets. I was wearing blue slacks. They wear navy blue jump suits. And I certainly wasn't stopping anybody from going into that building. I didn't scan anyone who didn't voluntarily agree to be scanned. I never blocked their way. Stood off to the side all the time."

Justice Breitner joined in. "You were wearing a Sam Browne belt, one of those military belts that goes across from your shoulder to your hip, is that correct?"

"Yes sir."

"And you were wearing a helmet?"

"I was."

"The kind of helmet worn by motorcycle police?"

"And everyone else who rides on a motorcycle."

"Yes. And you had a cell phone holstered at your hip, is that true?"

"I did. There's nothing wrong with that."

"Did it look like a gun?"

"I didn't think so."

"Didn't several women testify at your trial that they thought you were wearing a pistol?"

"Yes. But I wasn't."

"Bottom line, Mr. Wright." O'Leary picked up the questioning. "Bottom line was that you were trying to look like an authority figure, if not a policeman, then a security guard, but at least someone who had a right to stop people and check them out before they entered the building. Isn't that what you were doing?"

"Sure I was trying to look like a security guard. That's what I was doing out there. Acting as a security guard. I don't see what's wrong with that."

"Who asked you to be a security guard?" Justice Germaine wanted to know.

"Nobody. I just went there on my own. Look your Honors, I'm pro life. Strong pro life. Always have been. I think it's a crime what is going on in that clinic. Unborn children being slaughtered every day, and nobody to speak for them. But I am also sick to death of the violence and the killing that is being done in the name of the pro life movement. It doesn't help the cause when these mental cases go charging into abortion clinics shooting up the place and killing doctors and nurses. I want to prevent that sort of thing. Not just to protect the people inside, but to protect the credibility and the reputation of those of us on the outside who are trying to get our message across."

"A noble speech, Senator." Templeton's voice dripped with sarcasm. "Is that why you filed an assumed name in Berrien County to do business under the name of The Army of Righteousness?"

"I wasn't aware that there is some law against righteousness, your Honor."

"There are laws against trespassing on other people's property and exploding fireworks in crowded cities without a permit. Isn't that what your Army of Righteousness does?"

"I never had anything to do with any of that. And I am not charged with doing anything like that."

"We will try to keep our questions on the case at hand, Mr. Wright. Do you have any further argument?" Chief Justice Malloy was indirectly admonishing Templeton.

"That's about it, Your Honor. Tempest in a teapot if you ask me."

"One more question, if I may, sir." Breitner again. "After you searched these people, didn't you give them some of your pro life literature?"

"I did, if they wanted to take it."

"I see. After this man in uniform stops me and searches me, I am supposed to brush him aside if he tries to get me to take a brochure. That about it?"

"That's not the way it was. I never intimidated anyone. Never scared anyone. Just tried to be polite, efficient, and businesslike."

"Just as you would if you were working for the clinic. Right?' Templeton again.

"I was working for the clinic. I was performing a service for them. Donating my time to make sure nobody went in there with a gun."

Wright sat down. Frank Buchanan, Kalamazoo County prosecutor stood up.

"Frank Buchanan for the people. We charged the defendant with two counts. Impersonating a police officer and acting as a security guard without a license. He was convicted on the first charge and the judge dropped the other count. We think he is guilty of one or the other.

"It's clear that the defendant was dressed in paramilitary garb. It's clear that he was conducting himself in a manner that would lead people of ordinary intelligence to assume that he had some authority to do what he was doing."

Justice Henry leaned forward and addressed counsel. "If the defendant had just been standing there, dressed as he was, but just standing there doing nothing, would you have brought these charges against him?"

"Probably not."

"If, in addition to standing there, he had been asking everyone who entered the building if they were carrying a weapon, would that have been an offense in your opinion?"

"Just asking them?"

"Yes. Just saying 'Excuse me, are you carrying a gun?' Would that have been a crime or misdemeanor on his part to do that?"

"Well, I suppose not, if that's all he did."

"Was it a crime for him to ask people if they would permit him to scan them for metal?"

"I think that was very intrusive, your Honor. I think that's where he crossed the line."

" There are security personnel right outside the door to this courtroom who frequently ask people to allow themselves to be scanned for metal. Do they commit crimes by doing so?"

"Of course not. But they work for the court, don't they?"

"So you think the crucial fact is whether or not the security person is on the payroll, is that right?"

"Whether or not they are authorized to do what they are doing, yes."

"Authorized by whom?"

"By the owner. By the clinic."

"He was not on clinic property was he?"

"No, he was out in front. On the sidewalk."

"On the public sidewalk, isn't that right?"

"Yes."

"And does the clinic own the public sidewalk?"

"Of course not. But when you are standing in front of a building, the natural assumption is that you are working for the people who own that building."

"Or you are working for somebody who has a legitimate interest in protecting the people inside that building, right?"

"That's right."

"Someone who really doesn't want any violence to occur in that building, right?"

"Right."

"Like, for example, someone who might be falsely blamed for any violence that might be caused by someone else at that place?"

"I suppose that could be, Justice Henry, but that's not what most people would expect, in my opinion."

"Thank you, counsel."

***

In the conference room, Doris Templeton was highly animated. In fact, she was agitated.

"These terrorists have got to be stopped. This dreadful menacing intimidation is taking place all over the country. I can tell you from personal knowledge that they are scaring the living daylights out of poor innocent young women who are just trying to get proper medical care."

"Or keep hubby from knowing they have been fooling around?" Alton Henry could always find a way to pick a fight.

"I seem to remember that the supreme court of the United States has said that a woman has a right of privacy which allows her and her doctor to decide whether to terminate a pregnancy. If you've got a problem with that, write them a letter." Templeton roared back.

"I think we ought to focus on the facts of the case before us." The chief justice was trying to head off another tiff between Henry and Templeton. "Doesn't this case involve a charge of false personation? Shouldn't we stick to that matter?"

Breitner picked up the ball. "That's right. We need to decide if this fellow was acting like an authority figure, a peace officer. That's all there is before us."

"The issue is tighter than that, as I see it," O'Leary chimed in. "Wright was convicted by a jury. If the jury was properly instructed, and there was evidence at the trial from which the jury could fairly have reached its verdict, then we should affirm. It doesn't matter whether we think he acted properly or not, if the jury had a basis to do what they did."

"Well, that may be so, Bob," Van Timlin observed. " But this is an appeal from denial of a motion for judgment notwithstanding the verdict. Wright's complaint to us is that the trial judge should have overruled the verdict. So our job is to decide if the trial judge was wrong in refusing to do so."

"Technically that is the posture of the case, Van, but as a practical matter, the trial judge should have looked at the jury's verdict just as we do. If they had a basis to do what they did, we should leave it alone," O'Leary insisted.

Malloy intervened. "The jury's verdict isn't entirely sacrosanct, Bob. I spent eight years on the trial court, and I can tell you they make lots of mistakes. When a jury is moved by passion or prejudice, it is the trial judge's duty to set the verdict aside."

"But not just because he disagrees with them. He has to find that there was not sufficient evidence for them to conclude as they did."

"I agree," the C.J. replied. "But in this case, there are almost no disputed facts. Wright admits to everything charged here except for the legal conclusions. If the facts are not in dispute, the jury has no function. The case becomes a simple matter of law."

"Well I say that as a matter of law, he is guilty as hell," said Templeton.

"Would you say the same thing if he had handed out pro choice leaflets instead of pro life leaflets?" Henry was back, too.

"Good question." Hilda Germaine commented thoughtfully. "Does his purpose in dressing as he did, and acting as he did make a difference?"

"What are you saying, Hilda?" Doris was confused, surprised by her colleague's question.

"I'm just saying that we ought to ask ourselves whether the gravamen of this offense is acting like a police officer or tricking people into taking pro life literature."

"Is there a difference?" asked Breitner.

"I should think so." Germaine answered. " I don't know that there is any law against tricking people into taking propaganda.

I mean, if someone was standing on the street telling people he was handing out free tickets to the baseball game, and the hand outs were actually advertisements for a restaurant, would anyone think he should be prosecuted?"

"Maybe we can narrow this down a bit." Malloy picked up the discussion. "The security guard statute only forbids unlicensed guarding when it is done commercially, for money or compensation. Are we all agreed on that? Can we agree that the charge of acting as a security guard without a license was properly dismissed?" Affirmative nods around the table showed consensus.

"Are we all agreed that Wright was not wearing a badge or the uniform of a Kalamazoo police officer?" Silence.

"Do we agree that the offense of false personation requires a *mens rea*? That the defendant must have intended to impersonate an officer?"

"Wait a minute," Breitner cut in. "If he acted in a way that would lead reasonable people to believe that he was a policeman, that's all the prosecution has to show."

"Not quite, Ed. If the offense requires *mens rea*, and I think it does, then the question is not what the other people may have thought, but what the defendant intended. The outward appearances of his actions are only relevant if they prove that he must have known people would think he was an officer. The law presumes that people intend the natural consequences of their acts."

"That's right, and if reasonable people would think he was a policeman, the law will conclude that he intended to be taken for a policeman." Breitner was emphatic.

"Quite so, Ed," the C.J. rejoined. "But I have gone over this record very carefully, and my law clerk has been over the record with a fine tooth comb, and we cannot find one iota of testimony from anyone that they thought he was a policeman."

"Wait a minute," Templeton jumped into the fray."Didn't a Mrs. Fellrath, or Fellpausch, or something like that testify that she thought he was an officer?"

"Fellpath. Nancy Fellpath." the Chief was reading from his notebook. "She testified that she thought Wright was a security guard. Page 65 of the record."

"And he's not charged with impersonating a security guard, Doris," said Hilda Germaine calmly. "Maybe we ought to take a careful look at this matter."

"Well, I'm going to vote to affirm. I don't care if the ghost of Judge Learned Hand appears to me in a dream with a writ of hocus pocus. These right wing crazies belong in the slammer." Templeton thumped her book shut and pushed back her chair.

"Who else is leaning toward affirmance?" Malloy asked it with a smile. Breitner and O'Leary signaled yea.

"The clerk will draw a name for assignment of a majority opinion to reverse. See you all tomorrow."

***

Malloy stopped at the hospital on his way to the office on Monday, June 10th. Doctor Carnahan was there. He had good news. The babies were about ready. On Saturday, June 15, amniocentesis would be performed to determine if the babies' lungs were developed fully enough, and if so, a cesarean section would be performed. Margaret, weary of her bedridden ordeal, was clearly relieved to have a tentative date set for the birthing. Jim assured her that all was well at home, and promised to return later in the day with the children.

Entering the outer office of the C.J.'s suite in the Law Building, Malloy was somewhat taken aback to see a young man sitting on the edge of his secretary's desk. She was far too fastidious to allow such things, and obviously didn't like his presumptive familiarity.

"This is Raymond Tibson, from the Detroit First Press, Mr. Justice. He would like to interview you."

Malloy shook hands firmly, pulling Tibson off of the desk in the process. "Pleased to meet you, sir. Just have a seat here, and I'll be with you in a moment." Malloy then asked his secretary to come into his office, which she did, closing the door behind her.

"Let's not leave that fellow out there by himself for very long. What does he want?"

"I don't know, Judge. He just said he wanted to talk to you."

"Give me about five minutes, and then send him in."

Malloy called Mike Delbert, the clerk of the court. He always had his ear to the ground. What would the First Press want from him? The clerk was no help. No major cases had been released or filed, so far as he knew.

Shortly, Tibson was across the desk from the C.J. "Very impressive office, Mr. Chief Justice."

"Thank you. It was all here when I arrived. A little too big, if you ask me."

"Some folks would say you were pretty lucky to have an office like this."

"I guess I am."

"I hear you are having lots of good luck these days."

"I don't know what you have heard, but I do consider myself to be very fortunate, not only to be chief justice, which was a complete surprise to me, but also because my wife is going to have twins next Saturday."

"Next Saturday?"

"Yes. They are going to induce labor. She has been in the hospital for five weeks now."

"Rumor has it that you hit the jackpot down in Florida."

"Oh yes. The lottery. I still can't believe it."

"Where were you in Florida?"

"Largo. It's a suburb north of Saint Pete. My folks have a little place down there."

"Is that where you bought your winning ticket?"

" Come on, Raymond, you don't expect me to tell you where to buy winning tickets do you? That's a gambler's secret."

"Just curious. Some folks say that maybe you didn't buy that ticket at all."

"Some folks?"

"You know, news room gossip. I'm sure you have heard about the Chicago pols who had the incredibly successful lottery pool. Kept winning all the time."

"Cook County is an interesting place. I saw something about that, but I never heard what if anything was going on. Have there been some new developments?"

"Only the network TV story about the American Lottery Exchange."

"What's that all about?"

"You've never heard of the American Lottery Exchange?"

"I've heard of it, but I don't know what it's all about. Do you?"

"Just that it's supposed to be some kind of a money laundering scheme. A way for crooked politicians to take bribes and cover it up. Like that. That's all I know."

"Well, I assure you that I know where my winning ticket came from, and I did not buy it from the Lottery Exchange, or whatever it's called."

"How much did you win?"

"I'd rather not say. It was a sizable amount."

"In the millions?"

Laughing. "Not exactly."

"More than a hundred thousand?"

"I said I'd rather not tell you."

"Anyway, a substantial amount?"

"You could say that."

"By the way, has there been any more fall out from that business of the Guatemalan flag being hoisted in the plaza?"

"Fall out?"

"You know, the business of somebody supposedly on your staff ordering the flag put up in connection with that fireworks caper that the Army of Righteousness pulled off."

"I don't know what you mean by fall out. I told everyone at the time that my office had nothing to do with it. I don't know who used my name or why. But it wasn't me or my staff. We have no one here by the name of Sandy, and no public relations officer, or whatever she claimed to be. As far as I am concerned, that matter is a closed book."

"I was in the courtroom the other day when Wallace Wright was arguing his case. I noticed that he said he worked on several supreme court campaigns. Would one of them have been yours?"

"Yes. I've known Wright for a long time. He's a very popular fellow over in the western part of the state."

"Isn't he the President or the General or Commander in chief or whatever of the Army of Righteousness?"

"I hadn't heard that until it came out in court. Apparently he has filed an assumed name certificate claiming that he is doing business under that name. I can't imagine why."

"Hey, the AOR has made a lot of noise in Michigan and all around the country. Wright has positioned himself as the official spokesman for that organization. That's especially true as long as nobody else has come forward or admitted being involved in those bombings."

"Bombings?"

"You know, fireworks bombs."

"I thought I heard Wright say he had nothing to do with those things."

"Sure he denied it. What else would he do?"

"You're saying he lied in open court, in front of the whole supreme court?"

"Why not? Lawyers do it all the time."

"I think our interview is over, Mr. Tibson."

"Just one more question. Yesterday, the jury came back in the Durnacky case. You know, Mr. Death, the assisted suicide guy?"

"And?"

"And they acquitted him, just like his lawyer said they would."

"I'm not surprised."

"Doesn't that make you and the other justices who voted to make him go to trial look foolish?"

"Not if you know the difference between an appellate court and a jury. We have our job to do, and the jury has its job to do. It's not the same thing."

"Maybe not, but jurors are all registered voters. It looks like your decision was out of tune with the majority of the people who put you in office."

"The decisions of the supreme court are not based on the Gallup poll or the latest newspaper editorial. We are obliged to follow the law, no matter how unpopular. That's the role of the courts in our system of government, to protect the citizens against the tyranny of the majority."

"May I quote you on that?"

"The line is not original with me. It probably came from Oliver Wendell Holmes. But you can always quote me on anything I say. Now, if you will excuse me, I have a number of things to do this morning."

***

After a sleepless night, Saturday morning found Malloy as nervous as a bridegroom. He showered, shaved, dressed and hurried to the kitchen to fix breakfast for the children before Alice, the sitter, arrived.

First, of course, they would have cereal. With milk. He went to the refrigerator, took out a new carton of milk, and attempted to open it. He opened the ridge along the top of the carton at one end, then spread it in two wings, which he pinched together to cause the sprout to pop out. It didn't. He tried again. The two wings simply collapsed without opening the spout. Frustrated, he started for the drawer to get a paring knife, intent upon cutting the carton open. That's when he realized that he had been trying to open the wrong end of the ridge along the top of the carton. By harking to the plainly visible legend, 'Open This End', he found that a spout was quickly and easily formed.

Next, he confronted the cereal box. Again, a new box. Unopened. The constant challenge of commercial packaging. Inside the cardboard box was a plastic bag, sealed along the top. He took hold of both sides of the plastic bag and pulled. The seal on top scarcely budged. He pulled harder. The seal gave a little more. Again, he pulled mightily. This time, the sealed top of the plastic bag almost separated. Only a bare thirty-second of an inch remained to be parted. One last pull, with gusto, and the bag ripped wide open, the entire box being jerked violently to one side, and the toasted contents leaping to freedom and falling like snowflakes on the kitchen floor. Malloy cleaned up the mess, mumbling a vulgar benediction upon the packager, and poured cereal for Jimmy, Paul and Mary Ellen.

Orange juice. What is breakfast without orange juice? In the freezer, Malloy found a small cardboard container with metal top and bottom labeled frozen orange juice. He got out the electric can opener, and attempted to remove the top. No go. The opener would not bite on the ridge around the top. He tried again and again. The frozen juice inside began to melt. The cardboard sides of the container began to buckle. Malloy began to lose patience. Jimmy, the ten year old, came suddenly to the rescue. "Mom just pulls that little tab on the side." He informed his father. It worked.

When Malloy arrived at Margaret's bedside, he learned that the amniocenteses had been done several hours before. The Go, No-go decision would be made within the hour. Twenty minutes later, Doctor Carnahan came in, and matter-of-factly described the cesarean procedure. He made it sound quite routine, and Malloy was put somewhat at ease. Margaret, whether from prior instruction, or just general knowledge, seemed to be completely informed, and quite comfortable with the process.

By 10:40 AM, Malloy was scrubbed and standing expectantly in the birthing room, marveling at the efficiency of the doctors and nurses. For them there were no mysterious plastic containers, no reticent caps, no contents jumping out to spill on the floor. They moved with swift and certain hands, deftly employing the tools of their art, never missing a beat, never stumped or stumbling.

Holding his wife's hand, and watching with excited interest, Malloy was suddenly reminded that a cesarean section is, in fact, a surgical procedure. The instant Carnahan's scalpel sliced across his wife's belly, Malloy lost all enthusiasm for watching the birth of his twins. A surge of nausea almost forced him to turn away, but he did not want to embarrass himself or panic Margaret. With his free hand, he began vigorously rubbing his eyes, feigning an irritation. Then he turned his head and coughed, all the while keeping his eyes closed. He kept it up until one of the nurses handed him a glass of water, which he accepted. When these diversions were over, he risked another peek at the site of the operation, and was amazed to see the form of an infant emerging from the mass of bloody tissue.

Theresa Ann was born at exactly 11:03 AM. Theodore Clifford came just seconds later. Carnahan addressed the distraught father. "Do you think you could calm down long enough to cut the umbilical cords, Judge?" he asked with a grin. Malloy nodded gravely, still not fully in control of his woosey stomach. He took the surgical scissors from the nurse, and while the Doctor held the cords, he severed the twins from their mother. Tiny, wrinkled and scrawny, they were quickly whisked away to the neo natal unit of the hospital's pediatric ward. They would later learn that Terri weighed in at two pounds three ounces, and Teddy at two pounds seven.

The little girl cried when she was born. It was a comforting sound, frail and squeaky as it was. In Malloy's untrained view that meant she was breathing. Teddy, on the other hand, uttered not a peep. Malloy wondered what that meant. Was is unusual? Was the little boy in trouble? He dared not ask in Margaret's presence.

And then they were alone. Mother and father. Not knowing what the fate of their two tiny newborns was or would ultimately be. Jim leaned over the bed so Margaret could hug him. Spent, wearied, and worried, she pressed her face against his neck, and sobbed softly.

Malloy stayed with his wife until she dosed off. Then he went to the nursing station to inquire about the twins. Both were in the plastic domed cribs in the neo natal nursery. Bathed and naked but for a diaper and a knitted cap, they lay motionless a few feet beyond the glass viewing window that separated the nursery from the corridor. A nurse approached Malloy, as he stood on tip toes trying to get a better view of Terri's face. "You know, it's all right for you to go inside. You're the father aren't you?" she asked.

"I'm the father alright. Those are my twins." Malloy felt a sudden rush of pride, as he said the word 'twins.'

"Well, come on, let's get your hands washed and you can go inside to get a closer look." She led him to a sink in the corner of the nursery. "You can touch them by reaching through the openings on the side of the plastic canopy. They're not quite as fragile as they look. Don't be afraid of hurting them."

Her counsel was wasted. Malloy was in absolute awe of the infants who were barely larger than his hands. He was not about to handle them.

Alone in the nursery, Malloy stood over Teddy's crib. If the baby was breathing, it was so shallow and slow that it could not be detected even a few feet away. Terri's color was a bit better, but she also showed no sign of movement. Next to the sink in the corner of the room were some small plastic cups. Malloy filled one cup about half way, maybe two ounces of water. Then he returned to the babies.

Leaning over Teddy, Malloy poured a few drops of water on

the tiny forehead.

"I baptize you in the name of the Father, the Son, and the Holy Ghost." Then he lifted the edge of the knitted cap and dabbed at the beads of water on the wrinkled, motionless face.

Approaching the baby girl, he repeated the process, dripping a dollop of water on her head while pronouncing the ancient ritual of Christian initiation. Terri opened her eyes for an instant, then skewered up her face and let out a minuscule whimper.

Malloy heaved a sigh and left the nursery to return to his wife's room. When he took her hand, she opened one eye.

"Hi, handsome. How did we do?"

"Great. The girl is two pounds three and the boy is two pounds seven. A couple of gorgeous, skinny, little runts. How are you feeling?"

"Tired, but happy that it's over. I asked the nurse if I could go and see them, but she said she didn't think I could walk that far yet. All this time in bed makes you weak."

"Want to try?"

"I couldn't."

She had hardly spoken the words when a nurse entered the room pushing a wheel chair. "How would you like to go for a ride, Mrs. Malloy?"

Moments later, Margaret and Jim were peering into the little cribs together, making all the familiar nonsensical noises that new born humans inspire.

***

Sunday morning, Malloy picked up a copy of the Detroit First Press after 8:30 Mass. He had been watching the Firp all week, expecting a negative story would follow his raspy interview with Tibson. Parked in front of a convenience store, he opened the paper to the second front page. There it was:

CHIEF JUSTICE PLAGUED BY RUMORS

When newly elected Supreme Court Justice James P. Malloy was tapped by his fellow Justices to succeed long time Chief Justice Edward Breitner, many eyebrows were raised among veteran court watchers in Lansing.

This week, the skepticism directed toward the freshman justice reached a new crescendo, as he admitted winning a substantial amount of money in the Florida lottery amid revelations that lottery winnings apparently have been used in other states to launder drug money and effect political pay offs.

Interviewed by the First Press this week, Malloy declined to say where or when he bought or acquired the winning ticket, reputedly worth nearly two hundred thousand dollars.

Last month, the television magazine 'That's Three O' carried an expose' of the American Lottery Exchange, a West Virginia based scheme to buy and sell winning lottery tickets. A number of politicians in Chicago and elsewhere have recently cashed in winning lottery tickets, a form of extra income which would be totally legitimate, if the ticket was actually purchased from a lottery dealer. Agents of the Federal Bureau of Investigation are known to be examining the affairs of the Exchange to see if its clientele includes known criminals and persons who might be interested in concealing the true source of their income.

So far, no one has accused Malloy of receiving any illegal payments. The chief justice denies any wrongdoing.

Malloy, who was recently implicated in an unsolved bombing incident at the state Capitol, apparently carried out by the right wing terrorist group known as the 'Army of Righteousness,' was elected to the high court by a scant 12,000 votes last November. He defeated long time and highly respected Justice Douglas Green of Dearborn.

Malloy admits being supported in his election by leaders of the 'Army of Righteousness', but vociferously denies any part in the bombing.

In an opinion authored by the controversial young chief justice, the court last month ordered Detroit's 'Mr. Death', Morris Durnacky, to stand trial for manslaughter in the assisted suicide death of a suffering, terminally ill Wayne County man. Durnacky was acquitted by a jury last week in Recorder's court.

A First Press survey taken the following day revealed that 72% of county residents agreed with the verdict, and felt that the supreme court was wrong in requiring Durnacky to stand trial.

Jim Malloy dropped the paper to the passenger's seat, shaking his head from side to side, while feeling the anxiety rise in his belly. He wondered why they didn't mention that he didn't know how to open a can of orange juice.

CHAPTER 14

JULY 1991

By statute, the Circuit Judges of Michigan are organized as the Judicial Conference. They are required to attend an annual in service training program designed by the supreme court to keep them up to date on changes in the law and trends in the administration of justice.

There are only a few facilities in the state large enough to accommodate the nearly two hundred judges, their wives, guest speakers, and assorted employees. One of those places, a perennial favorite with the judges and more particularly with their spouses, is the Grand Hotel on Mackinac Island. The gracious white frame hotel, with its world famous front porch, elegantly decorated salons, sumptuous meals, and unparalleled hospitality, sits majestically on high ground overlooking the quaint autoless village, where the clop, clop of horses' hoofs mingles with the groaning of ships' horns in a cacophony of vacationer activity.

Fudgees, they are called. They come in summer, those hundred days when this tiny island is the destination of thousands from down state, out state, and all around the world. They loiter, wide eyed, near the fudge makers' shops, watching mesmerized as the smooth brown goo is ladled and coddled and worked over with skills passed from father to son to granddaughter, until irresistible chunks of chocolate decadence are lined up like brazen temptresses in the shop windows. Then they go inside and taste. And buy. And tell each other they are bringing home to friends and family what they know they will naughtily consume before the hydroplane gets back to St. Ignace or Mackinaw City.

Those judicial conferences have many purposes, not the least of which is to get judges from all around the state acquainted with each other, talking to each other, learning from each other.

240

How do you handle plea bargains? Motions in limine? Child support delinquencies? Is your docket getting bigger? Smaller? What do you think of the new crop of lawyers? Fast and lasting friendships blossom at judicial conferences.

The supreme court, of course, is always prominent at those events. Some of the justices participate as discussion leaders or seminar presenters. Some just mingle and press the flesh with old friends. Often they talk to each other about court business. About their cases. About the politics and the gossip that cling like barnacles to the vessel of jurisprudence.

In 1991, the conference was scheduled for the last week of July, with Judges arriving on Sunday the 28th. By Tuesday, the 30th, it was in full swing.

Van Timlin, Templeton, and Germaine were standing in the main lobby, engaged in some obviously engrossing gossip, when the chief justice emerged from the stairwell and greeted them. They shook hands all around and exchanged pleasantries about the weather, the agenda, the meals, and the vigorous socializing of the night before. To a casual, even a perceptive observer, these were just four colleagues interacting genially. But Malloy read non verbal signals as they chatted. There was something in the look in Van's eyes when he said hello. Something in Hilda's body language when she shook his hand. Some extra standoffishness about Doris' posture that turned on the intuitive warning light in the C.J.'s subconscious. He broke off cordially, and headed for the bar. It was the cocktail hour. O'Leary would be there.

He was. Martini in hand. Pontificating to three Yooper Judges about Upper Peninsula justice. Malloy pulled a chair over from a nearby table, and ordered a beer.

"So, what are you gentlemen learning that you didn't already know?" the Chief asked playfully.

"Keltner here says that there are no deer on this island. He says they have tried many times to keep deer here, but every time they do, the animals cross over to the mainland as soon as

the straits freeze over in the winter." O'Leary reported.
"I'd say they've got more sense than the human population."
"The herd instinct in both species is very strong," noted
Keltner, a circuit judge from Menominee. "You take this bill in
the legislature to provide special punishment for terrorists. Talk
about lemmings to the sea. I can't believe the stampede to
support such a phoney law."

"Why phoney?" Malloy was curious.

"They want to double the punishment for any crime
committed as an act of terrorism. So if I steal a loaf of bread to
eat, or sell, or give away, that is a one year offense. But if I steal
the same loaf of bread to eat at the church picnic, sell to support
a political party, or give away to people at a campaign rally, it's
a two year offense." Keltner shook his head in disgust.

O'Leary was confused. "I don't get it. Why should it matter
why I stole the bread?"

"That's the dumb part about this terrorism law." Keltner
enjoyed instructing the supreme court. "It says a crime
committed as an act of terrorism is more serious. Then it defines
terrorism as 'any act done to promote or defeat a political or
religious cause or organization, or to prevent or discourage any
person from the exercise of their religious or civil rights, or
committed as a member of a street gang or other combination
of persons for nefarious purposes.' "

"So you are saying that the terrorism law makes crimes
committed for religious or political reasons more serious than
crimes committed out of plain old greed or passion?" Malloy
wondered.

"You've got it. The star chamber is back."

"A chilling thought," observed the chief justice as he downed
his beer and prepared to leave. Turning to O'Leary, he asked,
"Got a minute for some supreme court business?"

"Always. What's up?"

Keltner and the other two Circuit Judges suddenly
remembered having other places to be and things to do. Soon

the two high court colleagues were alone.

"What's going on, Bob? I sensed that Doris, Hilda and Van were talking about something they didn't want to share with me a while ago. They all acted uneasy when I saw them in the lobby."

"I'm afraid our friend Breitner has dropped a cow chip in the punch bowl, Jim. I just saw it this afternoon, and was going to get together with you on it tonight."

"What are you talking about?"

"The memo, Jim. Haven't you seen the memo?"

"What memo?"

"Breitner sent a memo around to the justices, apparently everyone except you, suggesting that the court ask the tenure commission to investigate you."

"He what?"

"He wants us to ask the tenure commission to look into your lottery win and that business about the fireworks and the flag."

"You gotta be kidding!"

"Nope. I wish I was. That's not all. He wants the court to remove you forthwith as chief justice."

The waitress came by. Did they want another round? Malloy said absolutely, and ordered his second beer. O'Leary took another martini.

"Have you talked to Henry about this?"

"No." O'Leary mumbled. "I haven't talked to anybody."

"Well, you are going to have to talk to some people. You know how I got that lottery ticket. You were there. So was Flynn. If I remember correctly, buying tickets was Flynn's idea. We all bought them."

"That's right, we did. But you're the only one who won."

"So? Is there something wrong with winning?"

"Heck no. But are you sure that Art didn't get that ticket from the Lottery Exchange, or someplace like it?"

"I'm not sure, but I will be. As soon as you told me about that 800 number, I called in the FBI to check the whole thing out."

"The FBI? You called the FBI?"

"Damn right I called the FBI. I told them to find out whether the ticket I got came through the Exchange, and if so who put up the money to buy it. I want no part of anybody's dirty little secret."

"Aren't you afraid that they will come back on you?"

"Who?"

"The FBI. Aren't you afraid they will end up accusing you?"

"Of what, trusting Wilhelm?" Malloy was getting annoyed. "I did nothing wrong. If Wilhelm did, I'll expose him, and he can take the consequences."

"You told the FBI about Wilhelm?"

"I told them everything I knew, yes. Why shouldn't I?"

"No reason." O'Leary grew silent, then sighed deeply. "I'm sure glad I didn't win anything."

***

Malloy stormed through the hotel looking for Breitner. He buttonholed judges, collared clerks, and queried court personnel. Nobody had seen him. Then he went to the front desk and learned that Breitner had checked out late that afternoon, choosing to skip the last day of the conference.

Malloy spent a near sleepless night, tossing and turning and muttering epithets about his predecessor in the center chair. Finally dozing off at 5 AM, he woke with a quick start at 6:45. As was so often the case, the short sleep not only refreshed him, but supplied dreams which helped him to focus on his problem. Decision dreams he called them. In this one, he was alone with Breitner in a boat, fishing in a lonely lake. Malloy was catching all the fish. Breitner was crying. Whether a byproduct of the dream or of his long night of mulling, Malloy knew what to do. He had to find Breitner and talk to him. Face to face.

Malloy found Elizabeth Breitner having breakfast in the main dining room. She confirmed that Ed had left the day before.

"Poor boy, he has been working too hard, he looks terrible. I told him to just go up to his cabin and rest. He always looks better after he has been up there a while."

"I'd like to do some of that loafing and fishing myself, Elizabeth. Just where is Ed's cabin? Maybe I'll go and join him."

"I'm sure he would enjoy that, Jim. But I'm afraid I can't give you very explicit directions. I've never been up there myself. Too far from my hairdresser, if you know what I mean."

Malloy gave the remark a mandatory chuckle. "You have no idea where it is?"

"It's at a place called Whitefish Lake. Near Wawa somewhere. Of course, you can always reach him by leaving a message on his car phone's answering machine. I have his phone number right here in my purse someplace." She struggled unsuccessfully with her purse for several minutes. Malloy sensed that she was annoyed that he had interrupted her meal. He told her not to bother as he had the number at his office, and wished her safe travels back to Bloomfield. She replied that she was going to Harbor Pointe to visit friends. He said goodby, then spotted Mike Delbert.

The supreme court clerk usually knew everything. He didn't know exactly where Breitner's cabin was located. Somewhere up in Ontario, near Wawa. "There's a phone at the cabin," Delbert offered, "but it's a party line, and there is no answering machine. I've never had any luck reaching Breitner on that line."

Gulping coffee and wolfing down some toast, Malloy motioned the court administrator, Caroline Greenwald, over to his table. He told her that he was going to have to leave the island early as some urgent court business had come up. She assured him that the program was going well, and he would not be needed for the final sessions. Within an hour, he was packed, transported by carriage to the dock and waiting for the boat back to the mainland.

The trip across the Straits of Mackinac on a hydroplane takes about twenty minutes. Sitting in the enclosed cabin, watching water spray against the windows, Malloy imagined his meeting with Breitner. Suddenly heavy eyelids drooped into fitful cat naps. Short vignettes played themselves out on the big screen of his fancy. Sometimes he would take Breitner by the shoulders and shake him, yelling angrily. Asking over and over, Why, Why, Why?

Sometimes the dream would become a nightmare. Breitner would have the entire court behind him. Mom and dad Malloy would be with Breitner, too. Malloy would be alone. All alone. He would call for Margaret. She would be locked in a room with no telephone. Holding babies. Singing to babies. Unable to hear him.

On the dock at Mackinaw City, retrieving luggage, getting the car, chatting with two circuit judges who were chagrined to be caught skipping the day's seminar in favor of golf at Boyne Highlands, Malloy felt reinvigorated. Soon he was driving his car hundreds of feet above the blue water flowing from Lake Michigan into Lake Huron, leaving the mitten shaped land mass behind, enjoying the sense of passage that only the Mackinac Bridge can offer.

Exiting the bridge, and realizing that he was actually heading toward Sault Saint Marie and northern Ontario, Malloy felt a pang of doubt about his decision to seek out Breitner. He was on his way into a vast, largely uninhabited land with no real notion of where the hell he was going. Elizabeth's clue, that the cabin was at Whitefish Lake, yielded only minimum guidance. The road atlas didn't even show Whitefish Lake.

Working the car phone as he drove north, Malloy first called the operator for the area code in Wawa. 705. Then he called information and asked for the number for Edward Breitner. The operator said there was no Edward Breitner in the 705 area, but there was an 'E. Breitner.' Could that be it? Malloy asked where the phone was listed. Whitefish Lake. Any street address? None.

Just Whitefish Lake. No help there. Taking down the phone number, he placed a call to Breitner's cabin. The phone rang for five minutes. He hung up. He called the Chamber of Commerce in Wawa. There was none, but he did find a Visitor's Bureau. They told him Whitefish Lake was near a town called Hawk Junction. There was no Hawk Junction on his map.

In Michigan, Malloy would call the register of deeds or the assessor's office. But he knew nothing about Canadian land titles. He called information again, looking for the tax assessor's office. No luck. Their records were all by parcel and not by name. Maybe, he thought, he could go to their office and leaf through the books trying to spot the name Breitner. Not a very hopeful approach for such a long drive. He tried the Ministry of Natural Resources, which has jurisdiction over the Provincial Parks. The ranger, or whoever it was that answered the phone, could not place the name Breitner.

Soon he was approaching the Soo. Should he go on? Was this a fool's mission? Then it dawned on him that the cabin would probably have electricity. Perhaps a lead could be gleaned from talking to the electric company. He worked the phone some more. Most rural electricity, he discovered, would be supplied by Ontario Hydro.

Malloy called information, got the number for Ontario Hydro, and was about to call them when a thought occurred which caused him to hang up and reflect. He was going to ask for the billing department, and pretend to be Ed Breitner calling about some confusion in his billing. He hoped to induce the operator into inadvertently giving him some useful information from which he might locate Breitner's cabin. Two concerns concurred in his mind. First, the operator would surely be under instructions not to divulge information over the telephone, especially if she had no way to be assured that she was talking to the actual electric customer. Second, he would get one and only one chance at this charade. A second call might get the same operator, or somehow trigger suspicion in the billing office. He could not risk being traced or having his call bumped up to a supervisor.

Malloy called the supreme court clerk's office in Lansing, and asked to be put though to the payroll clerk.

"This is the chief justice. I'm trying to locate Ed Breitner's cabin up in Ontario. You don't happen to have an address for him up there do you?"

The payroll clerk checked, came back on the line and said she found nothing.

"Well, then give me his home address and phone number in Bloomfield Hills."

She did.

"And how about the address and phone number of his apartment in Lansing?"

She gave him that, too.

"One more thing, just in case I need it. What's his social security number?"

The clerk read the number to the chief justice.

***

"Ontario Hydro? Give me the billing department please."

"Billing department? My name is Ed Breitner. I have a problem with my cabin up on Whitefish Lake, or my cottage, I can't really tell you which. I used to get bills on the cottage regularly, but I haven't gotten a bill on that property for several months and last time I was up here, I had electricity at the cabin where I wasn't getting the bills anymore, but on the cottage where I was paying the bills, the electricity was turned off. I don't know, I just seems to me that you folks have got my billing all screwed up. I don't mind getting electric service where I don't pay the bill, but I sure as heck would like to have the lights on in the place where I am paying the bills every month, if you know what I mean."

A very pleasant, professional voice, with the familiar hint of

Canadian pronunciation, responded. "I am very sorry, sir, if you have been having trouble. I will be happy to assist you. May I have the correct spelling of your last name, please."

"It's Breitner. B-R-E-I-T-N-E-R. Edward Breitner."

"Mr. Breitner, what is your billing address?"

"That may be part of the problem. I used to get all my bills, on both properties at my office in Lansing, then I changed the billing address on one of the places, I forget which one, to have the bills sent to my house in Bloomfield Hills."

"What is your address in Bloomfield Hills?"

"3954 Drury Lane. Zip code is 48241"

"That is the only address I have for you, Mr. Breitner."

"Is that the billing address on both pieces of property, both locations? The cabin and the cottage?"

"I am only showing you as being billed at one location."

"That's what I'm trying to tell you, miss. I'm paying the bill, I think, on the location where I'm not getting electric service, and I'm not getting any bills for the place where I'm getting electric service, and I don't know if this one bill is supposed to cover both the cottage and the cabin or if its just for one or just for the other, or which one it is. I'm really all confused, and I think you folks must have your records all mixed up or something."

"I am very sorry, sir, if you have been inconvenienced in any way. If you are not receiving bills for one of your properties, you are going to have to come into the office and fill out an application for new service. Or if you wish, I will send you an application, and you can mail it back to us, eh?"

"That's nice of you, miss, but how can I make out an application if I don't know which property you are billing me for now and which one you are not billing me for?"

"The service location is printed in the upper left hand corner of your electric bill."

"I know that. But I'm calling you from my car right now, and I don't have my bill with me. All I know is that I'm not getting electric service at my cabin and I am getting it at my cottage. And when I paid the bill last time, it looked to me that you were billing me for the cabin and not for the cottage. Now I don't care if you turn off the cottage because I won't be using it until my brother in law and I come up in the fall, but I sure would like to have electrical service at the cabin when I get up there later today. So if you have me shut off for non payment, it's only because you haven't been sending me the bills, or you have got the address of the upper Whitefish Lake property mixed up with the lower Whitefish Lake property."

"I am sorry sir, if you have been inconvenienced in any way. As I said, we only have one service location on this billing, and that is the property on the Whitefish Lake Road. If you are supposed to be billed for some other property, you will have to fill out a new application."

"Well, I guess that's what I'll have to do. Where is your office located? I'll stop by there on my way, if I can."

The Ontario Hydro billing clerk gave Malloy the directions to their office. He thanked her and hung up. It was not a very useful clue to be informed that property on Whitefish Lake was located on Whitefish Lake Road. But it was a start. He followed the signs directing him to the International Bridge.

When he had crossed over the locks in the Saint Mary's River, Malloy tried Breitner's phone again. This time, a whining racket from his car phone assaulted his ear. That's when he discovered that there was no cellular service north of the Soo.

***

With so little to go on, it would be no easy task to find the cabin. Malloy began asking directions almost as soon as he spotted the massive statue of a bird on Queen's Highway 17 which reminds the modern, English speaking world that 'Wawa' is an Ojibway word meaning 'Wild Goose'.

The first several locals he asked-- the owner of the Wild

Goose Motel where Malloy took a room for the night, the diner waitress, the service station attendant, and the convenience store clerk-- didn't have a clue. They could verify that Whitefish Lake is up near Hawk Junction, but none had ever heard of Ed Breitner nor could they suggest how Malloy might go about finding him. The crowd of colorful townsfolk at Mary's in Hawk Junction had never heard of Ed Breitner either, but they told Malloy that Whitefish Lake Road was about ten miles east off Route 101. He found the road easily enough, but its winding course forked many times, and there were few cottage signs. None that read 'Breitner'. When he saw something that looked like a driveway running off in either direction, he followed it to the end. Sometimes the two car tracks would simply peter out in the middle of nowhere. Sometimes he ended up at a cottage or cabin. If he did, he got out of the car and tried to find out if it was Breitner's place or if the owner knew where Breitner's might be.

Most troublesome were the occasions when there was no one home. Then he would have to poke around hoping for some sign of his colleague. He felt very much like an intruder or trespasser as he knocked on cottage doors and peeked in cabin windows.

Some of the drives were blocked off with gates or ropes a few yards in. He decided not to pursue those, at least not until all the unblocked paths had proved wrong. At one of these sealed-off passages, he saw a bright blue jeep parked near a log cabin, in front of some kind of a storage shed.

Malloy began to think he was on a wild goose chase. Wild Goose. *Wawa. Wawa. Wawa.* He found himself tapping the steering wheel, singing an old college drinking song, the words to which had long since embedded themselves in the most inactive reaches of his memory. *Wawa, Wawa, Wawa. Where the hell is Breitner? Wawa Wawa Wawa. Where can his cabin be?*

One false trail meandered through the trees in a seemingly

aimless pattern, then, abruptly ended at a dilapidated gate, drooping from one hinge, on which was posted a faded sign: Northstar Gold Mine. No Trespassing. *Wawa. A wild goose chase*. Malloy, with great difficulty and much backing up and going forward, managed to turn his car around and retrace his unproductive detour.

He came upon a fork one prong of which was marked with an arrow pointing to Totomenai Lodge. He found the lodge, but no one there knew Breitner either. Discouraged, Malloy decided to return to town and try other ways to locate his quarry. Retracing his route, however, he noticed that the blue jeep was gone from where he had seen it before. And, the gate, previously closed, was open. He decided to chase one more goose.

The cabin could have been Abe Lincoln's. A rough hewn log structure, with a stone chimney, a door and window in front. It could have been Lincoln's except for two things. The electric line running into the cabin from a pole at the water's edge, and the aluminum shed standing about five feet to the right of the cabin. The shed was perhaps eight or ten feet wide, and stood just over six feet tall.

Malloy stopped his car, got out, and approached the cabin. On such a warm summer afternoon, the smells and sounds and sights of the place were intoxicating. If this was Ed's place, he could see why his colleague loved it here. And it gave him a different picture of the man. Hard to stay angry at someone who likes to be in a place like this. The warm fuzzy came and went. Malloy remembered why he had come all this way.

The door was locked. Nobody around. Peeking through the windows was no help. He could see nothing to help him identify the owner of the cabin. No clue that this was Breitner's place. Daunted, Malloy wandered around the cabin, then turned to the storage shed. It had no windows. Only two doors hinged to open like french doors. Mini garage doors, Malloy thought. A mini garage? He examined the ground in front of the shed. Sure enough, there were car tracks. He tried the doors. Locked. He tried to peeking between the doors, but the quarter inch clearance was not enough to permit a view of the dark interior.

Malloy went to his car trunk, got the spare tire jack and a flashlight. He forced the jack between the doors near the bottom, and pried. The aluminum bent and opened a crack about an inch wide. Malloy pointed his flash light through the crack and craned his neck around to see inside. He could see a parked car. More peeking, more craning. Then he saw it. The familiar Michigan license plate. MSG 004.

This was Ed Breitner's cabin. He had found it. But where was Breitner? His car was here. He couldn't be far. Malloy walked to the water's edge. A row boat was pulled onto the shore. No sign of beaching of another boat. No oil slick near the edge of the water. Would Ed be out walking someplace? Was he close by? Malloy returned to his car and leaned on the horn. The blast of alien noise offended the sacred sounds and silence of the forest. He honked some more. And then again. He waited. Then honked some more and waited some more. Nothing. No Breitner. No response.

Then it occurred to the C. J. that Breitner could possibly have driven someplace. Maybe someone had picked him up to go fishing or something. Or maybe, just maybe, Breitner had another car. That's it, Malloy thought. That's why he has this aluminum shed. To keep his other car in, when he was gone. Of course--the blue jeep. That must have been Ed. Malloy jumped back into his car, turned it around, drove back to the highway. There he stopped. Which way did the jeep turn? West toward Hawk Junction, or east toward Chapleau? Hawk Junction was closer. Malloy turned right and headed west.

A few miles east, highway 547 runs north from 101. It traverses some six thousand meters to the village of Hawk Junction. Then it stops. Its only function is to connect the 350 souls who call Hawk Junction their home to the outside world. Malloy canvassed every street in the town in less than five minutes. No blue jeep. He stopped at Mary's Place, the town gathering spot. The same crowd he had seen earlier was there. Sitting in the same chairs. He wondered if they had left and come back, or if they never leave. More inquiries. The men in this neck of the woods seem all to be between thirty five and forty five. The younger ones have long hair. They all wear caps.

There is a fellow who comes to town once in a while in a blue jeep, eh? That's right, I seen him. Me too. Always goes east off 547. Must be from Chapleau, eh?

Malloy accepted the verdict of the local jury. He drove the 120 kilometers to Chapleau, where he repeated the investigatory ritual he had gone through in Hawk Junction and Wawa. Gas stations, restaurants, bars, anywhere he might find people. Do you know Ed Breitner? Five eleven. Black hair. Greying at the temples. Brown eyes. Drives a blue jeep. At Myrtle's Cafe he spoke to the only person in the place, the owner. No she didn't know anyone named Ed Breitner. The only blue jeep she had ever seen belonged to Earl Boatman, her waitress's husband. Earl's hardly ever around. Some kind of sea captain, always sailing away to some place or other. The waitress had gone home, as there wasn't much dinner trade. "Pot roast is the special today. You ought to try some. You won't get a better meal in Chapleau," she bragged.

"Where does this fellow Boatman live?"

"Forest Street. Up the hill. Near the end of the second block. I don't know the number."

Malloy thanked her and left. Up the hill. Forest Street. Second block. There it is. The blue jeep. *Wawa Wawa Wawa. Where are you, Edward Breitner?* He got out of the car, walked up the steps to the front door, rang the bell and waited. And waited. C'mon, there must be someone home. The car is out front. Finally, it opened. The attractive young woman's feet were bare, her hair disheveled, and her attitude somewhat embarrassed. She was tying the cincture around her bathrobe. And she wasn't standing in a puddle, or dripping water any place.

"Excuse me, Ma'am. I'm awfully sorry to bother you. Is your...er...is your...ah, husband home?"

"He's not...available right now. What do you want?"

"I'm looking for a man named Ed Breitner. I thought your husband might know him or know where to find him."

"I don't know anyone by that name."

"I think I saw your husband's car at Mr. Breitner's cabin this afternoon, that's why I thought your husband might be able to help me."

"Earl goes all around fishing. He was fishing this afternoon. Maybe that's where you saw him."

"I'm sure. Anyway, let me give you my card. If your husband knows Mr. Breitner, ask him to have Breitner call me at The Wild Goose Motel in Wawa. The number is on the back of this card. I'll be there at least until noon tomorrow."

She took the card and looked at it.

"You are a judge?"

"Yes Ma'am. But don't hold that against me."

She smiled. "I'll give this to Earl. Maybe he knows your friend."

Malloy thanked her and left. He passed up the pot roast at Myrtle's in favor of a steak at Mulligan's Irish Cafe in Wawa. Later, from his room at the Wild Goose, he tried Breitner's cabin phone at midnight. No answer. He tried again at 2:00 AM. When the phone had rung nearly fifty times, a very angry gentleman answered.

"I don't know who the hell you're calling mister, but they're not home, God damn it. Now will you please hang up, eh? And let the rest of us on this party line get some sleep, eh?"

CHAPTER 15

AUGUST 1991

If the doorbell had rung six minutes earlier it would have occasioned *coitus interuptus*. As it was, the disruption had interfered with a tender connubial aftermath, a moment when Earl and his wife Valarie, united after another of his long seafaring absences, lay entangled, spent, at peace with the physical universe, and secure in the knowledge that three-year-old Billy was safely committed to the care of a neighbor who had five children of her own.

Returning to the bedroom, Valarie tossed aside her bathrobe and slid back into the king size bed beside her man.

"Who was there?" The man wanted to know.

"Some guy looking for a friend of his. I didn't know him."

"Why did he come to our house?"

"Says he saw a car like yours near his friend's cabin. He thought you might know him."

Boatman subconsciously gave way to Breitner. His pulse quickened.

"Who did he say he was looking for?"

"I don't know the name. It's written on the back of his card. I laid it on the dresser. Over there."

Breitner sat up, threw his legs over the side of the bed, stood and walked quickly to the dresser.

"What's the matter, Earl? Is something wrong?" She could sense the sudden change in him. The tension.

"It's nothing Val. Nothing. Just wanted to see if it might be somebody I know."

"Is it?'

"Nope. What was that guy at the door, some kind of a judge? His card says chief justice of Michigan."

"He said he was a judge."

"No kidding. What did he look like?"

Valarie described Malloy. Breitner knew his lair had been found. A cold chill ran down his spine. This was the moment he had feared and dreaded for so long, and pushed from his conscious mind so many times. He knew instantly that he had to put an end to his idyll. Now. Today.

He crawled back into bed and lay there staring at the ceiling. Grateful that he had the foresight to put the house and car in her name, Breitner mentally walked through the steps that would have to be taken. After a long silence, he leaned over and kissed Valarie softly, warmly, affectionately, sadly. His heart ached. His throat choked with painful emotion. A tear fell from his cheek to hers. She opened her eyes as their lips parted, and looked into his eyes with a forlorn, questioning, frightened face.

"I love you, Val." He said it. He meant it. More than he had ever meant those words in sixty years.

"I love you too, Earl." Val meant it, too. "I wish you could stay here with me always."

"So do I." Breitner meant that, too.

"I tell you what. You fix dinner. I'll go to Cramers and get Billy. We'll have a nice family evening, and I'll call the Shipping Line and see if I can stay an extra few days."

Valarie was thrilled at the idea. Earl had never tried to extend a homecoming before. Her euphoria was to be short lived. After dinner, Breitner, pretended to call the shipping line which was Captain Boatman's employer. When he hung up, he announced sadly that he had to be in the Soo by noon the next day to catch a freighter heading to Cleveland. He would have to leave early in the morning, and would be gone a very long time.

Breitner was up early on Thursday, August first. By the time he was dressed and ready to leave, Valarie was sitting in her favorite rocking chair, holding her son in her arms and crying softly. Her life had been a series of hard, disappointing, painful events. The hurt was back again. She could not make it go away. She could only let it flow over her in ever more gripping waves, until she was one complete open wound, fresh, bleeding, unattended.

Breitner stood at the door, looking at them. He wanted to hold them in his heart. He wanted to tell Valarie everything. He wanted to tell her nothing. He wanted to stay forever. He wanted to be instantly gone. He opened his mouth and tried to say, "Goodby sweetheart." His lips moved but there was no sound. He knew that he could never see her again. He knew that tonight, Earl Boatman would die. Again.

Breitner drove the jeep to a point about a mile east of his cabin where the shoulder of the road had been widened for some construction work. He pulled the jeep off the road, walked around to the right rear tire, stooped, loosened the valve, and drained the air until the jeep settled on the rim of the wheel. Then he walked briskly along the other side of the road to Whitefish Lake Road. Malloy, after all, was only minutes away in a motel. He might get a notion to come back looking for him. Might even be at the cabin waiting for him. He could not risk exposing the connection with Boatman's jeep any further.

There was no sign of Malloy at the cabin, although Breitner did notice the damage to the shed door. After locking up the cabin, Breitner opened the shed, and slipped behind the wheel of the Oldsmobile. He would never be Boatman again. From now on, he would be the justice. Former chief justice. Distinguished, honored, celebrated jurist. He pointed the Olds west toward Wawa. In a few hours he would be back in the United States. For keeps.

At the Soo, when his cellular phone was again in range, he called Valarie, told her that the jeep had a flat tire, that the keys were under the front seat, that she should go and get it, have the tire fixed and keep the car until he returned. He told her that he had hitch hiked to the Soo. Then he said goodby one more time. Somehow, Valarie knew there would be no next time.

***

Malloy waited at the motel most of Thursday. No call came from Breitner. Mid-afternoon, he tried his message service again. Breitner's voice was recorded. "I got your message, Jim. Sorry I missed you at the cabin. I was fishing just a few yards down the shore all day. Now I'm heading back to Lansing. Maybe we can meet in your office early next week. I agree that we have much to talk about."

Malloy slammed the phone into its cradle. What a waste of time. What a wild goose chase. He told himself that he should have left a note for Breitner at the cabin, telling him to call the motel. Obviously that fellow Boatman was a false lead. Or maybe his wife didn't even give Boatman the message. She looked a little spacey.

Disgusted, the C.J. packed up, checked out of the motel, and started for home. *Wawa. Wawa. Wawa. Wild goose chase. Wild goose chase. Wawa. Wawa. Wawa.* He couldn't get the stupid tune out of his mind.

Returning to Michigan at Sault Saint Marie, Malloy called his home and spoke to Margaret for the third time that day. They had brought the twins home just two weeks before. They were doing well for premature infants, but it was still dicey business. Fortunately, Alice Newton, their close neighbor and faithful baby sitter, had fallen instantly in love with Teddy and Terri, and she was at their house almost constantly. A big help. Of course, Margaret couldn't attend the Mackinac Conference as so many of the Judges' wives did. In truth, she didn't want to. Not this year.

Satisfied that all was well on the home front, Malloy decided to take a brief detour to Munising and visit O'Leary. He found the senior Celtic jurist lounging on his front porch, gin and tonic in hand, enjoying the view across the road where mighty Lake Superior splashed against the craggy shore.

"Well look who's here! Did you come for a swim? Too late.

Summer was on a Tuesday this year. Tuesday last week."
"I'm no polar bear, Bob. And my radiator won't hold enough
antifreeze to get to the first sand bar. How are you doing?"
"Do I look overworked? I am you know. The damn chief
justice who runs our court has me writing so many opinions..."
"How...many...opinions...do...you...have...to...write?" Malloy
recognized the old comedic routine.
"I have to write so many opinions that my fountain pen has
carpel tunnel syndrome."
"Rim shot, " Malloy responded, rapping his index fingers on
the porch railing like a night club drummer punctuating a stand
up comedian's one liner.
Shortly Malloy was also sipping gin and tonic, and the two
friends were intensely analyzing Ed Breitner's memo, his
motives, and his methods. They talked about the possible line up
of justices if Breitner pushed his idea to a vote. Assuming a
party line split, there would be four votes to refer to the Judicial
Tenure Commission, and two votes against. Malloy, since he
was the subject at issue, could not vote on the motion. Since
Alton Henry was a staunch supporter of Malloy, they agreed
that he would vote against Breitner's motion.
But Van was the wild card on this one. Malloy had seen him
talking to Doris and Hilda in the lobby of the Grand. He might
think that removing Malloy as chief would put him back in the
running. O'Leary asked Malloy if the governor would step in
and push Van to support Jim.
"I'm not so sure. The Firp is all over me. I suspect that I am
a political liability at this point, and there's no reason for
Edwards to expend political capital on me. No, I think he'll stay
out of it, at least publicly."
"And privately?"
"I don't know. It doesn't hurt to ask. Maybe he will at least
let one of his minions drop a hint to Van."
They pondered and speculated over a barbequed steak and
baked potatoes. His host downed several bottles of beer with

the meal, but then O'Leary wasn't driving. Jim had only one. He left near sundown, and was growing sleepy by the time he crossed over the bridge to Mackinaw City. He called Margaret, told her he would not make it home that night, pushed on, intending to stop at a motel at Gaylord.

Malloy was thoroughly confused and frustrated. Why hadn't Breitner answered his phone at the cabin? If he wasn't there, where was he? Was it possible that he changed his mind and didn't go to the cabin? Had he gone somewhere else? Is it possible that Breitner is traveling somewhere at this very moment? Malloy picked up the car phone and dialed Breitner's car phone number.

"Hello."

"Ed? Is that you?"

"Yeah. Who is this?"

"Malloy. Where the hell are you?"

"Indian River. Just coming back from my cabin. Sorry I missed you there."

"Yeah. I'll bet you are. Listen, Ed, we've got to talk. Where are you staying tonight?"

"I've got a room at the Indian River Motel. I just went out to get something to eat, and I'm on my way back there now."

Malloy's tone of voice was firm and demanding as he said, "Stay there. I just got over the bridge, and I'll be at Indian River in twenty minutes. I want to talk to you."

"I'm in room seven. I'll be waiting."

Malloy leaned on the gas pedal. He had been rehearsing speeches to Breitner for two days. Now he was ready to deliver. At the motel, Malloy's car skidded to a stop next to Breitner's, and the chief justice knocked heavily on the door to number seven. As Breitner dropped the chain lock and opened the door, Malloy charged into the room past Breitner, then swung around and demanded, "What they hell do you think you are doing?"

"What do you mean, what am I doing?"

"You know damn well what I mean. Your sneaky memo to

the court about me. Who do you think you are, pulling a stunt like that?"

"It's no stunt. I just did what I think is best for the court. Somebody has to think about the reputation of the supreme court. You sure as hell don't."

"Don't give me that. You never worried about tabloid press stories when you were chief. They don't mean a thing and you know it."

"I don't know any such thing. I know that you got a couple hundred thousand dollars from some suspicious lottery scheme, and you haven't any explanation for it. I know that you have been playing footsie with those right wing crazies who set off bombs all over the place. We never had this kind of trouble before you came on the court."

"You can't be serious. Do you really think that I am connected in some way to the Army of Righteousness?"

"Aren't you?"

"Of course not. What on earth would give you such a paranoic idea?"

Breitner reached into his pocket and pulled out a folded piece of paper. He handed it to Malloy. "What am I supposed to think when I get stuff like this?"

Malloy took the paper, unfolded it to its full letter size, and read aloud, "YOUR SILUS OPINION STINKS, BREITNER. GET ON THE BANDWAGON WITH MALLOY OR SUFFER THE CONSEQUENCES."

"Where did you get this?"

"I found it stuck under my windshield wiper last week when I came out of the office. Let me show you what else I found at the same time."

Breitner got up and walked to the door. Malloy followed. Outside, Breitner pointed to the hood of his car. The letters AOR, about five inches high, were scratched into the enameled surface. The two men stood looking at the vandalism in silence, then returned to the motel room and sat down.

"Look, Ed," Malloy began. "I don't blame you for being upset by what those sick people have been doing. But you are taking the wrong track here. This is something we all have to face and fight together. You certainly don't think I had anything to do with that note or the damage to your car, do you?"

"What am I supposed to think? Whoever is doing this is obviously a friend of yours."

"The hell he is. No real friend of mine would do a thing like that. The only person I know who has anything to do with the Army of Righteousness is Wallace Wright. And as far as I know, he is a harmless zealot who likes to get his name in the paper. I've never known him to do anything rash or criminal. He was an elected public official for nearly twenty years, for God sake. How crazy could he be?"

"I don't know Wright, and I don't know who he hangs around with. But he is obviously not the only one doing these things."

"I agree with that. But the right thing to do is to get the state police involved. Let's find out who sent you that note, if we can. Let's take some security measures so this won't happen again, or so we can catch whoever is doing it. But for God's sake, let's be together as a court, not wrangling among ourselves or accusing each other of complicity."

"You want me to trust you? You, who went behind my back, conspiring with that old Neanderthal Alton Henry to take the chief justiceship away from me? You, who twisted the arms of your Republican cronies to take over the court on the very first day you arrived. You want me to think of you as a friend? Someone I can trust? Get serious."

"You just can't get over it can you? What ever gave you the idea that you have a divine right to be the chief justice of the supreme court? How long do you have to be in politics to learn how the system works? You'll have another crack at it in 1993 and every two years after that."

"I don't have to wait until 1993. I think I can muster the votes to kick your ass out of the center chair right now. How do you like that for politics?"

"Hey, I didn't say you're not entitled to try. Go ahead and challenge me if you want to. Only for God's sake don't pretend you're doing it for the good of the court. You're splitting the court down the middle, distracting us from the cases we are supposed to be deciding, stirring up emotions and conflicts that should be left on the back burner until the next regular election of the chief."

"Nobody knows what's going to happen between now and 1993. The court can't wait that long, and neither can I."

Malloy stood, walked to the door, opened it, and turned slowly, deliberately toward his adversary. "You go ahead and do whatever you want, Breitner. But let me tell you this, as long as I am chief justice, nobody is going to threaten a member of the court or damage one of our vehicles and get away with it. I intend to call the state police, even if you won't. If you think you are going to parlay this AOR nonsense into another term as chief justice, you've got another think coming, mister."

"Fuck you, Malloy," Breitner snarled as Malloy slammed the door shut. Malloy stopped with his back to the door. The manager of the motel and a prospective guest were walking past on their way to inspect a room. Inside, Breitner was shouting at the top of his lungs. "FUCK YOU. YOU SELF RIGHTEOUS SON OF A BITCH. YOU CAN JUST GO FUCK YOURSELF. DO YOU HEAR ME? GO FUCK YOURSELF."

Malloy smiled at the passers-by, jerking his head back toward room seven. "Class act there, wouldn't you say?"

The two men laughed, uneasily.

***

Friday, August 2nd dawned somewhat overcast. Malloy started slowly, being in somewhat of a disheartened mood. He really didn't have a plan to ward off the Breitner offense, except to try to dissuade him. And, after last night's confrontation, he wasn't very optimistic about that. Even if a majority of the court did not vote to refer him to the Tenure Commission, any public disclosure that some of his colleagues thought he was guilty of improprieties would be devastating. The newspapers, particularly the First Press, would have a field day.

Driving south on Interstate 75, Malloy's introspection was jolted by the sight of three state police cars racing north, flashers in full spin, sirens wailing. Must be some big accident behind me, Jim thought. Moments later, two more state police cars roared by in the north bound lanes. Malloy flipped on his radio. Maybe he could pick up a local station with some information about the accident.

The only station he could get was carrying a network talk show. Some inane drivel about rap music. A controversy of no interest to him. Then, it came on.

"This is Charles Folio in the newsroom at WINR. We interrupt this regularly scheduled broadcast to bring you a special report. At 6 o'clock this morning, the body of an unidentified, white male approximately sixty years of age was found, riddled with bullets, in the parking lot of Cross in the Woods Shrine in Indian River. Just moments ago, WINR learned that the victim was Edward Breitner, a Justice of the Michigan Supreme Court. Reporter Al Nolan is at the scene now, and we have him on the line. Al, what is happening in out there at this time?"

Jim Malloy's heart was in his throat. Pounding. Choking him. He felt nauseous. He pulled the car to the side of the road and turned up the volume of his radio.

"Well Charlie, quite a crowd has gathered here at the parking lot. There are at least a half dozen state police cars, as well as the sheriff. Several TV stations have sent their mobile equipment in here, and there are reporters and photographers by the dozens, as well as a lot of curious citizens. We were able to get through and talk with Sergeant Tom Norton of the state police, and he informed us that their check on the license number of the blue Oldsmobile revealed that it is a state owned vehicle issued to Justice Edward Breitner of the Michigan Supreme Court. In addition to that, a number of people, police and newspaper reporters, who have been able to get close enough to see the body, have told me that they recognized Breitner."

"What was he wearing, Al?"

"He is dressed casually, Charlie, as you might expect in this area at this time of year. A golf shirt and slacks. The rumor here is that the justice has a cabin up in Canada, and presumably was either coming from or going to his cabin."

"Has anyone been arrested yet?"

"No, and we haven't heard any suspects mentioned so far. Just moments ago, a 38 caliber pistol was found in the tall weeds just a few feet from Breitner's car. Police are proceeding on the theory that it is the murder weapon. So far, there's no report of fingerprints or anything like that."

"So they have no clue as to who might have been responsible, is that right?"

"Not exactly. There are a couple of suspicious things the police have been talking about. I'm told that the justice had some sort of paper, a letter or something, in his possession which might give a clue. Also, the letters AOR were found scratched on the hood of his car, apparently by a key, or similar sharp object."

"AOR? Do they know what those letters mean?"

"One of the reporters here told me that AOR stands for Army of Righteousness. It's a militant right wing group, mostly known for anti-abortion activity."

"Why would they target Breitner?"

"I'm told he was a very outspoken supporter of pro choice legal decisions. One theory is that the AOR has been terrorizing judges in order to get the abortion laws changed. That's strictly speculation by the press though, Charlie. I haven't heard anything like that from the police or the sheriff."

"Is anything else happening at this time?"

"An ambulance just arrived. It looks like they will be taking the body away very soon."

"Thanks, Al. Keep us posted on any new developments, will you?"

"Will do."

"That was Al Nolan, reporting from the parking lot of the Cross in the Woods shrine in Indian River, Michigan. That beloved religious symbol will perhaps never be the same again after the gruesome events which occurred there last night, or early this morning.

"At 6:15 this morning, a caretaker of the shrine discovered the brutally murdered body of Michigan Supreme Court Justice Edward J. Breitner riddled with bullets and slumped in the back seat of his state issued 1991 Oldsmobile. The car was parked in the paved parking lot where hundreds of visitors stop each day, and leave their cars to walk into the forest to see and venerate the largest crucifix in the world.

"As you heard just moments ago from our reporter on the scene, police are saying they have no clues as to who might have been responsible for this horrible crime, except that the letters A-O-R were scratched on the hood of Breitner's vehicle. We are being told that A-O-R stands for Army of Righteousness. That would be the same anti-abortion terrorist group responsible for a number of abortion clinic fireworks bombings over the last year.

"If the AOR is responsible, it would be ironic indeed that Justice Breitner was martyred by an organization claiming to be dedicated to righteousness, and that the terrible deed was done within a few hundred yards of the great symbol of Christianity, the cross upon which Jesus Christ was similarly martyred almost two thousand years ago. This is Charles Folio in the newsroom of WINR, Indian River, Michigan. We return you now to our regularly scheduled network programming."

Malloy was stunned, didn't know what to do, who to call,

where to go. Finally, he got on the phone and called the Michigan state police post at Gaylord.

"This is Chief Justice Malloy. I'm in my car, about twenty miles south of Gaylord. Do you need me to go to Indian River?"

"No, Mr. Chief Justice. The body has already been removed and is being taken to Detroit by a local ambulance company. We're giving it an escort."

"What about the other members of the court? They could be in danger. Is anything being done to increase security?"

"I don't know, your Honor. That would all come out of the Lansing office. You should check with them."

Malloy hung up. Then he dialed state police headquarters. He asked to be put straight through to Colonel Rosewall, the head of the department.

"Colonel? Jim Malloy here. I just heard about Breitner on the radio. I'm in my car, about twenty minutes south of Gaylord. I can't believe what has happened. I just saw Ed last night in his motel room at Indian River. He showed me a note that was left under his windshield and some scratching on the hood of his car. I told him we should contact the state police and get some sort of an investigation going. I want you to know that the court is very anxious to get to the bottom of this. We will assist your people in every way that we possibly can."

"I appreciate that, Mr. Chief Justice. We intend to make a very thorough investigation, rest assured."

"In the meantime, Colonel, shouldn't we provide some greater protection for the members of the court?"

"As I see it, Judge, this is an act of political terrorism. Justice Breitner, so I'm told, was the leader of the liberal wing on the court. He was apparently murdered by some right wing crazies. I don't think all of the members of the court are likely targets for those people."

"I'm not really comfortable with that, Colonel. I think every member of the court should have all the protection they may think necessary. The state police shouldn't be making political judgments about who needs protection."

"I understand your position. We'll do whatever you ask."

"Well, you can start by contacting each Justice and asking them what, if anything, they want you to do for them."

"O.K. I'll start with you, sir. What do you require?"

"You can send a car around to my house, and keep an eye on it until I get home. My wife will be frantic when she hears what happened to Ed."

"It's done. Do you need anybody yourself?"

"Not now. I'm a moving target at the moment."

***

For the second time in less than a year, the supreme court of Michigan was in mourning. To say that the Breitner murder was received with shock and dismay by the justices and other court personnel would be a gross understatement. Everyone was devastated. Their grief was palpable. But there was an aspect of the killing which made it even more painful than the unexpected passing of a valued colleague. The political overtones of the homicide pervaded the halls of the Law Building and tinged every hushed conversation among insiders. Breitner's seat would be filled by a Republican governor. Pro-life forces would clearly have the upper hand, with five out of seven justices holding strong conservative views. The Army of Righteousness had effectively changed the court by the heinous crime. Doris Templeton, in particular, dropped drippingly sarcastic observations which suggested that she did not believe the chief justice and some of his followers were all that broken up about Breitner's death. While she didn't come right out and accuse Malloy of complicity in the murder, she never missed the chance to remind her colleagues of their decision in *People v Wright*.

Ed Breitner's funeral was a production worthy of an Oliver Stone. The governor, lieutenant governor, attorney general, secretary of state, the chief justice and associate justices of the supreme court, the entire court of appeals bench, a United States senator, four congressmen, the mayor of Detroit, a caucus of legislators from the Capitol, and quorums of county commissioners, city councilmen, and township trustees.

Saint Mark's Episcopal Church on Quarton Road in Bloomfield had never seen such an array of public officials, police cars, television cameras, newspaper reporters, lawyers, judges, law professors, politicians, educators, civic and religious leaders, community volunteers, automotive big wigs, banking, insurance and shipping magnets, media groupies, and just plain friends and family.

Elizabeth, felled by grief on Friday, stood tall in dignified mourning by Tuesday when the casket was convoyed in solemn procession from the funeral home to the church. She entered the vestibule behind the coffin, embracing her son and daughter, supporting them as much as they were supporting her. They walked slowly down the long cathedral vaulted aisle, heads up, gazes fixed straight ahead, gait steady and perfectly balanced. The nave was packed, every pew bulging at its ends with the unaccommodated arms and legs of the last mourner or spectator crammed into it. The mood was austere, grave, full of pomp and saturated with significance.

On the altar, enrobed in their most ceremonial garb, watching the Breitner family move proudly and painfully toward them, stood the Episcopal Bishop of Michigan, the Archbishop of the Roman Catholic Archdiocese of Detroit, and the Dean of the Metropolitan Rabbinical Council. Over the next forty seven minutes, the three clergymen inveighed the blessing of the Deity upon the soul of Justice Breitner. Their prayers were generously sprinkled with references to the deceased's life work, his community service, his scholarship, leadership, fellowship, and firm, sure guidance of the judicial ship of state. At the conclusion of the religious ceremony, the presiding Episcopal Bishop requested that the congregation remain seated for some commemorative remarks by one of Justice Breitner's closest associates on the Michigan Supreme Court, the Honorable Doris Cummings Templeton.

Doris rose from a front pew, and, eschewing the raised pulpit, walked to the reader's lectern. She carried a ring binder which she opened when she reached the microphone. She began by addressing the grief stricken family in front of her.

"Elizabeth, John, Clara, all of us...everyone here in this church today...want you to know how deeply we feel and appreciate the pain you must be feeling. You have our condolences and our sympathy, love and affection. I say that without exaggeration." Templeton was speaking softly, gently. Now her voice became almost a whisper, as though every word had to be dredged up from the very bottom of her heart. "Every person in this church loves each of you because, John and Clara, all of us loved your father. And Elizabeth, I'm sure you know that we loved your husband."

She inhaled deeply and spoke with more force. "Edward Breitner was a man who commanded respect, and who earned the love and affection of every one he worked with throughout his life. The man was a leader, truly a leader, in every sense of the word. People wanted to go where he was going. People wanted to be with him. To be part of his plans, part of his team. He had the courage to be out in front, to speak up when others shied away. He could be tough if he had to be, but he was always civil, always thoughtful of other people, sensitive to their feelings, concerned for their welfare. He had the best global view of society and the legal system of anyone I ever knew. In his mind, the various traditions and trends in the development of the common law occupied just the right space, received just the proper deference and emphasis. He knew when to hold fast to the old, when to embrace the new."

Throughout the church, men and women were nodding their heads in agreement. Breitner's reputation permeated the room as the common bond that conjoined the eulogist and all the mourners. "Ed Breitner was, throughout his life, an inspiration to me, personally," Templeton acknowledged with pride, "and to many, many others like me. His death was tragic and senseless."

Templeton seemed to grit her teeth. Suddenly, her voice became hard, her manner intense, almost bellicose. "Every decent citizen of this country is repelled, sickened, by the ugly, vicious, criminal act which ended this brilliant jurist's career before his time had come. No one can or will defend the twisted mentality which conceived of the idea of killing Ed Breitner as a way to advance their own political agenda. In his lifetime, Ed Breitner was a champion of liberty. He stood tall against those who would put this nation under the boot of despotic leaders bent on forcing their outmoded ideas of morality on the vast majority of Americans who do not subscribe to their beliefs. Now he has given the last full measure of devotion to that same cause. Ed Breitner lived for the cause of liberty and he died for the cause of liberty."

Templeton looked directly at her colleagues who were seated just a few rows from the front. She made eye contact first with Alton Henry, then with Jim Malloy. Her words now came venomously. "Those enemies of freedom who have perpetrated this outrage on all of us, who tore Ed Breitner from the loving arms of his family and the fond association of his friends and co-workers, will learn that even in death he is far more powerful than their puny schemes and pitiable crimes. For they have assured by their sacrilege that the name of Edward J. Breitner will live forever in the annals of human liberty; that his spirit and his dedication will ennoble the hearts of generations to come, so that as long as men and women shall inhabit these beautiful Michigan peninsulas, the dastardly cowards who opposed him in life and hastened his passing will never inherit the land he loved and gave his life to protect and defend."

So saying, Justice Templeton closed her notebook, nodded to the clergy, and returned to her seat. She was among the first to follow the family and the casket out of the church, but she did not go to the cemetery. Instead, she drove inconspicuously out of the parking lot and turned south toward the interstate. Within minutes, she was on her way to Chicago.

***

Born last Friday, he had just come home today, Tuesday, August 6, 1991. Eight pounds three ounces. Twenty inches long. Black eyes that would mellow eventually into deep brown. Scraggly black hair that someday would be brown, too. A loud, insistent, irrepressible cry. And of course, he had the undivided attention of the four cooing adults who surrounded him and vied for his attention and the chance to hold or cuddle him, coax a burp from his little round belly or just touch the magicly velvet new skin on his face, arms or feet.

Three generations of forbears peered down at him: his great grandfather, Arthur Cummings Templeton, his grandmother, the Honorable Doris Cummings Templeton, his mother, Cheryl Templeton, and Roger Foresberg, a friend of the family for whom the child bore a remarkable resemblance.

"All right, Cheryl, you win, he is adorable," the Justice conceded. "Now for the sixty-four dollar question, what will you name him?"

"I've given it a lot of thought, Mom. Gramps and Roger and I talked about it all day yesterday. We think it should be Edward Breitner Templeton. What do you think?"

Doris glanced quickly at Roger and then at her father. Both were smiling. She placed her hand on Cheryl's shoulder, nodded affirmatively, then, without a word, left the room.

CHAPTER 16

SEPTEMBER 1991

The Breitner murder was a continuously breaking story in all the media through the summer and into autumn. On Tuesday, September 3rd, the court convened to hear its September docket. The empty chair shouted down all attempts at conversation in the conference room. The justices were distracted and curt with counsel during oral argument. At day's end, they didn't much want to be together and adjourned early without real discussion or tentative decisions on any of the cases on the call.

The Detroit Evening Paper carried a scurrilous article which hit the streets about one o'clock in the afternoon, claiming that, only a few days before he died, the late Justice Breitner was rumored to have filed a petition with his colleagues on the court to censure Chief Justice Malloy for actively supporting the Army of Righteousness. The rumor mill was further quoted as saying that Malloy was livid with anger over the charges, and had left the judicial conference at Mackinac Island early for the purpose of finding Breitner and confronting him over the issue. One source, who refused to be quoted or identified for fear of reprisals, said that the chief justice had appeared angry enough to kill somebody when he left the island.

Malloy's telephone rang incessantly that afternoon. By the time he reached his office at 3:45 PM, no fewer than 18 news sources had requested interviews. Television stations, newspapers, wire services, radio networks. They all wanted a piece of the chief. Malloy walked down the hall to talk to O'Leary. Evelyn told him that O'Leary had left. He had a headache and needed to take something for it.

"Scotch?" asked Malloy, annoyed.

"He has a lot on his mind, Mr. Chief Justice. You don't

understand."

"I understand, all right. I understand that if he doesn't ease off on the booze, he's going to have some very serious problems. Right now, I've got too many problems of my own to fret about Bob. I'd hoped to get some help from him, not the other way around. Tell him I was looking for him will you?"

"Yes, sir."

On the way back to his office, Malloy heard Hilda talking to her secretary. The Detroit based Justices had offices in the Law Building, sparsely furnished, and used mostly as temporary bases of operations during the week of oral arguments. Hilda was just gathering up her papers for the long commute.

"Hilda, do you have a minute? I'd like to talk to you if you do."

"I can spare a little time, but not much. I'm due to take Melissa to her piano recital at six o'clock."

"Just a couple minutes would help."

They stepped into Hilda's office and closed the door.

"Did you see the article in the Evening Paper this afternoon?"

"No Jim, I haven't seen a paper all week."

He handed her a clipping which he had in his shirt pocket.

"Wow. Tough stuff. Where do you suppose they got this?"

"I don't know, Hilda, I just can't imagine." Malloy shook his head. "Every newspaper in the state is looking for me. What am I supposed to do, call a press conference and deny that I killed Ed Breitner?"

"And confirm that you stopped beating your wife."

"Exactly. It's a no-win situation. If I refuse to comment, it looks like I'm hiding something. If I answer questions, they can crucify me with innuendo. Catch 22. The old rock and hard place syndrome."

"What does your gut tell you, Jim?"

"It says call all the bastards together and give them hell."

"Answer all of their questions?"

"Yes."

"Truthfully?"
"Of course."
"Can you?"
"Absolutely, Hilda. I've done nothing wrong. I've got nothing to be ashamed of, nothing to hide."
"Including the lottery thing?"
"Including the lottery thing."
"Then go do it, Mr. Nutcracker, and good luck to you."

***

Mike Delbert, the court clerk arranged the press conference in the lobby outside the supreme court chamber. By 5:15 PM, the appointed hour, a hastily assembled podium was laden with a dozen microphones, drenched in klieg lights, and surrounded by folding chairs groaning under tons of sweating, cursing, expectant reporters. Right at five fifteen, Chief Justice Malloy entered the foyer from a side door and strode to the lectern. His face was somber, his demeanor serious.

"Ladies and gentlemen, I thank all of you for cooperating in this press conference. I know it's late for many of your deadlines, and that some of you tried to see me earlier, but I felt it was only fair to talk to everyone at once. That's why we've handled your requests in this fashion. I hope no one is too greatly inconvenienced. Now I think I have a pretty good idea of what you want to talk to me about today, but I don't have any kind of a prepared statement or speech to make. I am simply making myself available to answer any questions you may wish to put. To make it as fair as possible, and give everyone a chance, I have asked Mr. Delbert to take the names of those who wish to speak. He will call out the next questioner in order as he receives the names. I'll answer one or two follow up questions, but I can't let any one person monopolize the time we have here. Do we have a questioner?"

The clerk had been working the crowd for fifteen minutes. He had a stack of three by five cards in his hand. "Avery Townsend, Associated Press."

"Mr. Chief Justice, where were you on the night of August first, and the early morning of August second, when Breitner was shot?"

"I was on my way home from Justice O'Leary's house in Munising. I stopped to see him after going up to Canada to talk to Justice Breitner. I was not able to contact Justice Breitner in Canada, but after I got across the bridge, I called him on his car phone, and we arranged to meet in his motel at Indian River. That was about ten o'clock at night. After our meeting, I drove to Gaylord and stayed at a motel there until the following morning."

"Were you in your room all night?"

"Yes."

"Can you prove that?"

"What do you mean, can I prove that?"

"Can you prove that you didn't leave you motel room later that night when Breitner was killed?"

"I can state categorically that I didn't leave my room that night."

"All we have is your word on that, is that correct?"

"I think I have answered your question. Let's pull another name, please."

"Mary Zyngol, Flint Bugle."

"Justice Malloy, is it true that Justice Breitner was trying to get you removed as chief justice before he was killed?"

"He wrote a memorandum to the other members of the court. I was not given a copy. That's what I went up to Canada to talk to him about. I have since obtained a copy of the memorandum, which I will make available to all of you. Mike, you can distribute those copies of the memo now."

There was a great stir in the room, as Breitner's memo was hastily circulated. Zyngol, speed reading the memo, continued her questioning. "This memo seems to confirm the rumor that

Breitner was trying to oust you from the chief justiceship, if not from the court. That made you pretty angry didn't it?"

"It certainly did."

"Angry enough to kill Breitner?"

"Of course not. That's an impertinent question. But I'll say this: I was angry enough to drive up to Canada to talk to him face to face. When I finally caught up with him at Indian River, I told him in no uncertain terms that I did not appreciate what he had done, and that I thought it was quite improper."

"What exactly did you say?"

"I can't give it to you verbatim. Let's just say we had words."

"Did you come to blows?"

"No."

"Shouting?"

"He did. I didn't."

What action has the court taken on this memo?"

"None. It has never been discussed by the court."

"None of the Justices have ever talked about it?"

"I didn't say that. The court has never discussed it in a meeting at which it was an agenda item for discussion."

A new questioner was selected. Aaron Feller from the First Press.

"Justice Malloy, you have a lot of friends in the Army of Righteousness. Don't you?"

"I wouldn't know. I don't ask people about things like that."

"Would it surprise you to learn that at the Malloy family reunion at Kensington Park last July there were at least five cars in the parking lot which had Army of Righteousness decals in their windows?"

"It would surprise me to learn that the First Press has nothing better to do than spy on family picnics, but as far as decals are concerned, my sisters and my brothers in law are particularly active in the pro life movement. They go to Washington D.C. every year in January to march in protest of *Roe v Wade*. I understand that those decals have been liberally distributed during those demonstrations. I do not understand that there is any organizational significance to them. It's just a general expression of good prevailing over evil."

"I don't hear you making any public statements condemning the terrorist acts that the AOR has been responsible for. Do you condone them?"

"I don't condone terrorism in any form by anybody. And I certainly condemn the actions of the person or persons responsible for the death of Justice Breitner. But I do not accuse decent law abiding citizens of criminal actions just because they have a political decal on the windshield of their car."

The Lansing paper was next.

"We are hearing people say that the lottery ticket you won money on was purchased from some money laundering broker by some wealthy conservative business interests associated with the Army of Righteousness, is that true?"

"That, sir, is vicious nonsense, and if you had any integrity as a newspaperman you would not even think of asking such an irresponsible, libelous question."

Station WOKJ Grand Rapids. "Mr. Chief Justice, have you ever been able to find out who used your name to get the Guatemalan flag hoisted for that fireworks display here in the Law Building Plaza?"

"No I haven't. We have worked closely with the State Police on that matter, and so far as I know, they've been unable to identify the source of that request, or locate the persons responsible for the bombing. The box that held the rockets, as you may know, was of a fairly common type. The fireworks appear to have been of a kind commercially available from many sources. There were no fingerprints or other identifying marks on the box. I've asked the investigating officers to keep me informed, as I highly resent having my name and my office used by anyone for such an improper, illegal purpose."

WSNT Ann Arbor.

"You have never revealed where you got the lottery ticket, have you?"

"No, I haven't. I assure you it was all open above board and legal."

"Did you buy the ticket yourself?"

"A friend of mine bought it when he went to Florida. He bought tickets for several of us, and brought them back when he returned."

"So it's possible that your friend could have bought the ticket from a broker, right?"

"I don't know why he would do that. But I suppose it is theoretically possible."

"Can you tell us who the friend was?"

Malloy paused. *Think it through, Jim. Think it through.*

"I'm not going to reveal the name of the person who bought that ticket for me. Not now. Not yet, at least When I heard about the allegations of money laundering in connection with lottery tickets in Chicago and elsewhere, I made an investigation of my own to determine if such things were really being done. When I realized that the things being claimed on TV and in the newspapers were at least possible, I called the Federal Bureau of Investigation, and informed them of my personal experience. They're checking to see if there was anything improper about the ticket I cashed in, and they've promised to keep me informed. If it appears that a crime has been committed, or any illegal or improper thing done or attempted, I assure you I'll see that the persons responsible are brought to justice. And I also can tell you categorically, that I will not profit by any improper or unethical scheme."

"Are you saying that you'll rat on your friend who bought the ticket?"

"I've already given his name to the FBI. I have no intention of taking dirty money, even after it has been through the laundry. Anybody who thinks I would is no friend of mine."

The lead on the evening news on almost every channel was

that Chief Justice Malloy called in the FBI to investigate his own lottery winnings. The Detroit Evening Paper led with the headline "I WON'T TAKE DIRTY MONEY SAYS C.J."
   The First Press story was titled "MALLOY LACKS ALIBI IN BREITNER SHOOTING."

***

The governor's people were in a quandary. Chief Justice Malloy was generating so much negative publicity that the fall out was beginning to stink up the executive office. Mark Edwards had been elected on a socially conservative platform, with strong support from the right-to-life crowd. That was all well and good. Identification with main stream pro-life activists was a definite political plus. But his advisors desperately wanted to keep him away from any taint of association with right wing extremists, most particularly the Army of Righteousness. Now he was obligated to fill a vacancy on the Michigan Supreme Court. It was his first opportunity to do so. It was the most important appointment he had yet made in the executive office. The circumstances which gave rise to the appointment, however, would surely color the way in which his appointee would be viewed. If, indeed, he were to take advantage of the Breitner murder to stack the court with fellow pro-lifers, the papers might well begin to insinuate that the governor himself was privy to the execution-type homicide.
   The executive staff cast about for someone who would diffuse the highly explosive situation. One of the staffers mentioned Julia Hudson. At first the idea was dismissed. Hudson, after all, was a federal judge, having been appointed to the United States District Court for the Eastern District of Michigan, Northern Division, only three years before. Federal judges serve for the duration of their good behavior. Which means, for all practical purposes, they are appointed for life. If they retire, which they may do after age 65, they continue to receive their salary for the

rest of their lives. Most, however, choose not to retire, but to take what is known as 'senior status,' which entitles them to continue sitting on the bench, but with a substantially reduced, convenient workload. Senior judges, unlike retired ones, participate in all salary increases granted to the active judiciary.

The idea that a federal judge would leave a secure, lifetime position in favor of an elective office seemed at first, totally improbable. Still there had been some notable exceptions in Michigan history. And Judge Hudson's appointment to the high court would certainly be well received by the press. Although she had never taken a public position on the critical life issues, abortion and euthanasia, she was generally regarded as being middle of the road on both. Some preliminary phone calls established that she would not be opposed by the MEA or any of the other groups which habitually stalked the governor. The big question was, would she take it?

***

On Saturday, September 7, 1991, to celebrate Julia's forty-third birthday, Tom Hudson took his wife out to dinner. To their very favorite restaurant, indeed Detroit's favorite restaurant, Joe Muer's on Gratiot Avenue. The third generation seafood eatery was always an experience, especially for someone like Judge Julia Hudson. Everybody who was anybody was at Muer's. Always. Lunch, dinner, it didn't matter. Sometimes both. In fact, many a legendary lunch had run into dinner, as Detroit's movers and shakers drew diagrams on the tablecloths and did deals eye ball to eye ball over clams, oysters, black bread and bean salad.

The drive from Flint, just a little over an hour, was well worth it. After all, where else could you go and find yourself instantly in the middle of a party attended by so many of your friends? Julia swept into the lounge, a few steps ahead of Tom, nodding, waving, shaking hands, hugging and bantering with many of the patrons. The Michigan bar standing two deep at Muer's bar.

It was a perfect dinner date. Tom gave Julia a diamond pendant. She was thrilled. Not so much with the pendant as with the fact that he had remembered to buy a gift. The man was generous to a fault, but he was also annoyingly forgetful.

Julia and Tom had met in Washington, D.C. when she was a young associate with the law firm of Winston and Cramer and he was a defensive safety for the Washington Redskins. Julia won a scholarship to Vanderbilt as a swimmer. She narrowly missed a berth on the U.S. Olympic swim team in her senior year. They were never introduced really, and years later neither could remember how they actually met. In truth it was a process of osmosis. Two beautiful people parading around a health club in scant athletic garb, checking out the opposite sex like shoppers in a Turkish bazaar. When a fellow takes a good long look at a girl's legs, then lets his eyes slowly move up to take in the rest of her shapely body, until finally he focuses on her face and finds himself looking her squarely in the eyes, there is nothing left to do but smile. Tom smiled, and Julia smiled back. That's how they met, though neither would admit it, even to themselves.

After a series of shoulder injuries sent him to the hospital for surgery, Tom gave up the NFL in favor of a career in the business world. He first purchased a franchise for a health club. After running it successfully for several years, Tom felt ready to go out on his own. He incorporated and started a fitness center under the name "Super Jock." The selling point was simple enough. For a reasonable fee, members could participate in the kind of training programs which had been perfected and used in the National Football League. Weight lifting. Flexibility. Balance. Coordination. Tom lined up many of his old friends from his football days to make appearances at his clubs. Just a brief twenty minute talk about fitness, with lots of NFL war stories thrown in. Usually the seminars were held in the locker rooms, with all the ambience that location suggests. It was a guy thing and it worked. Within a few years, Tom Hudson had a chain of fitness centers with locations in several major markets. When he began franchising in 1990, things really took off. Soon, he would be looking to diversify.

Julia enjoyed her work on the trial bench, but it was not exactly her best suit. Along with her swimming, she had been an excellent student at Vandy. At Wayne State, she had been near the top of her class in the law school. Later, working in D.C., she had earned an LLM at Georgetown. Julia loved the law library. She loved to read the law, research its esoteric points, browse among the ancient and modern authorities in search of the occasional, soul satisfying peeks at pure truth and time-tested wisdom.

The trial bench was no place for a scholar. Too many cases. Too much to do. Decisions had to be made off the top of your head. Right there. Right now. The jury is waiting. The lawyers are waiting. The courtroom is quiet. It's your turn to speak. Is the evidence admissible or isn't it? Flip a coin. Call the shot. On to the next question. Julia felt frustrated as a trial judge. She wanted to read the law. Mull over each point. Find the right answer in every case. You just couldn't do it in a busy trial court.

So the phone call from the governor's office which had come on Thursday was still churning in her head on Saturday night at Joe Muer's. After the key lime pie, she broached the subject to her husband.

"You know that phone call I got from the governor's office the other day?"

"Yeah. They want you for the supreme court. Have you decided?"

"I'm still thinking about it."

"I thought you were going to take it. After all, it's a honor to be on the highest court, isn't it?"

"I said the governor called, not the president, "Julia responded, laughing.

"It's only a matter of time. You'll hear from the president soon enough. One promotion at a time."

" I'm not so sure this would be a promotion. The pay is about the same, but my job is a lifetime appointment while the supreme court is an elective office with an eight year term. If I take this, I'll have to run for Breitner's unexpired term in 1992, then run again in 1998, assuming I win the first time."

Just then a handsome African American couple, who had been sitting across the room, got up to leave. Their path to the door took them right past the booth where Tom and Julia were sitting. The two women greeted each other warmly.

"Hilda, how are you?"

"Well for heaven's sake, Julia Hudson. What are you doing so far from home?"

"Celebrating a birthday, but don't tell anyone."

"Really? I'll promise not to tell if you return the favor. My birthday is in ten days."

Ben Tuttle leaned over and stage whispered to Tom, "She only mentioned that because she thinks I forgot."

"I almost did. Why don't you two sit down with us and let's toast the two birthday girls."

Hilda glanced at Ben. "Why not?" he asked, anticipating her question.

"Why not indeed," said Hilda, sliding into the booth next to Julia.

"This is still a great place for fish, isn't it?" Julia asked, making small talk.

"The best," Ben rejoined. "Do you come here often?"

"Yes, and my sign is Pisces, and I am majoring in journalism." Julia quipped.

Everybody laughed. Hilda let out a big sigh. "Ah yes, how well I remember those days. The dating scene, the singles bars. Ugh. I'm sure glad you know how to dunk, Ben." She winked at her husband.

"Local joke." Ben explained. "Hilda was a Greenwich Village

recreation league basketball groupie when we met."

The tuxedoed waiter appeared. He knew from experience that when couples got together like this, there would be another round of drinks. And there was.

"What's this I hear about you being considered for the supreme court?" Hilda surprised Julia with her question.

"Bad news travels fast. Doesn't it?" Julia's reply was typically self effacing.

"Good news in my book. Real good news." Germaine was serious. "You would be a wonderful addition to our court, Julia. I'm sure that leaving the federal bench isn't easy, but you could make a real contribution in Lansing."

"And hey, what about this," Ben jumped in with a brilliant idea. "The two of you and Doris Templeton could bill yourselves as the 'Supremes'."

"Yes," said Hilda in a scolding tone of voice, "and we could affirm all the malpractice verdicts against doctors with outlandish senses of humor." She dismissed her husband with a wave of the hand and addressed Judge Hudson. "Seriously, Julia, it would be just wonderful to have you with us. Appellate work is very different from the trial bench, as I'm sure you know. There is so much interaction among the members of the court. It really is important to have compatible colleagues."

"I think I know what you are saying. And believe me, the opportunity to work with you, especially, is one of the most tempting things about the idea." Julia meant what she said.

"You flatter me. But we do have an interesting court, even though right now, we are still largely debilitated because of Ed's death."

"That certainly was tragic." Tom observed. Then, recalling the Tuttle boy's murder, he added, "I'm sure you folks must wonder when it will end. The senseless killing."

Ben and Hilda mumbled agreement. They went back to drinks and visiting about the play Ben and Hilda had seen the night before at the Music hall. Shortly, Doctor and Mrs. Tuttle took their leave, amid warm well wishing.

"Nice folks," said Tom.

"I don't know how she survived it. The very thought of losing our Zachary puts me in a state of panic." Julia observed, with a slight catch in her voice.

"She seems like a good person to work with."

"The best. It would be fun."

"So do it. Like the Nike people say. Just do it."

"But the money..."

"Damn the money, sweetheart, do what your heart says you should do. Be happy. That's all any of us have. You certainly don't have to be concerned about security. As long as I'm around, we'll always have plenty. When I kick the bucket, you'll be rich beyond anything decent. So if you feel like doing it, just do it."

Julia Hudson reached across the table and took her husband's hand in hers. He had just given her a birthday present that would change her life. And she was grateful.

***

On Monday, September 9, Governor Edwards announced the appointment of Federal District Judge Julia Hudson to the Michigan Supreme Court. The chief justice had been given no advance notice. When he learned about it, he called her right away.

"Congratulations, Judge. I'm delighted to hear that you have accepted the governor's offer."

"I am really pleased to be joining you, Hilda and the others."

"When will you take the oath?"

"Does it matter?"

"I think so. Remember, this is an elective office. You should start right now to build up the political base you will need next year. A swearing in ceremony is a good vehicle to generate some enthusiasm among friends and supporters. I suggest we do it on the first day of the term next month. That would be Tuesday, October 8th. Give you some time to get out invitations, and such."

"Do you think I should wait until then to join the bench?"

"Heavens no. The ceremony is just for show. You are on the payroll as soon as you sign the oath in the Clerk's office. The sooner the better."

"Is tomorrow soon enough?"

"Julia, I think you are going to be a real asset to the court. Welcome to the bench."

CHAPTER 17

OCTOBER 1991

The Hudson appointment played well in the press. Moving to the attack, the governor called for a grand jury investigation of the Breitner murder. He urged that a so-called one man grand jury be appointed by the court of appeals, and the grand juror be given plenary power to conduct investigations in any part of the state.

Michigan has a long and rather interesting history of one man grand jury investigations. The statutes of the state, curiously, do not mention the phrase 'one man grand jury.' The law simply authorizes a judge to conduct an investigation into possible crimes that may have been committed in his or her jurisdiction, subpoena witnesses, grant immunity, compel testimony, and issue indictments. This is done, typically, when a petition is filed by the prosecuting attorney. When the possible criminal conduct may have occurred in more than one county or judicial circuit, the court of appeals is authorized to hear the petition for a grand jury and grant it.

One man grand juries have always been favored by the media. In a word, they're 'sexy.' The process reeks of drama, secrecy, intrigue, and ultimately news, news, news. In years past, one man grand jurors have emerged as leading candidates for higher public office. Kim Sigler, a grand jury special prosecutor in the early 1940's, was catapulted into the governor's chair by the notoriety he received. Homer Ferguson became a United States Senator. All grand jury proceedings are held in secret, and it is a crime to reveal information learned during grand jury proceedings, except to the extent that indictments are returned. Obviously, not everyone called to testify before a grand juror is under investigation, but the media love to speculate on why so and so has been called, and what they might be telling the grand juror. Grand jury proceedings may be convened anywhere, and in years past have been called in hotel rooms, meeting halls, even private homes. The reason is to avoid publicity, which is often harmful to the investigation. Or dangerous. Especially in the investigation of organized criminal activity, threats against potential witnesses are common.

The newspapers picked up the drum beat. TV got on the bandwagon. Soon everyone knew there would be a grand jury. The only questions were who would be appointed, and who would be investigated. On Monday, September 30, a petition was filed in the court of Appeals, signed by the attorney general and the prosecuting attorneys of most of the major counties around the state. Twenty three days later, on Tuesday, October 22, Shiawassee County Circuit Judge Kenneth Pershing was appointed by the court of appeals to investigate the death of Justice Breitnor and "any and every criminal action done or taken in the State of Michigan by any terrorist organization or combination of persons who may have conspired to violate the law to further their political, religious or philosophical goals, corrupt or interfere with the administration of justice, or otherwise disturb the peace and good order of the people of Michigan." A broader charter could hardly have been imagined.

Pershing was a quiet, hard nosed, seasoned trial judge. He would brook no nonsense, had no political ambitions beyond the desire to stay in his own judicial office until retirement, and enjoyed a reputation as a plodding, methodical, persevering worker. He set up shop in his courtroom in the gracious old court house in Owosso. No special accommodations were made for the media.

***

October began on a Tuesday and the supreme court convened for oral arguments. Busy all day, the bench heard four cases, the last of which, *Danken v Danken* ended at 3:45 PM. The justices, filing into their conference room and doffing their robes, were treated to a ribald dialog between O'Leary and Henry; a mock debate about which of them should wear his robe when they go to dinner. The silliness was occasioned by the *Danken* case, an action by one Ericka Danken, claiming to be the widow of Theodore Danken, deceased, against Hans Danken and Frederick Danken, children of Theodore by his first wife, Bertha, seeking the widow's share of Theodore's estate, consisting of a three unit shopping strip in Fenton.

Theodore divorced Bertha in Genessee County in 1978. He moved to Denmark in 1979, and entered into an "Agreement of Cohabitation" with a man named Eric Vorsberg. The agreement was accompanied by a will, which, under Danish law, validly left Theodore's entire estate to Eric. In 1981, Vorsberg underwent a sex change operation, thereafter taking the name Ericka Danken.

"Damn you, Alton, you got to wear your robe last time. It's my turn to go in drag." O'Leary's raspy falsetto announced.

"You're so mean to me Robert," Henry rejoined in an equally uncharacteristic voice. "I'm sick and tired of your bullying. I'm going to go to dinner with Van." As he said it, Henry reached over and touched Van Timlin on the arm. The older man had not been listening, being deeply engrossed in reading a brief. He looked up with a start.

"Dinner? Are we going to dinner already?"

Malloy was still chuckling as he attempted to call the court to order and initiate discussion of the cases. Doris Templeton preempted him. "I don't think you male chauvinist pigs are very damn funny. *Danken* is a serious lawsuit by real people with real problems. The parties are entitled to our best thinking. No nonsense, no comedy routines."

Chastened, Malloy hastily agreed. "You're right, Doris. Absolutely. Why don't you get us back on track by leading off the discussion. What do you think we should do with this thing.?"

"I'd start with the most important point. In my opinion, the plaintiff here is a female. She says she is a woman, and her complaint describes in detail how she came to that conclusion. The defendants here are not disputing those facts."

Henry spoke up. "The defendants don't dispute that he or she had the operation. They do, however, dispute the conclusion that the plaintiff is the widow of Theodore."

"Isn't that a question of the legal effect of the cohabitation agreement?" Germaine asked no one in particular. And no one answered.

"Well, my grandparents were married in the Netherlands," Van Timlin observed. "And when my grandfather died, my grandmother inherited the farm here in Michigan. Certainly a foreign marriage is valid here in the United States."

"Sure, Van," said O'Leary, "but was this cohabitation agreement, so-called, a foreign marriage, or something else, entirely unknown to our law? I'm inclined to think it was the latter."

"Plaintiff is Theodore's widow in Denmark, why isn't she his widow here in Michigan?" Templeton demanded.

Julia Hudson moved forward in her chair, but didn't speak. Malloy noticed, and thought that she, being a new member of the court, was reluctant to chime in.

"Julia, what's your view?" Malloy prompted.

"As I read Section 700.113 of the Probate Code, an alien may inherit property in Michigan, just the same as a citizen," offered Hudson.

"Nobody questions that, Julia." Alton Henry was lecturing. "But the code also says that Michigan real estate passes according to Michigan law. The Danish will has never been offered for probate here, and I doubt that it would make a difference, anyway."

"Are we all agreed on that?" The chief was looking for some consensus. "Do we agree that this property will pass according to the intestacy laws of Michigan?" Heads nodded. Nobody disputed the point.

"Let's say that it does," Templeton again. "Under Michigan law, the widow gets one third. That's what the plaintiff is asking for. Just what the Michigan law says she is entitled to."

Henry shot back. "The Michigan law doesn't entitle HIM to anything. HE is not Danken's widow. Not in Michigan he isn't. Not yet, anyway, thank God."

"And I suppose you don't think Rene Richards should have been allowed to play tennis professionally in Michigan either, do you?" Templeton spat the question at Henry.

"Sexual identity is hardly an issue in women's sports from what I hear," Henry zapped in rejoinder.

"That's enough!" The C.J. took over. "Let's get back to Doris' original proposition. This is a real case and a serious one. We are the supreme court of Michigan. This is no place for waging the War of the Roses. Particularly in light of the gender division of the court, it behooves us to respect each others' views, and listen to each others' opinions. And try to see the legal basis for each others' arguments. Now, if no one has an objection, I'd like to take the straw vote on *Danken v Danken*. Those who think we should reverse the court of Appeals, and allow the Plaintiff to collect the widow's one-third, please signify by the usual sign."

Templeton, Hudson and Germaine raised their right hands.

"Those opposed?"

Henry, Van Timlin, and O'Leary signaled their opposition. The chief didn't vote. Instead, he turned to the Mike Delbert, who always attended the conferences, sat at a small table in the corner of the room, and never spoke unless spoken to. "Mike, whose name is up next to write the majority opinion?"

Delbert scanned his notebook.

"Yours," he replied.

The chief justice's ears turned red while his six colleagues were united in uproarious laughter.

"We are adjourned," said Malloy. He gathered up his papers and left the room. He could still hear them laughing as he turned the corner at the end of the hall.

***

FBI agents George Gronski and Marvin Smith were waiting in Malloy's office. They had come to report on their investigation of the Lottery Exchange.

"Our people in West Virginia were very familiar with the American Lottery Exchange. It's run by a lawyer named Gary Behlin. He keeps records of all the tickets he buys and sells. Our agent down there went through his records carefully and did not find your ticket. We are satisfied that the ticket never came through his shop."

"That's some consolation, anyway."

Smith joined in. "We have checked it out with the Florida State Lottery Commission. Your ticket was purchased at a convenience store in Miami. Do you know if your friend Wilhelm was ever in Miami when he was down there?"

"I think he goes to Marco Island. I'd be surprised if he went to Miami, though I suppose it's possible."

"Anyway, Mr. Chief Justice, that's about all we can tell you." Gronski stood up as he was speaking. "We don't see any Federal offense here. Since the state authorities now have a grand jury working, we're going to stay out of it unless we are invited in by the local law enforcement people. We'll send a report to the grand juror, and then close our file."

Malloy thanked them. When they had left, he called Art Wilhelm's Chicago office. "Is he there?"

"Yes, he is, Mr. Chief Justice. I'll put him on the line." Sally Remington, Wilhelm's assistant, was always cheerful and helpful.

"Hi, Jim. What's up?"

"Just a heads up for you, Art."

"I read in the papers that you already turned me over to the FBI. What else can you do to me?"

"The FBI confirmed that the ticket wasn't purchased from the American Lottery Exchange."

"I told you it was clean."

"They also found out that it came from a convenience store in Miami. Were you in Miami in February?"

"Now what, you're playing detective?"

"Don't jack me around, Art. If it's going to be either your ass or mine, I vote for yours."

"No, I wasn't in Miami. But I have friends who were. I told you before, and I'm telling you again, I did not know that ticket was a winner. If I had known, you never would have seen it. You can be damn sure of that."

"I believe you, Art. I really do. But you may be called by the grand jury to answer some questions about it."

"Pershing?"

"Yup. The FBI guys said they were getting out of it, but they were turning over their file to Pershing. When he sees that the ticket was bought in Miami in the week before February 16, he is going to want to know if you were there and if you can prove that you were there."

" I appreciate the heads up, Jim. I'm not afraid of the grand jury. I have nothing to hide. If he calls me in, I'll tell him everything I know."

"And you're sure that none of it will embarrass me?"

"Absolutely, unless you are embarrassed about being a lucky Irish son of a bitch, which you are."

"Your envy has you looking green enough to be Irish yourself, Art. I'll see you at the gin rummy table."

***

On Saturday, October 12, 1991, Doris Templeton busied herself with preparations for a luncheon. She didn't do a lot of entertaining. Hadn't for a while, anyway. Not this kind. Having the ladies for lunch was not a Doris Templeton thing to do.

Entirely too domestic. Still, she was very much looking forward to it. She had extended the invitation to Hilda and Julia, almost on a whim. The three women had been chatting in the rest room. Julia said something like "The three of us ought to get together for lunch sometime." And before she knew what she was saying, Doris had extended the invitation, noting that her Birmingham condo was between the homes of the other two. Acceptances were immediate, and the date was made.

Now as she set the table with her rarely used good china, arranged the centerpiece just delivered from the florist, and checked the progress of the hot chicken salad in the oven, she kept one eye on the television. Clarence Thomas was defending his nomination to the United States Supreme Court. Accused of sexually harassing Anita Hill, an employee under his supervision, the federal judge relied upon his past reputation in an effort to defuse the furor created by her startling testimony Whether that testimony should be called revelations or accusations depended on one's point of view. The case had become a metaphor for the battle of the sexes. Across America, a dichotomy developed. Men believed Thomas. Women believed Hill.

Hilda Germaine was the first to arrive.

"Doris, your place is just charming," she said as her hostess took her coat.

"A little nest to hide in, safe from the man's world outside."

"It's beautiful, really. Ben and I often talk of getting into something smaller. How long have you been here?"

"I bought the place three years ago. With I-75 nearby, I can be downtown in about 30 minutes."

"And Lansing?"

"About an hour and forty. Depends on the time of day."

The phone rang. It was Julia, looking for directions. She was in her car, only a few blocks away. Doris returned.

"Julia. She'll be here in a minute or two."

Hilda nodded. "I like her, don't you?"

"She seems to have a good head on her shoulders. Not afraid to go to the books. Doesn't have the God complex most federal judges get."

"That's for sure. If anything, she appears a little reticent."

"She'll get over that. If Henry keeps on goading her like he did on the *Danken* case, she'll bust him in the chops."

Hilda laughed. "Or hit him with her purse, which is more lady-like."

"She better have a lead pipe in the purse, to make a dent on his thick skull."

The two women adjourned to the living room and became engrossed in the televised senate confirmation hearing.

Shortly, Julia arrived, and a glass of wine was poured.

"To us!" Hilda said it with a smile. They clinked glasses and toasted themselves, while across the living room, Clarence Thomas squirmed.

***

Doris' luncheon was eminently successful. The chicken salad, the sesame rolls, the herbal tea and apple cobbler, all came out well and were served with aplomb. But more delicious than any of these, the gossip was titillating. Of course, the principal targets of their conversation were the four men with whom they served on the court. One by one, they analyzed, criticized, and pulverized their colleagues. Van was old, old, old. Henpecked by his wife, Gertie. His kid was a slob. Totally predictable. Rock ribbed, unreconstructed Republican. Male chauvinist. On the up side, polite, generous, kind, courtly, courteous, and a fine legal mind. When he was awake.

Henry came in for Doris' most stinging evaluation. Mean spirited, vicious, cruel, Neanderthal. Self important, arrogant, pompous, banal, sneaky, two faced, despicable. After one particularly eloquent diatribe, Julia was moved to laughter. "Are you sure Alton isn't your ex husband?" Her question had them all howling.

O'Leary drew more sympathetic comments. Doris told Julia of Bob's personal tragedies. Julia didn't even know Bob was an amputee. And she had never heard the story of the death of his wife and his son.

"Bob is a good Judge," Hilda noted. "But I do worry about his drinking. We often go to lunch together at the country club the week of arguments. He will have two or sometimes three martinis with lunch. If we have lunch brought into the conference room, as we sometimes do, he goes back to his office before he eats, is gone fifteen minutes to a half hour, and comes back reeking of gin."

"Does it affect his performance on the bench?" Julia asked.

"Not so far," Doris answered. "But it's hard to tell. I think he's one of those functioning alcoholics who never seem quite drunk, but never seem quite sober, either."

At last, the talk turned to Malloy. It was almost as though they had avoided the subject. Once his name was mentioned, and the flow of conversation would ordinarily have veered toward the chief, an uneasy silence set in. Finally, Hilda spoke.

"I like Jim. He's a good man and a good judge, though he's an awful clutz. I feel terribly sorry for him with all this bad publicity he's been getting. Mostly, though, I feel sorry for his wife. Margaret simply doesn't deserve the stress and anxiety."

"What is the business about a lottery ticket? I haven't been following it in the papers." Julia wanted to know.

"Malloy won a bunch of money," Doris offered. "They say over a hundred thousand. The press is insinuating that somebody gave him the ticket as a bribe or pay off or something. Nothing has been proven so far, but Malloy isn't helping any by refusing to tell when and where he got the ticket."

"I thought he told the papers he got the ticket from a friend," said Hilda.

"He did. But he hasn't said who the friend is, or why the

friend gave it to him. That leaves the door wide open for speculation and rumor," Templeton rejoined.

"Well, there sure are rumors." Julia acknowledged. "If it were me, I'd just give the money back and be done with it. Stifle all the rumors."

"Easier said than done, Julia. Malloy has five kids. Margaret doesn't work outside the home. Ben makes a good income from his practice, but even with our two paychecks, we have to watch our family budget." Hilda shook her head. "I don't know how he supports seven people on what he makes."

"That's his fault." Doris spoke while gathering up dishes and cups. "He's nothing but a big, dumb, Catholic stud who thinks every woman should be in the kitchen, barefoot and pregnant." Julia played uneasily with her dessert spoon. Hilda stiffened noticeably. Their silence followed Templeton to the kitchen. "O.K. Strike the 'Catholic' part, but I stand by the rest." Doris tossed the words back over her shoulder to the dining room.

CHAPTER 18

NOVEMBER 1991

The headline in the Capital City Tribune blared the news that
the bill had passed, proclaiming:

STATE OUTLAWS TERROR

Alton Henry was reminded of Franklin Roosevelt's
pronouncement of the so-called four freedoms. Freedom of
Speech. Freedom of Religion. Freedom from Fear. Freedom
from Want. He looked up from the paper at the chief justice
sitting at the other end of the conference table, pouring over his
notebook. The two men had arrived early this fifth day of
November, the first in the current term. They were alone in the
room.

"Well Jim, I hope you are as relieved as I am to know that we
shall never more experience the emotion of terror."

"What?"

"Terror. The newspaper says there will be no more terror in
Michigan. Tornados will have to be toned down. Lightning will
be kept on the distant horizon. Armed robbers shall henceforth
conduct themselves with due regard for the feelings of their
victims." He held up the paper so that Malloy could see the
front page.

"Wonderful," Malloy reacted. "Next perhaps the legislature
will be good enough to outlaw stress and anxiety."

"I can see it now: 'Nervousness Banned' or how about
'Annoyance Verbotin'"

"Enough, already. Is that the so-called Tuttle Bill, the anti-
terrorism law?"

"One and the same. Did you hear how they worked it through
the legislature last night?"

"No, what happened?"

300

"The thing would have been dead in the water. They needed five votes in the senate and a dozen or more in the house to pass the conference committee version of the bill. Then somebody, I think in the governor's office, came up with the brilliant idea of making terrorism murder a capital offense. Punishable by hanging by the neck until dead."

"You're kidding! We don't have the death penalty in Michigan and they know it. How could such a thing get through the legislature?"

"A little slight of hand. The act says that it becomes effective when and if the constitution is amended to permit the death penalty for terrorism. Then the legislature promptly passed a joint resolution placing an amendment to the constitution permitting the death penalty for terrorist murder on the November 1992 ballot."

"And it passed?" asked Malloy.

"Overwhelmingly. The conservatives wanted the death penalty restored, and the liberals wanted the terrorism law. They put something for everybody in the bill. The only ones left out were the true moderates, and there aren't many of them," Henry opined. "It's an unholy alliance if you ask me."

"I thought you favored the death penalty."

"I do, but not just for political criminals. I'm not so sure it does any good in political cases. You end up creating martyrs. The kind of guys you maudlin, sentimental Irishmen sing songs about."

"Thus inspiring another generation to take up arms. Would you like to hear a few bars of *Four Green Fields*?"

"I'll pass."

Just then Doris and Van came in. Henry continued his preachment. "Good morning fellow travelers. You are just in time to pay homage to the new era in taxpayer comfort. We are now to be free of terror."

Templeton rose to the bait. "I saw the headline. About time somebody laid the law down to those right wing idiots who run around killing people and call themselves pro life."

Van Timlin seemed surprised. "I would have counted you as being against the death penalty, Doris. Am I hearing otherwise?"

"Not across the board, no. I don't think the death penalty really deters crime. Especially murder, which is almost always committed in the heat of passion. But these political crimes are different. These people kill to influence the body politic. It's a form of blackmail or coercion. It's almost always deliberate, cruel, and heartless." Templeton spoke with conviction.

Germaine arrived and Hudson was only a few steps behind. Julia nodded to the chief justice and took her seat in silence. Waiting for O'Leary, the justices continued their dialog about the terrorism law and the death penalty. The political compromise which ushered the bill through the legislature continued to muddy the philosophical waters as the legal ramifications of the new law were discussed. Would the governor sign the act? Would the voters approve the constitutional amendment? There were pros and cons from both liberal and conservative perspectives.

The State of Michigan was the first sovereign government in the English speaking world to abolish the death penalty for murder and lesser crimes. The death knell of its death penalty began in 1830. Despite the resignation of the sheriff, who refused to be the hangman, a public execution, replete with a brass band entertaining some two thousand spectators, took place that year in Detroit. It disgusted the decent citizens of the town. Newspapers chastised the mob, and calls for reform were heard from responsible quarters.

Then in 1838, a year after Michigan was admitted to the union, a man named Fitzpatrick was convicted of carnal knowledge--statutory rape--of a nine year old girl in Windsor, Ontario, just across the border. There were two suspects arrested. Fitzpatrick, being Irish, was thought the more likely perpetrator. After he was hung, the other suspect made a deathbed confession to the crime. The reaction in Detroit triggered the abolition movement. The press railed against the gallows as a cruel holdover from draconian feudal days, when hands were chopped off for petty theft, and the penalty of death extracted for a long list of offenses. The Michigan legislature, in the eighth year of statehood and still a vigorously youthful deliberative body, responded swiftly and dramatically. The penalty of death, by hanging, was retained for only one crime, treason.

In the intervening years, there were several attempts to reinstate the death penalty, but in 1963, when the people of Michigan last rewrote their constitution, the prohibition was not only retained, but enshrined in the constitution itself, and extended even to the crime of treason. By the last decade of the twentieth century, however, weighted by citizen fear of rising crime rates, the pendulum was swinging back toward reinstatement. Public opinion polls showed that over sixty percent of the population favored it. Only concerted, ever vigilant effort by its supporters was keeping the historic prohibition on the books.

Against this background, the 'Tuttle Law ' compromise loomed large. Stemming religiously inspired activism was a primary goal of many on the far left. Executing murderers topped the wish list of most right wingers. The package seemed to have an almost irresistible sway. It appealed to the extremes on both left and right. The middle of the road looked exceedingly narrow to the pollsters.

About the time the justices agreed that the so-called 'Tuttle Act' would, if signed into law by the governor, surely be submitted to the supreme court for an advisory opinion, Justice Bob O'Leary sauntered in. Eyes red and gait unsteady, even for a man with one leg, he looked at the clock, noted that his watch was slow, mumbled a weak apology, and took his place at the table.

"I'm afraid we haven't time to listen to morning reports, ladies and gentlemen. Counsel are waiting in the courtroom, and the appointed hour has arrived. Let's put on our robes and go to work."

So saying, the chief justice cast a reproving scowl at his good friend Robert Allen O'Leary.

***

It's pretty hard to get in or out of the courthouse in Owosso without being noticed, even in ordinary times. The heightened security associated with the Pershing Grand Jury made it literally impossible. Art Wilhelm didn't even try. Running the gauntlet of radio, television, and newspaper reporters who lined the walls from the double doors at the head of the steps in the front of the building to the double doors at the end of the hall in the back of the building, the former Illinois congressman appeared to be making a campaign sweep, nodding, smiling, shaking hands, and bantering with his many acquaintances in the fourth estate.

The preliminaries took but a few minutes. Introductions. Pictured identification. General instructions on the secrecy of grand jury proceedings. Administration of the oath. Judge Pershing, sitting at his usual post on the bench, but without the customary black robe, flashed a polite little smile as he welcomed the witness. The only other persons in the room were a deputy sheriff, the court reporter and the prosecuting attorney, Emmet Fournier. Fournier began the questioning.

"For the record, please, your name is?"

"Wilhelm. Arthur Wilhelm. I live at 2332 Hampton Towers, Chicago, Illinois."

"And by whom are you employed?"

"I am a Senior Vice President of The Barrows Group, a public representation firm, based in Washington, D.C."

"What are your responsibilities with that firm?"

"I am liaison to various public bodies in Michigan, Illinois and

Washington."

"Is it fair to say that you are a lobbyist?"

"The best."

"Yes?"

"Yes."

"Is one of the public bodies you liaison with the supreme court of Michigan?"

"No sir. Our firm does not lobby courts. That would be unethical if not illegal. We only work with legislative bodies and administrative agencies."

"So you don't lobby judges at all?"

"Let me qualify my answer. There could be some occasion, for example, if a court were considering adopting a new court rule, when the court is acting in a legislative capacity, and then we might have a reason to try to influence the action of the judges on behalf of our clients. But never concerning a lawsuit."

"The grand jury has been given reliable information that you gave a lottery ticket to Chief Justice Malloy that was worth some one hundred and eighty thousand dollars. Is that correct?"

"Yes and no. I gave him the ticket, but he paid for it. All I was doing was buying a ticket for him. An errand boy."

"Where did you buy the ticket?"

Wilhelm paused thoughtfully.

"I didn't exactly buy the ticket."

"How did you get it?"

"I won it in a poker game."

"You won it?"

"That's right. A bunch of us old timers have a poker club down in Naples. We meet twice a month from October through May. Different guys. Depends on who's in Florida at the time. There are maybe thirty of us. We meet on Wednesday nights. At the high point of the season, January and February, we'll have maybe three tables going."

"Is that legal in Florida?"

"I don't know, but years ago, one of the fellows came up with the idea of playing for lottery tickets. His theory was that we are not gambling unless we are playing for something of value. You know, if we used toothpicks or match sticks, we wouldn't be gambling. He argued that lottery tickets have no value unless you win, and winning the lottery is not against the law. So he figured it was no crime to play poker for lottery tickets. I don't know if the theory would hold up, but we have never been arrested, and the chief of police of Fort Meyers has played with us a few times."

"So you won this ticket in a poker game. When was that?"

"Tuesday, February 12 th."

"And the drawing was on what day?"

"Lottery drawings in Florida are always on Saturday nights. Whatever Saturday was. 12, 13, 14, 15, 16. February 16. Saturday February 16."

"When did you give the ticket to Justice Malloy?"

"Sometime in March. Late March, after I came north from Florida."

"So at the time you gave Malloy the ticket, it was already a winner, worth over a hundred eighty thousand dollars, is that right?"

"Yes."

"So you just gave the chief justice all that money, is that what you are saying?"

"That's what I am saying."

"Mr. Wilhelm, did the Barrows Group at that time have any clients who had business before the supreme court of Michigan?"

"Probably."

"What do you mean, 'Probably'?"

"Mr. Fournier, Barrows is one of the largest, most respected public affairs representatives in America. We have literally hundreds of clients. Big ones. Insurance companies who write liability insurance. Their whole business is to defend lawsuits. They are in court all the time. Every day. I doubt there is a court of any size in America which doesn't have Barrows clients in some pending litigation."

"Well did Barrows have any particular client with business in the Michigan Supreme Court in February and March of 1991?"

"Yes."

"Who would that be?"

"Missaukee Mutual Insurance Company, for one."

"What litigation were they involved in?'

"Missaukee had the coverage on the *Grand Haven* hospital in a case involving a judgment for so-called wrongful birth."

Fournier approached the bench and conferred with Judge Pershing.

"Wait here a moment, Mr. Wilhelm," the judge said, as he stepped down from the bench and followed Fournier into his chambers. Moments later, they reappeared. The prosecutor continued.

"Mr. Wilhelm, could that matter have been the case of *Silus v Grand Haven Community Hospital?*"

"That was it, yes."

"And wasn't that the case in which the supreme court reduced the Plaintiff's verdict from five hundred thousand dollars to one dollar?"

"Absolutely."

"And Justice Malloy voted with the majority didn't he?"

"Yes, I believe he did."

"So you gave Malloy $183,000, and in return, he got the court to overrule the judgment in the *Silus* case, saving your client half a million dollars. Is that about it?"

"No, Mr. Fournier, that is not it." Wilhelm spoke through clenched teeth. "That is emphatically not the case."

"Then what exactly is the case, sir? Just why did you give Malloy one hundred eighty-three thousand six hundred dollars?"

"I didn't give him one hundred eighty-three thousand six hundred dollars. I gave him a lottery ticket worth that much. But I never gave him any money."

"What is the difference?"

"There's a very large difference. I had no idea the lottery ticket was worth anything. I thought it was a loser."

"Are you trying to tell the Grand Jury that you didn't know it was a winner?"

"That's exactly right."

"Isn't there a 900 number on the back of those tickets? Couldn't you just pick up the phone and see if you won?"

"Yup. But I didn't. I never do. I come home from Florida with a bag full of lottery tickets from two months of poker games. This year, I bet I won over two thousand tickets down there. Some of those games get pretty serious. I'm sure as hell not going to sit there and call the Florida Lottery Commission two thousand times to find out how many tickets are winners. My secretary does that for me."

"And did your secretary do that on this ticket?"

"She told me she did. But she didn't. After I got back from Florida, I had to go to Michigan. I often play gin rummy with Justice O'Leary and his cousin, Harry Flynn. Sometimes Malloy plays with us. I took money from all those guys to buy lottery tickets in Florida, and I had to give them some tickets. So I asked my secretary to save a bunch of the losing tickets after she called Florida on them. I took what I thought were losing tickets to Michigan and gave them to the guys."

"So you want us to believe that you didn't know the ticket was worth anything, is that what you are saying?"

"You got it. Believe me I was not happy with my secretary."

Judge Pershing took over the questioning. "Mr. Wilhelm, I'm curious about something here. You say that you gave Malloy the ticket by mistake, right?"

"Right."

"Did you tell Malloy about the mistake?"

"No sir."

"So as far as Malloy is concerned, he thinks you knew the ticket was valuable when he gave it to you, is that so?"

"I told him that if I had known the ticket was worth anything, I never would have given it to him."

"And you think he believes that you didn't know?"

"I don't know what he believes, Judge. The plain truth of the matter is that I am very embarrassed about the whole business. I certainly can't tell those three friends of mine that I stiffed them deliberately."

"Stiffed them?"

"You know, gave them tickets I already knew were losers. They gave me money to buy lottery tickets that at least had a chance of winning. I forgot to buy tickets for them. I should have just given them each their money back, but I didn't want to admit that I forgot about them, so I gave them a bunch of losing tickets. Or I gave them what I thought was a bunch of losing tickets."

Pershing leaned back in his chair, deep in thought. Fournier spoke again. "Mr. Wilhelm, do you have any way of proving that you didn't know that the ticket was worth anything when you gave it to Malloy?"

"I thought you might ask that. Yes, I do."

"How?"

"My secretary, Sally Remington, is across the street in the coffee shop. She can testify, if you wish."

Thirty minutes later, the grand jury reconvened. Sally Remington was in the witness chair, sworn and answering questions.

"Mrs. Remington, what can you tell us about the Florida Lottery ticket which ended up in the hands of Chief Justice Malloy?"

"I can tell you this. I almost lost my job over it."

"How so?"

"Well, I was supposed to call the 900 number on all of Mr. Wilhelm's lottery tickets. I always did. That was my responsibility. This particular day, I was very busy with office work, and he asked me to give him some of the losing tickets to take with him to Michigan. I gave him all I had, maybe two or three dozen. I don't keep them, you know. Just toss them in the waste basket, usually. But he wanted me to save some of the losers, so I did. But when he looked at how many I gave him, he said, 'Is that all you've got? I need a few more.' So I just grabbed a handful from the pile I was working on and gave them to him. I mean, they're almost all losers. Maybe one out of two or three hundred is worth anything. Then it's usually only 30 or 40 dollars. I just took a chance. Assumed they were all losers like they usually are."

"So what happened next, Mrs. Remington? When did you learn of the mistake?"

"It wasn't for a couple of months. Maybe April sometime. Anyway, Mr. Wilhelm came storming into the office that morning fit to be tied. He was yelling and screaming at me, I thought he was going to have a heart attack, or he was going to kill me or fire me, I didn't know what. It was just awful. Really awful. He slammed the door to his office so hard that the glass in the door broke. I had to have a glass company come out and fix it. Cost three hundred and some dollars. The telephone man who was there installing a new line for our computer modem was as scared as I was."

"There was a telephone repair man in your office at the time?"

"Yes. He was putting a new line in for our computer, like I said."

"And you say you think he was as scared as you were?"

"I know he was."

"How do you know he was?"

"Because he called the police."

***

The headline in the Detroit First Press on the morning after Wilhelm's appearance in Owosso proclaimed:

MALLOY PAL MUM ON LOTTERY

The lead paragraph told the whole story.

"Arthur Wilhelm, often identified as a close associate of Chief Justice James P. Malloy, refused to say whether his testimony before the Pershing Grand Jury related to the $183,600 lottery ticket Malloy claims was given to him by a friend."

The story went on to say that both Malloy and Wilhelm refused to answer questions about where the ticket had been purchased or by whom. To that was added a paragraph recounting the recent revelations about Chicago politicians winning large lottery pay offs and the subsequent investigations of the lottery in Illinois, and another paragraph repeating the disclosures made on television about the American Lottery Exchange.

Next to the story was a picture of Wilhelm taken as he left the courtroom, surrounded by barking reporters, jostled by TV cameramen, and being escorted through the crowd by a deputy sheriff. Under the photograph was the legend, "Reluctant witness Arthur Wilhelm is led from the courtroom"

***

Not a week after Art Wilhelm left the Owosso courtroom, Wallace Wilson Wright was summoned to appear before Judge Pershing. Wright was ready. He had already suspected that grand jury investigators had been sneaking around, talking to his friends, probably tapping his phone. For more than a month, he had made it a habit to use pay phones whenever talking to people who shared his conservative views or were interested in helping him with the work of the Army of Righteousness. When he filed the assumed name certificate, claiming to be doing business as the Army of Righteousness, he thought he had cornered a wonderful publicity platform for his conservative causes and possible future candidacies. His Kalamazoo security guard operation, and the attendant publicity as his case wound its way up to the supreme court, and was decided in his favor, had fostered immense interest in the Army. Phone calls came from all over the state, indeed from all around the country. He had become an icon of resistance to legalized abortion. Many of his new contacts lived in the nether world of conspiratorial communication. They left coded messages, sought clandestine meetings, spoke in tongues.

The Breitner murder brought a new and more ominous dimension. Now there were official ears listening. Ears that belonged to the minions of law enforcement, but lived in the same nether world of whispered codes and secret rendezvous. Wright was now under suspicion for murder in the first degree. The subpoena to appear before the grand jury was no surprise to him. He had already hired the best and most expensive criminal lawyer in the state.

In the late 1980's the Michigan grand jury law was amended to allow witnesses to be accompanied by their lawyers. Before that, a witness was entitled to the advice of counsel, but the attorney had to remain outside the courtroom when his client was testifying. The result was that a wary witness would have to ask the court's permission to talk to his lawyer after every question was asked, causing great delay and inconvenience for everybody. Thus the amendment.

Wright's lawyer took no chances. He advised Wright to answer no questions beyond his name and address. He was given a three by five card on which were written the words he was to use. He read the card every time a question was asked. "I refuse to answer the question on the ground that my answer may tend to incriminate me.'

Judge Pershing and prosecutor Fourier realized that they had called Wright as a witness prematurely. They really had little to ask him, because they had very little evidence about his activities. But the newspapers insisted that Wright be called. After all, the Army of Righteousness was apparently responsible for the murder of Justice Breitner, and Wright was the only person officially associated with the AOR. At least he should be questioned.

So when Wright refused to answer any questions, the grand jury was put to a difficult decision. They could grant Wright immunity from prosecution and force him to testify under penalty of being jailed for contempt of court. But if they did that, and he was in fact responsible for the killing, he could not be prosecuted. Immunity was best used to force testimony from people who knew who did it. Not from the people who actually did it.

So the Wallace Wright appearance garnered nothing for the grand jury. But it was a cornucopia of news for the famished media.

MALLOY SUPPORTER CLAMS UP

Amid speculation that he had taken the fifth amendment behind closed doors, Wallace Wright, the archconservative leader of the Army of Righteousness, and admitted campaign worker for Chief Justice James Malloy, refused to comment after his appearance before the grand jury in Owosso today.

Wright, who was recently exonerated by a divided supreme court after conviction by a jury for impersonating a police officer in front of a Kalamazoo abortion clinic, was summoned by Kenneth Pershing,

Owosso Circuit Judge investigating the
murder of Justice Edward Breitner,
Malloy's chief rival on the court.

Breitner's bullet riddled body was
found in the back seat of his car in a
northern Michigan parking lot. The
letters AOR, the abbreviation for Army
of Righteousness were scratched on
the hood of the car.

Malloy, who has admitted he
quarreled with Breitner on the night of
the murder, denies complicity in the
killing, but has no alibi for the actual
time of the murder.

CHAPTER 19

DECEMBER 1991

Judge Pershing held a press conference early in December. No, there were no indictments being handed down. No, there would not be any big news forthcoming soon. No, he would not comment on what he had learned so far from the various witnesses called. No, he had not spoken to Chief Justice Malloy. No, he had no present intention to call Malloy as a witness. But he did have a statement to make about the progress of the grand jury.

"There is a great deal of preliminary investigation which needs to be done by the prosecuting attorney's office and the attorney general's office before we can resume calling witnesses. I am the only circuit judge in Shiawassee County, and I have my own docket to handle as well as the grand jury. I have a number of civil and criminal cases to dispose of this month. Therefore, I am announcing today that there will be no more witnesses called before the grand jury until next month." The press conference ended abruptly as the press corps talked about breaking camp until after the new year.

Back in his office, Pershing called Malloy. "Jim? Ken Pershing here. Got a minute?"

"Of course. How are you?"

"Up to my ears. Between the grand jury and my regular call, I have a full plate."

"I can imagine. What's up?"

"I just had a press conference. I told them that I would not be calling any more witnesses this month. Frankly, Jim, this thing is going nowhere. I'm getting a lot of pressure to talk to you, and I don't know how to handle it."

"You can subpoena me. I'm willing to testify. I'll tell you anything I know."

"I'm sure you would, Jim. But I don't want you to be hounded by the press, and I don't think a lot of speculation about you being investigated is good for any of us."

"I couldn't agree more. These last months have been a nightmare."

"Why don't we get together informally, just you and I? If what you tell me privately suggests that you should be called as a witness, we can always do that later. Are you comfortable with that?"

"Sure. When and where?"

"I'd like to do it someplace where the rat pack isn't hanging around. Out of state maybe. Are you going to the American Bar Association mid winter meeting in Dallas?"

"I could. I marked it as a tentative date."

"I'm on the council of the Judicial Section, so I plan to be there from January 30th through the 9th of February. I'll be at Loews Anatole. We could get together then."

"Can you can wait that long.?"

"The wheels of justice grind slowly. And besides, my prosecutor needs about a month to finish some things he's looking into. I'll be in a better position to talk to you then."

"It's a date, Ken. I'll see you in Dallas."

"Sounds good. Oh, by the way, Jim, there is one more thing. You know of course, that I can't reveal anything I hear in testimony as a grand juror."

"Yes, I know that's the law. I don't expect you to violate the law, and I expect that I'll be bound by the same obligation when we talk."

"That's right. But there is one name I would like to pass along to you which was not mentioned in testimony, but turned up in our investigations."

"What was that?"

"A man named Bill Carpenter who works for Ameritech in Chicago. A repairman. You should talk to him."

"About what?"

"Ask him if he knows Art Wilhelm."

***

Cindy surveyed the breakfast table. Oatmeal, sausage, fresh strawberries and melon, homemade biscuits and piping hot coffee. She went to the foot of the stairs and summoned Hilda for the third time.

"I fixed a nice breakfast for you darling. C'mon down here."

The answer came from beyond the bedroom door. "I'll just want a cup of coffee, mother. I have to be in Lansing this morning. Got to run. Go ahead and start without me."

Muttering to herself about her daughter's frenetic life style, Cindy forced herself to sit down to the meal. In a few minutes, Hilda appeared, poured herself a cup of coffee, snitched one of the biscuits, and sat on the edge of a chair at the end of the table.

"At least you have time to tell me what's happening in the court."

"Oral arguments today, mother, like always on the first Tuesday of the month."

"I know that. I wanted to know about the judges. How's the new girl getting on?"

Hilda smiled. "The new 'girl' as you call her, is doing fine. She's a good lawyer, a student of the law."

"And what about the chief justice? They going to throw him in jail?"

"Not hardly. Though it seems that the newspapers want him drawn and quartered, doesn't it?"

"Sure does. You think he has done wrong, Hildie?"

"I don't know. There are so many unanswered questions. But my heart tells me we shouldn't jump to conclusions. He's a good family man. I just can't believe he would do anything seriously wrong."

"Family tells lots about folks, I always say. How's that

friendly Irish judge. The one with the wooden foot?"

"O'Leary? He's fine I guess. He worries me though. I told you about his wife and son didn't I?"

"Oh yeah. You told me all right."

"I think he gets very sad, sometimes. I wish he wouldn't drink so much."

"Demon rum brings a whole lot of good men down, and that's a fact."

Hilda checked her watch. "Got to go, mom. What are you up to today?"

"Going down to see that friend of yours at the Police Athletic League."

"Really? What for?"

"He promised to get me a some CD's for Jeremiah."

Jeremiah again. Every time Hilda heard the name, her stomach pinched with pain. She knew Cindy had been seeing the boy regularly. She knew, because her mother reported in detail, how her son's killer had progressed under the close supervision of Benny and Nora Oldsmer. How he had shown a remarkable talent for music, indeed had been labeled by his teachers at Holy Trinity school as a child prodigy, a budding piano virtuoso. How he practiced long hours on the Oldsmer's old Baldwin upright, picking out tunes from phonograph records and disk jockeys on the radio. How Benny, who played the piano himself, had taught Jeremiah the proper hand movements, and even had him reading music and playing classics.

Hilda was very proud of her mother. She marveled at Cindy's strength of character. She marveled at her mother's involvement in the boy's rehabilitation. Marveled, but could not bring herself to share in it. Could not forgive. Could not forget.

***

Jeremiah Wheatley and Chief Justice Malloy were also the subjects of a conversation between Justice O'Leary and his secretary, Evelyn Mentash. As Christmas neared, the justice extended his customary invitation to his long time, trusted assistant to join him for dinner. For him, it was an expression of appreciation for another year of faithful, competent, reliable service. For her it was a date. The one big date of her otherwise dateless year. She came to work that Thursday dressed to the nines. Hair coifed. Nails done. Face carefully and glamorously made up. Despite eight hours at her work station, she still looked like a queen at five o'clock when O'Leary announced that it was time to go.

He took her to a gourmet restaurant in East Lansing, a campy place where students, faculty, townies, professionals, and politicos mingled in casual elegance. A corner table added a sense of intimacy to their dinner.

"You never told me whether you went to see that boy who lost his foot. The one who shot Hilda's son." Evelyn raised the subject because it was about her boss's kindliness.

"Didn't I? I thought I mentioned it. That was almost a year ago."

"No. You never said anything after I gave you the clipping. I thought it would be very difficult for you to relate to him under the circumstances. So I guess I just assumed you didn't go."

"I went. And you're right. It wasn't easy. But if I was queasy about going to see him, I got a real lesson in Christian charity from Hilda's mother."

"Hilda Germaine's mother?"

"Yes. I ran into her at the hospital. She was there to see the boy, too."

"Really?"

"Uh huh. And I understand she has stayed in touch with him. Has had quite an influence on him as I hear it."

"That's remarkable. I don't think I could bring myself to do that."

"It takes a very special kind of person."

"The talk among the secretaries is that Justice Germaine has made a very good recovery from the loss of her son. They see her as a strong person."

"She is. For example, I think she has taken Ed Breitner's death better than most. Doris Templeton, on the other hand, was devastated. She still seems to be embittered by it."

"Do you think she blames the chief justice?"

"I think she harbors a lot of resentment against Malloy. Sees him as a catalyst for many things she doesn't like."

O'Leary motioned the waitress over and ordered a second martini. Evelyn passed. She was still nursing her Margarita. She was still nursing it as well when he ordered his third cocktail. She warmed to the intimacy of their shared gossip. It was a chance to get him talking about how he felt, what he thought. To reveal himself to her. That was what she longed for. As she longed, pined, to reveal herself to him.

"Do you think that Justice Malloy has done something wrong? Is he really in trouble?"

O'Leary sighed a long sigh. "I don't know, Evelyn. I just don't know. I do know this, however. Art Wilhelm gave him the winning ticket, and Art Wilhelm knew about the lottery ticket exchange and the way they use it to launder bribe money. And I know that Malloy was up to his ears in debt after his campaign. I suppose it is possible that they cooked up a deal to get clean money into Malloy's hands. Maybe it wasn't a bribe. I wouldn't think Wilhelm would try to bribe a judge. He's too smart for that. Frankly, he's too honest. I've known him a long time."

"Then you don't think there was anything fishy about the winning ticket?"

"I didn't say it was above suspicion. I still wonder if it wasn't Wilhelm's way of getting around the ethical ban on post election fund raising. It would be like him to make some phone calls to a few discreet party leaders, raise the money to pay off Malloy's debts, then figure out a way to get the money to Malloy without Malloy knowing it was being done. Sort of like that television show about the eccentric millionaire who is always helping people without their knowledge."

"So you are saying that Malloy could be innocent, but Wilhelm be guilty, is that it?"

"Sort of, but Wilhelm isn't guilty of anything, unless he was trying to influence Malloy in some way. And if he was deliberately concealing the fact that he was helping Malloy, how could he be trying to influence him?"

"Wouldn't it be illegal for Wilhelm to give Malloy the money?"

"No. Not if it was anonymous. Assuming the money is legal in the first place."

"Legal?"

"Yes. Assuming the people he got it from gave him their own funds, on which they had paid taxes. The ethical rule about raising money after the election only applies to the judges. It is part of the judicial ethics code. It doesn't bind people who are not judges. So it's not illegal or improper for somebody to donate to a judge's campaign after the election. It's only unethical for him to accept it."

"And if he didn't know it was a campaign contribution, he is in the clear?"

"That's the way I see it. But you can just imagine how it would play in the newspapers."

The conversation continued through dinner, two bottles of wine, and several stingers after dessert. Evelyn nursed the wine and cordial as she had her cocktail. She didn't need alcohol. She was intoxicated by the voice of the man who was giving her his undivided attention. They talked of many things. His daughters. His life. Hers. He moved his face closer to her as he spoke. She looked straight into his eyes. As was often the case, O'Leary showed almost no sign of intoxication. The more he drank, the more he talked. The more he talked, the more eloquent and poetic he became. The little slurring of the words somehow added to their charm. He was Mister Wonderful.

Until he paid the check and attempted to stand up. Then, he staggered precariously, bumping into the table, spilling the coffee, showing his inebriation. She excused herself, went to the ladies room, and on returning, walked to the front door to wait for him to come out of the men's room. By the time they reached his car, he was incoherent. Evelyn managed to get his car keys away from him, then shoved, cajoled, and poured him into the passenger's seat, fastened his seat belt, rounded the car and drove him home to Harry Flynn's apartment.

Flynn's was dark. O'Leary was asleep in the front seat. Evelyn went to the front door and rang the bell. It was after midnight. Nobody answered. She rang again. Still no answer. So Evelyn Mentash did what she had always wanted to do. She took the justice home to her house. There she laboriously maneuvered her boss into the living room, stretched his six foot frame out on her couch, removed his shoes, coat and tie, unbuttoned the top three buttons of his shirt, kissed him squarely on the mouth, then built a fire in the fireplace and sat on the floor between O'Leary and the crackling hearth until five o'clock in the morning.

***

In five days, it would be Christmas. The tree in the corner of the Oldsmer living room cast multicolored shadows on the walls and ceiling. Benny was in the basement, fixing something. Nora was in the kitchen fixing something else. Jeremiah was in the living room. He needed to fix something, too. His ball point pen moved slowly, unsteadily across the oversized Christmas card.

"I am so very sorry for what I did to your son Josh. I hope you can someday forgive me. I know Jesus died for my sins. So did Josh. I will always pray for him and for you all."

Ben helped him address the envelope and Nora found a postage stamp to put in the upper right hand corner.

PART THREE

YEAR TWO

CHAPTER 20

JANUARY 1992

MORNING REPORT
FROM THE COMMISSIONERS TO THE
JUSTICES

PEOPLE v BARNISH

Defendant, a psychiatrist, treated one Forrester, who suffered from severe depression and anxiety because of being care-giver to his wife. She was in the late stages of Alzheimer's disease, in no pain, but incontinent, unable to recognize anyone, and completely dependent. Forrester, for financial and emotional reasons, refused to put her in a nursing home, but pleaded with Barnish to give him a prescription that would put her out of her misery. It is alleged that Barnish authorized a massive purchase of the tranquilizer he had been giving Forrester, informing him that exceeding a certain dosage would be fatal. Defendant charged Forrester a substantial fee of $3,000 in consideration of 'the risk involved in this sort of thing.' Forrester gave his wife a lethal dose of the prescription, which was revealed by autopsy. Confronted with a charge of open murder, Forrester pled guilty to manslaughter and blamed the doctor for having made the homicide possible by his assistance. An indictment was returned against the doctor for conspiracy to commit murder and he was bound over for trial. The court of appeals refused to take an interlocutory appeal from the circuit judge's denial of defendant's motion to quash and an emergency application for leave to appeal to the supreme court was granted.

"I assume you have all read the morning report on *People v Barnish*. It's the only case on our docket for today. We should have time to discuss it and some other pending matters after we hear the oral arguments." The chief justice looked around the conference table. "Anyone have something to add before we take the bench?"

Justice Hudson raised her right hand."I wasn't here when leave to appeal was granted. Why did we take this case?'

"Because four of us had real questions about whether the doctor should be put on trial for murder under these facts," answered Templeton directly. Hudson shrugged her shoulders. "I see," she said quietly.

The courtroom was empty except for the two lawyers and a handsome greying man sitting on the last bench. Malloy wondered if it might be Doctor Barnish. "People versus Peter Barnish. Are the People ready?"

"Yes, your Honor," said the prosecutor.

"And the defendant?"

"Ready, your Honor."

"Go ahead counsel," said Malloy addressing the prosecuting attorney.

"If the court please, the defendant is the appellant here. He should go first."

"Quite so," Malloy flushed at his mistake. "You may proceed, Mr. Lambert."

"If it please the court, my name in Oscar Lambert. I represent Doctor Barnish. My client is a licensed physician, a graduate of the University of Minnesota medical school, a member of the American College of Psychiatric Medicine, and an adjunct Professor of psychiatry at Wayne State University Medical School. He is a highly respected member of his profession, against whom no charges or complaints of improper practice have ever been made or filed."

Justice Henry interrupted. "Mr. Lambert, even the great ones fall from grace sometimes. Let's get off of the commercial and get to the meat of this case."

"Your Honor, I was just trying to set the scene. The prosecuting attorney would have you believe that Doctor Barnish is some kind of a fly by night charlatan, grubbing for money, and recklessly dishing out huge doses of poison to people who want to commit murder. Nothing could be further from the truth. My client is a reputable, ethical physician. He did what he felt was proper and necessary to treat his patient's depression. The prescription he gave Mr. Forrester was the same prescription he had been giving him for over three years. The dosage, which was plainly marked on the bottle by the pharmacist, in accordance with the doctors instructions, was the same dosage he had prescribed for Mr. Forrester all during the time he treated him. If Forrester took the medicine according to the instructions on the bottle, there was no danger to him or anyone else. Nowhere did Doctor Barnish authorize Forrester to give the medicine to his wife. The prescription was for Forrester. Not his wife. She was not a patient of Doctor Barnish. That particular medicine would never be prescribed for someone with Alzheimer's disease."

"What do you make of the three thousand dollar fee?" Henry asked the question.

"My client denies that there was anything out of the ordinary in that charge. It was an accumulation of fees over a long period of time, for many services. Mr. Forrester was a very needy patient. He frequently called the doctor at odd hours, came to his house to see him, even found him in a restaurant once and interrupted his dinner to get medical advice. The fee was barely compensatory for all the trouble Forrester had given my client."

"Aren't all those things matters to be presented to the jury?" Julia Hudson wanted to know.

"My client shouldn't have to go before a jury, your Honor.

There simply isn't enough here to bind him over for trial."

With that, Lambert sat down and the prosecutor, Hugh Ramsey, stood, approached the lectern, and introduced himself.

"If the court please, this is a charge of conspiracy to commit murder. Forrester is the unindicted co-conspirator. He swears that he and the doctor had an agreement. They conspired together to kill Mrs. Forrester. He testifies that the doctor knew what he intended to do with the prescription. That's why Barnish wrote the prescription for 200 milligrams. Two hundred milligrams, if the court please, would have been enough to keep Forrester in pills for six months at his regular dosage.

"The real issue here, may it please the court, has nothing to do with the size of the dosage. It has to do with whether the doctor was justified in helping Forrester to dispose of his wife, as a means of treating Forrester's depression."

"Wait just a minute, Mr. Ramsey," Hilda Germaine interrupted. "Are you telling us that the doctor gave Forrester this large prescription to eliminate his wife as a means of curing HIS condition?"

"Exactly, your Honor. Doctor Barnish has published several articles in medical journals in which he has argued that the best, most effective treatment for depression is to remove the source of the worry and anxiety. If a patient is depressed over losing his job, the best treatment is to get him another job. If someone is depressed over an impending divorce, the best treatment is a reconciliation. If a teenager is depressed over an illegitimate pregnancy, the best treatment for her depression is an abortion. And, if a man is depressed over his wife's terminal Alzheimer's disease, the best thing for him is that she should die."

"He wrote that in a medical journal?" Malloy was incredulous.

"Words to that effect, your Honor."

"Anything else counsel?"

"No, your Honor. Just that we would like a chance to tell a jury what really happened here."

Lambert rose for rebuttal.

"If the court please, my client is a medical scholar. What he writes for publication in scholarly, theoretical journals has nothing to do with his day to day practice. The prosecutor wants to punish my client for his ideas and his theories. That is hardly consistent with the tradition of academic freedom we hold so dearly in America."

***

Back in the conference room, Alton Henry took to his soapbox. "There you have it, ladies and gentlemen. Physician assisted suicide has just become physician assisted mercy killing."

"Well, I don't call that a mercy killing." Van chimed in. "The wife wasn't in any pain. The claim was that she could not feel much of anything in her condition."

"How far down into the gutter do we have to let Alzheimer's patients slide before we allow them to die with dignity?" Doris Templeton wanted to know. "Does anyone here think she was going to get better? Do any of you know what it is like to see someone you love die of Alzheimer's? My mother had it. I can tell you, it isn't pretty."

"So her death by poisoning was to prevent the husband from having to see her die of the disease, is that it, Doris?" O'Leary asked the question.

"Would you feel better about it if he had taken the pills himself so he wouldn't have to see her die?" Templeton's question was rhetorical.

"Where are we on this?" asked the C.J. "How many to affirm?"

Six hands went up. Doris Templeton looked around. "I'll submit a dissent," she murmured.

***

There were 56 Bill or William or Willard or W. Carpenters in the Chicago phone book. Malloy had obtained a list of them and over the weeks since talking to Ken Pershing, he had been systematically calling them. None turned out to be employed at the telephone company. Toward the end of January, while sitting at his desk reading a long, dull, ponderously written brief in a complicated corporate litigation, Malloy seized, belatedly, upon the idea of calling the phone company. Probably they wouldn't give out the home phone number of one of their employees, but perhaps he could speak with the repairman while he was at work.

It turned out to be surprisingly easy. He called the phone company. The operator asked the name of the repairman he wanted to talk to, and in seconds responded with the man's office telephone number. Malloy called the number, asked for Bill Carpenter, and promptly heard a man's voice on the other end of the line.

"Carpenter."

"Bill Carpenter?"

"That's me."

"Mr. Carpenter, this is Judge Malloy. Chief Justice Malloy, of the Michigan Supreme Court. I'm sorry to trouble you at work like this, but I could not locate your home phone."

"That's all right, judge. What can I do for you?"

"Do you know a man named Art Wilhelm?"

"I guess I do. I wouldn't have been able to answer that question a few weeks ago, but I got some calls from some investigators up in Michigan, and now I know who they were asking about. Wilhelm is a lobbyist down in the loop, right?"

"Right. You know him then?"

"Not exactly. But I have met or at least seen him."

"When was that?"

"Last year. End of April some time. I was in his office installing a new line for a modem, when he came in and started yelling at his secretary. Throwing things around the office. Mad as hell. I thought he was going to hurt her. I didn't want to get involved, so I called the police."

"Did they come?"

"Yeah. In about five or ten minutes. They got Wilhelm calmed down. I finished up and left right after they came."

"What was Wilhelm yelling about?"

"Something about a raffle or lottery ticket. Best I could figure she, the secretary, had goofed up somehow. Didn't check to see if the ticket was a winner. Apparently he gave the ticket away to someone thinking it was not worth anything. He claimed she made him lose a lot of money. I don't remember exactly how much, but I do recall he said it was enough to pay her salary for five years."

Malloy thanked the gentleman, and hung up the phone. Smiling. Then the smile broke into laughter. All alone, sitting at that big, imposing desk, amidst all those weighty law books, Jim Malloy laughed out loud. He roared. Then he called Margaret.

"Guess what, Mag. My good friend Art Wilhelm tried to stiff me and it backfired."

"I don't get it. What are you saying? What happened?"

"Nothing happened. I just got off the phone with a telephone repairman in Chicago who was in Wilhelm's office when Art was chewing out his secretary because she didn't check to see if my lottery ticket was a winner. He thought she had. The son of a bitch thought he was giving me a bunch of losing tickets."

"I don't get it."

"Don't you see? Wilhelm had his secretary check to see if any of the tickets were good. If they were, he was going to keep them for himself. If they weren't any good, he would give them to us, and tell us to call and find out if we won anything. He was stiffing us for a lousy twenty or thirty bucks apiece. But the secretary forgot to call on this one ticket. Maybe on all of them, I don't know. Anyway, she didn't catch the winner I ended up getting, and Wilhelm was madder than hell at her. Made such a fuss, the telephone man called the cops. Can you believe it?"

Margaret was laughing now, too. Then quickly appreciating

what the news meant, she got serious.

"Too bad you can't call the First Press. I'd love to see them eat their ugly insinuations about you."

"Why can't I call them?"

"Trust me. I'm the journalism major. How would you look calling your friend Art Wilhelm a petty welcher? Anyway, I doubt that the Firp would believe you. They would run to Art, and he would be awfully embarrassed. By the time he got through hemming and hawing, they would be convinced he was covering something up. It would just be an occasion for them to repeat all the other stuff they keep saying about you. No, honey, at this point, no news is good news. Best to leave it that way."

"I guess you're right, Mag. But it isn't fair."

***

The *Danken* case, involving the putative, sex-changed widow, posed a particularly troubling dilemma for the chief justice. The straw vote had come up three against three, with his colleagues divided along gender lines. He had attempted to be a peacemaker in the war between the sexes, and had ended up being ridiculed by both sides, when his name was drawn to write the majority opinion. One thing was certain. He would be authoring a majority opinion. Either way he chose to decide the case, he would be speaking for the majority. If he held in favor of the alleged widow, he would get the concurring signatures of the three women justices. If he came out against the claimed widow, he would have the support of his three male colleagues.

After much research, conferring with his law clerks and careful writing and rewriting, Malloy crafted an opinion which he felt offered an amicable solution. His opinion traced the origin of the statutes protecting widows. All of the ancient rules, Malloy argued in his opinion, were made for the obvious purpose of protecting women who lacked the legal status or practical means to fend for themselves. The typical paradigm was the housewife and mother, without financial resources of her own, fully dependant upon her husband for support.

Malloy's thesis was that the court must determine whether the plaintiff was the deceased's widow within the meaning of the Michigan intestacy laws. He was careful to refer to the plaintiff throughout his opinion in the feminine gender. He took the position that the plaintiff was a woman, and that the sex change operation was irrelevant.

The real question was whether the Danish cohabitation agreement made her the deceased's spouse, in the sense intended under Michigan's protective laws. Malloy dissected the cohabitation agreement. It did not purport to be an agreement of marriage. It did not refer to the parties who signed it as husband and wife, but as domestic partners. He pointed out that there was no such thing as common law marriage in Denmark, nor in Michigan. Just living together would not make a man and woman husband and wife in either country. He concluded that the term widow as used in Michigan's law meant the female spouse--the wife--of a deceased man. Surviving domestic partners were not widows, he said, any more than surviving business partners were widows.

Malloy's opinion went on to point out that in modern society, many people enter into domestic partnerships which are not marriages in the classical sense. They do not carry with them the unwritten assumption that one of them will be the bread winner and the other will be the homemaker. Thus, there is no basis for the law to extend any special protection to the survivor in such an arrangement.

When he approved a final draft of the *Danken* opinion, Malloy felt good about it. The men would sign it, because it came out the way they voted. He felt that the women, while not concurring in the opinion, would not find it so objectionable as to warrant particularly vigorous dissent. He was wrong.

Doris Templeton had been working on a dissenting opinion from the day the case was argued. She simply assumed, correctly as it turned out, that the women would be in the minority. Her opinion carried some blistering dicta to the effect that the court's majority were living in the dark ages. Before women worked outside the home. Before they voted. Before they could even own property. She trumpeted the coming of the age of feminism, and predicted that the precedent being set by the majority would fall as soon as women made up the majority of the court.

Of course, Alton Henry could not let the gauntlet fall unchallenged. Hardly had Malloy's majority opinion and Templeton's dissent been delivered to the offices of the justices when Henry's concurring opinion landed on their desks. He agreed with the result reached by the chief justice, but for very different reasons. In Justice Henry's view, the plaintiff was not the widow of the deceased because the plaintiff was a man. Sex change operation or no, she was a he. At least she was a he when the domestic arrangement was made. The law of this state, Henry pointed out, still defines illicit cohabitation between two males as a criminal offense. "Those closed minded radical fanatics bent on destroying the moral fiber of the nation who feel otherwise have no business sitting in judgment upon their fellow citizens, and certainly add no honor to the great history and tradition of the Michigan Supreme Court," his opinion stated.

Malloy reread Henry's opinion. He reread Templeton's opinion. Then he told his secretary that he wanted to see both of them in his office. ASAP.

***

It took the chief justice's secretary several days to arrange the meeting. Phone tag. Scheduling conflicts. Gamesmanship. Henry called Malloy several times. What was this all about? Why do I have to be there with Templeton? Malloy stone walled. Important court business. That's all he would say.

The day came. Henry arrived first. Malloy occupied him with small talk. Doris arrived a few minutes later. Malloy greeted her cheerfully, asked her to take a seat across his desk and next to Alton. Malloy began by thanking both of them for coming.

"I know it is unusual for justices to be summoned this way, and I apologize for the inconvenience. But I feel there is a very important issue to be resolved and it is absolutely necessary to talk to both of you at the same time. It's about your opinions in the *Danken* case.

"My opinion speaks for itself," Templeton was quick to announce.

"So does mine." Henry insisted.

"I understand how both of you feel. But there is more at stake here than the expression of your personal views. Our opinions are published in the official reports of the Michigan Supreme Court. They go into law libraries all over the country. All over the world. They are permanent records. They reflect on this institution. We simply can't publish opinions that contain personal references to each other which are critical or derogatory. It's not good for the court, and it certainly isn't good for either of you."

"*Scripsi scripsit.* What I write is written, " Henry spoke in a low, firm voice. "That's all I have to say."

"I do not frequently agree with my brother Henry, but he has my unmitigated concurrence on that point. My opinion stands." Templeton was adamant.

"I was afraid that you folks would feel this way. I prepared redrafts of both of your opinions, in which I excised only the words I felt were beyond the pale of propriety." Malloy slid copies of the two revisions across the desk to each of them. Neither picked them up.

"If you don't want to talk about toning down your words, I won't demean you or waste my time by jawboning. But I will tell you this: the case of *Danken v Danken* will not be decided by this court as long as I am chief justice and either of your opinions remains as written."

"You can't do that," Templeton challenged the C.J. "Under our rules, you must either submit your opinion or sign one of ours by a fixed deadline. You know that."

"I also know that the clerk of the court and the official reporter take their orders from the chief justice. And I am telling you this case is not going in the books with these scurrilous opinions you two people have written as long as I am the chief."

"Well, then maybe we will just have to get another chief," said Alton Henry.

***

The work day was about over when Evelyn Mentash asked to see the chief justice. Malloy welcomed her into his office and gestured toward a wing back chair to one side of his desk. That way he could remain behind the desk, a position of authority, but have nothing between them, a relationship that suggested openness and willingness to listen. It was the way he always met with staff people. His secretary left the door open, as she had been told to do unless instructed otherwise. Especially if the visitor was a woman.

Evelyn nodded her head toward the open door. "This is rather sensitive, can we be heard?" Malloy got up, walked across the room, bid his secretary and law clerk good night, and closed the door.

"What's on your mind?" he asked.

"It's about Justice O'Leary. I'm worried."

"Worried about what?"

"His drinking. It's gotten worse. I'm scared. Scared he his going to destroy himself, and I don't know what to do."

With a little prodding from the Chief, Evelyn proceeded to detail events over the last months and weeks which clearly raised danger signals. Drinking in the office. Drinking in the morning. Blacking out. Failing to recall what he did or said when drinking. Missing appointments. The whole tragic scenario.

The chief justice praised her for her courage in coming to see him. He thanked her personally and on behalf of the court. He told her that he would look into the matter, and gently, sympathetically ushered her from the office. Then he returned to his desk, sat down with a great heave of a sigh, looked for a phone number in the yellow pages and dialed the local office of Alcoholics Anonymous.

***

On Friday, January 31st, Malloy found O'Leary alone in his office. He closed the door behind him, and after the usual chit chat, took a seat along side O'Leary's desk.

"I hear you have Alton Henry's underwear all bunched up, Jim. Did you really have to do that?"

"I owe it to the memory of our sainted colleague, Chief Justice Breitner. After all, I criticized him for not controlling those two warriors. At least I have to make the effort."

"Henry doesn't like to be tackled by members of his own team. You'd better watch out."

"I will, Bob. But that's not what I came to see you about."

"No? What then?"

"Bob, I don't like to have to do this, but I am going to ask you to take some time off."

"Time off? What for? I don't know what you mean."

"I think you do. It's your drinking, Bob. It's got to stop. You've got to stop. I love you like a brother. You know that. I just can't sit back and let you destroy yourself. You've got to get help."

O'Leary's face reddened. He stood and walked around the desk. Walked to the window. Walked to the door. Then he walked back to where Malloy was sitting. He stood next to Malloy's chair, leaned down until his face was within inches of

Malloy's.

"Listen here, you self righteous son of a bitch, who the hell do you think you are coming in here preaching to me like some damn teetotaling cheerleader? I can handle my booze. I know when I've had enough. You don't ever see me miss a court date do you? Haven't I got all my opinions up to date? What the hell business is it of yours what I do on my own time? I don't see you turning down drinks or asking for lemonade."

"This isn't about me, Bob. It's about you and your health."

"The hell it isn't about you. You're up to your ass in bad ink in the newspapers, you've pissed off your buddy Henry, now you want to come and take it all out on me. You've got a nerve getting on my case. You and your cozy little lottery deal with Art Wilhelm. Your skirts aren't so very clean, Mr. Chief Justice."

"Some day I'll tell you about the lottery ticket, Bob. It's a great yarn, and we'll have a good laugh on Art. Meantime, I'm talking about you and your problem. It's going to be a problem for all of us on the bench, and a black mark on this institution if you don't get help."

"Bullshit," said O'Leary, as he sat down on the couch against the wall. Malloy ignored him, charged full speed ahead.

"I called AA. They gave me the name of a facility in the area around Howell. I called them. They want you to come in for sixty days. It's a quarantine period. I told them it wouldn't work unless you could get out for all regular court dates. They balked, but finally agreed, as long as you return immediately after court. I've talked to your law clerk and your secretary. They will maintain absolute secrecy on this and cover for you completely."

"You talked to John and Evelyn?" O'Leary was incredulous.

"I have. And they are both very relieved that you'll be getting help. They both care about you as much as I do."

O'Leary fell silent. Malloy let his words hang in the air. Finally, O'Leary, got up from the couch, walked slowly to the chair behind his desk, and after sitting down, put his hands on top of his head and leaned his elbows on the desk.

"I can't believe this is happening. I just can't believe it."

Malloy came around behind O'Leary and put both hands on his shoulders, massaging the back of Bob's neck with his thumbs. "I told the nurse to expect you by supper time on Thursday, February 6. You can leave right after our conference. John can drive you. Margaret and I will be praying for you, Bob. We love you very much."

As Malloy closed the door behind him, he had no idea whether his mission had been accomplished. Much would depend on whether O'Leary's clerk and secretary backed up what the chief justice had said. He would not know until February sixth whether his associate would keep the date to enter treatment.

Inside the office, Bob O'Leary's hands moved down to cover his face. Soon his hands were wet with tears. Tears shame. Tears of anger. Tears of pain.

He reached for the knob on the bottom left hand drawer of his desk, pulled the drawer slowly open, and stared at the bottle of Seven Crown, peering out of its royal pouch.

Then he opened it and took a long, defiant swig.

CHAPTER 21

FEBRUARY 1992

Thursday, January 30, 1992. Six-thirty in the morning. Jim and Margaret Malloy made their way through cold, dark city streets to the edge of town and Capital City Airport. They left the car in the short term parking lot. It would be picked up later by Malloy's clerk. Margaret was apprehensive. This trip to Dallas would be her first over night away from the twins. They were seven months old now, both doing well. Teddy weighed fifteen pounds; Terri, twelve. Alice Newton, of course, was staying with the children. The woman was a real blessing. Still, after all the worry and all the anxious moments with two premature infants to care for, Margaret found it hard to relax. Hard to feel young and free of the gnawing burden of responsibility.

And she wasn't really thrilled with the idea of going to Dallas. It would have been nice if she and Jim could just get away someplace by themselves. Someplace romantic. Someplace far away from courts and lawyers and newspapers and politics. Someplace where they could just be Jim and Margaret again, if only for a few days.

But that was not possible. Jim had to be in Dallas for a secret meeting with Ken Pershing. The ostensible purpose of the trip was to attend the annual meeting of the Fellows of the American Bar Foundation, an elegant black tie affair, at which all the big players of the American legal establishment could be seen.

As always when they flew together, Margaret insisted on the aisle seat, and dug into the airline's complimentary travel magazine as soon as her seat belt was fastened. She would attack it ferociously until after the plane was on the runway. Then she would reach over, take Jim's hand, and start to talk. About anything. Where they were going. The kids. His job. The

339

weather. The other passengers on the plane. Taking off made her nervous. She was a chatterbox until the cruising altitude was reached.

This morning, Malloy listened with one ear. He longed to talk to Margaret about his upcoming visit with Ken Pershing. Speculate about what Pershing might be after. About what was on his mind. Get Margaret's common sense evaluations. She had a great instinct for people. Their motives, their predilections. That conversation would have to wait until they closed the door of their hotel room.

Dallas provided some relief from the winter chill. The Malloys spent their first day in Texas getting registered, greeting old friends, just milling around. Margaret found a museum tour for Friday which interested her. She knew that Jim would be looking for Pershing and would need to have the room to himself. Her job was to be inconspicuous.

As it was, she could have stayed in the room. Ken Pershing had apparently surrendered to the cloak and dagger syndrome. Waiting for Malloy at the front desk when he registered was a sealed envelope. Inside was a slip of paper. It read, "Hotel Argonaut. Room 1211. 10:30 AM Friday." This was not the hotel where Pershing was staying. Malloy shook him head in amused disbelief, as he thought of Ken Pershing, an otherwise pedestrian small town trial judge, renting a room at the Argonaut, a third rate hotel, under an assumed name. The meeting, already shrouded in secrecy, took on an aura of recondite mystery.

The setting tempered Malloy's feelings as he entered the small lobby and waited for the elevator. Pershing was an old acquaintance. They had served together on the Board of the Judges Association when Jim was on the trial bench. Malloy regarded Ken as a straight shooter, a good man. He thought Pershing had an equally good opinion of him, and had been prepared to have an open, hair down discussion. Now, the elaborate security of their meeting made him uneasy. He wondered what Pershing was really after.

The door to room 1211 was partially open. Malloy knocked. No answer. He pushed the door inward. Could see no one. He stepped into the room. "Ken? Are you here Ken?" At that moment, he heard the toilet flush. Smiling, Malloy shut the door, returned to the room and sat on the edge of the bed. "You certainly are taking no chances, Ken. I'll bet this is the first time a Michigan grand jury has ever convened in this flea bag hotel."

The bathroom door opened and Raymond Tibson, premier investigative reporter of the Detroit First Press, appeared.

"Good morning, Mr. Chief Justice. It was nice of you to take the time out of your busy schedule to grant me this personal interview. My editor will be especially pleased to know that you have decided to be open and candid with the people of Michigan who elected you to the supreme court."

Malloy swallowed his Adam's apple. He wanted to run out of the door. He wanted to take this twerp by the collar and throttle him. He wanted to yell and curse and shake his fist at the sky. He wanted to know why a merciful God in Heaven would let him be tortured like this. *Steady, Jim. Easy does it. Play it cool.*

"I'm certainly relieved to see you here, Tibson. I couldn't imagine who would have left me that anonymous message, except maybe Judge Pershing. I was afraid he had flipped out and was starting to imitate the CIA."

"You hadn't planned to meet with him in Dallas?"

"I certainly hadn't planned to sneak around in hot pillow joints to meet with him, no."

"But you were planning to meet?"

"I knew he would be here in Dallas, and he knew I was coming. We expect to run into each other, yes."

"Is he going to call you as a witness?"

"I don't know. If he does, I will testify, of course."

"You won't take the fifth amendment?"

Malloy laughed uneasily. "No, I don't expect to have to take the fifth amendment."

"Even if he asks you about your ties to the Army of Righteousness?"

Malloy was up and walking toward the door. "Even if he asks me about my secret meeting with Ray Tibson. I have nothing to hide from Judge Pershing. And I have nothing more to say to you. Good day sir."

***

Back at his own hotel, Malloy, still shaking with anger, decided to kill some time and calm his nerves by meandering among the dozens of exhibits that the American Bar Association convention had attracted. Computer software vendors, legal publications, travel agents, secretarial services, expert witnesses, accident reconstruction specialists, and a host of other law related enterprises had come to Dallas to sell their wares. The great hall was abuzz with lawyers asking questions and loquacious salespeople demonstrating the latest gadgets and electronics. Malloy was engrossing himself in a video lecture by the nation's foremost expert on demonstrative evidence, when he felt a tug on his sleeve. He turned to see the smiling face of Ken Pershing, Owosso Circuit Judge.

"Going back to law school, Jim?"

"Just want to keep up on the law of evidence so that I can correct all the mistakes you fellows make in the trial courts. How are you doing?"

"I finished my business with the Judicial section. I'm looking to get out of here later today if I can change my flight. I overdose on this convention business very quickly."

"I know what you mean. Do you have a minute to hear about my adventurous morning?"

"Sure, Chief, let's move out of the traffic pattern though."

The two men chatted as they walked to a less congested part of the hall. Out in the open, but sufficiently distant from the exhibits so that no one would be close enough to hear their conversation, they were able to talk without concern for security. They had a right to speak to each other. There was nothing sinister about a circuit judge talking to the chief justice.

"How in the world would Tibson have known we were planning to meet down here?" Pershing wondered.

"I doubt that he did. But it was easy for him to know that you and I would be here. We are both registered with the bar as convention participants. The list of the registrants and their hotels is available to any one at the bar's registration desk. I'm sure he could have gotten a copy of the roster out of the Chicago headquarters a week ago," observed Malloy.

"These media guys have more nerve than brains. They drive me nuts." Pershing was serious.

"Got to live with it, Ken. Freedom of the press, you know."

"I know. But it's hard to ignore them, and they can screw up an investigation. Take Wright, for instance. We were weeks away from calling him. Maybe months, or maybe we never would have called him as a witness at all if we couldn't find anything to tie him to the Breitner murder. But the newspapers were all over us like white on rice. Even the little Owosso paper wrote an editorial demanding that we call Wright. My wife, for crying out loud, couldn't understand why I hadn't subpoenaed him. So we brought him in. He takes the fifth, and we're back where we started. Is he the head bad guy or not? We haven't a clue. We can't even say that he was involved."

"I can't help you there, Ken. All I know about Wright is that he has been a very active conservative politician in the southwestern part of the state. Served many years in the legislature. Damn effective campaigner. Seems to know everybody in the Republican Party."

"We do know this, his phone has been ringing off the wall ever since he got in trouble over this Army of Righteousness thing. He gets calls from all over, and the people who call him include a lot of kooks and suspicious characters. We know he has had contact with a very militant bunch up near East Tawas.

Ex Viet Nam guys, originally, but they've added a number of younger men in recent years. They own a hunting camp up there, about three hundred acres. Local scuttlebutt is that they have military games every summer. They use some kind of cartridges that contain vegetable dye to shoot at each other. I would call it kid stuff, if it weren't for the fact that they seem to be so serious about it."

"Is the Tawas thing recreational, or does it have political overtones?"

"A couple of the major players in that operation are pretty outspoken radicals. One of them refused to pay his income taxes a few years ago. Ended up doing some time before he finally paid up. But we have found nothing concrete to tie them to the killing."

The two judges wandered over to the coffee bar, got decafe, and strolled away from the crowds again. Malloy told Pershing about his trip to Wawa. How he had been angry at Breitner for the memo urging his removal, how he had managed to find Breitner's cabin, but was unable to make contact with him while in Canada.

"It was a real wild goose chase, Ken. So I came back to Michigan and went over to see Bob O'Leary in Munising. We had dinner, and I left early in the evening. About the time I crossed over the Mackinac Bridge, I called Breitner's car phone for the umpteenth time, and he answered. We set a meeting at his motel in Indian River."

"How did that go?"

"It was ugly. I chewed him out for the memo. He showed me an anonymous note which complained about his opinion in the *Silus* case and threatened him if he didn't back me."

"We've got the note. It was in his pocket when his body was discovered."

"He also showed me the scratches on his car."

"The AOR scratched on the hood?"

"Yeah. He said it had been done the week before, and that the anonymous note was on the windshield when he found the scratching."

"Did he say anyone else knew about the scratching?"

"No. As a matter of fact, that was a bone of contention between us. I thought, instead of blaming me for the scratches and the note, he should have come to me and together we could have tried to find out who did it. He didn't even report the incident to the police. I told him I was going to report the matter to the state police, myself, whether he did or not."

"How did you leave him?"

"He was pissed. He yelled at me as I was leaving. The manager heard it."

"And you never saw him after that?"

"No. I drove to Gaylord and got a motel room there."

Pershing grew pensive, looking down at his feet and stroking his chin. "Do you know of any reason why someone might have been trying to blackmail Breitner?"

The thought had never occurred to Malloy. "Blackmail? No, I can't imagine why anyone would be doing that. Why do you ask?"

"We found a pattern of unexplained cash withdrawals from Breitner's bank account. Could be nothing. Could be anything."

"Have you talked to Elizabeth?"

"Yeah. But she's no help. They had a very strange, distant relationship."

"I know."

"By the way, who else knew he was at Indian River?"

"I don't know. But something strange was going on with him."

"What do you mean?"

"For one thing, the message he left on my car phone's answering service was peculiar. He said he was sorry he missed me at the cabin and that he wanted to talk to me. He couldn't have known I was at his cabin, unless he also knew where I was staying, because I left that information with the wife of one of his fishing buddies. So I couldn't understand why he didn't call me in Wawa. Then there was his telephone. I must have called his cabin a dozen times at all hours. He never answered."

Pershing seemed distracted. "We had the Canadian authorities check into his cabin, They could find nothing there that would help us, except maybe the fact that the door to his storage shed looked like it had been tampered with."

"That was me."

"You?"

"Yes. I told you I had to pry at the door to see inside and identify Breitner's car."

"Oh yes." Pershing looked at his watch. "I'm going to have to go. I'm checking out today."

"Just one more thing, Ken. Did the Canadian people find any sign of another car at Breitner's cabin. A Jeep?"

"No. They would have mentioned it."

"Are you sending anyone up there to do some more investigating?"

"I don't see the need of it. The Mounted Police are very thorough. I trust them. And the taxpayers of Michigan don't need to pay for any more wild goose chases."

Malloy laughed. "You're probably right about that."

***

On Monday, February third, Malloy stopped by Van Timlin's office for a chat.

"Another first Tuesday tomorrow, Van. Are you all ready?"

"Well, I am about as ready as I should be, I suppose. I've read all the briefs anyway."

"You always do. By the way, it looks like we may have some excitement at our meeting tomorrow."

"What kind of excitement?"

"I think Alton will make a fuss. Try to rake me over the coals."

"Because?"

"Because I leaned on him and Doris for their nasty opinions in the *Danken* case. Have you seen them.?"

"I most certainly have seen them. And in my opinion they are a disgrace. You know, Jim, there seems to be a terrible trend in our profession, a lack of civility. Lawyers calling each other names. Lawyers making unflattering personal references about judges. And judges themselves tearing each other apart and publicly berating the attorneys who appear before them. Used to be, when I was a young lawyer, that a judge would never criticize a lawyer in front of the client. If he had something harsh to say, he would always take the attorney into his chambers and say it there. Nowadays..."

"Nowadays, it's no holds barred. Right?"

"Quite right. And here we have justices of the state's highest court, the very people who are supposed to set the tone, engaging in what the lawyer's oath calls 'offensive personalities.' I'm appalled by the sight of it."

"Makes you long for the good old days when every lawyer was 'my learned brother' and every judge was 'this honorable court,' doesn't it?"

"It sure does. Did you say that you admonished Doris and Alton?"

"Took 'em to the woodshed, Van. That's my job, isn't it?"

"I don't envy you. When I was chief justice, civility and politeness were the rule. We didn't always agree, and in fact we didn't always respect each other, but we always were agreeable and treated each other with respect."

"A good way of putting it."

"Anyway, I admire what you did. I don't think Alton will do you any permanent mischief."

"I hope not. Thanks for your kind words."

Malloy went back to his office and called Hilda Germaine. Just to say hello. Just to touch base.

***

The C.J. was the last to enter the conference room. It didn't take much clairvoyance to smell the odor of mutiny. Malloy took his place at the head of the table, dispensed with small talk, and called for review of the morning report on the first case to be heard that day. Before anyone could speak, Alton Henry took the floor. "Mr. Chief Justice, there have been three opinions circulated in the *Danken* case. Yours for the majority, Doris Templeton's dissent and my concurring opinion for affirmance. I move that we sign those opinions right now and release our decision in the case."

"My opinion isn't ready to go yet, Alton. I still have some revisions to make. I thought I told you about that last week."

"You told me you would never let that case come down. I say it's ready to go, and I move that we sign our opinions right now."

Doris agreed, and seconded the motion.

"Your motion is out of order. Our next opinion conference is Thursday. You can make the motion then." Malloy returned to his notes on the morning's docket.

"That's about all of your high handedness we have to take, Malloy. I move that the chief justice be removed from office and Justice J. Frederick Van Timlin be elected chief justice for the remainder of the unexpired term."

"Support," thundered Templeton.

Fat's in the fire, Jim. Keep cool. Play out the string.

"Your motion is out of order, Alton. That matter is not on our agenda. And it will continue to be out of order until the court rules are amended. The constitution says that the supreme court shall select one of their number to be the chief justice, according to rules to be adopted by the court. The only rule we have ever adopted is Rule 7.323 which says that we elect a chief justice at our first meeting in every odd numbered year. There is no court rule providing for removal of a chief justice. Until we adopt such a rule, I am sitting right here."

Henry blustered, looked around the table, and renewed his attack.

"You rule me out of order? You think I'm out of order? Well, we'll just see about that. I appeal the ruling of the chair."

Steady, Jim. Steady as she goes.

"An appeal of the chair's ruling, according to Robert's Rules of Order, is not debatable. Shall the decision of the chair stand as the decision of the court? "

Justices Germaine, Hudson, and Van Timlin raised their right hands. Henry glared at Van Timlin. "Aren't you with us? I just said I want to put you back in the chief justice's chair."

"Well now, Alton, that's very nice of you, and I appreciate the honor you pay me by placing my name in nomination. It surely is a gratifying thing to be thought so well of by one's learned and esteemed colleagues. Any other time, under any other circumstances, I am certain that the compliment you pay me would embolden me humbly to accept the singular recognition you propose. But I happen to agree with Justice Malloy's view that it is the responsibility of the chief justice to assure that our official opinions contain no vituperation, and therefore, I am going to cast my vote to sustain the decision of the chair."

***

On the afternoon of February 6, after the court's opinion conference, the chief justice was driven to Capital City Airport by his law clerk. Just in time to catch the commuter flight to Chicago's O'Hare International Airport, the first leg of a trip to Seattle to attend the annual meeting of the National Conference of Chief Justices. He was alone this day, Margaret having declined to do any more traveling after the Dallas trip only a week before.

His plane left at 5:05 and arrived at 5:05, a function of the change from the eastern to the central time zone. With time to kill at O'Hare, Malloy found the frequent flier's executive club and staked out a telephone. He called the court. An assistant in the crier's office answered. No one else was there. Malloy fumbled in his suit pocket for a notebook, and leafed through it until he found a phone number. Then he dialed the number, listened, dialed his credit card number, waited, then said, "Evelyn, it's the chief. What happened this afternoon? Did Bob go to Howell?"

He listened.

"Uh huh. At your apartment? With John Hayes, his clerk?"

He listened again.

"What did you say to him?"

Silence. Listening.

"Uh huh. He did, eh? So how did you handle it?"

Malloy tapped his fingers on the ledge as he listened some more.

"I see. Well, I guess that's it then. How are you doing?"

More silence.

"Yes, I know, Evelyn. These things are very difficult. You and John deserve high praise for service above and beyond the call of duty. Believe me, what you did means a lot to me and to the court. God bless you both."

Malloy hung up. He let out all the air in his lungs. O'Leary was at the treatment center in Howell.

He sat for a long time just staring out the window, watching the big jets come and go. Then he absent mindedly picked up a magazine and began leafing through it. One article caught his eye:

MAKING THINGS WORSE: WHY YOU SHOULD NEVER CONFRONT AN ALCOHOLIC WITHOUT PROFESSIONAL ADVICE.

The article began with the story of a 53 year old advertising executive whose boss had called him into the office, dressed him down for coming back to the office drunk after lunching with a client, accused him of being an alcoholic, told him to take two weeks off to dry out, and threatened to fire him the next time he touched a drop of anything alcoholic.

Hours later, the man's body was fished out of the East River.

Malloy wondered what they said to new patients in Howell.

CHAPTER 22

MARCH 1992

Malloy was in Seattle when Tibson's Dallas datelined story in the Detroit First Press hit. Margaret called him at his hotel and, in a voice choked with anger and hurting, read the story.

MALLOY TO TELL ALL
Embattled Chief Justice Agrees to Testify
If Called By The Pershing Grand Jury

DALLAS, February 7, 1992. Michigan Supreme Court Chief Justice James P. Malloy, long regarded as a key witness in the terrorist murder of his colleague Edward Breitner, has agreed to take the stand and testify under oath concerning the August 1991 slaying.

Malloy, who has repeatedly refused to comment publicly about his role in the Breitner affair, told the First Press in an exclusive interview that he will answer every question without invoking the fifth amendment protection against self incrimination.

Malloy continues to insist that he is innocent of any wrongdoing. Kenneth Pershing, the Owosso County Circuit Judge appointed by the court of appeals to conduct the investigation could not be reached for comment. It was known however, that he was in Dallas earlier in the week and that he

was expected to confer with the chief
justice during his stay here.

The story went on to repeat all of the previous rumors and
speculation about Malloy, including his lottery windfall, his
supposed connections to the Army of Righteousness, his rivalry
with Breitner, the Breitner memo urging his ouster, his angry
trip to Wawa, the confrontation at Indian River and his night in
the Gaylord motel.

When she had finished reading, Margaret was in tears. Malloy
tried to calm her down, to no avail. She was angry about the
press coverage, but as she continued to talk, it became apparent
to him that she was also angry at him.

"I studied journalism. I know how these people think and how
they work. You can't just go around blurting out everything to
the newspapers and expect them not to use things against you.
They're in the business of selling newspapers. Can't you get
that through your head? They don't know you and they don't
care about you. They are going to write the story the way it
looks the most interesting to their readers. And if that means
trashing you, that's what they will do."

"I think I know that, Margaret," Malloy said, trying to keep
his voice level.

"You don't act like it. You never call me. You never talk to
me before you shoot your mouth off. I would have told you not
to say a thing to Tibson."

"What was I supposed to do in the Argonaut Hotel, say,
'Excuse me, I have to call my wife'?"

"No but you didn't have to grant him an interview."

"I didn't grant him an interview."

"No? Then where did he get all this about you going before
the grand jury?"

"I dunno. I suppose I said something like that as I was
walking away. I didn't talk to him any longer than it took to get
out of the room."

"Yeah. I'll bet. If I know you, you were playing the nutcracker. Trying to match wits with the guy. You'll never learn. And of course you never think of the children or me. How do you suppose I feel when you get this kind of ink? How do you think it makes the kids feel when they have to go to school and listen to their friends taunt them about their father?"

Malloy didn't answer. He sat with the phone to his ear, listening to her weeping fifteen hundred miles away. Wishing he could take her in his arms and hold her and tell her he was sorry for the pain he had caused her.

"You just don't care about us. All you care about is getting your name in the paper. You don't care what they say about you as long as they spell your name right."

Malloy bit his lip. *Easy, Jim. Don't escalate the war.*

Best to try to change the subject. "How are the twins?" he asked, incongruously.

"The twins are fine. So are Jimmy, Paul and Mary Ellen."

"What did you have for dinner tonight?"

"Chicken. Why do you ask?"

"I just wondered what kind of garbage you're going to wrap in that newspaper tonight."

"Real funny, Malloy. You just don't get it, do you?" Margaret was not amused. More silence.

"Well, I gotta go, Mag. Got a big day tomorrow."

"So do I."

"I love you."

"I love you, too."

"Good night."

"Good night."

Malloy sat on the edge of the bed, holding his head in his hands. *"As long as they spell your name right."* The words lingered, burning, in his ears. Did she really think he felt that way? Didn't she realize that he was whistling in the dark? You never let a bully know he's hurting you. He'll only want to hurt you all the more.

Jim recalled his 'Nutcracker' days. The sequel to his famous attack on the bully, Clyde. When Clyde caught him alone, in Finnegan's alley, and slammed his head repeatedly against the back wall of the garage. With every slam, he had spit in Clyde's face and growled through clenched teeth, "You can't hurt me, Fatso."

And neither can you, Tibson.

***

O'Leary attended the Thursday conference on February 20th. He looked nervous, anxious, uncomfortable. He said little during the meeting and avoided Malloy's eyes. Immediately after adjournment, he was gone. On checking with Evelyn Mentash, O'Leary's secretary, Malloy learned that Bob's clerk had picked him up in Howell, delivered him to the court, and spirited him away as soon as the conference was over.

The other two Thursday conferences in February were canceled, since there were not sufficient opinions ready for discussion. So Tuesday, March third, the first session day of the next monthly term, loomed rather large for Justice O'Leary. He had been in treatment almost thirty days. He was about to spend three consecutive days away from the center, mingling among judicial colleagues, experiencing the stress of debate and decision making, feeling the old insecurities and longings. The things that led him to drink. The subtle sirens of fermentation and distillation.

Throughout the short drive, O'Leary was ambivalent. In one way, he was feeling fine. Better than he had in years. He was beginning to sleep better. In fact the last four nights were the first in years that he had been able to get through without waking. Even once. Even to go to the bathroom.

On the other hand he was disquieted for some reason. Learning to take one day at a time wasn't easy. Every time the thought occurred to him that he would never, ever again be able to lift a festive toast to his lips, he felt deeply sad. Deprived of the joy of living. Denied the right to pursue happiness. Separated from his friends. Ostracized. Rejected. Wounded. Deprived. It was as though the crippled leg had taken over his whole body. His very soul was now crippled.

Torn between rehabilitation and debilitation, he was not ready to return to work. The staff at the treatment center knew he wouldn't be. That's why their program is designed to last sixty days. From experience, they know it takes that long to refocus. To get ready for a new and different life. Bob's position and the need to keep his condition secret conspired to wreck his chance at resurrection. He felt cheated. He had no time to get well. He had to be well.

Entering the conference room, O'Leary mustered all his inner metal, put on a happy face, and greeted his colleagues as cheerily as he could. The response was less than heartening. It seemed to O'Leary that the justices were all grumpy, distant, unfriendly. Did they know? Was his secret out? Were they disapproving of him, branding him a hopeless drunk? Or worse, pitying him as a hapless, helpless alcoholic?

Caught up in his own thoughts, O'Leary read every non-verbal communication as though it had something to do with him. Of course, the fact was otherwise. Henry was still stinging over last month's rebuff of his effort to oust Malloy. Templeton was equally miffed over the hold up of the *Danken* case. Hudson was wondering what kind of a zoo she had allowed herself to be sent to. Van was as oblivious to O'Leary as he was to everything else. Hilda's pleasant smile never faltered, and her facial expression rarely gave away her inner feelings. And Malloy, the only one who really knew of Bob's situation, was absorbed with his own problems.

O'Leary sat down, opened his notebook, and waited for what seemed an eternity for someone to speak, something to happen. Then suddenly he heard himself talking. Spilling his guts. Like this was an AA meeting. Like these people cared. Like they were his friends. His confidantes. Like they could be trusted.

"Before we begin to talk about today's cases, I want to express my apologies to all of you for anything I may have done or failed to do over the last several years which you may have found offensive or hurtful. And I want to express my deep gratitude to the chief justice for making me confront the condition which has caused me to behave less than appropriately over the past several months. You may or may not know that I have checked myself into an alcohol recovery center since our February conference. I am staying for the entire program. I'm learning so much about my condition and myself. It has been a seminal experience. I hope to be able to say years from now that these weeks have been the turning point of my life. All I know now is that I need the prayers and good wishes of all of my friends and associates. I'm telling all of you these things because I think the court has the right to know about the personal problems and difficulties of its members. I don't ask any special consideration or favors from any one. I only ask for your friendship and that in the interest of preserving the public image of the court, if not mine, you help me to get past this difficult time without the embarrassment of public disclosure."

The silence in the room was palpable. The chief justice wanted to say something. He could think of nothing.

Templeton rose, walked around the table to O'Leary's chair and extended her right hand. "Congratulations, Bob. You have real guts, and I am proud to be your colleague on this bench." Simultaneously, Hudson and Van Timlin burst into applause, which was joined in by the others.

Hilda Germaine summed up the feelings they held in common. "We have our differences around here, but there is one invariable rule, Bob. We all want what is best for this court. Usually that is the same thing as wanting what is best for each and every one of us, because our success and wellness as individuals is what gives the court its vitality. You have done something that is very good for the Michigan Supreme Court,

Bob. We all know it, and we appreciate it. I think you can count on every person in this room to keep your confidence and lend you their encouragement and support in every possible way."

O'Leary bowed his head and let tears of gratitude flow. His were not the only tears in the room. Van Timlin took out his handkerchief and blew his nose, wiping his eyes in the bargain. "I don't know what you're crying about, Van," chided Alton Henry. "You're not on the wagon." Laughter broke the serious mood; Malloy rang for the clerk and asked for comments about the first case on the day's docket.

***

On the Wednesday of session week the women made it a point to have dinner together. Usually at the Lansing City Club, where the hostess accommodated them in a private room. On March 4, the talk turned to the chief justice, as it often did.

"That fellow Art Wilhelm has been subpoenaed to testify before the grand jury again. I hear he is a friend of Malloy's. Do you think this has something to do with the lottery scandal?" Hudson asked her companions.

"I heard he's the one who gave Malloy the ticket, supposedly at O'Leary's house. Some people are saying O'Leary may be involved, too." Hilda Germaine noted.

"I know Wilhelm is a wheeler dealer. I remember him from my days in Washington," added Templeton "He was in the congress at the time. I wouldn't be surprised to see a headline about unethical acts on his part. Once a sleaze, always a sleaze."

"I just wish Malloy, or Wilhelm or somebody would come out in the open and say what really happened. If that lottery ticket was legitimate, there should be no reason why the whole story can't be told." Hudson's comment drew nods of agreement.

"Maybe O'Leary can break the log jam," Doris wondered aloud. "Do you suppose he feels up to doing something?"

Julia interjected. "What would he do?"

"Maybe he could convince Wilhelm or Malloy to talk to the media. Maybe he himself knows the story. Even if the truth were only leaked to the papers, that would help. It's this dark cloud of suspicion that has hung over the court for almost a year now that is so destructive." Templeton spoke with conviction.

"You're right, Doris," rejoined Germaine. "Maybe one of us should have a talk with him. I think he can have occasional visitors now."

"Do you think it's good to get him involved in a stressful situation?" Julia asked. "I mean just when he is recovering and all."

"I'm not so sure this wouldn't be exactly what he needs to get his mind off of himself." Templeton observed.

"At least we could ask him. He ought to know what he can handle and what he can't," offered Germaine.

"Good idea, Hilda. You should go. He trusts you," Templeton urged. Hudson agreed.

On Thursday, the conference ended shortly after lunch. Germaine pulled O'Leary aside as they were breaking up. "I'm going back to Detroit alone, Bob. I would be happy to drop you off in Howell. No need for your law clerk to make the round trip." O'Leary agreed. He welcomed the company of another justice. It was an affirmation.

In the car, Hilda wasted no time getting to the lottery business. "The grapevine has it that you know the story about Malloy's big lottery win. Is the rumor mill accurate?"

"Only partly, Hilda. I know that Jim got the ticket from Art Wilhelm, but I don't know where Wilhelm got it." O'Leary told Germaine about the gin rummy games and the way the ticket purchase came about. "We all got tickets from Wilhelm. He bought them with our money."

"But you really don't know if Wilhelm bought Malloy's ticket at a convenience store or from a money laundering exchange."

"No. I really don't. And I don't think Jim knows either."

"So the only one who can tell where the ticket came from is Wilhelm?"

"That's right."

"What would it take to get him to talk publicly about it?"

"That would be tough. Art has been around the track in Washington and elsewhere. He's not likely to open up if it would embarrass him, his clients or anyone else."

"What if you or Malloy revealed that Wilhelm was the source of the ticket? Wouldn't that create a lot of media heat on Wilhelm? Wouldn't he have to speak up sooner or later?"

"Maybe so, Hilda. But I don't see how I could bring myself to do that to him. He's still a friend of mine, and just now I need all the friends I can get. And besides, to be honest, I'm not looking for any added stress. Just remember where you're dropping me off."

Hilda realized the idea of involving Bob was not fair. There would have to be another way to break the story.

***

On March 16, just after supper, O'Leary called Malloy at home.

"I haven't missed Mass at Holy Trinity Church on Saint Patrick's Day in years, Jim. I don't know if I can handle it, but the doctor here thinks I can if I go with someone like you. Can you do it?"

"Done deal," The chief replied quickly. "I'll pick you up at 6:30 in the morning." Malloy's big blue Oldsmobile was out in front waiting the next morning at 6:25.

"Thanks for coming, Jim. I sure hope I can do this. I hope I can get through this day."

"Not to worry, Bob. We're in this thing together. You and I are going to do Saint Patty's day in Detroit on mineral water and Seven Up. We'll set the world's record for deliberate, conspicuous, stubborn, Irish sobriety. Here, put this on." Malloy handed O'Leary a small gold lapel emblem, the symbol of the Pioneers, a long establish society of Irish teetotalers.

"I've heard of them. I had an uncle who wore one of these. He died of consumption, but his liver was donated to science."

O'Leary was in a good mood, but still a little apprehensive. To ease his anxiety, he broached a subject that had been on his mind for a long time. "You told me once that we would have a good laugh on Art Wilhelm when you described how he came to give you the lottery ticket. I'm ready to laugh now."

Malloy told the story of the telephone repair man. O'Leary didn't laugh right away.

"You're saying that Art deliberately stiffed us? That he knew all of our tickets were losers?"

"He thought they were, anyway."

"No wonder he doesn't want to go public with it. But why don't you say something? You're the one who gets all the bad press on this."

"Think about it, Bob. How am I going to look if I accuse Wilhelm of trying to cheat his card playing buddies out of, what was it altogether, eighty bucks? I shutter to think of the field day the First Press would have with that one."

They arrived at the Fisher Building just a little after 7:30. J.P. McCarthy, the quintessential drive time radio personality, was holding forth, as he always did on the seventeenth of March, in a restaurant in the first floor of the midtown skyscraper. McCarthy was unique in the world of talk radio. For more than a generation, he had dominated the powerful signal of WJR, which billed itself as the 'great voice of the great lakes'. McCarthy knew everybody who was anybody in Detroit, and they all knew him. Moreover, McCarthy knew literally thousands of people who were not somebodies. The working, voting, buying class. They were his people, and he was their celebrity.

Malloy and O'Leary were immediately identified as important guests, and admitted to the overcrowded room. Standing room only. Elbow to elbow. The bar was open, the drinks were flowing. Bloody Marys. Screwdrivers. And, what else? Green Beer. Pitchers of draft beer, deeply colored with green vegetable dye. At 7:30 in the morning. Only the Irish would welcome such an affront to the pallet. Malloy and O'Leary moved quickly to order soft drinks. This was no day to be standing around without a glass in your hand.

J.P. was way in the back of the room. Flanked by the Irish band known as 'Blackthorn,' and a coterie of politicians and newsmen, McCarthy spewed his fabled charm and wit into a hand held microphone, which he periodically shared with selected guests. McCarthy was a world class interviewer. He knew everybody's business, could call up names, places, events and facts like a veritable human computer, and presented it all with such benign good humor that even the targets of his rare but real wrath regarded him with fond respect.

O'Leary and Malloy had just about worked their way up to see their host, when they heard McCarthy greeting a familiar political personality.

"And here, ladies and gentlemen, among our most preeminent guests this fine morning is a well known man about town, raconteur, and bon vivant, the distinguished former congressman from our neighboring state of Illinois, the Honorable Arthur Wilhelm. Greetings, Art. What brings you to Detroit?"

"Where else would anyone want to be today, J.P.?"

"Tell us, Art, what will they be doing in the windy city of Chicago on this day of days?"

"Chicago has a great Irish community, J.P., as I'm sure you know. The Chicago River will be dyed green today, as it always is. And of course, Chicago's Saint Patrick's Day parade is among the biggest in the country. By three o'clock this afternoon, there won't be an empty seat at the bar anywhere in the loop, I can tell you that."

"We're delighted to have you with us, Art. And I see some

friends of yours and of all of us have just come in. Chief justice Jim Malloy and Justice Bob O'Leary. Come on up here gentlemen." Malloy and O'Leary doubled their efforts to elbow through the mob, and in a moment were next to McCarthy and Wilhelm.

"Ladies and gentlemen, let's give a big welcome to the distinguished jurists from our supreme court in Lansing." Applause and whistles greeted the justices on cue. "Good morning, Mr. Chief Justice. You and Justice O'Leary, I see, are properly decked out in green ties. Will you be celebrating the entire day with us here in the Motor City?"

"Wouldn't miss it, J.P." answered Malloy. "We'll be sharin' the green at Holy Trinity this noon as well."

"That's wonderful. Bob O'Leary, it's great to see you, too. Tell me, can you still do some of the classic Irish jig steps?"

"Is the Pope Catholic?" replied O'Leary. "You never forget those things."

"Alright, lets have a demonstration!" The crowd cheered and applauded. The band struck up a jig. O'Leary dropped his arms to his sides, and began the familiar bouncing steps, punctuated with stomping, best suited to hard soled dancing shoes. The routine took only a few seconds, but it brought the house down.

"Amazing," McCarthy pronounced as O'Leary finished."Truly amazing that you can do that difficult step. You lost your left foot in Viet Nam, didn't you?"

"Never have to worry about fallen arches, J.P." O'Leary joked. More applause, mingled with laughter.

Turning to Malloy, McCarthy's insatiable curiosity prompted another question. "And speaking, as we were, of wearing the green, you certainly have the luck of the Irish, Mr. Chief Justice. Didn't the State of Florida present you with a nice bouquet since last time I saw you?"

"Nearly enough to buy your sailboat, J.P. Is it on the market?"

"Not as long as there is a race to Mackinac Island. Now tell me something, Jim. Mr. Justice. Just between you and me and the few hundred thousand folks who might be in their automobiles driving to work this morning, just where did you get that winning lottery ticket?"

Malloy's ears reddened. *Hold on, Jim. Keep cool. Keep it light.*

"The man who bought it for me is standing right next to you, J.P. You ought to ask the congressman to buy you some lottery tickets, he's mighty good at it."

McCarthy, never at a loss for words, hesitated for just a split second. Then he motioned the band leader with his left hand, and turning to Wilhelm, smiled and said, "Stick around Art, I may want to rub your nose for some Irish luck. But first, let's take a station break." The music came up on cue.

***

Holy Trinity Roman Catholic Church is one of the oldest in Detroit. Located a stone's throw from the ball park, its spire demarcates a neighborhood once known as Corktown because of its predominate Irish population. In the mid twentieth century, Holy Trinity achieved a special prominence in the city because of the presence in its rectory of a saintly pastor named Clement Kern. Monsignor Kern was a dynamo of Christian charity and social action. He supported the organization of unions, fought city hall, helped budding young attorneys and politicians, established a credit union, legal and medical clinics, and an annual tradition called the Sharing of the Green. Nobody ran for public office in Detroit without giving due deference to Clement Kern and Holy Trinity.

On Saint Patrick's Day, the tiny, old church was always packed to its doors. Standees lined the walls. Folding chairs diminished the aisles. Worshipers, patrons, new and former parishioners began arriving before eleven for the noon Mass. Ecumenical ushers, recruited for their celebrity, greeted and seated the crowd. Later they would pass the traditional collection plates for the support of the many impoverished men, women and children who turned hopefully to Holy Trinity in their time of need. The collection at Mass was the frosting on the cake. Detroit's Irish, previously canvassed by mail, would have already filled the church coffers somewhere in the seven digits.

As in every election year, on this Saint Patrick's Day the crowd swelled to absolute maximum. Sitting room gave way to standing room, which then shrunk to elbow room, which in turn was subsumed by breathing room. Just getting one's wallet out of a back pocket presented a gymnastic challenge. Malloy and O'Leary managed, however, and each dropped a fifty dollar bill as the basket passed. Public servants rarely used envelopes or wrote checks. Not that anybody really noticed what they gave. But you can never be too sure.

Latecomers who could not get into the church milled about on the sidewalk, pretending to have just come out with everyone else, gabbing excitedly, greeting old friends, relatives, rivals, and enemies with equal good cheer.

The annual ritual then required a stop at the school. Holy Trinity Elementary School was one of the few in town that still boasted a contingent of nuns. Not many, but enough to set the tone of discipline and fervor. There were no Irish children in the school any more. Hadn't been for years. Mostly, the kids were Spanish, Mexican, and African American. On Saint Patrick's Day, however, they all wore green and sang songs from the old sod. Napertandy. Danny Boy. The Black Velvet Band. The Wild Colonial Boy. They sang and they played the instruments the nuns had taught them to use. Guitars. Tambourines. The saxophone. The piano. Entering the plain square room which served as an auditorium, Malloy and O'Leary were handed green photocopied flyers which served as programs. They were mostly full of Hispanic names. One name which was not Hispanic caught O'Leary's eye. Jeremiah Wheatley.

He looked around the room at the children who lined the walls waiting for their turns to perform. The third youngster left of the piano was black. Taller than O'Leary remembered him, but recognizable. The scars from his burns were visible, though muted by growth and time. The program wore on for forty minutes. The kind of thing that usually appeals only to grandparents. On Saint Patrick's day, however, all of Detroit was grandparent to these striving children. Then it was his turn. Jeremiah walked to the piano stool, showing only a little sign of his disability. He opened his sheet music, placed it on the piano's easel, sat down, and began to play. Jeremiah was good. Really good. He played an Irish reel. He played it with vigor and he played with verve. Toe tapping verve. Step dancing verve.

Bob O'Leary got up from his folding chair and walked to the front of the room. For the second time this March seventeenth, he did his famous Irish step dance. The little black piano player looked at him quizzically at first, then breaking into a wide toothy grin, Jeremiah began to beat the rhythm of the tune on the hard wooden floor with his hard plastic foot.

CHAPTER 23

APRIL 1992

Tuesday, April 7, 1992 was one of those big days in the Michigan Supreme Court. In fact, it was officially designated a 'solemn occasion.' The first case on the call, and the only one the court would hear this morning was entitled *'In Re the Constitutionality of Act 201, Public Acts of 1991.'* The governor had requested an advisory opinion. Under the constitution he could do so only "on solemn occasions."

Act 201 was the much publicized and highly controversial anti-terrorism law, which was variously referred to in the media as the 'Tuttle' Law, the 'Breitner' Law, or the 'Tuttle-Breitner Anti-Terrorism Act.' It was also called the 'death penalty law' because it proposed to reinstate capital punishment in Michigan for the crime of 'Terrorist Murder' as defined by the legislature.

The advisory opinion case was particularly sensitive because 1992 was an election year and the legislature had decreed that there was to be a referendum on the death penalty on the November ballot. The ballot issue was directly tied to Act 201. It was posed in these words:

SHALL THE CONSTITUTION BE AMENDED TO ALLOW THE PENALTY OF DEATH FOR TERRORIST MURDER AS DEFINED BY LAW?

The issue divided the state along unusual and volatile lines. It fostered the strangest of political bedfellows. Basically, Act 201 and the related death penalty referendum pitted the extreme right and the extreme left against the middle of the road or the political mainstream. In general, the intelligentsia, the press, the legal profession, the top people in both Republican and

367

Democratic Parties, and the organized civic, business, and community action groups were opposed to both the terrorism law and the death penalty. Many trade unions, taxpayer groups, splinter parties, right and left wing radicals, and just plain unorganized, usually non-voting citizens, supported both the terrorism law and the death penalty amendment to the constitution.

It was impossible to run for public office in Michigan in 1992 without coming to grips with the issue. Every voter information survey, every citizen's forum, every newspaper and television station wanted to know where the candidates stood. No office was exempt. From drain commissioner to United States Senator, candidates were put to the test. For or against. Pro or con. Make up your mind. And, of course, almost every candidate tried to waffle. Find an answer that offended no one. Find some safe ground where you can hide out until after November. After the people have spoken. After the winning side has been identified.

Of course, the best way to waffle was to pass the buck to the Michigan Supreme Court. The court would decide whether the Tuttle Law was constitutional. Let the court decide. Let the rule of Law prevail. Let the system work. But don't ask me. Not yet, anyway.

When the seven robed justices entered the courtroom that April morning, the scene greeting them was shocking. Almost every seat in the chamber was occupied by a person wearing a blue denim shirt, over which a black Sam Browne belt reached diagonally from right to left. They all wore black four-in-hand ties--both men and women. All wore ties. In the few seats they had not preempted, newsmen, law clerks, and representatives of the governor's office vied for space. A clamor at the courtroom door evidenced the fact that many who wanted to enter were unable to do so.

The chief justice called the case. The attorney general was, in effect representing both sides. He had assigned a team of able lawyers on his staff to research and argue in favor of the constitutionality of the law, and another equally competent task force of staff attorneys to oppose it. In the state law library, the two squads had come to be known as the 'Pro Team' and the 'Con Artists.'

In addition to the attorney general's people, many legislators and political and civic organizations had filed *amicus curiae* briefs, supporting one position or the other. One such brief was filed by 'The Army of Righteousness, an unincorporated association.' Three attorneys were named on its cover as counsel for the AOR; the senior partner in a well regarded ten lawyer firm in Mount Clemens, an associate professor on the faculty of the Detroit College of Law, and a retired circuit court judge from Cadillac. Their brief argued that the terrorism law was unconstitutional because it was vague and indefinite, and because it operated to chill the exercise of federal constitutional liberties, particularly the rights of free speech and freedom of religion.

The chief justice nodded to the lead attorney of the Pro Team, and leaned back in his chair to listen with interest. He looked past the well dressed woman at the lectern and tried to assess the impact of a packed courtroom of paramilitary spectators. Obviously, this was the Army of Righteousness. They were here to defeat the Tuttle/Breitner Law. Malloy agreed with their purpose, but not their method. Their action had backlash written all over it. Their presence on this day, here in this room, he thought, would project upon the mental screen of every justice on the bench a haunting image of Ed Breitner's automobile, with the letters, 'AOR' scratched on the hood, and their colleague's bloody body slouched inside. An image demanding justice. Demanding retribution.

As Malloy's eyes wandered around the room, his attention was abruptly captured by one of the uniformed visitors. Unlike all of the rest, whose countenances were serious if not somber, this fellow was smiling. Smiling, Malloy suddenly concluded, directly at him. *Good heavens. Could it be? No, it couldn't be. Oh yes it is. That's Pat. Pat Sheehan. My sister Molly's husband, for God's sake.*

The chief justice averted Sheehan's gaze, and mumbled under his breath, "What the hell is my damn fool brother-in-law doing here in the courtroom with those goofy trouble makers?" Then he got mad. Mad at his brother-in-law. Mad at the clowns who engineered the Christmas fireworks. Mad at the idiots who used his name to hoist the Guatemalan flag. Mad at Wallace Wright and his right wing pals. And absolutely furious with whoever had murdered Ed Breitner in the name of righteousness.

Malloy leaned forward and tapped the gavel crisply just once. "Excuse me, counsel. I am sorry to interrupt your train of thought. We will give you a chance to start over again in just a little while. The court is going to take a brief recess at this point. The crier and the clerk will kindly clear the courtroom of all spectators and then report to me in the conference room." Malloy rose, and his colleagues, wondering what was going on, followed suit.

In the conference room, Malloy slammed his notebook down on the table, and let off steam. "I never let anybody pack my courtroom when I was a circuit judge, and I'm not about to let them do it now. When Mike gets the room fully cleared out, I will have him issue numbers on blue paper to everyone with press credentials and on white paper to every one else. Then I will instruct him to draw forty blue numbers and one hundred white numbers. The people Mike calls will be admitted to the courtroom, and nobody else. Does anyone have a problem with that?"

Justice Henry definitely had a problem with it. "You have no right to do that on your own authority. What if there are more than forty reporters? Do you give press priority to little small town weekly papers? We can't do this now, today, without the court adopting guidelines."

Templeton agreed. So did Germaine and Van Timlin. The

discussion continued until the clerk arrived to announce that the courtroom was cleared. Malloy handed Delbert a piece of paper on which he had been writing during the discussion. The clerk read it, nodded, and left the room. Malloy allowed the discussion to continue for another ten minutes. Then he stood and said, "You folks can make all the guidelines you want for next time somebody tries to pack the courtroom. Today, I'm making the rules, unless the court chooses to overrule me. Does anyone wish to make a motion?" In silence, the justices picked up their materials, and lined up to return to the bench.

Back in the crowded courtroom, Malloy was relieved to see that the AOR presence had been reduced to a scattered handful of blue shirts. Pat Sheehan was not among them.

***

The advisory opinion case, with its interruptions, and the wide public interest it held, went on until nearly 1:30 PM. The court broke for lunch, then returned to discuss the case in chambers for the rest of the afternoon. At day's end, it appeared that a majority, while being generally opposed to the law as a question of public policy, could see no valid legal premise upon which to strike it down. Julia Hudson's name came up to write the majority opinion. She asked the others to send her memos on their views, and promised to get out a preliminary draft opinion before circulating anything final.

O'Leary was tired. It was his first day out of the treatment center. He had graduated the previous night. The staff had a small party. Ice cream and cake. Fond farewells and Godspeeds. They were great people, all of them, Bob thought. They had been his home and family for nearly two months. They provided security, a sense of discipline and purpose. From now on he would have to make it on his own. Of course, Alcoholics Anonymous would help. He had the addresses of all the local meetings, and had already attended several and met the people.

One group, composed entirely of lawyers and judges, made him feel especially welcome. And it was a great comfort to know that certain of his long time friends were in the program and had been for years without his knowledge.

At five o'clock, he sat at his desk, catching up on new applications for leave to appeal. Evelyn came into his office, asked if there was anything she could do for him before leaving, and when he said no, asked if she could talk to him for a moment.

"Sit down, Evelyn, " O'Leary said warmly. "What's on your mind? How are you doing?"

"I'm doing fine. How are you?"

"Hanging in there. It will be hard, but I'm pretty sure that I can take things one day at a time."

"Good. I know you will. I believe in you."

"Thanks. I don't know what I would do without you, Evelyn. You've been a great source of strength to me."

"Not always. For a long time, I'm afraid, I was an enabler. I made excuses for you. Covered up. Lied to myself about how bad your drinking was. Lied to myself and to everybody else. No more. I can't do it any more. I can't come in here day after day and just do whatever you want me to do, without questioning whether I think it is what should be done or not."

"I've always valued your input, Evelyn. I need your advice and counsel."

"I won't quarrel with that. But you also need a secretary. Someone who works for you. Thinks of you as the boss. The one with all of the answers. Blind loyalty and obedience. That's what you need. Every justice needs a secretary like that."

"I don't know. I've been pretty happy with the way you and I have worked together."

Evelyn fell silent. She rolled the pencil in her hand around in her fingers as though reading the legend printed on it. When she spoke it was softer but more decisive. "I'm leaving you, Mr. Justice. Giving you my notice. Now. Tonight. I'll be gone in two weeks. That should be long enough for you to find someone else. I'll help with the interviews if you want me to."

O'Leary was stunned. He didn't know what to say. Her statement was so unexpected, yet so final. He dismissed his first instinct to forbid her to quit, and his second impulse to beg her not to quit, and went with a third idea. "What are you planning to do?"

"I would like to get married. That's what I plan to do, though I'm not sure my plan will work."

"Married? I didn't know you were seeing someone. Tell me about him."

"He is just a big dumb Irishman who lives in the upper peninsula and desperately needs a woman like me to make a home for him, look after his health, spoil his grandchildren, entertain his family and friends, and make him feel like the wonderful human being he really is." Evelyn was up and walking toward the door. "The only problem is he doesn't realize that he loves me. Maybe he never will." She turned, and disappeared into the outer office, where she snatched up her purse and coat and literally ran down the hall to the elevator.

Bob O'Leary shuffled the papers on his desk and prepared to leave for his AA meeting. He would have much to tell tonight when it was his turn to share.

***

That night, Malloy called his brother-in-law from home, and gave him a thirty minute lecture on why a military approach to political issues had no place in a free and democratic society. When it all passed over Sheehan's bullheaded understanding of moral absolutes, Malloy turned to personal persuasion. "Just do me a favor, will you Pat? Stay out of my life with your AOR stuff. I have enough troubles of my own without having to explain why you do what you do." In twenty minutes, his sister Molly called to apologize for her husband, and assure Malloy that Pat was turning in his Sam Browne belt. Jim thanked her, and hung up the phone wondering how long poor Sheehan would languish in penitential celibacy. Those Malloy girls were tough, tough, tough.

***

Evelyn's last day was April 22nd, a Wednesday. The staff at the supreme court had a long tradition of observing birthdays, anniversaries of marriage or employment, retirements, or separations with a reception. In fact, these events generally gave staff members an excuse to eat homemade goodies throughout the day.

On this day in 1992, the secretaries, law clerks, court clerks and criers, security guards and two of the Justices gathered in the chief justice's conference room for cake, cookies, coffee and fond farewells to Evelyn Mentash, who had faithfully served the supreme court since 1987 when she came to Lansing with her long time employer, Bob O'Leary. They toasted Evelyn, presented her with funny greeting cards, hugged her affectionately and wished her well in her future endeavors. No one knew what her plans included, however. There were rumors, the most persistent of which was that Evelyn was getting married. But she had not confirmed it, and there was no known prospective groom. That, of course led to the wildest speculation that the romantic imaginations of the secretarial staff could conjure. From a mysterious Greek shipping mogul, ala Aristotle Onasis, to a handsome movie star like Tom Cruise. Some of the farewell messages and greeting cards were hilarious.

Her fellow secretaries had purchased a small gift for Evelyn, and presenting it was to be the highlight of the reception. After that, those who had other places to go, could leave without giving offense. The only problem was, Bob O'Leary, Evelyn's employer for nearly twelve years, beginning with his freshman term in Congress, wasn't there.

His absence made everyone uneasy. He, above everyone else, ought to be there to wish her well. Was he miffed because she was leaving? Was there a larger story about her separation than any that had surfaced during the two weeks since she had announced her intention to leave? What was the real scoop?

Finally at quarter to six, when the crowd was about to leave, grand finale or no, O'Leary showed up. He strode into the room and briefly acknowledged Malloy and Van Timlin, the only justices present. Then he walked straight to where Evelyn was sitting, eating a piece of angel food cake. Without a word of explanation or salutation, he got down on his left knee, opened a small jewelry box and said, "Evelyn, darling, will you do me the honor of becoming my bride, the love of my life and comfort of my loins, the queen of my castle and solace of my senility, until death do us part, so help you God?"

As Evelyn giggled and the staff applauded, he took her left hand and pushed a two caret diamond ring on the third finger.

***

For over a year, the Detroit First Press had been on a crusade to discredit and ultimately oust Chief Justice Malloy. Hardly a week would pass without some little shot being fired. By and large, the Firp was alone in its efforts. The other major metropolitan daily, the Detroit Evening Paper, generally limited its coverage of the chief justice to actual events, without reporting courthouse speculation. The lesser papers around the state were equally uninterested in the Firp's advocacy journalism project.

Then on Sunday, April 26, 1992, a new voice was heard. The Detroit Evening Paper, which boasted the largest circulation in the state, carried an in-depth feature article entitled, "JAMES MALLOY: IS HE REALLY ABOVE THE FRAY?" The article recounted the various events of the last year. The lottery win. The Guatemalan flag incident. Malloy's trip to Canada seeking Breitner, on the eve of Breitner's brutal murder ostensibly by the Army of Righteousness. And of course, the fact that Malloy was the last person to have seen Breitner alive on that fateful night. The story told of the chief justice's connection with the AOR through his political contacts with Wallace Wright. It included a recap of Malloy's biography, and some quotes from lawyers and court watchers who were acquainted with him, describing Malloy as one who usually kept his own counsel, was generally regarded as honest and hardworking, but had a fairly volatile temper, a certain innate clumsiness, and a tendency toward activism when he thought he was in the right, which was most of the time.

A separate side bar accompanying the article, framed in a box and superimposed over the main body of the story, revealed that Malloy's brother-in-law, one Patrick Sheehan, had been identified as an active member of the Army of Righteousness.

CHAPTER 24

MAY 1992

At four thirty in the afternoon, the sky had turned ominously dark and threatening. Springtime in Michigan is tornado time. Violent storms rise up almost without warning. Sometimes the sirens wail. Take cover. Stay away from windows. Head to the basement now. Right now. Take candles and matches. Blankets. Some fresh water. Huddle in the southwest corner. The storms usually blow in the from the southwest. This day, a funnel cloud touched down near Battle Creek. Ominous clouds blanketed the capital throughout the day.

The supreme court's opinion conference, on this stormy day, lasted longer than usual. There were a number of matters on the agenda. Quite a bit of time was devoted to further discussion of the terrorism law case. Justice Hudson had compiled an extensive list of precedents both in Michigan and in other states, interpreting laws dealing with the subject of terrorism. They were, to put it mildly, all over the map. None appeared directly on point. The language of Michigan's new terrorism law broke untested judicial ground.

The *Danken* case was also on the court's long opinion agenda. Despite vigorous protest by Justices Henry and Templeton, the chief justice continued to refuse to release his opinion and allow the case to be decided and printed in the Michigan Reports.

Doris Templeton went down the hall to her small Lansing office when the conference concluded. She had a headache. She was tired. She had driven up to the capital alone, leaving her law clerk to work on pressing matters back in her downtown Detroit office. Now she faced the hour and a half ride back to the metropolitan area on I-96. Ugh. She picked up the phone and called Cheryl. Doris was, after all, a grandmother. And

while she was hardly your typical, chicken soup and Vics
Vaporub grandmother, or your garden variety Barbie Doll and
tea party grandmother, she was a real, honest-to-God
grandmother, in an important-public-official-with-a-life-of-my-
own way.

"How's Eddy?"

Cheryl launched into a detailed account of her son's weight,
height, clothing, bowel movements, eating habits, crawling
motions, sitting up efforts, smiling tendencies, and the numerous
evidences of his genetically endowed intellectual superiority. All
of which was received on the Lansing end of the call with such
enthusiasm and appreciation that time slipped away unnoticed.
Suddenly, a clap of thunder outside brought Doris to look at the
clock.

"My Gosh, it's after 6:30, Cheryl. I've got a long drive, and
it looks like we are going to have some nasty weather."

Cheryl coaxed one last cooing sound out of her offspring and
they said goodby.

***

Alton Henry's eight year term of office expired at the end of
1992. Unlike his colleagues, who faced the electorate in pairs,
Henry ran all alone. Someone had to; after all, the court had
seven members. Henry was the odd man out. Of course, in
1992, Justice Julia Hudson would run for the unexpired term of
office of the late Justice Breitner, so her name would be on the
ballot as well as Henry's. But they would be in separate races,
each facing their own opponents. Henry was not an official
candidate in May. He would not be a candidate until early in
June, when he would file an affidavit of candidacy with the
secretary of state.

But the fact that he was not yet officially running did not deter
Henry from seeking support among the electorate. Beginning in
January, he had started to accept all the bar association, service

club and citizen group invitations that he routinely threw in the wastebasket during the seven years since he last faced the voters. On the first Thursday in May, Alton Henry was due in Charlotte at seven o'clock for a meeting of the Eaton County Bar Association. He had used the time after the court's opinion conference to review and revise his fifteen year old standard speech to the lawyers.

Henry glanced at his watch. After six thirty. Time to go.

***

Doris Templeton entered the elevator and pushed the button for G1, the upper level garage floor. As the door of the elevator was about to close, a man's hand reached around and arrested the progress of the automatic double door. Presently, the body connected to the hand appeared in the open elevator entrance. Alton Henry. Seeing Templeton, he hesitated a split second, like a halfback doing a stutter step. Then he entered, said nothing and turned to face the closing doors.

***

The winning dart in a game of 301 could not be hurled with more accuracy than the lightning bolt which struck the Law Building on May 7th. It careened through the open louvers of the air vent in the rooftop structure housing the electric motors which operated the west bank of elevators, literally melting the computer controls. Nine stories below, the elevator carrying Justices Henry and Templeton ground to a complete stop, somewhere between the first floor and the upper level of the garage. The elevator cab was instantly bathed in utter darkness. Total darkness. The kind of debilitating pitch black that challenges the sense of balance, and makes every familiar object unknown and potentially dangerous. Doris Templeton was the first to speak.

"Shit."

"Shit," Alton Henry pontificated, "as I have often read on the rear bumpers of automobiles, happens."

"Well, it doesn't have to happen to me. Certainly not in the present company."

"The feeling is mutual, I'm sure."

"Doesn't this thing have an emergency button or something?" Templeton at last demanded.

"I don't know. Aren't the controls on your side?"

"I thought they were over where you are," Templeton ran her hand along the wall of the cab until it reached the front, then felt up and down the front panel in search of controls. "Must be. They're not over here."

Henry, in the meantime, was doing roughly the same thing. His groping was better rewarded. "Yeah. Here they are." He ran his hand down the buttons, pushing each as he went. Nothing happened. No lights went on. No beeps. No response whatever. He found a toggle switch, and flipped it up and down. Nothing.

"These controls are all dead." Henry pronounced.

They fell silent and stood stiffly in place. Waiting for the lights to come back on. Waiting for the elevator to begin moving again. Waiting for this uncomfortable situation to come to an end. Minutes passed. Two, three, four. Six, seven, eight. Twenty, maybe thirty minutes. In the dark, in the silent dark, minutes stretch to hours. Dead silence yields to the howl of live breathing.

"This is ridiculous," observed Henry finally, " How long do you suppose..."

"Hush. I think I hear someone coming."

Silence. Listening. Far off, faintly, unintelligible noises. Human voices. Talking? Calling?

As though guided by the downward thrust of a maestro's baton, Templeton and Henry began in unison to pound on the door of the cab. "Help!" They yelled. "HELP!" Then they began to improvise.

"WE'RE OVER HERE" Henry yelled.

"WE'RE STUCK IN THE ELEVATOR." Templeton screamed.

Bang, bang, bang went their fists on the door. Bang, bang, bang.

HELP, HELP, HELP. They yelled, and hollered, and shouted and screamed. HELP, HELP, HELP.

More improvisation. Templeton shouted, "HELP. THIS IS JUSTICE TEMPLETON OF THE SUPREME COURT, SOMEONE PLEASE COME AND OPEN THE ELEVATOR DOOR. LET ME OUT OF HERE."

Alton Henry, not to be outdone, chimed in, "THIS IS JUSTICE HENRY. I'M IN HERE, TOO."

Silence. Weary, panicky silence. Then Templeton, angry, frustrated, and impatient, burst forth anew, pounding ferociously on the door. "HELP, GOD DAMN IT, HELP ME. I'M STUCK IN THIS GOD DAMN ELEVATOR WITH THE GOD DAMN PRINCE OF DARKNESS, ALTON FUCKING HENRY HIMSELF. WON'T SOMEBODY PLEASE, FOR CHRIST'S SAKE, COME AND LET ME THE HELL OUT OF HERE BEFORE I PUKE ALL OVER THIS UGLY OLD SON OF A BITCH."

"HELP ME, SOMEONE. ANYONE." Yelled Henry, as Templeton leaned against the back wall panting, trying to catch her breath. "HELP ME BEFORE I PERISH IN THE UNWELCOME COMPANY OF THIS FLATULATING, OBSCENE, DEMENTED, BLASPHEMOUS, SUPERANNUATED HAG OF A WITCH WHO THREATENS TO FLAIL ME WITH HER BROOM AS SURELY AS SHE MALIGNS ME WITH HER MALEDICTION." Henry's big, heavy hands beat a tattoo on the elevator doors which gradually subsided, gradually slowed. BAM. BAM. BAM. Bam. Bam. Bam. bam. bam. bam   bam   bam   bam. "Oh, shit." said Henry.

"That's what I said in the first place."

"Then I concur in your opinion."

"About time, I'd say."

Silence. Long, tired, defeated silence.

"'Maligns me with her malediction?' Did you say 'Maligns me with her malediction?'" Doris began to snicker. Her snicker matured into laughter. Alton couldn't help himself. He began to laugh, too. Soon they were both laughing uncontrollably. Laughing at themselves. At their predicament. At their foolish, panicky attempt to attract attention.

"Prince of darkness?" Alton forced the words out between peals of laughter. Causing him to laugh all the harder.

"Superannuated hag?" Doris choked the words and redoubled her laughing.

"Oh, shit?" asked Alton. And they both howled.

"Oh, shit!" cried Doris. And they both hooted some more.

Alton Henry laughed so hard, he felt weak in the knees. He leaned against the back wall, and felt himself sliding down the wall to a sitting position. The more he slid, the louder he laughed. Soon, the seat of his pants hit the floor with a thud, and he laughed even harder. Hearing his voice descending, Doris Templeton was overcome with the improbability of it all. Her laughter got out of control, too. She dropped to her knees, then, attempting to assume a sitting position, began falling to her right. She stuck out her right hand to brace herself, and pushed it squarely into Alton Henry's face. Still laughing hilariously, she tried to extricate herself from him as he attempted to keep her from falling on top of him. The net result was a grotesque entanglement in which her arms were around his waist, her head on his chest, his arms draped over her back, and his nose buried in her hair.

The more they tried to get loose from one another in the pitch darkness, the more they laughed and the more they laughed, the more intertwined they became. Alton finally fell into the corner, with Doris on top of him, laughing uncontrollably into his left ear. Bracing his right hand against the wall, he pushed himself and her into a sitting position. As he did, her mouth brushed against his left cheek, and for an instant, he thought she had kissed him.

In a moment they were quiet. Sitting side by side on the floor of the elevator. Exhausted from laughter, weak from fear. Some how calmed in the knowledge that they were not alone.

Alton was the first to break the silence.

"Am I imagining things, or is this episode a metaphor?"

"A metaphor? How so?"

"For the court. A metaphor of what we do as justices of the supreme court. We're together. Alone. In the dark. We don't know what to do. We don't really have all the answers. We don't agree with each other, but we're stuck with each other. Whether we like it or not. Whether or not we like each other, we're all in the same boat. Our success or failure is a shared thing. We need each other."

"I must be getting disoriented in the dark. I thought I heard Alton Henry say something wise and sensitive. Can it be that beneath the hide of a male chauvinist pig there beats the heart of a human being?"

"One learns many things in the dark. Not the least of which is that you smell like a lady."

"And perhaps that you can act like a gentleman. Would you mind helping me up?"

Henry leaned forward to brace himself against the front wall to stand up. His hand touched something only two feet above the floor. He ran his hand over the object. A plate of some kind. No, it has hinges. And a little ring to pull. He pulled the ring. The little door opened. He reached inside, in the darkness, groping to feel what was in there. Some kind of an implement. Ah Ha. A familiar implement. A telephone.

He reached down and took both of Doris's hands in his, then pulled her gently to her feet. "Doris, I think we are not going to have to spend the night together. I just found the emergency telephone."

"That's too bad, Alton. I was starting to look forward to the prospect."

***

Circuit Judge Kenneth Pershing picked up the file labeled 'press clippings.' It bulged with recent stories. They would all have to be added to the fat scrapbook his secretary was keeping on the work of the grand jury. In addition to the Detroit Evening Paper's feature story on Chief Justice Malloy, there were articles and editorials from Flint, Saginaw, Grand Rapids and Traverse City. Plus a wire service blurb that had been picked up in Chicago, Philadelphia and New York. The universal thrust was that the grand juror ought to call the chief justice as a witness.

Pershing didn't want to do it. He knew Malloy, and liked him. More importantly, Pershing respected the C.J. Thought him a man of honor and integrity. Hardly the criminal type. Hardly a murderer. And Pershing knew what calling the chief would do. How the very fact of his appearance before the investigatory body, with nothing more, would create an atmosphere of suspicion and speculation. The kind of gossip that destroys reputations.

But Ken Pershing had an agenda of his own, albiet a modest one. He wanted to stay on the bench. He liked his job and his life. He had no intention of allowing his service as grand juror to become the occasion of his return to the practice of law. And so he reluctantly weighed the impact of the mounting publicity. As long as it was merely bad press for the chief justice, Pershing could ignore it. But now, as he read the clippings, he sensed that the thrust of the editorial criticism was beginning to be directed toward him. Why doesn't the grand juror call Malloy? Is Pershing holding back? Will Pershing white wash the chief justice's role in the Breitner affair? What is Judge Pershing hiding? What is he afraid of? Why won't he do his simple and obvious duty?

These were the kinds of questions that Ken Pershing didn't want to hear. And didn't want to have to answer. Dropping the clipping file, Pershing picked up the telephone, checked his roladex, dialed the number of an old friend, and waited while the connection was being made into the offices of the supreme court.

"Alton Henry, please."

"This is Alton Henry."

"Mr. Justice, Ken Pershing calling. How are you?"

"Fine, Ken. I haven't seen you in a long time. How are things in Owosso?"

"Things would be fine if I could get all these nosey reporters out of my courthouse."

"I'll be happy to trade places with you. I'll need all the publicity I can get this year."

"That's right, you are running this year aren't you?"

"Yup. And I couldn't get my name in the papers if I bit a dog. Judicial candidates are like lepers to the media."

"I suppose I'll be back to where you are soon enough, but right now I can't go out for a hamburger without being accosted by some hotdog with a press card or a TV camera."

"Look at the sunny side, Ken. If you don't screw up, your next election should be a breeze."

"That's what I'm calling you about, Alton. I need your advice. You've always been straight with me from the time I clerked in your office as a law student."

"Glad to tell you whatever I can, Ken. You know that."

"Well, I've been getting plenty of heat from the press and broadcast people critical of me for not calling Jim Malloy as a witness. I know you and Jim have been close since he went on the supreme court. I don't want to call him, but I don't know how much longer I can hold off without doing myself real harm politically."

"Malloy can take care of himself. You call him, Ken.

Nobody's going to take care of you if you don't do it yourself. Do you think Malloy would hesitate for a minute to remove you from the bench if the Judicial Tenure Commission recommended it? You didn't get chosen as the grand juror because somebody thought you would be squeamish. Do your duty as you see it."

"Easy enough, theoretically. But I doubt that I would think it was my duty to call him if it weren't for the negative ink."

"You wouldn't have any problem calling Joe-Average-Citizen if as much suspicion were pointing at him as points to Malloy. A convenient big lottery win with unanswered questions about where the ticket came from. Admitted ties to the Army of Righteousness. His office apparently calling Capitol Security to get the Guatemalan flag raised for the AOR. His brother-in-law dressing up in one of those uniforms. The mystery trip to Canada on the very day Breitner was murdered. And the undeniable fact that Breitner was out to remove him as C.J. Not to mention that Breitner's death gave him another Republican vote on the court. What else do you need? If all of that doesn't raise your eyebrows, they must be locked in a muscle spasm."

"I guess you're right, Alton. It makes me sad to think that even Malloy's friends are beginning to doubt him. I sure appreciate your candor. I know you wouldn't be talking this way if you thought there was nothing to these things. Thanks for the guidance."

Pershing heaved a deep sigh after he hung up. Then, steeling himself, he made the courtesy call he knew he would have to make sooner or later.

"Mr. Chief Justice? Ken Pershing here. Do you have a moment?"

"Sure, Ken. What's on your mind?"

"I'll get right to the point. Unhappily, I am going to have to call you as a witness in the grand jury probe. I can work with you on the timing to a degree, but it will have to be done."

"Thanks for the heads up, Ken. I can appreciate the pressure you've been under. Send your man around with a subpoena whenever you're ready. But I would like at least thirty days before I have to appear."

"We can do that, Jim, and I'm glad to oblige. But from now on, I guess we'll have to avoid private conversations. At least until this thing is over."

"I understand. Thanks again. I'll see you in court, as the saying goes."

"Goodby, Jim. And good luck."

Malloy dropped the phone into its cradle and stared out of the window at the gathering storm. He knew what Margaret and all of his friends and relatives would say. Get yourself a lawyer. Only a fool represents himself. This is serious business. Mere innocence is never a perfect defense. The truth doesn't always win. You could be the victim of a frame up. Don't let your ego permit you to play into the hands of your enemies.

He imagined himself in the witness chair, stone walling. Repeating the bunker defense which belonged almost exclusively to the guilty. 'I refuse to answer on the ground that my answer may tend to incriminate me.'

The prospect made him sick at heart.

CHAPTER 25

JUNE 1992

There were times when Jim Malloy had to talk to his wife. Not that he couldn't or wouldn't make decisions himself. He always did and she knew that. But talking through a problem needs a good listener. And Margaret Malloy knew how to listen, how to ask questions, how to challenge, when to encourage, when to instill doubts, when to respond and when to keep quiet. She was a world class listener.

The problem was that she had a life of her own. She was engaged in, and engrossed in, the rearing of five children. No doubt in the big scheme of things a much more important vocation than her husband's. Certainly it was as time consuming and more physically tiring

All of which meant that there were times when Jim Malloy wanted to talk with his wife, but it was not possible for her to talk with him. So he would stand around, just like Jimmy, or Paul, or Mary Ellen, trying to get her attention, and she would try to listen while doing some other urgent, unavoidable task.

"I'm listening." She would say. But then she would turn to Paul and tell him to redo the map for social studies class because Montana is not south of Idaho. Or tell Mary Ellen won't you please stop fussing with my hair brush and put your pajamas on. Can't you see I am talking to your father?

This early June evening, Malloy really needed her undivided attention. He undertook to put the children to bed. If he could just get them all asleep before his wife collapsed with fatigue, maybe she would have time for him. Jimmy and Paul relished these times. Dad would try to be tough. No nonsense, off to bed with you both. They would tease each other and tussle like two bear cubs, until Malloy got mad and picked them up and physically threw them into their beds. That was a blast. When dad threw them in bed. They could bounce off the mattress onto the floor and he would pick them up and do it again, and pretty soon it would be major league rough house with both boys tickling their father and him pretending to be angry and tickling them back so hard they had to go to the bathroom and when they did it was all over and they had to go to bed for keeps.

So finally it was ten o'clock and Jim and Margaret could sit at the kitchen table with a cup of tea and she still had enough energy to listen.

"I know it defies all the conventional wisdom, but I just don't want to have a lawyer with me when I go to the grand jury. It will cost a fortune and I already know what he will tell me to say."

"What about Joe? Your brother would be glad to represent you, wouldn't he?"

"He might not. Criminal law is not his thing."

"Don't you know any good criminal lawyers?"

"Lots, but they would all tell me to clam up. Say nothing. Or worse yet, negotiate a grant of immunity to tell everything I know."

"So what's wrong with a grant of immunity? Doesn't that mean you can't be prosecuted?"

"Sure. But it also means that in everyone's mind I am guilty of something. Like Richard Nixon being pardoned. Nixon never admitted anything, but he might as well have pled guilty. The pardon had the same effect as a plea of guilty as far as the public was concerned."

"What would the public know? Aren't grand jury proceedings supposed to be secret?"

"Supposed to be is the operative phrase. Most of them leak like a sieve."

"I don't know. This whole thing scares me. I just wish it was over. I wish it would go away."

"There is only one thing that will make it go away, Mag. They've got to find Breitner's killer."

"Do you think they will?"

"Not the way Pershing is going about it. I'm disappointed in him."

"How so?"

"He's not aggressive or inquisitive enough. He's letting the media lead the investigation. He acts as though his job is to follow up on whatever he reads in the paper. I think he is just scared to death of the big city newspapers."

Margaret thought awhile, then asked the question that put everything in perspective. "Jim, what would you do if you were the grand juror?"

Malloy didn't hesitate for a second. "I'd send somebody up to Wawa. Better yet, I'd go myself. Whatever happened to Breitner started to happen at his cabin. I'm convinced of it."

"Why don't you tell Pershing to go?"

"I did. He thinks it's a waste of money. He got a report from the Canadian authorities, and he is satisfied there's nothing else up there to discover."

"And you think there is?"

"Everything in my gut tells me so. First of all, when Breitner went up there from Mackinac, he intended to stay at least several days. Elizabeth said as much. She was gong to visit friends at Harbor Pointe. I'm sure she expected him to be at the cabin for some time. So why did he leave so unexpectedly?"

"Maybe he was just trying to dodge you."

"That's possible, but what would be the point of it? Remember he left a message for me saying that he wanted to get together back in Lansing. We were going to have to talk sooner or later."

"Maybe he just didn't want to talk to you up there."

"Or perhaps there was some other reason why he left. Pershing thinks Breitner may have been being blackmailed. If so, maybe he was under some pressure to hurry back."

"You mean to meet with the blackmailer?"

"Possibly. Or possibly to get away from a blackmailer or someone else. There were too many things that just didn't make any sense. Where was he when I found his cabin? Why didn't he answer his phone? I called at all hours of the day and night."

"Well did you stop in town and ask people about him?"

"Yeah. That was another thing. No one knew him. No body had ever heard his name. He has been going up there for years. I can't believe there isn't someone who can tell us what he did when he was there. Who he hung around with. Hawk Junction is the nearest town, Mag. There are only 350 people there. Wouldn't you think after years and years, somebody would have known him?"

Once again, Malloy's chief advisor became pensive. Taking both of his hands in hers, Margaret fixed her eyes on her husband and said, "Then go back to Wawa, Jim, if you think that's what's necessary."

***

It was grey and desolate when Malloy reached Breitner's cabin. He couldn't get inside. The Mounties had padlocked the door. They had also sealed the aluminum shed. Wawa Wawa Wawa Wawa. Another wild goose chase, Malloy told himself. He stood at the shore, gazing over the still waters of Whitefish Lake. He thought of Breitner's last message. Pershing had asked for the tape. Malloy listened to it over and over before sending it to the grand juror.

'Sorry I missed you at the cabin.' Sorry I missed you. Sorry I missed you. How did Breitner know that Malloy had been at the cabin? And why did Breitner lie about fishing nearby? If Breitner had been anywhere around the cabin he would have to have heard the commotion Malloy raised, yelling and blowing his horn.

A lone fisherman came into view, as he lazily putt-putted toward a shady cove across the lake in his little boat. His boat. The man in the boat. Boatman. Boatman. That's it. That was the name of the fellow with the jeep. Suddenly, a light went on inside of Malloy's head. *Boatman DID see Breitner! That's how he knew I had been at the cabin. Boatman must have told him I was here. Of course. How could I be so dumb? Earl Boatman knew Breitner. He must know something that would help unravel the mystery. Why didn't I see that until now?* Malloy scolded himself, as he dashed back to his car.

He covered the 120 kilometers to Chapleau in record time, the metric speedometer showing unfamiliar numbers like 136 and 141. It took a few wrong turns before he found the Boatman house. No jeep out in front. This time, he had to identify the place from memory. Not easy. So many looked alike. But when he thought he had found it, he was pretty sure. No one home. He would wait, maybe come back later.

It was getting along about lunch time, and Malloy was hungry, so he started looking for a place to eat. The first place he saw was Myrtle's. He remembered that Myrtle's was where he had first learned about Boatman. Maybe he could find out where the Boatmans were from the lady who owned he diner. Anyway, he was hungry enough to try the meatloaf she said was so good the last time he was there.

Malloy sat down in the diner and gazed around the room to find a waitress. When he caught her eye, he knew she was Mrs. Boatman. She took his order, and gave Malloy a second look, thinking for a moment that she should know him, then dismissing the thought. Lots of people come in to Myrtle's more than once.

The meatloaf wasn't all that bad. Pretty good in fact. He paid his bill in American money. When she returned with his change, he handed her his business card. "Perhaps you remember me. I would like to talk to you if I may."

Valarie looked at his card, then stuffed it in her apron pocket. "What about?"

"Actually, I'm looking for your husband. Where might I find him?"

"I'd like to know myself, mister. He's been gone for a year."

"I'm sorry to hear that. You have no idea where he is?"

"None. I called the place where he was supposed to be working. They never heard of him. I've started a divorce."

"When was the last time you saw your husband, Mrs. Boatman?"

"Last August first. Listen Mr....." She fumbled for the business card in her pocket. "Mr., er, Judge Malloy, I'm busy here and I can't talk now. If you want to ask me more questions about Earl, you'll have to see me after I get off work."

"Shall I come by your house?"

"If you want. Or you can wait here. I don't know how much more I can tell you."

Malloy waited at the diner. Then he followed Valarie as she drove the blue Jeep to pick up her son from the baby sitter's and continued home. She invited him to come in. He told her about the death of Justice Breitner, the man he had been looking for when he had come to Chapleau the year before.

"It just seems odd that your husband disappeared the same day Breitner was murdered. Was he planning to leave on August first?"

"No, he wasn't. As a matter of fact, it was very sudden, like he changed his mind, or something. He never told me very much about his business. I never asked. That's just the way it was between us."

Responding to his questions, Valarie told Malloy how she had met Boatman, and how they fallen in love. She told him of her husband's strange comings and goings, and the fears and worries she harbored whenever she wondered what secrets he kept from her.

Malloy's curiosity was compounded.

"Didn't Earl leave any papers, or documents that would help you figure out where he might have gone, or what he might have been doing?"

"Like what?"

"Bank statements, for one thing. Did he have a bank

account?"

"Yes. I never had anything to do with that. Just wrote myself a check every month, like he told me to. I never opened the statements, at least not until he had been gone a couple months. When I did open them, I saw that he wasn't making bank deposits like before, so I took the rest of the money out of the bank."

"Was there anything odd about his finances? Big deposits or withdrawals about the time he left?"

"Yes. There was a large check he wrote to a company of some kind. I never could figure out who they were."

"Do you remember the name of the company?"

"Some initials, I think. I don't really remember. Should I go and get the statements?"

"If you don't mind. Maybe I can help you in some way."

Valarie went upstairs. Her son stood in the dining room staring with wide, inquisitive, dark eyes at the stranger. Malloy smiled, and Billy ran into the kitchen. In an instant, he returned, and announced with obvious pride, "My daddy catched a big, big fish."

"That's wonderful." Malloy was accustomed to little boys' overtures. From across the room, he could see a photograph on the mantle. A man holding a large fish, a little boy standing next to him. "Is that your daddy?" The justice pointed to the snapshot.

"Yup," said the boy. "You want me to show you the big fish? I can show you."

"That would be nice."

Billy climbed onto the back of a chair and reached up to the mantle, removed the picture, and bounded across the room.

"See. There's the big fish. And there's my daddy. And there's me, too."

Malloy did a double take. "This is your daddy?"

"Yup. And that's the big fish, too. And that's me with my daddy and the big fish. We ate him."

Malloy looked closer at the black and white photograph. There was no doubt about it. 'Daddy' was Ed Breitner. Ed Breitner and Earl Boatman were one and the same person. Malloy was still trying to comprehend the import of his discovery when Valarie returned. She was carrying a cardboard box, maybe three times the size of a shoe box. She placed the box on a table next to the chair where Malloy was sitting.

"Judge, do you think Earl is a criminal? Do you think he has done something wrong? Is that why he left me and Billy?"

"I honestly don't know," Malloy replied, as he began to examine the bank statements. He stifled his initial instinct to tell the woman who her husband really was. "But I do think he may have been the last person to see Justice Breitner alive. That's why I am so anxious to find him."

Malloy could tell she was fighting tears.

"If Earl was a criminal, I don't want to know. He was good to me, Judge. He surely did love Billy. And I know he loved..." She faltered. "..me, too. I don't care who he was or what he was."

She was crying now. "He made me happy. He gave me a wonderful son. He left me some beautiful memories. That's enough. It's more than many people ever have. He never beat me, never got drunk. Never hit Billy or cussed him out. Never broke up the furniture like my old man did. I've got no complaints about Earl Boatman. I'd like to leave it that way."

She picked up the photograph, started to put it back on the mantle, then changed her mind, and jammed it unceremoniously into a drawer.

"Actually, I'm starting to date someone else. I want to put Earl in the past. Those are all his papers. Everything I know about him."

The statements were from the Royal Bank of Canada. They showed a clear pattern. Periodic monthly deposits of around twelve or thirteen hundred dollars. Regular monthly withdrawals of one thousand dollars each. The names printed on the face of the checks were Earl and Valarie Boatman. The one thousand dollar monthly withdrawal checks were all signed by Valarie Boatman. Because the deposits were always more than the withdrawals, a balance of a little over fifteen thousand dollars accumulated and was withdrawn in December of 1991. The account was apparently closed at that time. The December check was also signed by Valarie.

The only debit transactions which varied from that pattern consisted of a series of five deposits beginning in May of 1991, and continuing until late June of the same year. The amounts varied from sixty-two hundred and something to sixty-eight hundred and change. A total of ten deposits. Sixty-six thousand seven hundred fifty-two dollars in all. The only unusual credit transactions were two checks. One written on May 12, 1991, in the amount of thirteen thousand four hundred nine dollars, and one written for a similarly odd amount a little over fifty three thousand. The two checks roughly equaled the total of the ten deposits. The second check, the larger one, was dated August 1, 1991, the day Ed Breitner was killed. These two checks, unlike the monthly withdrawals, were signed by Earl Boatman.

Malloy examined the back of the May 12 and August 1 checks. Both had been endorsed with a rubber stamp, and deposited at the Automotive National Bank. Both were made payable to 'L.R., Incorporated.'

Anxious to leave when he finished looking at the bank statements, Malloy moved toward the door. As he stepped out on the front porch, Valarie caught his sleeve and pleaded with him. "Please, Judge, leave me out of whatever you are doing. Me and Billy. Leave us alone. We haven't done anything wrong. Whatever Earl did, leave us out of it, please?"

"I'll try, Mrs. Boatman. I'll certainly try."

Malloy hurried back to his motel in Wawa. He dialed the 517 area, got the number of the corporation and securities division of the Michigan department of commerce, spoke to a clerk, told her he was Chief Justice Malloy, and was informed that the most recent annual report of 'L.R., Incorporated' showed it to be a wholly owned Michigan corporation. The sole stockholder, director and officer was a woman named June Flanders. Malloy asked for, and was given Flanders' home address, as shown on the official public corporate record.

He didn't know for sure, of course, but Malloy surmised that the odd amounts of the various checks were a function of the premium on United States funds which occurs when they are translated into Canadian dollars. Regular deposits of one thousand dollars U.S., would result in the roughly thirteen hundred dollar monthly deposits in the Royal Bank. Deposits were being made in American, withdrawals in Canadian. Thus the build up which was taken out when the account was closed. That hypothesis, when applied to the Earl Boatman transactions, gave Malloy another interesting clue. The odd amounts of the May and June deposits would indicate that Boatman was intending to make a pay-out in U. S. currency. If that were the case, the two checks he wrote approximately equaled ten thousand and forty thousand American dollars respectively.

Malloy kept thinking of the photograph of Breitner, his son, and the big fish. Ed Breitner was smiling in the picture. It was a mischievous smile. Like a kid caught with his hand in the cookie jar. The great Ed Breitner was a bigamist. Hard to believe. But now Pershing's blackmail theory was beginning to make sense.

***

At the court's opinion conference later that month, the case of *Danken v Danken* was finally decided. Justices Alton Henry and Doris Templeton withdrew their previously submitted opinions. Henry signed the chief justice's majority opinion, and Templeton joined in a short dissent filed by Justice Hilda Germaine.

CHAPTER 26

JULY 1992

When Malloy returned from Canada with the evidence of Breitner's bigamy, he was optimistic. He really believed he had cracked the case, that the true story of Breitner's death was beginning to unfold. In truth, it was not that easy. Judge Pershing not only would not delay Jim's appearance before the grand jury, set for the second week in July, he would not even talk to Jim or send an investigator around to see him.

Malloy had minimal luck running down the lead to L.R., Incorporated. His brother Tom worked at the bank, and was able to confirm that deposits of ten and forty thousand were made in 1991 on the fourteenth of May and the fourth of August respectively. He also discovered that June Flanders was the only signatory on the account. But he had not been able to access the microfilmed canceled checks of L.R., Incorporated to see who received payments from the account. That was the key fact, since the firm's account appeared to be a mere conduit, with checks being written in the same amount as each deposit within a few days of each receipt. Only a small balance sustained the account otherwise. The Breitner payments stood out, as most other deposits and withdrawals were less than five thousand dollars.

On Sunday night, Malloy awoke at 2:45 and couldn't get back to sleep. He prowled around the house, raided the refrigerator, watched infomercials on TV, tried to read a novel, a newspaper, a magazine and a self-help manual. All to no avail. His movements aroused his wife, a light sleeper. She found him in the den, scribbling notes on a yellow pad.

"Can't sleep, huh?"

"One of those nights."

"What are you writing?"

"Nothing. Just trying to get my thoughts straight for the

398

Honorable Ken Pershing next week."

"Worried?"

"I guess. A little. I sure wish we could crack that June Flanders thing. Who the heck is she? Why would Breitner give her all that money? Pershing thinks Breitner was being blackmailed. Maybe Flanders is the conduit to the blackmailer."

"I'll bet that's it, "said Margaret. "Breitner's a bigamist. Somebody found out about it, and they're making him pay to keep it quiet."

"It certainly makes sense, though it hardly explains the murder. I sure would like to learn more about Flanders, though. I've checked with everyone I know in Berkeley where she lives. No leads. She apparently rents her apartment. I had someone who subscribes to credit services run her through Dun and Bradstreet. They got nothing but the same bare bones corporate information I already had."

"Can't you hire a private eye?"

"I did. Cost me three hundred dollars. For that I learned she drives a green two door 1988 Cutlass, license number DRC 769, and has an unlisted phone number."

"Can you have her followed?"

"I thought of that. Called a couple other private investigators. They both wanted a thousand dollars a day and neither could start on the case until next month. Too late to help me. I'd go down and follow her myself, but it's too risky. If I was discovered the papers would crucify me."

Margaret walked over and put her arm around Jim. "Don't worry, you'll think of something. Now get back to bed and get some sleep. I'll tidy up here and join you in a minute."

Malloy kissed his wife and went back to bed. She sure was a steadying influence. Margaret looked over Jim's scribbled notes. One said, '4789 Bluebird Court, Berkeley, MI. DRC 769.' Margaret folded the note, went into the kitchen, and tucked it under her appointment calendar.

***

4789 Bluebird Court turned out to be a townhouse in a nice, but modest neighborhood. There were no garages in the development. Residents parked their cars under open carports clustered randomly among the units. The green Cutlass was there at 7 AM. It was still there at eight and eight-thirty. At eight-thirty-three, an attractive brunette in a flowered blouse and navy blue skirt came out of 4789, and went to the car. Sitting in her van, pretending to read a newspaper, Margaret Malloy's heart raced wildly. This was not fun and games. She waited until the Cutlass had exited the parking area and turned south on Coolidge Road before she started up. Traffic held her at the first intersection and she almost lost her subject before her tailing began. But she did a little aggressive driving and had the green car well under surveillance by the time it entered the John C. Lodge expressway.

Tailing another car on the freeway during morning rush hour was easy. Margaret stayed three or four cars behind and did nothing that would arouse any suspicion. It did, in fact, begin to feel like a game. Or maybe she was in a movie. She shook off the fantasy. Serious business, Mag. Real serious business.

The Cutlass exited at Larned Street, and turned into a parking ramp at its intersection with Griswold. Margaret was right behind the green car by then. Flanders found a parking spot on the third level. Margaret could not. She hurried up two more ramps before she could beach the van. Now the race was on. She dashed to the elevator, luckily was picked up within seconds, and dashed out onto the sidewalk just in time to see Flanders' flowered blouse crossing Congress Avenue, a block to the north. Margaret had dressed like a working women would, and the heels made running a chore, but she had no choice. So she ran. Entering the Penobscot Building less than a minute later, she told herself to catch her breath quickly. She certainly didn't want to look like she was chasing someone.

Flanders was waiting for one of the elevators that served the upper floors. Margaret stood fairly close to her, looking up at the moving dial. Momentarily, the elevator came. Flanders and Margaret were two of the four people entering. After her quarry had pushed the button for the twenty-second floor, Margaret pushed it again, trying to look absent minded. When they exited at 22, Margaret consulted the room number directions on the wall pretending to be looking for a particular office. Flanders walked briskly to the left and entered suite 2234.

Margaret strolled past 2234. 'Finch, Wolmar and Feldman, Attorneys at Law.' Was Flanders an employee, a lawyer, a client? Jim should have known if she was a lawyer. That would be a simple matter of looking up the name in the Michigan Bar Journal. At the end of the hall were the offices of a theatrical company. Margaret tried the door. It was locked. Returning to the elevators, she saw a ladies room. It too, was locked. She decided to entered the Finch, Wolmar offices, pretending to be a client of the theatrical agency wanting to use the ladies room. June Flanders was sitting at one of two desks in the outer office area. Apparently she was a legal secretary. Margaret decided to change her ploy and addressed June Flanders directly. "Does Mr. Finch handle theatrical contracts?"

"I don't know, ma'am," said June. "Mr. Finch's secretary isn't here. I work for Mr. Wolmar. He does mostly criminal work."

"I see," said Margaret. "I have an appointment down the hall, but the office isn't open. I'll stop back later."

Thinking about it driving back to Lansing, Margaret concluded that her ploy had not been half so clever as she imagined. But it got the job done. Jim would be very pleased with her sleuthing, she thought.

She thought wrong. He was madder than hell. "What if you got caught? It would be the end of me for sure. You didn't have to do that. We could have found out some other way."

Margaret was disappointed and not a little angry. "I thought you would be pleased. After all, I did it for you."

"I know you did, honey. And I appreciate your efforts, but I just wish you would tell me about things like this first. We need to be careful."

"Oh sure, like you talk to me before you blab to the newspapers."

Malloy could see this was going nowhere he wanted to be.

"O.K." He sighed. "What did you learn?"

"Not much," Margaret answered smugly. "Just that she is a legal secretary for a man named Perry Wolmar."

"PERRY WOLMAR? Did you say she works for Perry Wolmar?"

"Why, do you know him?"

"Do I know Perry Wolmar? Do I know Perry Wolmar?" Malloy leaped to his feet, took his wife in his arms and danced her wildly around the room, laughing and clapping his hands.

Finally, Margaret settled him down. "What is so good about Perry Wolmar?"

"Margaret Mary Malloy, you are a genius. A cotton picking, ever loving genius. Do you realize that you just told me that Ed Breitner gave forty thousand dollars on the day he died to the secretary of the attorney for Morris Durnacky, the infamous Mr. Death?"

"I did?"

"You sure did. You just solved the mystery of the decade. Ed Breitner, God help him, committed suicide."

"And tried to make it look like he was murdered?"

"And made it look like he was murdered."

"I can't believe it, Jim. It's so bizarre."

"Bizarre, yes. But I have to believe it's true. Especially if he was being blackmailed by someone for something. Don't you see? The blackmailer demands more and more money, maybe actually starts to leak the blackmail information. Breitner can't face the consequences, so he takes the coward's way out."

***

Cindy Germaine stopped to see Nora Oldsmer, for a little chat. The women had become good friends as a result of their respective connections to Jeremiah Wheatley. And, of course, he was the subject of their conversation. He always was.

"Sometimes, Cindy, that boy gives me fits. Just when I think he is making progress, leaving all that nastiness behind him, up pops the devil again."

"Is he still having those awful tantrums?"

"A little less, but he still has them."

"I thought last Christmas, when he sent the card to Hilda and Ben, he was showing a clean heart."

"So did I, but there seems to be something deep down troubling that boy. It's like he hates himself sometimes. Thinks he must be Lucifer himself. Then he tries to act like it."

"Being a mom isn't easy, is it?"

"Hardest thing I ever did, Cindy. Got to be after Jeremiah twenty four hours a day. Cleaning him up. Dusting him off. Bringing him around. Working him over. Cheering him on. It's wearing me down."

"You're doing good work, Nora. God's going to give you a great reward some day."

"I hope so. It just seems like he thinks nobody loves him. Like every one thinks he's a bad, evil person. Like God has given him a plastic foot to remind him that he is a sinner and is never going to be anything but a sinner. Like he has to hobble when he walks so people can see him and say, Here comes Jeremiah. The sinner. The murderer. Look at how he walks. He even walks like a sinner."

"I've seen that in him too, Nora."

"I don't know what I would do without you, Cindy. You are his only ray of hope. His only way to forgiveness and reconciliation. I don't think we could keep Jeremiah without your help. He would have been sent to reform school long ago, if you weren't on his side. God bless you."

"I only do what I think Jesus would have me do, Nora. Force of habit, more than anything else. I sure wish Hilda would bend a little to Jeremiah. She still hurts so, poor thing. Maybe she never will let go of the hurt."

"I know what you mean. I can imagine how she feels. Still, until she and Ben give the boy some small hope that he can get out of his terrible guilt, I don't think we're gonna be able to whip the nastiness out of him."

Cindy shook her head in agreement and regret. She reached for her purse, then turned back to Nora and asked, "Would you consider coming over, Nora? To our house, I mean. Would you come and talk to Hilda?"

Nora squirmed. The idea of approaching a supreme court justice was awesome enough. Much less the mother of the boy her foster son had killed. "I sure would be awfully scared, Cindy. Terrible scared."

"My Hilda won't hurt you, Nora. She never hurt anyone in her whole life. I think you two should talk. It would be good for both of you."

"I'll do it, Cindy, but only if Hilda agrees, and really wants to meet me. By the way, what do I call her?"

"She is Justice Germaine to all the lawyers and the newspapers, but her children's teachers always called her Mrs. Tuttle. Lots of people do, and she doesn't mind it. Especially if you are talking to her as a mother."

***

Malloy called Colonel Rosewall and arranged for a state police escort to Owosso. He had two purposes in mind. First, he knew that there would be a mob of reporters, cameramen and the like forming an obstacle course before he could reach Judge Pershing's courtroom, and he wanted troopers to run interference. Second, he wanted to appear as someone on the side of law enforcement. One of the good guys. The state police body guards would affirm that he was the chief justice. Like the governor or the president, someone who needed constantly to be protected from the bad guys. Furthering the image, Malloy had his law clerk chauffeur him behind the state police vehicle. And, of course, he went to Owosso without a lawyer.

At the Shiawassee County courthouse, things transpired much as Malloy has envisioned. There was a mob. Flash bulbs popped incessantly from the moment the two cars pulled up to the curb until the door to Pershing's courtroom closed behind the chief justice.

Inside, the scene was, by contrast, quiet and formal. Dignified almost to the point of solemnity. Pershing, robeless, was already on the bench. Fournier, surrounded by files and papers, sat at the counsel table. The court reporter sat at her station. No one else was present. After a few perfunctory, off-the-record greetings, Pershing began reading a prepared statement into the record.

"Let the record show that we have subpoenaed chief justice James P. Malloy to give testimony concerning the matters we presently are investigating. I want it clearly understood that Justice Malloy's appearance here today does not, in any way, imply that he is under suspicion of any wrongdoing or that he has been heretofore implicated in any crime or impropriety by any witness previously testifying here or by any demonstrative evidence we have uncovered or received in these proceedings. Madam Reporter, would you please administer the oath to Justice Malloy?"

Malloy, who had already taken the witness chair, stood as he took the oath. Fournier rose and addressed him as Malloy sat down again.

"For the record, your name please."

"James Patrick Malloy."

"And you are the chief justice of the Michigan Supreme Court?"

"By the grace of God and the sufferance of my colleagues, I am." Malloy figured Fournier had to be loosened up. He was too somber.

Fournier didn't loosen.

"Justice Malloy, will you please tell us about the Florida lottery that you won last year?"

Pershing interrupted. "Now wait a minute, counsel. I thought you and I agreed that the lottery ticket business was all cleared up when we had Wilhelm and his secretary in here. Why are you bringing that matter up again?"

"Your Honor, I just want to make sure that the witness confirms what Wilhelm told us. I just want to hear his version of it."

"All right, go ahead. But don't waste a lot of time with it."

"Tell us, Mr. Justice."

Malloy described how he had given Wilhelm twenty dollars at Flynn's house after Flynn had suggested buying Florida lottery tickets. How Wilhelm had brought tickets to the card game when he returned from Florida, and how Malloy had called the 900 number and discovered the good news. He went on to tell of his conversation with O'Leary in the hospital, and how he called 1-800-I WON BIG to verify that winning lottery tickets could be purchased. Malloy continued his testimony, describing his call to the FBI and his meeting with the two agents. Finally, he told Pershing and Fournier how the FBI people had reported that Wilhelm's ticket was not sold through the exchange in West Virginia, that they were closing their file and sending it to the Pershing grand jury.

"I presume you know what happened after that, counsel." Malloy concluded.

"Yes, of course. Now Justice Malloy, are you telling the grand jury, under oath, that you did not then, and do not now, know who purchased that ticket from the Florida lottery agent, or whether the ticket had been sold to anyone since it was issued, and if so for how much or by whom it was purchased?"

"I have told you all I know about it, counsel."

"So it could have been purchased by Wilhelm or one of his clients for the very purpose of giving it to you, isn't that true?"

"That is quite true. And that is the very reason why I called the FBI. And I certainly hope that if this grand jury, with its power of subpoena, and its power to grant immunity, is able to uncover anything suspicious or improper about my winning the Florida lottery, you will inform me promptly, so that I can take the proper steps to return the money, or do whatever I have to do to disassociate myself from any impropriety whatsoever."

Pershing interjected. "You have my word on that, Mr. Chief Justice. Now, Mr. Fournier, will you please get off of that subject?"

Fournier walked to the counsel table and looked at some papers.

"Alright, Justice Malloy, let's talk about the fireworks in the Law Building plaza." With that, Fournier embarked upon a long, detailed exploration of the Guatemalan flag episode. Malloy, as he had publicly, denied any knowledge of the origin of the call which purportedly had come from his office. Again, Pershing had to push Fournier to drop the subject and move along with his questions.

"Would you tell us please, what, if anything, you know about the murder of Justice Edward Breitner."

"I think I can tell you who did it."

Pershing leaned forward. "You can?"

"I think so, Judge. But I am going to have to ask your indulgence on something. I have received some information in confidence. Admittedly, the communication was not legally privileged, and, like a newspaper reporter's source, would have to be disclosed if you insist upon it. But I've given my word that I would try to keep this person out of any investigation, and I mean to do what I can to keep that promise. Your Honor, I don't think it will be necessary to know my source in order to get at the truth here. And I can assure you that my source has committed no crime. The reason for confidentiality has to do with personal feelings and preference."

Pershing leaned back and closed his eyes for a moment. Then he said, "Mr. Justice, this is a highly unusual request, and I'm not at all comfortable about it. But because of my respect for you personally and the office you hold, I'm going to defer exploring your source at least for the time being. I want to hear who you believe to be responsible for the death of Justice Breitner."

"I think Ed Breitner committed suicide."

Pershing was startled. Fournier was aghast. Even the court stenographer sat bolt upright, eyes popped wide open.

Fournier took over. "Are you aware that Justice Breitner was found in the back seat of his car riddled with bullets? And the murder weapon found thirty feet away in the weeds? Just how do you suppose he managed to fire six shots into various parts of his own body and then throw the gun into the weeds?"

"I don't know exactly how he did it, counsel. I just know that he had some very serious problems which might well have caused him to be depressed or even panicked. And I have it on good information that, on the day he died, he paid a large sum of money to a person who is in the business of assisting suicides."

Pershing sat forward again. "You mean Mr. Death? What's his name, Duracky?"

"Durnacky. Morris Durnacky. His lawyer is Perry Wolmar of the Detroit law firm of Finch, Wolmar and Feldman. Wolmar's secretary, a woman named June Flanders, is the sole stockholder, director and officer of a corporation called 'L.R., Incorporated.' Breitner paid L.R. ten thousand dollars in May of last year, and another forty thousand on the day he died."

"And you got this information from your so-called confidential source, is that what you're telling us?" Fournier spit the question at Malloy in a doubting manner.

"You don't have to take my word for it, counsel. You have

subpoena powers. Get the bank records. Get the corporate records. Get Ms. Flanders in here and ask her all about it. See if I am not telling you the truth."

"I can assure you, Mr. Chief Justice, the grand jury will find out who is telling the truth and who isn't," Pershing announced. Then he excused the witness to await a further call from the grand jury, if needed.

***

The really difficult part about appearing before the grand jury began when his appearance was over. The mob outside the door wanted satisfaction. It wanted news. It wanted blood. The state troopers were prepared to usher Malloy to his car. They shoved their way through the crowd until they reached the outer door and the front steps leading down to the sidewalk. Reporters shouted questions at Malloy all the way down the hall. Cameras followed him. Broadcasters tried to stick microphones in his face. Malloy made another of his snap decisions.

Sorry, Margaret. No time for consultation.

"O.K., O.K. I'll answer questions. But let's get organized. He positioned himself on the front porch of the courthouse facing down the steps toward the street, and directed the media people to gather on the steps below him. He stationed the troopers on either side of him, and directed them to keep the top step open. When most of the commotion was settled down, the cameras all pointed up at him, and the microphones grouped in front of him, Malloy said, "O.K., first question," and pointed to one of the reporters.

"Did you take the fifth amendment?"

"No."

"Did Pershing grant you immunity?"

"No."

"Did you tell him where the lottery ticket came from?"

"I told him where I got it, yes."

"Where did you get it?"

"From Art Wilhelm."

"What did you do for Wilhelm?"

"Nothing."

"Did they ask you about Breitner?"

"Yes."

"What did you tell them?"

"Everything I know about it."

"What do you know about it?"

"I do not think he was murdered by terrorists."

"You don't think the AOR did it?"

"No. I don't"

"Who did it?"

"I don't know for sure, but I believe the grand jury has sufficient information so that with diligent investigation and thorough questioning of the right people, they should be able to solve the mystery and assess responsibility for Justice Breitner's tragic death. Now if you will excuse me, I must return to Lansing."

So saying, Malloy moved through the still questioning crowd to his waiting automobile and was driven off.

***

The chief justice dominated the evening news that night. The coverage was generally fair, and Malloy came off quite judicial, in control, and definitely one of the good guys. In the First Press, however, a front page photograph appeared showing Malloy between two uniformed state troopers, entering the courthouse. Above the picture were the words 'MALLOY BROUGHT IN FOR QUESTIONING.'

Margaret was livid. "What's the matter with those people. Don't they have any professional integrity at all?"

Malloy shrugged his shoulders. "You win some and you lose some. How did they spell the name?"

If looks could kill, the glance Margaret threw at her husband would have been a felony. This was the aspect of politics that she hated. For all the supposed honor of holding important public office, it seemed to her that shame and embarrassment were more often the reward. What was it about newspapers, she wondered, that made them think their job was to belittle and carp. And how could Jim be so indifferent to the hurt?

She was still awake when Jim crawled into bed beside her. She felt his hand gently caressing her neck and shoulder. She bit her knuckle and forced back the tears.

CHAPTER 27

AUGUST 1992

August is usually a slow month in the Michigan Supreme Court. That's when most employees take their vacations. No cases are set for oral argument, and no opinion conferences are scheduled. Only those justices who have opinions to write can be found in their offices. September starts the new judicial year. Every member of the bench is expected to have all of his or her opinions finished by then. In the jargon of the bench, they had to be 'fully written.'

Doris Templeton was fully written, and spent the first week of August in Chicago visiting her daughter and grandson and her father. Arthur was getting on in years. Doris was beginning to worry about the old man, and the reversal of their roles was very difficult for her. He had always been so strong, so independent, so reliable. The thought of him becoming needy and dependent troubled her deeply. Fortunately, old age comes slowly. She would have time to get used to the idea.

On this summer Saturday, her father was still his old self, hosting a birthday party for his great grandson. The breeze-whipped waves of mighty Lake Michigan splashed rhythmically over the sandy shore as Arthur, Doris, Cheryl, Roger Foresberg, and of course, the guest of honor, one year old Edward Breitner Templeton gathered in the park. After their picnic, while Cheryl changed Eddy's diaper and Arthur loaded the car to return home, Roger approached Doris.

"May I talk with you a moment, Justice?"

"Sure, Roger. What's on your mind?"

"I have been clerking at Katman, Milliken this summer, as you know."

"I've heard. Good firm. Do you like it?"

"Very much. And what's better, I think they like me. One of the associates told me she thought I would be getting an offer

412

from their hiring committee."

"Congratulations, Roger. That's great news."

"Thanks. But that's not all. I really wanted to talk to you about Cheryl and me."

"What about Cheryl and you?"

"We're in love. We want to get married."

"So?"

"So?"

"So what? So why are you telling me? If you want to get married, get married. You're both old enough. You don't need my permission."

"I wasn't looking for your permission, Madam Justice. I hoped to get your blessing."

Doris broke out into a big grin. She put both her arms around the young man's neck and kissed him. "You've got my blessing, you big dope. I was wondering when you would say something. Mazeltov."

***

Alton Henry spent August campaigning. First, there was the Democratic State Convention in Detroit. A hot, sweaty, crowded, noisy, nerve-wracking affair, full of people he didn't know and who didn't know him. He was nominated without fanfare and with very little opposition just because he was the incumbent, was historically nominated by the Democrats, and nobody strong enough wanted to take his seat away from him. Besides, the party knew it was going to have to spend a ton of money trying to defeat Mark Edwards, the Republican governor, and they had no desire to divert precious party funds to unimportant sideshows like the supreme court race.

After the convention, Henry was on his own. He dutifully answered all of the candidate questionnaires he received, usually with long, convoluted replies which offended no one and got him no votes. And, of course, he went to meetings. Every group he could wrangle an invitation to address. Women's groups. Lawyers groups. Women lawyers groups. Ethnic groups. Old folks. School kids. College campuses. Anywhere and everywhere. He put thousands of miles on his state owned vehicle, spreading the gospel of law and order, and condemning ambulance chasing lawyers. Except of course, when he was speaking before groups like the Michigan Trial Lawyers Association.

One invitation came from McBain, a small farming village halfway up the mitten. Candidates' night. Every taxpayer in the county would be invited to the high school auditorium. No candidate could hope to carry the county without speaking before the McBain Citizens Forum. Alton Henry drove north for two and a half hours, stopped for dinner in Claire and arrived at the McBain High School fifteen minutes after the appointed hour. He was disappointed with the crowd. No more than fifty people in the room. He handed his card to the lady at the table just inside the door. She passed it along to another lady who took it to the gentleman who was sitting next to the speaker. The speaker, it turned out was from Traverse City and was running for Trustee of Michigan State University, an unpaid constitutional office.

When the trustee candidate sat down to perfunctory applause, the gentleman to whom Henry's card had been handed stood and took the microphone. He was, apparently, the chairman of the gathering. He called on another speaker, a candidate for the state legislature. Thereafter, he called on many, many speakers. Candidates for lieutenant governor, secretary of state, regent of the University of Michigan, Members of the board of governors of Wayne State University, county prosecutor, county drain commissioner, register of deeds, sheriff, state senator, county commissioner, county clerk, village clerk, village trustee. On and on they went, sometimes three or more candidates for the same office. Then came the judicial offices, district judge, probate judge, court of appeals judge, circuit judge.

Each candidate was given three minutes to make a presentation. The lady who delivered Henry's card to the chair was the time keeper. She was a stickler, who yelled "TIME" in a loud voice precisely at the three minute mark. Each speaker left the room after making his or her remarks.

By the time Alton Henry's name was called, the crowd, which had consisted almost entirely of candidates waiting to be called on, had dwindled to five people. The lady at the door, the timekeeper, the chairman, one old woman crocheting in the front row, and a hapless candidate for sheriff who had come in after Alton Henry.

Functioning in the near hypnotic daze that marks one as an actively campaigning candidate for public office, Alton Henry rose, walked to the front of the room and delivered, by rote, his canned, revised, audience-tested, number one speech. At exactly three minutes, when Henry was about to begin the part about liberty being the precious gift of our nation's founding fathers which we have no right to squander on hair brained social welfare schemes, the timekeeping lady rose from her chair and shouted, "TIME." Alton Henry glared at her for four seconds and then spoke.

"Madam, I am a justice of the supreme court of Michigan, elected by the suffrage of ten million American citizens, and charged with the constitutional responsibility of interpreting the laws which govern every facet of social, economic, and environmental life in this sovereign state. I have driven over two hundred miles to be up here speaking to you and the other four people in this room, and by God Almighty I am going to finish what I came here to say, if my last words are heard only by the brick walls of this school building. So sit down and shut up."

***

Pershing issued subpoenas to Perry Wolmar and June Flanders. When they came to Owosso, they did not go directly to Pershing's courtroom, where the media people maintained a tireless watch. Instead, they went into the county clerk's office, looking much like a couple in search of a marriage license, or a lawyer and his client seeking to examine some unremarkable legal documents.

At the clerk's counter, Wolmar identified himself, asked to see the county clerk herself, and was admitted to the inner office with Flanders in tow. On reaching the clerk's private office, he informed her that they were there to see Judge Pershing, and had been instructed to come through the clerk's office to avoid being seen by the media. She ushered them through the back hall to the judge's entrance to the courtroom.

Pershing and Fournier began by interrogating Wolmar. Yes, he knew about L.R., Incorporated. He had set up the corporation for a client. His secretary, Ms. Flanders acted as a bookkeeper for the corporation, which Wolmar described as 'just a holding company.' The sole function of the corporation, according to Wolmar was to receive and record the income of his client from certain enterprises.

"Who is your client?" Fournier wanted to know.

"That is privileged information." Wolmar responded.

"No it isn't." said Judge Pershing. "Answer the question."

Wolmar squirmed, then told Pershing that his client was Morris Durnacky, the man known as Mr. Death. Beyond that, Wolmar was no help to the grand jury. He never saw any of the checks that came through the corporation. He had no knowledge of who any of Durnacky's customers or clients were. He said that Ms. Flanders handled all of those things.

June Flanders was called as a witness. Perry Wolmar stayed in the room. He was then acting as attorney for his secretary. Flanders was a very forthcoming witness. Yes, she was the sole incorporator, stockholder, director and officer of L.R. Yes, she received all the money, deposited it to the corporation account and disbursed it to Mr. Durnacky. That was the whole purpose and business of the corporation. Durnacky paid an annual fee for the service. That was the corporation's only income. Yes, she brought the bank records with her. Yes, they showed deposits of ten thousand dollars on May 14, 1991 and forty thousand dollars on August 4, 1991.

Fournier questioned her about the deposits. "Now, Ms. Flanders, according to your records, from whom were those two checks received?"

"My ledger says they came from a Mr. Earl Boatman."

"Earl Boatman?"

"Yes. B-o-a-t-m-a-n." She spelled the name." Earl Boatman. That's what my record shows."

"You are sure it was not Edward Breitner?"

"Positive. I make photo copies of every check. I have all my copies right here." She opened her brief case, and took out a manila envelope.

"Would you please locate the May and August checks we have been discussing?"

She leafed through the file and presented the checks to Fournier.

"These checks are not in the amounts you testified to, Ms. Flanders. The May check is for over thirteen thousand, and the August check is for more than fifty thousand."

"That's correct, Mr. Fournier, but you will notice that the checks are drawn on the Royal Bank of Canada. They are payable in Canadian funds. According to the rate of exchange on that day, they yielded roughly ten and forty thousand U.S. dollars respectively. The exact amounts are shown there on the bank statements."

"Then this man Boatman was Canadian?"

"Apparently so. I know nothing but what is on the check."

Fournier read from the checks. "Let the record show that these checks were written on printed forms identifying the account owners as Earl and Valarie Boatman, 217 Foster Street, Chapleau, Ontario."

Later that afternoon, Fournier called Valarie Boatman in

Chapleau. She told him her husband had left her, that she had no idea where he was, that he had lied to her about his place of employment, that she didn't know where he worked, that she had filed for divorce, that she had never heard of Morris Durnacky, and that under no circumstances would she come to Michigan to testify about anything.

***

Malloy got the call at home.

"Jim, Ken Pershing here. I'm calling off our communications embargo. Are you willing to talk to me?"

"Sure, Ken. What's on your mind?"

"We struck out with Wolmar and his secretary. Seems the two checks you thought were from Breitner were actually from some Canadian fellow named Boatman. She had photocopies of them to prove it. Flanders is clean, Jim. And we're back to square one."

"Not so, Ken. You're hot on the trail."

"I don't know how that can be. We called Boatman's wife. She says he left her, she's divorcing him, she doesn't know where to find him, and she won't come down here and testify."

"If that's all she can tell you, her testimony wouldn't help anyhow, would it?"

"Nope. Just another dead end."

"What about Durnacky? What does he say?"

"We haven't called him."

"Why not?"

"C'mon, Jim, you know why not. He'll have Wolmar with him. And Wolmar will tie us up in knots if we don't already have concrete evidence to connect Durnacky to Breitner."

This was the point Malloy had feared and fretted about. Should he reveal that Breitner was Boatmen and Boatman was Breitner? He had labored over it for weeks. He and Margaret had talked about it long into the night. Revealing it would clearly help solve the mystery. But working against that were two factors.

First, Valarie didn't know that her husband was a justice of the Michigan Supreme Court. To discover that her marriage was bigamous would surely be a heartbreak. She didn't want to be involved, and Jim had pledged to try to keep her out of it. And if she found out who he was, there was always the possibility that she would do a complete reversal, go public with it, maybe sue Breitner's estate.

Not good ink for the court.

That brought Malloy to the second reason for keeping quiet. He didn't want to embarrass Elizabeth. He didn't want to shame Breitner's memory. Breitner after all, had died a hero. A martyr. Whether he really was a martyr was not as important as the public perception, Malloy felt. Why drag the court through that kind of negative sensationalism? Malloy tried to think of other reasons why Pershing should call Durnacky as a witness.

"At least you could call him in and ask him about Boatman. Didn't you tell me you thought Breitner may have been the victim of blackmail? Was Durnacky blackmailing Breitner? If so, what for? Maybe Boatman was a friend of Breitner's who Breitner used as a conduit to pay the money to Durnacky. After all, if he wanted his death to appear like a murder, Breitner wouldn't want canceled checks to Morris Durnacky in his bank statement."

"That might work Jim, but I'm very apprehensive about this suicide theory. If the press gets wind that we have called Durnacky they are going to be all over me like a cold sweat. What can I tell them? Heck, I don't even believe it myself."

"Look, Ken, I have an idea. Let me flesh it out, and I'll get back to you."

"O.K. Chief. But you damn well better get me out of this fix pretty quick. My one year as grand juror will be up at the end of October, and I have absolutely no desire to keep this fiasco going one minute longer than is necessary."

Malloy laughed. "Relax, Ken. We'll have you back hearing divorce cases in no time."

***

The lady dialed 1-800-GOODBYE. When the recording came on, she set up a meeting the following evening at seven o'clock at an address in Northville. The house was a frame ranch on one acre which had once been the dream house of a World war II veteran and his bride. They were both gone now. He to his eternal reward, and she to a nursing home. Their children could not agree to sell the place while mother was still living. They rented it, furnished, month to month. When they could find a tenant.

Morris Durnacky arrived on time. He was observant. The Green Berets taught him that. Only one car in the drive. A compact, two years old. Probably a lonely old widow, he thought. Kids grown. Arthritis. Maybe cancer. This would be routine. He rang the bell. To his surprise, it was answered by a much younger woman. In her late forties, perhaps. Well dressed. A secretary, or professional of some kind. He had hardly settled himself in a chair at the dining room table, preparing to open his brief case, when she handed him a subpoena from the grand jury in Shiawassee County. It directed him to appear that very evening in that very house to give evidence concerning matters then under investigation.

Durnacky rose to his feet, and began to stammer a question to the woman, when Circuit Judge Kenneth Pershing, and Chief Justice James Malloy appeared from the bedroom.

"Good evening, Mr. Durnacky," said Pershing, "I trust you will pardon this rather unorthodox means of getting together. We wanted to protect you from undue and unwelcome notoriety."

Durnacky was dumbstruck. "What the hell is this? What's going on here?"

"You have just been subpoenaed to testify before me as the one man grand jury appointed to investigate the murder of Justice Edward Breitner. This lady here is the official court stenographer. She will record every word that is said. We want to ask you some questions. Justice Malloy here is another grand jury witness. He has been sworn to keep secret whatever he may hear you say, as am I, except if you are indicted. In that case the record of your testimony will be available to the prosecutor."

"I'm entitled to a lawyer aren't I?"

"Certainly. Your attorney is Mr. Wolmar, isn't that so?"

"Yes."

"He should be here any minute. He was called this afternoon, and told to meet you here."

Durnacky fell silent. The reporter set up her machine, and took a position in the corner of the room. Pershing sat at the head of the dining room table, opposite Durnacky. Malloy sat at one side of the table. In less than ten minutes, the doorbell rang. The court reporter answered it. Perry Wolmar asked for Morris Durnacky, and was invited in. When he saw Pershing and Malloy, sitting at the dining room table with Durnacky, he stopped dead in the center of the living room.

"O.K. What's this all about? Morris, did you set this up? What's going on?"

Pershing explained calmly. "Mr. Wolmar, we have subpoenaed your client, Mr. Durnacky, to testify concerning the Breitner murder. We think he knows some things that will help us. We set this meeting here, without notice, because we wanted to protect him and the grand jury from unwelcome and possibly harmful publicity."

"There is no way I'm going to let him testify in this kind of a star chamber. No way, Judge."

"He has two choices. Either we talk here and now, or I bring him to Owosso with a brass band. One way or the other, I want to hear what he has to say."

Wolmar stroked his chin. "Can I talk to him privately for a minute?"

"Sure. Use the bedroom."

They left and returned about twenty minutes later.

"O.K. He'll talk now," said Wolmar.

Pershing explained the secrecy rule, assured Wolmar that Malloy was covered by it, and asked the reporter to swear in the witness. Pershing asked the questions, beginning with the usual identification. He then took Durnacky through his connection to L.R., Incorporated. Durnacky described it as his company, and admitted receiving the Boatman checks.

"What services did you perform for Mr. Boatman?"

Wolmar objected. "Your honor, Boatman was a Canadian. He lived in Ontario, did business with my client in Canadian money. I don't think this grand jury has the authority to investigate Canadian crimes. Whatever he did or didn't do for Mr. Boatman is entirely out of the scope of your inquiry."

Pershing was stumped. He conferred with Malloy, then continued. "Did you kill Justice Breitner?"

"No."

"Did you shoot Justice Breitner?"

"No."

"Did you receive any money from Justice Breitner, or from anyone else on behalf of Justice Breitner?"

"No."

Pershing conferred with Malloy again. They went into the kitchen and talked heatedly.

"I knew this wouldn't work, Jim. He is going to stone wall. We won't break him."

"I think he has been telling you the truth, Ken. I think he didn't know he was dealing with Breitner. That's why he says he took nothing from him. Try one more, direct question concerning his whereabouts."

The two judges returned to the dining room and sat down.

"Where were you on the night of August 1, 1991, and the

early morning of August 2, 1991?"

"Different places. I was traveling on I-75."

"Specifically, were you, at any time that night and early morning in the parking lot across the road from the Cross in the Woods Shrine at Indian River?"

Durnacky conferred with his lawyer. Wolmar asked for time to talk in private. They went into the bedroom, and stayed there for forty five minutes, talking anxiously. Then they returned to the table. Wolmar spoke.

"Your Honor, I have advised my client to take the fifth amendment to that question. He is, however, willing to testify to everything he knows about this matter if you will give him complete immunity from prosecution."

Now it was time for the judges to confer again. Back to the kitchen.

"What do you think, Jim?"

"I think Durnacky will solve the whole mystery. But something bothers me."

"What is that?"

"If he testifies the way I think he will, you are going to have to report to the court of appeals that no crime has been committed. If you do that, these grand jury records will be sealed and no one will ever know what really happened."

"That's not our problem, is it?"

"I suppose not, but I think the supreme court bench should know what happened to Breitner."

"I can see that. But what can we do?"

"Adjourn tonight, and reconvene in the chambers of the supreme court. Swear all the justices to secrecy, just as I have done, and take Durnacky's testimony in their presence."

"I guess we can do that, Jim." Pershing was shaking his head. "They sure didn't cover this stuff in law school."

CHAPTER 28

SEPTEMBER 1992

Monday, September 7, 1992, dawned grey and dreary. It was to be a day of destiny in the supreme court of Michigan, but for the court crier it was simply a pain in the neck. Arriving early, he busied himself arranging the seating in the court's conference room according to a detailed chart which the chief justice's office had given him Friday afternoon. The bench, it appeared, was going to have visitors. He was to arrange the justices' chairs along the west side of the conference table. It was not long enough to accommodate all seven of them on one side, so he had to bring in another long table to extend it. At the east end of the room, he was to set up a small table, and put a large leather chair, like those of the justices, behind it, facing west. On the north wall, he placed a single chair facing south, and another, just west of it, turned slightly southeast. Finally, another small table and two chairs were to be set up in front of the bathroom door on the south side of the room, facing north.

The crier didn't know it, but when he finished, he had created a miniature courtroom in which the seven justices were to be the gallery.

Malloy had difficulty persuading his colleagues to cooperate in his plan. The sheer novelty of the proceedings dampened their desire to participate. They were squeamish about doing something that might disqualify them from hearing some unidentified future legal dispute. Some were skeptical because they thought they were being asked to be party to an effort by Malloy to extricate himself from his troubles with the media. In the end, their curiosity got the best of them.

The Breitner killing was becoming known as the Michigan Mystery. Several television specials, billed as in-depth reporting, had been broadcast during the year that had elapsed since his body was found at Indian River. Some Hollywood types had been snooping around, looking to make a feature length movie about it. Elizabeth Breitner especially, felt the sting of unwanted notoriety, as agents hounded her to tell her story, sell her story, or simply appoint one of their clients to be the official chronicler of the mystery. Speculation, of the type, if not the intensity, of that stemming from the Kennedy assassination was rampant. One big difference; with Kennedy, there was the Warren Report, at least a common jumping off point. With Breitner, there was no official report. No compilation of known facts that could serve as a basis for deduction and hypothesis. Each day the mystery deepened, and the silence of the Pershing grand jury only exacerbated the situation.

And so the seven justices agreed to sit in on the grand jury proceedings as interested bystanders, sworn to absolute secrecy, powerless to react or respond to what they might learn, but intensely anxious to know the truth about their colleague's death, whatever that truth should turn out to be.

By nine-thirty that fateful morning, the chief justice and all six associates were in their chairs as Judge Kenneth Pershing entered the room, flanked by his reporter and Emmet Fournier, the prosecutor. Within seconds, Perry Wolmar, and his client, Morris Durnacky, appeared. The chief justice directed each to their chairs as they entered. There were no informal or cordial greetings. As soon as everyone was seated, Pershing motioned to his prosecutor to close the door. Malloy had already instructed the court crier to station himself outside the door, at a sufficient distance so that he could not hear the voices inside, but near enough to stop anyone who might try to enter.

Pershing began promptly at nine-thirty. "We are here this morning, convened as the grand jury ordered by the Michigan court of appeals on October 22, 1991, for the purpose of hearing the testimony of one Morris Durnacky regarding the events at Indian River on the first and second of August, 1991. Let the record show that the court has granted Mr. Durnacky full immunity under the statute in such case provided, so that he may not be prosecuted for anything which he tells this grand jury, nor any crime which may be subsequently revealed as a result of information gained from his testimony. The exception, of course, is that he may be prosecuted for perjury, should it appear that his testimony here is false. Do you understand all of this, Mr. Durnacky?"

"I do, your Honor."

"And you understand that you may not invoke the protection of the fifth amendment, is that correct?"

"Correct."

"Mr. Wolmar, have you fully advised your client of his rights?"

"I have, your Honor."

"And you are satisfied that he knows what he is doing and does this voluntarily?"

"I am."

"Alright, Mr. Fournier, you may question the witness."

Emmet Fournier was high. He was so keyed up he could hardly speak. His hands shook as he tried to assemble his notes. This was the biggest, most important, most memorable day of his life. He only hoped and prayed that he wouldn't blow it. Wouldn't make a fool of himself, right here in front of the whole supreme court bench. He got through the formal identification testimony without a hitch, and his blood pressure began to recede.

"Now, Mr. Durnacky, will you please tell the grand jury what you know about the demise of Justice Edward Breitner. Please begin at your first contact with him."

"That is a difficult question, counselor, because my first contacts were with a Mr. Earl Boatman. As far as I know, I never spoke to Breitner until August second."

"Then begin with your contacts with Mr. Boatman. When and how did you first meet him?"

"Boatman called my eight hundred number sometime in late April or early May of 1991. He set up a meeting in a motel near

Saginaw off I-75. I was to go to a certain room."

"Did you?"

"Yes. The door was open, as he had said it would be. I closed it, went to the bathroom door and said 'Hemlock.' Those were his instructions. He was in the bathroom and never came out while I was there. We talked through the door."

"What did he say to you?" Fournier asked.

"He said he wanted to die. That he had a very unfortunate personal situation that he could not get out of, and that he had pancreatic cancer which would kill him in a matter of months. He said he didn't want to die a slow, tortured death. Preferred to go out quickly while he was still fully functional."

"What did you say to him?"

"I told him that was his right, and I would help him to die in any way he preferred, whenever he thought the time was right."

"And then?"

"Well, then I told him what my fee would be, how we do these things, stuff like that. I asked him if anyone else would know what he was doing."

"What did he say to that?"

"He said no one knew, and he didn't want anyone to know. That's when he began to explain what he wanted me to do."

"What did he want you to do, Mr. Durnacky?"

"He wanted me to help him die in a way that looked like he was murdered."

Doris Templeton rose from her chair in a rage. "LIAR! YOU'RE A ROTTEN NO GOOD LIAR. How dare you...."

Pershing slammed his gavel on the table in front of him. "Justice Templeton, I am very sorry if this testimony is upsetting to you, but I cannot allow you to disrupt these proceedings. Please take your seat and remain silent while we are in session."

Doris slumped into her chair, her eyes red, her hands shaking, tears of anger streaming down her face.

Fournier fumbled a moment, then continued his questioning.

"What did you say to that?"

"I said we could do anything he wanted, but the price would have to reflect the difficulty of the assignment."

"Did you agree on a price?"

"We did."

"And what was it?"

"Fifty thousand dollars. Ten on the front end, forty at the time of performance."

"Did you discuss the manner of payment?"

"Yes. He said I would be paid in Canadian funds, but would receive the equivalent of fifty thousand U.S. dollars."

"Did he give you any money then?"

"Yes. He asked me how to make out the check for and to whom. The he slid it to me under the door."

"For how much?"

"Thirteen something Canadian. Ten thousand U.S."

"Did you know the rate of exchange?"

"No. I took his word for it. It sounded about right."

"Did you have a discussion at that time about exactly how, when or where this was to take place?"

"Not then, we didn't. He said he would contact me through my 800 number and set up another meeting. I told him I wouldn't do anything anyway until his check had cleared."

Judge Pershing interjected. "I am curious about that, Mr. Durnacky. You said he was to pay you the balance of forty thousand on the day of performance. How were you to know his check would be good?"

"We had to trust each other, Judge. He had to trust that I would carry out his wishes, and I had to trust that his check would be good. Like any business deal between men of honor." O'Leary whispered something to Germaine. Pershing glared at him, lifted the gavel, then set it down again. "Go on, counsel."

"What happened next? Did he call your number?"

"Yes. About a month later. He left a message telling me to go to the bus station in downtown Detroit and stand by a certain pay phone, pretending to talk in it, but keeping the line open for a call. He said he would call me there at a certain exact time."

"Did he?"

"Yes. He called and said he wanted to go over the details. He seemed to know all about the Epsilof case I had where the man shot himself in the motel room. He said he wanted to do something like that, but out someplace where it would look like someone else did it."

"What did you say?"

"I said there was real danger for me in that scenario, because if I pulled it off the way he wanted, I might be arrested for murder. I told him that the only way I would do it would be if I had some foolproof way of protecting myself if anything went sour, and I became a suspect."

"And how did you propose to do that?"

"For one thing, I insisted on a written contract. I always do."

"Do you have such a contract with Justice Breitner?"

"Not actually. My contract was with Earl Boatman." Durnacky reached into a briefcase on the floor beside him, removed a piece of paper, and handed it to Fournier. Fournier examined it, then handed it to the court reporter, who marked it as an exhibit. "Your Honor, exhibit one appears to be an agreement, entitled "Assisted Suicide Agreement" signed by an Earl Boatman for himself, and by Morris Durnacky on behalf of L.R., Incorporated." He handed it to the judge.

Pershing spoke. "Mr. Durnacky, I have been curious about the name of that corporation. L.R. Is that someone's initials? Do you have a partner in that business?"

"No, your Honor. L.R. stands for Last Rights. The corporation does business under the trade name Last Rights."

"I see. Now this agreement talks about assisted suicide. It does not mention faking a murder. Was that aspect of your arrangement reduced to writing anywhere?"

"No, your honor. He said he didn't want to discuss the gory details, that he was leaving the specifics up to me."

Fournier resumed questioning the witness. "When did you next have contact with Breitner or Boatman?"

"Boatman called my 800 number on the evening of July 31, at about 7:30. Left a message that it was an emergency, and I was to call him immediately at a number in the 705 area. He said he would wait for me to call."

"Do you have that number?"

"I can get it. It would be in my daily journal."

"What did he say when you called?"

"He said the deal was on for the next night. I was to meet him at Indian River, Michigan, in the parking lot of the Cross in the Woods. He asked me if I knew where that was, and I said I did."

"What time?"

"Three AM on August second."

"And did you meet him there?"

"I did."

"What happened then?"

"I inserted a hypodermic needle into his arm, then loaded it with a syringe containing 150 milligrams of morphine. I told him that when he was ready, he should push down on the plunger."

"Then what? Did he?"

"Yes. He did. Then he slumped over. I waited maybe fifteen, twenty minutes, removed the needle and felt his pulse. I could get no pulse, and I concluded that he was dead."

"What did you do then?"

" I went to my van, got a thirty-eight revolver with a silencer on it, and emptied it into his body. I removed the silencer and threw the gun into the weeds near his car. Then I left."

"When did you get the check?"

"I forgot to mention that. He gave me the check before I inserted the needle."

"When did you learn that the man you helped to die was Edward Breitner and not Earl Boatman?"

"The next morning. It was all over the papers and the TV.

When I saw Justice Breitner's picture in the paper, I realized that he was the man I met in the parking lot."

"Did you have further contact with Boatman?"

"I tried. I called his house a couple times. His wife always said he wasn't home. The last time I called she said he left her and she was divorcing him. She had no idea where to find him."

Fournier sat down and began to review his notes. Pershing took up the questioning. "Mr. Durnacky, you have told a most improbable story. There is no need for you to protect yourself by lying to this grand jury. We have given you immunity. Are you sure that you were not simply hired to assassinate the justice? Hired by someone who wanted him out of the way?"

"I have told you the God's honest truth, your honor. That's the way it happened."

Templeton was on her feet again, this time she would not be controlled. "The truth isn't in that man. HE'S A LIAR, JUDGE. A GOD DAMN LIAR. Ask him who scratched AOR on the hood of the car. Ask him if Boatman wasn't just the pay off man for the AOR terrorists. Ask him why we are supposed to take his word for it, the word of a man who admits he committed murder. Ask him...."

Pershing began to pound his gavel when she started her tirade, but stopped as Malloy and Germaine took Templeton's arms, restraining her, and helping her back into the chair.

"I do not condone that outburst, Mr. Durnacky, but surely you must realize that all of us in this room, the members of the supreme court who worked with Justice Breitner particularly, find it highly improbable that he would have acted as you have testified. What do you have which shows that Edward Breitner, as opposed to Earl Boatman, wanted to be killed? Have you any other proof?"

"Yes. I do, your honor."

"And what exactly would that be?"

"Well, I told you that I informed Boatman that I would not do this thing unless I was completely protected against being convicted of murder."

"Yes, I recall that you said that."

"I have it on tape."

"You what?"

"I have it on video tape. The whole thing."

Pershing, Fournier, the seven justices of the supreme court and the court reporter who was taking down the testimony were all stunned. Stunned in silent disbelief. Like they were witnessing a nightmare, and were somehow awake enough to realize that they were sleeping.

Finally, Pershing regained enough composure to ask,"Do you have it here?"

"I do, your honor. Would you like to view it?"

"I am afraid we have to," said Pershing in a monotone. Then he turned to Malloy. "Mr. Chief Justice, do you have a TV monitor available?" Malloy nodded affirmatively, reached over to the telephone on the credenza and called the crier's office.

In twenty tense, heart pounding minutes, punctuated by anxious, whispered conversations among the justices, the monitor was set up, the blinds were drawn, and the tape was inserted and running. It began with a picture of Durnacky, apparently made in an office, after the fact. He said, "This video tape was made in the early morning hours of August second, 1991 in the parking lot of the Cross in the Woods Shrine at Indian River, Michigan. The person in the back seat of the Oldsmobile is Earl Boatman, a resident of Chapleau, Ontario and a client of Last Rights. We have agreed with Mr. Boatman that this tape will never be shown except to prevent a miscarriage of justice by the erroneous prosecution of a person or persons associated with Last Rights."

At that point, the tape went blank for a few seconds. When it came up again there were gasps all around the conference room. Julia Hudson screamed. Alton Henry said,"Oh my God."

The scene was basked in an eerie light, like a policeman's flashlight pointed at post prom smoochers parked in a secluded lovers lane or like the lights that made the famous Rodney King tape possible. A glaring, out-of-place brightness, clashing with the pitch blackness all around it, illuminating the objects directly in front of it, but leaving the periphery eclipsed in shadows. It had a black and white quality, even though it was obviously a color picture.

In the center of the frame, sitting in the back seat of his car, was Justice Edward Breitner. No doubt about it. The rear door was open, so that his head and torso were visible. He was turned slightly sideways, facing the camera, which appeared to have been mounted about ten or twelve feet away from him. He was dressed casually. A soft collar golf shirt and khakis. His countenance was serious, but his expression was blank. There were no laugh lines crinkled by his eyes. The video image of Edward Breitner looked up, looked right at the seven supreme court justices staring incredulously at the TV monitor. Then he spoke.

"I have devoted my life to justice. I have given all I could give. It hasn't been enough. The forces of bigotry and violence, of hatred and tyranny seem to be growing stronger every day. Now my time to die has come. I cannot forestall it. I cannot prevent it. But I can use my death as I have used my whole life to further the cause of freedom and justice. What I do tonight I do willingly in a spirit of sacrifice for the good of our beloved state and nation. I hope this tape is never used, and that it will be destroyed in seven years as Mr. Durnacky promises to do."

With that, he matter of factly pulled his left sleeve up to his shoulder with his right hand. Another figure appeared from the camera's right. Durnacky. He inserted a hypodermic needle into the large muscle at the top of Breitner's arm, then plugged in a large syringe. Breitner reached around with his right hand and pushed the plunger down all the way. In seconds, he slumped over, his head resting against the back of the driver's seat ahead of him. Durnacky's arm, shoulder and hip could be seen at the right. He was standing there in silence. The conference room was equally silent, except for a muffled sobbing emanating from someone at the justices' table.

There followed an eternity of sixteen minutes and nineteen seconds, during which the otherwise motionless Breitner twitched several times and finally made a retching sound, half cough and half regurgitation, after which he slumped even further forward. Then Durnacky was seen to approach the inert figure in the car, remove the needle, and feel for a pulse. He stepped out of the picture to the left. Again, in a moment, he reentered from the left, turned slightly sideways. In his hand was a revolver, with a long extension on its barrel. He fired six rounds at the body, which bounced a little with each impact, slowly reclining to its right as the fusillade continued. The gunman disappeared again, and abruptly the screen went blank.

***

The grand juror and his people left shortly after Durnacky was dismissed. The seven members of the Michigan Supreme Court were alone in the conference room. They sat in stunned, speechless desolation, still lined up along the west side of the extended table. No one knew what to do or to say. At long last, VanTimlin, the senior person in the room, who happened to be seated in the center between Malloy and Hudson, reached out with both of his hands, taking Malloy's and Hudson's hands in his, and softly began, "Let us pray." Malloy and Hudson responded by taking the hands of Templeton and O'Leary respectively, and they in turn joined hands with Germaine and Henry.

"Heavenly Father," Van Timlin continued, "we humbly ask you to receive our brother Edward Breitner into your kingdom. He was one of us, and like all of us, he was full of good impulses and bad, moments of greatness and moments of wretchedness. Comfort us, Father, in our sorrow, strengthen us in the important work we must continue to do with heavy hearts, and lead us in the end to your eternal city where the riddles of our lives shall be revealed, and the darkness of our intellects made bright. Amen."

CHAPTER 29

OCTOBER 1992

Nora Oldsmer drove her husband to work so that she could use the car. The Tuttle's neighborhood was unfamiliar to her, and it took some exploring of the winding, tree lined streets before she located the address. One last, nervous, peek at herself in the rearview mirror, then up the walk to the imposing front stoop. She rang the bell, waited anxiously, and was relieved when Cindy opened the door.

"Good morning, Nora. You're right on time. Come in. Come in."

Nora entered the spacious foyer. Its floor was real Italian tile, the kind she had only seen in public buildings. The ceiling, twelve feet above the floor, was high enough to accommodate the elegant chandelier blazing above Cindy's head, as she directed Nora into the cozy, paneled den to her left.

Nora was not the only one who was nervous. Cindy had no little difficulty persuading her daughter to make this date, and as the days inched closer to the appointment, Hilda wished she hadn't agreed to the meeting. Josh's death had left such a void in the justice's heart that each day was a struggle to concentrate on other things. Time, the great healer, was only beginning to soften the intensity of her heartache. The gnawing emptiness in Hilda's stomach that woke her every morning was only starting to subside. This day would, Hilda feared, bring back the hurting. Bring back the vivid, persistent, mental pictures of her dear son's smile, his walk, his thoughtful deeds, his boyish charm.

As Hilda entered the den, Nora stood. Cindy offered a perfunctory introduction, which fizzled because it was unnecessary. Then, with a manufactured excuse about having something to do in the kitchen, she disappeared, praying that the conversation would go well, and wishing that she could be a mouse in the corner.

"Thank you so much for agreeing to see me, Mrs. Tuttle. You can't know how much it means to me to have this chance to speak with you."

"I'm sure it was not easy for you to come here, Mrs. Oldsmer. I admire your spunk."

"I was just so sure that if we talked to each other as mothers, you would understand how I feel. And I wish with all my heart that I could really appreciate how you feel. I simply can't imagine how you must have suffered."

"Death is part of life, Mrs. Oldsmer. We all experience it some time. And it is never quite what we expect."

"I believe that is so. But young people do not have the same familiarity with death that older people do. Jeremiah...." Nora paused, wondering if it was a mistake to mention the boy's name in front of his victim's mother.

"I'm sure Jeremiah still doesn't appreciate the seriousness of what he did," said Hilda, using the boy's name purposefully.

"He has had to learn a whole new vocabulary, Mrs. Tuttle. He had never heard words like sin or evil, or sorry or forgiveness before all this happened. He was a child of the streets. The kind we read about, and worry about, but don't often see, if we can avoid it."

"I know about the world he came from. It's the major social problem in America."

"I guess that's right. But seeing pictures of slums, inner city crime, riots, and the like is not the same thing as looking into the eyes of one certain human being who has been living like a wild animal in the jungle. It's scary, Mrs. Tuttle. Plenty scary. I don't know what we would have done without your dear mother, God bless her. She is the finest Christian woman I have ever been privileged to know."

"I quite agree. Except for her appetite for pancakes, she is perfect."

Nora smiled. "I've shared a few snacks with your mother, and

I know what you mean."

There was an uneasy pause. The lighter comment had broken some ice, but neither woman knew where the current of their words would take them. Hilda asked a question she thought proper, but didn't really want answered. "So tell, me, Mrs. Oldsmer, how is Jeremiah doing?"

"It's very hard to tell. Some days I think we are getting through to him. Some days, I wonder if we ever will. He's a very smart boy. Can learn just about anything if he puts a mind to it. Plays the piano really well."

"I heard."

"But then there's that mean streak in him. The nasties, I call it. He just gets the nasties sometimes, and I can't seem to reach him."

"What does he do then? When he gets nasty, I mean."

"Sometimes he throws things. Busts things up. Or he just yells and screams. Beats his fists on the wall. He never hit me or tried to, but he tried to hit my husband once. Benny slapped him good up side his head, and he never tried it again."

"Spare the rod, spoil the child, momma used to say."

"It's still true, I guess. But Jeremiah is so tough, I think he can take about anything without flinching. The only time I think he cares is when he sees me cry. Then he talks softly, and says he is sorry."

"I'd say that's a start, anyway."

"I think the boy carries a terrible burden of guilt. I don't think he knows what to call it. But that's what it is. At Holy Trinity School, they taught him to say the Lord's Prayer. I asked him to say it at home. When he came to the part about 'forgive us our trespasses' he asked me what trespasses were. I told him that's when you hurt somebody. He says, you mean like I hurt Josh Tuttle? And I say yes. Like that. He says, does the Father forgive everybody? And I tell him everybody that wants to be forgiven. And he says, Is God going to kill me for killing Josh? I say, no, boy. You don't have to die for your sins, because

Jesus already did that for you. He likes me to tell him that, Mrs. Tuttle. It makes him feel better."

"I'm sure it does."

"I told him that our trespasses are forgiven 'as we forgive those who trespass against us.' He said he never let anybody trespass against him, and he never would. I said. 'If somebody tried to hurt you, what would you do?' he said, "I'd hurt him first. Like I bit off the rat's tail before he could bite me' And I said, what if you hurt yourself like when you shot off your foot, who are you going to hurt then?"

"What did he say to that?"

"Nothing. He just started to cry, and then he said he didn't want to hurt himself any more. He didn't want to be a bad person any more, and just hoped that God the Father would forgive him even if he didn't deserve it because it was so painful to be a bad, guilty person and there was nobody he could hurt to make the pain stop because it was himself that was causing the pain."

Hilda felt her eyes beginning to burn. "He sounds like a troubled little boy.'

"Oh yes, Mrs. Tuttle. He's troubled. Wakes up screaming at night sometimes. I just don't know what to do. I guess I just hoped that maybe you or Doctor Tuttle could say something to him. Somehow let him know that he can be forgiven if he would just begin by forgiving himself." Nora went to her purse for a handkerchief. Tears were running down her cheeks, as she looked up at Hilda with pleading eyes.

"You love that boy, don't you, Nora?" Hilda's voice quivered.

"Yes Ma'am. I do. I surely do."

***

Early in October, the chief justice called Julia Hudson to inquire about the advisory opinion on the terrorism law.

"How is it coming, Julia? Are you making any progress?"

"Tough sledding, Chief. I can't seem to find any reliable precedents that will give us guidance. You would think that with so much terrorism in the world, there would be some other state that had experience with this kind of thing."

"You would think so. I'm concerned about the political ramifications, Julia. I was hoping we could get our opinion out this month."

"I don't understand about politics, Jim. I was a federal judge, you know."

"That's right. And above politics, right?"

"Next to God herself, hadn't you heard.?"

"Herself?" Malloy chuckled. "Have you been talking to Doris again?"

"Yes, but that's not where I get my theology."

"Seriously, Julia, the terrorism law is very closely tied to the referendum on the death penalty. I don't know if you've been watching the polls being reported in the newspapers, but it looks like the reinstatement of the death penalty might very well pass. It would be a sad thing for Michigan if it does."

"I certainly agree with that."

"Our tradition in this state has been a good thing for the courts, in my opinion. One of the worst evils about the death penalty is that nobody likes to carry it out. The result is an endless series of appeals, writs, emergency pleas, and eleventh hour maneuvers that take up the time and energies of the courts and make the whole criminal justice system look impotent."

"Which it usually is."

"Exactly. And even the victim's families are injured in the process. They wait and wait and wait for the sentence to be carried out and nothing happens. They get frustrated."

"And cynical, I might add."

"You bet. They expect the death penalty to be carried out and it isn't. In Michigan, we never have had that problem. Put a guy away for life and he goes to jail right away. He might file an appeal, but at least he is serving his sentence if he is behind bars."

"How do the other justices feel about the death penalty?"

"The only one who claims to favor it is Alton Henry, and he thinks it shouldn't be limited to terrorism cases."

"So what can the court do about it? The death penalty is up to the voters, isn't it?"

"Of course. Either the voters will amend the constitution or they won't. But the polls are saying that there is a big connection between the death penalty and the terrorism law."

"How so?"

"Well, the pollsters are claiming that a lot of people are going to vote for the death penalty even though they are not generally in favor of it, simply because it is limited to terrorism cases."

"I see what you're saying. You think that if we knock out the terrorism law, it will help to defeat the death penalty referendum."

"I believe it. Especially, if our decision is unanimous. If there is no terrorism law then a death penalty for terrorism murder is useless. If people see that, their enthusiasm should be dampened."

"Alright, let's suppose that you are right. There is still one rather significant hurdle."

"And that is?"

"That is the law. We certainly can't declare the terrorism law unconstitutional just because we don't like it, or just because we think it will help defeat the death penalty if we do it. There has to be a good, sound, legal basis for our decision. So far, I haven't found any."

"Maybe I can help you there. I think the answer is right on the surface, staring us in the face. The constitution says that death penalties are unconstitutional. Period."

"Yes, but didn't they get around that by making the act effective upon the amendment of the constitution?"

"That's what the act says. That's true. But take another look at the words of the constitution. It says, 'No Law shall be enacted providing for the penalty of death.' The key word is 'enacted'."

"I'm not sure I follow you."

"If the constitution said 'No law shall become effective, which provides for the penalty of death' I suppose you could argue that by delaying the effective date of the law, until the constitution is amended, the legislature did not violate the constitution. But the constitution doesn't talk about the effectiveness of a death penalty. It simply says no such law can be enacted. Period."

"So you are saying that it is the enacting of the law that violates the constitution, and not the effectiveness of the death penalty. Is that it?"

"That's the way I see it. The violation of the constitution occurred when the legislators pushed their voting buttons and lit up the big tote board. All the rest is window dressing."

"Maybe it will work, Jim. I'll put my law clerks on it right away."

"Let me know if you need help, Julia. We should get this thing down quickly if it is going to do any good on November 3rd."

***

On Monday, October 19, Circuit Judge Ken Pershing filed his final report with the Michigan Court of Appeals. The report was legalistic in form. It recited, at length, the various activities of the grand jury over the previous year. Sixty-two witnesses called. Over three thousand pages of testimony transcribed. Four hundred and nine exhibits admitted. Medical reports, coroners reports. Accident reports. Police reports.

But when the recitation of inventory was completed, the grand juror's final conclusions were far afield from what had been anticipated a year before when the grand jury was convened with fanfare and hoopla. Copies were made available for members of the press corps and the broadcast media. They stood around the appeals court clerk's office and read the summary with disbelief and disappointment.

"CONCLUSIONS

From the foregoing testimony and evidence, the grand juror has concluded as follows:

1) The identity of the person or persons responsible for the display of fireworks in the vicinity of the Twelve Oaks Mall on December 10, 1990, and similar fireworks in the plaza in front of the Law Building on March 26, 1991 has not been established, and in view of the fact that the incidents constituted misdemeanors and not felonies, no further investigation is warranted.

2) The grand juror found no crime or misdemeanor was committed in the obtaining of a winning ticket in the Florida lottery by Chief Justice James P. Malloy, either by the justice or by any other person associated with that transaction.

3) The grand jury has determined that Justice Edward Breitner's death was either not feloniously caused, or if felonious, the responsible person has been granted full immunity from prosecution. Therefore, no presentment or indictment will be returned in that matter.

Obviously, these conclusions did not satisfy the media. But they could not talk to Judge Pershing, as he had left for a much deserved vacation in Hawaii by the time his report was made public. Prosecutor Emmet Fournier steadfastly refused to make any public statement, as did the official court stenographer.

Pershing's report closed with the statement that all of the

transcripts, exhibits, and other records of the grand jury had been duly sealed as required by statute, and would remain so, subject to the call of the court, until such time as they were required by law to be destroyed.

The Detroit First Press headline the next day reflected the general attitude of the media:

MICHIGAN MYSTERY GETS PERMANENT SHROUD.

Its second headline, however, was not exactly the common understanding. The few other papers which mentioned Chief Justice Malloy at all, said something like 'Malloy Exonerated' or 'Malloy Cleared." The First Press' line was, 'Malloy Escapes Prosecution'.

***

The supreme court's decision on the request for an Advisory Opinion concerning the terrorism law was handed down on Thursday, October 22, 1992, just 12 days before the November election. The opinion was in *per curiam* form, which meant that it was the unanimous decision of the court, with no justice being named as the author of the opinion.

The media gave considerable play to the fact that among the justices voting in favor of the decision, which declared the law unconstitutional, was Hilda Germaine, mother of Josh Tuttle, whose murder by a street gang had largely inspired the enactment of the law. Other commentators noted that Justice Doris Templeton, who had been most outspoken in her criticism of the so-called Army of Righteousness, also sided with the bench in declaring the law unconstitutional.

Civil libertarians and opponents of the death penalty rejoiced upon hearing the news. Within 24 hours, the voter polls showed a substantial burst of strength for the anti-death penalty forces, which inched closer to a dead heat with the front running pro-death penalty faction.

***

Evelyn Mentash and Justice Bob O'Leary were married at Saint Mary's Cathedral in downtown Lansing during the eight o'clock Mass on Friday, October 23rd. The groom's cousin, Harry Flynn was his best man. His daughter Kathleen did the readings from scripture, and his daughter Nancy Ann was the maid of honor. Also present were the justice's law clerk, John Hayes, and Chief Justice and Mrs. James Malloy.

After the nuptial Mass, the group of eight went to the Parthenon restaurant for breakfast, and toasted the happy couple with fresh orange juice.

CHAPTER 30

NOVEMBER 1992

Freddie had gone to work, and Gertie was busying herself around the kitchen, cleaning up the debris of her son's lumberjack breakfast. Justice Van Timlin sat at the kitchen table, a cup of coffee in hand, reading a packet of materials which had arrived in yesterday's mail. The final documents relating to his Florida condominium included a certificate of occupancy showing that the unit was completed, inspected and ready for its new owners to move in. In addition, there was a report from the interior decorator, with photographs of each room, showing the furnishings, window treatments, and brick-a-brack she had selected, delivered and arranged in the unit. Down to the last detail, it was indeed, ready to receive the VanTimlins.

Van had long since informed Gertie of his impulsive decision to purchase the condo. They had not talked of it much, except as the place where they would be spend their customary two or three week winter vacations. Gertie thought it was a very expensive investment for so little personal use, and urged Van to consider renting the place when they were not using it themselves. Van would always answer with a non committal grunt.

"Well, Gertie, the condo is ready and waiting for us. Why don't we saunter on down later this month and see how it looks?"

"We can't do that, Van. I have too much to do here."

"What is so important here in Michigan that you can't get away for a while?"

"Thanksgiving, for one thing. I have to get ready for Thanksgiving."

"For heavens sake, Gertie, we don't have any big plans for

Thanksgiving. We can buy a turkey down in Florida just as easily as up here. Look here. Look at the picture of this beautiful kitchen. Wouldn't you like to fix Thanksgiving dinner in a kitchen like that?"

Gertie stepped over to the table, and craned her neck over Van's shoulder to see the picture. "It looks nice. But how could we have Thanksgiving in Florida? There is no place for Freddie to stay. You bought a condominium with only one bed room. You know Freddie can't sleep on a couch."

"If Freddie wants to join us for Thanksgiving dinner, he could simply rent himself a motel room nearby couldn't he?"

"That's ridiculous. Our own son staying at a motel, just to visit his parents. Our home is his home. He shouldn't have to do that."

"Well, Gertie, I've been thinking. And I think it's time we had a home of our own. One that isn't also Freddie's home."

"What are you saying?"

"I'm saying that I think it's time for us, you and me, to have a life of our own. Where we don't have to think about Freddie all the time and plan everything we do to accommodate him."

"But Freddie's our son!"

"Of course he is. As I was son to my parents and you a daughter to yours. But we didn't stay dependent on them all of our lives."

"That was different. We were married."

"Marriage isn't the only reason people leave home, Gertie. Some people leave their parent's home just because they have grown up and want to live on their own."

Gertie grew silent. She knew that Van was right, and deep down she often hoped that someday Freddie would no longer be a burden. But she didn't know how to let go of him. How to cope with the guilt of letting him fend for himself and fail. Again. If only she could be sure Freddie would be all right.

Van was silent, too. He knew the conversation had reached the sticking point. They had been there before. He finished his coffee, set the cup down in its saucer, and, staring at the empty cup, began to speak in a low voice.

"Gertie. I'm tired. This has been a terribly exhausting year at the court. Every year it gets harder to keep up. I see poor Henry running around the state trying to get himself reelected, and I thank God I don't have to run again. Then I think that when my term is up, I will be off the court, and the thought pleases me very much. I have been working man and boy for nearly sixty years. I think it's time for me to give it up. Time to quit. I'd like to have a few years of quiet enjoyment. Maybe watch the sun set."

"Are you sure that's what you want to do, Van? I always thought you liked going down to the court."

"I did and I do. But my term will be up in a couple of years anyway. So I really have no choice. The only question is, when do I go? I think the time is ripe right now. Now that we have the place in Florida."

"You would go there?"

"Oh yes. These Michigan winters are not for us old folks."

"You mean move to Florida?"

"We could always come back and visit."

"What about Freddie?"

"We could give him this house. He'll get it when we die anyway."

"But when would we see him?"

"We could visit in the summer. He will have enough room here to put us up. Unless, of course he gets married and has a bunch of kiddies."

"I don't see how I could do that."

"Well, Gertie, I've given the matter a lot of thought, and I am going to announce my intention to retire effective December 31st. My letter to the governor has been typed and is waiting for me to sign it."

"You're serious, then."

"Quite serious, Gertie. On Saturday, the second of January, I am going to move to Florida. I surely do hope you decide to come with me."

***

The sun came up at 7:14 AM on Tuesday, November 3, 1992. This day the people of the United States would elect a young Arkansas governor as President of the United States. The people of Michigan participated enthusiastically in the election. The state's highest voter registration, 6.1 million electors, yielded an enormous turnout, despite grey skies, temperatures ranging from the forties in the lower peninsula to the thirties in the U.P., and scattered light rain that failed to dampen the determination of the people to cast their ballots. Thousands upon thousands of new voters exercised the franchise for the first time in their lives. Long lines at the polling places taxed the capacities of the city and county clerks who were responsible for the orderly conduct of the election.

Alton Henry spent the evening at home, alone with his wife. It could have been any Tuesday night. After his customary vigil at the window, waiting for the return of the elusive woodchuck, Henry joined his wife in the living room, watched early, inconclusive election returns, and went to bed at nine o'clock. In the morning, he would learn that he had been defeated for reelection to the Michigan Supreme Court by a Republican woman, a lawyer and partner in the massive Detroit law firm known as Dikeman, Gottlieb. Her name was Florence Purdy.

During the campaign, Henry often referred to Florence Purdy as 'the purdy girl'. Indeed she was a pretty woman. High cheekbones and wide, blue eyes, set above a full mouth, and surrounded by smooth, pink skin that belied her 48 years, Florence was the epitome of brains and beauty. The paradigm for the feminization of the legal profession in the last half of the twentieth century. Another harbinger of the cultural sea change that was washing like a tidal wave over the nation's judiciary.

Florence Purdy had never run for office before.

When she was nominated by the GOP in August, she had almost zero name recognition among the state's voters. And yet, the very first poll taken early in September showed her in a neck and neck horse race with the long time incumbent from Hillsdale. The reason was very simple. The name Florence was a woman's name. The name Alton was a man' name. Male voters divided their ballots roughly equally between candidates with whom they were not familiar. Female voters who had no other reason to choose between the candidates, selected the woman by a wide margin.

***

All day long on November second, the exit polls were predicting that Michigan was about to reinstate the death penalty, allowing capital punishment for terrorist murder as defined by law. Of course, a new definition of terrorism would have to be adopted because the Tuttle Law had been scotched by the supreme court. But an affirmative vote on capital punishment was all the legislature needed to rush a new law to the governor for signature.

The O'Learys, Bob and Evelyn, were dinner guests of the Malloys at Rathcroghan. They didn't sit down to eat until the children were packed off to bed at 8:30. By then, the first scanty election returns had started to come in. So the television reports of vote totals provided the background music during their meal. After dinner, they adjourned to the living room, and began watching the TV in earnest. The first official returns on the death penalty referendum seemed to confirm the exit polls. At ten o'clock, the vote to amend the state's constitution stood at 101,437 Yes and 92,655 No. At eleven, it was Yes, 321,943, and No, 317,654.

Bob and Evelyn had planned to leave about eleven. But a horse race was developing, and both O'Leary and Malloy were acutely interested in the outcome. They speculated about where the votes were coming from, and whether the big turnout in Macomb county was good news or bad news for the opponents of the death penalty. Margaret made more coffee, and the O'Learys stayed.

At midnight, the count stood at Yes, 544,241 and No, 540,338. The gap had narrowed by only a few hundred votes. More coffee. More speculation. At one AM, the No vote made a surge, and was leading by two thousand votes, 702,117 to 700,098. The justices and their wives let out whoops of joy. Then the weary O'Learys said goodnight, and, thanking Margaret for the wonderful meal, took their leave. Jim helped Margaret tidy up the kitchen and dining room, then went back to watch for one more update. At 1:30, the television station reported that the Yes vote was back in the lead, 837,966 to 837,110. Malloy settled into his leather chair, as Margaret, exhausted, climbed the stairs to the master bedroom.

At two, the No vote held a paper thin lead. 67 votes. Malloy dozed fitfully in the big chair, waking every few minutes to see if there was any later news. At three o'clock, the anchorman announced that the station was concluding its election night coverage. Malloy went to bed. The No vote was leading, 1,001,997 to 996,415.

As the supreme court gathered in the conference room five hours later, a yawning chief justice and his colleagues learned from the clerk of the court that the death penalty referendum was unofficially defeated by over six thousand votes.

***

Wednesday was a regular working day. Cases were set for oral argument in Lansing. Alton Henry got the news of his defeat at the Still Valley Road diner, when he bought his usual copy of the First Press. It altered his routine not one whit. He walked home, watched the seven o'clock news, then changed clothes and left for the Capital.

He was back in his home office by 5:30, just sixteen minutes after sundown. He changed clothes, and went to the window to watch for his furry nemesis. At 6:10, in semi-darkness, the woodchuck appeared. Henry moved a little quicker than usual, and sent a twenty-two caliber bullet through the animal's heart.

Alton went outside and examined his kill. Satisfied, he entered the garage, got a spade, and carried the carcass on the blade of it to a place in the back yard about 70 feet from the house. There he set the animal down, dug a hole about three feet deep, and laid his long time opponent to rest. He pushed a few shovels of dirt back into the hole, covering the woodchuck, then walked to the woodlot in the back of his property, selected a maple sapling, dug it out, and returning to the woodchuck's grave, planted the tree over the dead animal.

He would miss old Woody, the son of a bitch, but the tree would remind the justice of the good times they had together.

CHAPTER 31

DECEMBER 1992

Hilda Germaine breathed a sigh of relief as she stuffed the last Christmas card into its silver and white envelope. She and Ben had an enormous list of friends with whom they exchanged holiday greetings. The list got larger every year. Only death eliminated a name. And sometimes that took a few years, if the person was a very old acquaintance who didn't usually respond. Looking at the box of fully addressed mail, she was rather pleased with herself. This was perhaps the earliest they had ever finished the cards. And finishing the cards was the first thing she had to do to get ready for the holidays.

So now she could charge ahead, finish the shopping and begin planning the family Christmas dinner menu. The thought of family stabbed her insides one more time. Since Josh's death at this time of year, Christmas would never be the same. How difficult it was to focus on the babe of Bethlehem when her own first born had been torn away so tragically. So ruthlessly.

Thinking of Josh was still painful, but somehow over the last weeks another emotion had crept into her heart. Hard to describe, really. Uneasiness. A different kind of sadness. A new dimension of pain and suffering. Was she actually beginning to feel sorry for that boy? She still had trouble even thinking his name. Jeremiah. She had seen the word 'jeremiad' somewhere. She went to the den and opened the large dictionary on its stand.

"Jer-e-mi-ad, [From Jeremiah, a biblical prophet] A lamentation; a prolonged doleful utterance; a lugubrious complaint."

Jeremiah, the prophet. She closed the dictionary and reached for the bible on the bookshelf. Absently, unconsciously, she leafed through the pages of the Book of Jeremiah. Chapter 30:15, 17, caught her eye. She read it once and then again.

453

"15 Thus saith the Lord: A voice was heard on high of lamentation, of mourning, and weeping, of Rachel weeping for her children, and refusing to be comforted for them, because they are not. 16 Thus saith the Lord: Let thy voice cease from weeping, and thy eyes from tears; for there is a reward for thy work, saith the Lord: and they shall return out of the land of the enemy. 17 And there is hope for the last end, saith the Lord: and the children shall return to their own borders."

Hilda closed the book. Her heart was indeed filled with lamentation. Her eyes full of tears. Tears for Josh. Tears for herself and for Ben. Tears for Jeremiah. Tears for a tortured, imperfect, humanity which seemed bent on always hurting itself, always causing itself pain.

Finally, she went back to the kitchen table, sat down with a heavy sigh of resignation, took pen in hand, and addressed a Christmas card to Jeremiah Wheatley. Inside, she wrote a note.
Dear Jeremiah:
Doctor Tuttle and I wish you a very peaceful and happy Christmas. We pray that the spirit of the infant Jesus, that wonderful spirit of forgiveness, will enter your heart and home as it has entered ours. You are very lucky to have Miss Nora as your mother. She loves you very much.
Hilda Tuttle Germaine

***

Anthony Montrose presided over the meeting in the plush conference room of his Chicago office in the Sears Tower. The chairman of the Starboard Society, a high powered, low profiled, political action committee, contributed generously to its causes, but it was hard to dominate a group like this. Among the two dozen assembled members were industrialists, financiers, real estate moguls, publishers. You name it. The power structure. All committed conservatives. All wealthy. All eminently patriotic.

To Montrose's immediate right, sat the executive director of the Starboard Society, a man with unquestionable political savvy, himself a former Illinois Congressman. Art Wilhelm.

The group was discussing the annual financial report. They had spent upwards of three million dollars in 1992 on various candidates and campaigns. One of the expenditures was called into question by Chet Cannery, a member from Saint Louis. It was an item for $65,000 disbursed for 'Malloy campaign.'

"I don't see any candidates by the name of Malloy on our 1992 election roster. Who is he, Art?"

"That's the supreme court Justice in Michigan that we helped back in 1990 and 1991. The $65,000 represented the balance of his campaign deficit, money we raised during this past fiscal year."

"How come we were still raising money in 1992 for a 1990 campaign?"

"It was an unusual case, Chet. Under Michigan's code of judicial conduct, Justice Malloy couldn't accept any campaign contributions after the election. We had to find a way to pay his campaign debts without him knowing where the money came from. And we had to get the money to him in some legal and visible manner."

"How could you do that?"

"Well, an opportunity came along for us to acquire a winning lottery ticket. Our bank balance was low at the time, so I went ahead and got the ticket, and submitted a request for reimbursement from the Starboard Society. It was all approved by our executive committee at the time."

Montrose chimed in. "That's right, Chet. We OK'D it back in 1991."

"So you are saying this fellow Malloy still doesn't know we helped him?"

"I'm sure he doesn't, " replied Wilhelm.

"Then why did we help him? What good did it do us?"

"The executive committee went all over that at the time,"

Montrose interrupted. "Malloy is a conservative, both on economic and social issues. And he's a good man. The kind we don't see enough of in politics these days. We gave him only token financial help before the election, because we didn't think he could win. When he won, Art recommended that we assist in retiring his campaign fund deficit."

"Sounds awfully damn complicated. Are you sure it wasn't illegal?"

Montrose intervened again. "We have an opinion of counsel that says we haven't violated any laws, Chet."

"What did the media have to say about it?"

"It was a little touch and go for a while," Wilhelm answered, nodding thoughtfully. "But I think we're out of the woods."

***

Mark Edwards had a birthday party every December 29th. On that morning in 1992, Margaret Malloy drove her husband to work so later they wouldn't have two cars downtown. She was going to Novi to return some Christmas gifts and do some bargain hunting, and promised to meet him that evening in the Lansing Center, at the Governor's two hundred dollar a plate dinner.

Near the end of the day, Malloy relaxed in his office. Sitting behind the big desk, in the big chair, contemplating the big responsibilities of the office of chief justice of the Michigan Supreme Court, Malloy smiled and allowed himself a moment of satisfaction. He had survived the onslaught of adverse publicity that marred his first two years as chief justice. He had done some positive things. Shown some leadership. He looked forward to the challenge of the next two years. With the unreliable Alton Henry replaced by a silk stocking Republican lawyer, and Van Timlin about to depart, giving the governor still another appointment, Malloy was confident that a new, strong, conservative majority would support his leadership. He liked the prospect of the future, both for the court and for himself.

Hilda Germaine poked her head in the door. She had spent the day working in Lansing because of a luncheon at the State Bar at which she was the guest speaker. "Got a minute, Chief?" she asked.

"Come on in, Hilda. I'm just relaxing. How was Christmas at the Tuttle house?"

"Too much food as usual. My mother insists on celebrating the holidays with one continuous banquet. How was yours?"

"Kiddie land. Fun but hectic. I had to come in to the office to get some rest."

Hilda laughed. "I can imagine."

"By the way," Malloy continued, "your Christmas card was one of the most beautiful I've seen this year."

"Thanks. It was pretty, wasn't it?" Hilda paused thoughtfully. "One bit of business, if I may, Jim."

"I'm always anxious to confer with you, Hilda. You know that. I count you among my closest friends on this court."

"I feel the same about you, Jim. You've done a very remarkable job as chief justice, especially considering all the flack that people have been giving you."

"No big thing," Malloy, bragged, feeling macho. "Just my thick Irish skin."

"I'm glad you're so tough, Jim. Especially glad that you don't take things personally, or pout when you don't have your way."

"I try not to."

"I just wanted to give you a heads up."

"About what?"

"The chief justiceship."

Malloy was confused. *What could she be getting at?* "What about the chief's job, Hilda?"

"Doris, Julia, Florence and I....."Hilda paused. "We sort of think that....."

Malloy broke into a huge, embarrassed smile. "You're

kidding."

"No, Jim. I'm not. We think it's time that Michigan had another woman chief justice."

Malloy shook his head in disbelieving resignation. "Why didn't I see it coming? I've got to be the original Charlie Brown."

Hilda laughed. "And who's your Lucy?"

"Good question. Who have the four of you settled on?"

"I drew the short straw, Jim."

Malloy stood and walked around his desk to Hilda. "You'll be a great chief justice. Congratulations." He extended his hand and she took it firmly. As she did so, he screwed up his face in an exaggerated scowl and said, "You'll get no help from me." Then he pulled her to him, and gave her a big hug. They both laughed heartily.

Still in his embrace, Hilda looked up at Malloy. "Jim, there is one thing I'm going to have to ask you to do for me."

"Anything, Madam chief justice. Just name it."

"Can you take over as chief during June and July?"

"Sure. Going on vacation?"

"Maternity leave," said Hilda demurely.

***

It was dark outside at five thirty when Malloy pulled on his overcoat. The offices of the supreme court were deserted. He didn't have to turn the lights out; they were operated by some distant central switch controlled by the maintenance staff. Before leaving his suite, Malloy looked around, letting the waves of nostalgia wash over his mind. It had been an exciting, stressful, productive, and unbelievably short two years. He thought of all the things that had happened in just a little over a hundred weeks. Looking back, the time seemed a seamless blurr of places, people, events and emotions.

Walking down the quiet hall toward the elevator, Malloy felt a mixture of sadness, relief and expectation. He had not done all he had hoped to do as chief justice. On the other hand, he had learned that it was not really possible to do as much in that office as he had supposed before it became his responsibility. There were limitations. Compromises that had to be made. Still, he could look forward to years of useful, satisfying work on the court. Whether as chief or associate, the job was important and interesting.

As he crossed the lobby toward the elevator, Malloy caught a glimpse of the portrait of the 'Big Four' displayed on an easel outside the courtroom. The nineteenth century jurists, wearing the stern faces so typical in portraits of that era, were enshrined in the collective minds and hearts of Michigan's legal community. From 1874 to 1881, Thomas Cooley, James Campbell, Isaac Christiancy, and Benjamin Graves wrote scores of historic legal opinions that shaped the common law of Michigan. Decisions so lucid, so scholarly, so well constructed and wisely conceived that they became models for appellate courts throughout the United States.

Malloy let himself be caught up in the moment. Standing there, alone in the lobby, thinking about the 'Big Four,' Malloy wondered how the bench on which he was sitting would be remembered. Perhaps they would never be revered as a great supreme court. But they were, to Jim Malloy, a very special group of human beings, who brought to their solemn responsibilities all the wisdom and dedication that frail human nature can muster. He was proud to be a part of this bench.

Outside in the early darkness, a soft snowfall dampened the sidewalks and flickered in the light of street lamps and Christmas decorations. The brilliant dome of Michigan's Capitol reflected in the windows of the Law Building and the Treasury Building across the plaza. Malloy's thoughts turned from his colleagues on the court to Margaret, his colleague in life. If these past two years had been difficult for him, they were surely as stressful for his wife. She had been a strong, reliable, and effective partner in his career. More important, she was the love of his life, whose laughter and companionship dwarfed every crisis, surmounted every problem. He wondered how soon she would be back from the mall. Aching to see her at that moment, Malloy conjured a vision of spontaneous romance, snapped his fingers to confirm an instant decision and quickened his steps as he detoured through the lobby of the Radisson Hotel.

At the Lansing Center, the crowd was gathering. As soon as he passed through the door, the din of happy conversation drew Malloy out of his introspection. He was suddenly thrust into a montage of laughing, talking, greeting, meeting, hand shaking, kissing, back slapping, elbow squeezing men and women. Most of them knew the chief justice of the Michigan Supreme Court by name. Malloy might, at the very most, recognize one face out of every fifty. Working his way toward the coat room, he fell into the politician's mantra.

"Hi there."

"How's it going?"

"Good to see you."

"Glad to see you."

"There he is!"

"Hello."

"Hello, there."

"Good evening."

"Nice to see you."

"Lovely dress."

"Hi, George."

"Looking good, man."

"Hey, pal, how are you?"

"Gimme five, old friend."

"Well, for heavens sake."

"Where's Charlie?"

"What's happening?"

"Well, look at you."

After checking his coat, Malloy moved through the crowd, still meeting and greeting, until he could position himself to watch the door for Margaret's entrance. A hundred handshakes later, the lights were flashed signaling that the cocktail hour was over and the dinner about to begin. The crowded lobby emptied. A few stragglers rushed in, checked their coats, and hurried through the double doors to the banquet hall. Maybe she wasn't coming. Maybe he should just go on in and be seated. Spotting a phone booth, Malloy ducked in and dialed his car phone number. "The cellular phone you have dialed is either not in service or has been driven out of the calling area." No help. He returned to the lobby.

Then he saw her. She had arrived while he was on the phone, and was checking her coat. She looked as stunning as he had envisioned, wearing the same little black dress that she had worn on the night of his election. He smiled as he recalled that episode, and felt a rush at the thought of staging an encore. As she approached him, Malloy extended his hand, as though greeting another political acquaintance.

"Don't tell me. Your name is on the tip of my tongue. You are...... You're..............."

Margaret grinned as she picked up on the farce.

"Malloy. Margaret Malloy. I'm the wife of the chief justice."

"I wouldn't be so sure about that if I were you."

Margaret looked quizzically at her husband. "Are you trying to tell me something?"

Guiding her toward the banquet room entrance, with a puckish grin, Malloy dangled a Radisson Hotel room key in her line of sight. "We'll have lots of time to talk about that after dinner," he whispered.

EPILOGUE

On April 28, 1988, The Michigan Supreme Court conducted a formal session in its former courtroom on the third floor of the State Capitol for the purpose of dedicating a bronze marker commemorating the old supreme court chambers.

Dorothy Comstock Riley, the second woman to serve as chief justice of the court, presided. The proceedings are recorded in Volume 430 of the Michigan Reports as follows:

> Chief Justice Riley:
>
> The history of the Supreme Court in these chambers ends in January of 1970. On March 3, 1970, the young Chief Justice of the Michigan Supreme Court presided over the ceremonies closing this courtroom. Those ceremonies are reported in volume 383 of the Michigan Reports, and thus we have a record of those who participated and what they said. The words of Thomas E. Brennan, Chief Justice on that occasion, bear repeating. Who better to repeat them than their author, and so I ask the former Chief Justice and President of The Thomas Cooley Law School, Thomas E. Brennan, to step forward.
>
> The Honorable Thomas E. Brennan:
>
> Madam Chief Justice, Justices of the Supreme Court, ladies and gentlemen, distinguished Senators and Representatives.
>
> I am doubly honored this day. I am honored, first, that the Chief Justice has asked me to speak, and second, that she has asked me to repeat what I said here when, as Chief Justice, I was privileged to preside at the final session of the Court held in these chambers. My remarks, reported as she notes in the Michigan Reports, were as follows:
>
> "We have come here to mark this occasion; to

observe this event with appropriate ceremony. It falls to me, as the Chief Justice, to make this opening statement. While the office I hold dictates that I should do this, I am warmly conscious of my poor measure to the task, for this is a time that fairly begs to be given over to nostalgia and filled with remembrances of other days and other faces; days before I came here and faces which I never saw. It is a time when the oldest man in this room should be able to recall with unseasonable clarity his earliest appearance at this bar. It is a time when names once familiar, but long unspoken, should be made to resound again upon these walls, so hallowed by their service, so honored by their lives. It is, in short, a time when men of sentiment and a sense of history are wont to look and listen for ghosts--and be most apt to see and hear them. For there is a continuity to human affairs and a life in human institutions which is more real than musty records and printed volumes can hold. And this is a place--and a mourning--in the life of the Michigan Supreme Court which needs to be seen with human eyes, and heard with human ears, and recorded in the mortal hearts and the immortal souls of human beings.

"It is good for us to do this and to remind ourselves that this old courtroom we close today has been the chambers of the Court and not the Court itself, because a Court is not a room or a building: it is people. This courtroom is old at 90 years; the Supreme Court is young at 133. Good men, brave men, wise men, strong and studious, dedicated and independent men, have in those 133 years, interchanged their ideas and entwined their lives to weave the fabric of Michigan's decisional law, and to bestow the gift of ordered liberty to generations of free men yet unborn. It is in homage to them, to those generous men, departed Justices and living former Justices who have graced this Bench, that our Court sits today in formal session."

Madam Chief Justice, I am loath to sit down without one further comment. The glorious past we mark in reverence here today is both glorious and past. It should be fondly remembered, but not slavishly imitated. Nothing more pointedly reminds us of the progress of the Supreme Court and indeed the advance of western civilization in the past 18 years than the one-gender syntax of my remarks in 1970. Those words were proper then, and indeed no female ever sat on the Bench in this old courtroom. But they fall far short of the mark today. In 1988, the homage we owe to Justices past is due both to men and women. The contributions which you and Justice Boyle and Chief Justice Coleman have made to our jurisprudence already echo through the Bench and bar as they have resounded in every community of our beloved State of Michigan.

Your appearance before the Legislature this morning, Madam Chief Justice and the numerous women Judges in attendance there and here, give cogent testimony that Michigan's One Court of Justice is graced by talented women whose leadership and service deserve to be recognized and appreciated. So let us mark this place and remember what happened here. But let us also rejoice that the past is past, that more history is being written in other rooms by other people, and that the warm glow of our yesterday is becoming the bright beauty of our tomorrow.